Image of a Lover

Books by Elisabeth Ogilvie

IMAGE OF A LOVER
STRAWBERRIES IN THE
  SEA
WEEP AND KNOW WHY
A THEME FOR REASON
THE FACE OF INNOCENCE
BELLWOOD
WATERS ON A STARRY
  NIGHT
THE SEASONS HEREAFTER
THERE MAY BE HEAVEN

CALL HOME THE HEART
THE WITCH DOOR
HIGH TIDE AT NOON
STORM TIDE
THE EBBING TIDE
ROWAN HEAD
MY WORLD IS AN ISLAND
THE DAWNING OF THE
  DAY
NO EVIL ANGEL

Books for Young People

THE PIGEON PAIR
MASQUERADE AT SEA
  HOUSE
CEILING OF AMBER
TURN AROUND TWICE
BECKY'S ISLAND
THE YOUNG ISLANDERS

HOW WIDE THE HEART
BLUEBERRY SUMMER
WHISTLE FOR A WIND
THE FABULOUS YEAR
COME ABOARD AND
  BRING YOUR DORY!

Image of a Lover
by Elisabeth Ogilvie

McGRAW-HILL BOOK COMPANY
New York   St. Louis   San Francisco
Toronto   Düsseldorf   Mexico

She, sleepless in summer, one midnight will discover
In a mirror, by candlelight, the image of a lover.

Book designed by Elaine Gongora

Copyright © 1974 by Elisabeth Ogilvie.

123456789BPBP7987654

Library of Congress Cataloging in Publication Data

Ogilvie, Elisabeth, date
  Image of a lover.

  I. Title.
PZ3.0348Im [PS3529.G39]   813'.5'2   74–5016
ISBN 0–07–047648–9

chapter 1

The bright day is done, and we are for the dark.

There is a photograph of us all taken one night that summer by Sam Baldwin. He was the itinerant photographer who used to make the rounds of the islands, mostly taking pictures of babies on the white fur rug he brought with him, and small boys and girls sitting astride his shaggy little ponies.

We are in the cottage, and Patrick is standing by the field-stone fireplace, with one elbow resting on the mantel beside my artistic arrangement of marsh rosemary and driftwood. His hand supports his brow in a mock intellectual pose, the other hand holds a book ostentatiously against his B-lettered chest. He holds your eyes in a sly, solemn, sidewise look, which, if you can keep your own to it long enough, is sure to dissolve into laughter and sweep you along with the flood. At least that is what you feel would happen. Even I feel it after all these years. After everything.

Meg Finlay, who'd come down to see if we were behaving ourselves and had walked in on our version of the Moulin Rouge can-can line (as taught us by Andrew, who'd actually seen it) is enthroned in one of the high-backed wicker rockers. She is smiling resolutely at the camera. It is a smile of iron. She plainly determined not to jump or even wince when the flash powder goes off.

Ian is sitting on his heels beside her chair, his serious expression preserved for as long as this browning old print shall last. He looks deeply concerned by the state of the world in July, 1896. He said afterwards that he was expecting Sam to blow the whole place up, Sam having come well-primed with Job Pease's West Indian rum.

Miranda sits on the floor leaning back against Meg's knees, laughing. Though she had begun doing her hair up in school, that summer she let it go loose or tied it back with a ribbon, and I wore mine in braids like a fourteen-year-old.

Andrew shows his beautiful Drummond profile to the camera because he can't stop looking at Jane. She gazes demurely at the camera, as if assessing Sam's skill; he is taking the group picture only so she can be in it.

Tom Finlay, Meg's son, is another lover, but you wouldn't guess it, because he too gives all his attention to the camera, gravely cooperative. With his black hair and eyes and his strong cheekbones he looks like an Indian among the fair-haired Drummonds.

The rest are young people from the village. Some of them are: Prissy Schofield, Rubens-lush with a bosom that incited either envy or contempt among other contemporary females. Faustina Pease, trying so hard for the right expression that her face is twice as long as natural, that of a suspicious horse. You can see a bit of Hugh Swenson's concertina past someone's ear, Hughie as usual is laughing at his own wit. His sister Jennie proudly holds her banjo. She is younger than most of us, between hay and grass. Dill Kalloch hunkers at one side, handsome the way a granite ledge can be handsome, and with just as much expression. Two brothers in their mid-teens are stretched out ornamentally in front, lying on their sides, head to head like bookends, each propped up on one elbow. They are the Awful Ansons. They have reckless, freckled, merry faces, their red hair cut off to short fur.

I am sitting directly behind them, cross-legged, my head showing between theirs, and I am grinning like a moon-crazed dryad over the silky ears of Charlie, Miranda's Skye terrier.

I was drunk that summer with a clear fiery joy because I'd found at twenty-two what I thought I'd lost forever at nine. That had been my last perfect summer until this one. Imagine an adult experiencing again the uncorrupted delight, the discoveries and enchantments, one believed only granted to children; to compensate, I always supposed, for the intensity of their woes, ranging from the rained-out picnic through the broken doll, the betraying friend, the move to another town, to the death of a parent. In between there had to be rapture in its purest essence, otherwise the child couldn't survive.

But to know that rapture again, as an adult! I wouldn't have believed it possible. And as an adult, I expected daily its departure.

We had a spell of reading Shakespeare, after the Players had been on the island and gotten us into the spirit of the thing. Old books in hand, we acted scenes from the tragedies, dying magnificently. Or we read out favorite sonnets, in love with the sound of our own voices. We liked best the despairing ones; we were children playing at funerals.

> *O! how shall summer's honey breath hold out*
> *Against the wrackful siege of battering days,*
> *When rocks impregnable are not so stout,*
> *Nor gates of steel so strong, but Time decays?*

Time couldn't decay us. Never *us*. At least not for another hundred years or so ... The photograph taken in the cottage that night is fading, and crumbling at the edges. And faint now almost beyond recall to the most sensitive ear of memory is the sound of singing on a summer night.

On the day when I went out to Drummond's Island, Miranda was seasick, but I was not. I admit that when we made the northeast turn outside the harbor of Rockland and were well out into the gray bay, I'd been appalled at the heaving hills and precipitous valleys of water before us. Until now my only experience with the ocean had been decorous ferry trips across Casco Bay in the very finest weather; Papa's delicate stomach couldn't stand even a slight ripple.

But Miranda never knew of my misgivings. She stood up there in the bow with her face into the wind, looking like a

Viking maiden if you could imagine a Viking maiden in caped mackintosh and headscarf aboard a snub-nosed little steamer. I stood there beside her, glad my gloves hid my white knuckles as I grasped the railing, and tried not to believe that the *Ocean Pearl* was going to sink without a trace because I had run away with Miranda, instead of going home to spend the summer as an unpaid nanny and music teacher to my father's second batch.

There were only two other passengers beside us, if you didn't count the cow on the lower deck. She had been escorted aboard with great patience and tenderness, and tethered where she would be as sheltered as possible. There was a middle-aged priest, weathered enough to be a fisherman or quarry worker, whom Miranda introduced as Father Emery. He was pleasant but preoccupied. The other passenger was a fisherman named Ethan Kalloch, who looked as if he'd had a week of hard nights ashore. After languidly acknowledging our meeting, he went into the passenger cabin and lay down on a locker and went to sleep.

No one was in the least concerned about the weather, no lifeboat drill was organized, no life preservers handed out, so after a while I decided that God had more important things to do than sink the *Ocean Pearl* in the Gulf of Maine just to show Seafair Bell that she couldn't defy her father with impunity.

"Home is out there," Miranda said, grandly waving as if the whole Atlantic were home and she a halcyon. She looked at her lapel watch. "We'll be there in three hours."

The tilting horizon was obscured by a silvery mist. *Something* might exist out there, but the only reality was the boat and the sea upon which the vessel rolled and plunged and shook herself. The water was forever shifting from one blue to another, then to a harsh vivid green, then through a whole range of pigeon-breast grays, while the distances seethed under the diffused light with a deadly luster.

But Drummond's Island did exist. Miranda was proof of it,

and the fisherman Ethan Kalloch, and the mail sacks whose labels I had read when they were brought aboard. Drummond's and Bannock were out there, substantial enough to have post offices. I stared into the mist until my eyes burned and watered, positive that my first glimpse of either island would be the most significant landfall of my life.

Suddenly Miranda said tensely, "I think I'll lie down a bit. I didn't sleep much last night. The hotel was so noisy." She had become very pale, her eyes a staring cobalt blue. "I don't want to arrive home in an absolutely exhausted condition—" She broke off and went quickly aft, holding to the rail and seeming to feel her way. I followed her into the cabin and she turned a white aghast face on me and said imperiously, "Go away."

Eyes shut, moving as if she were balancing an egg on her forehead, she lay down on a long settee. Keeping my balance by a marvel as the *Pearl* lunged like a bolting horse, I arranged the skirts of her mackintosh for modesty. "Don't you want something under your head?" I asked.

"Go away," she said again without opening her eyes. She crossed her hands on her breast as if to receive a lily.

"I thought you never got seasick. Shall I ask if the captain has a lemon?"

"Of course he hasn't got a lemon!" she snarled at me. "On this boat it's the mail and freight that's important, not the passengers. Someone's probably holding that cow's hand," she said bitterly, "but I could die, and they wouldn't care. Even *I* wouldn't care," she moaned.

"Shall I go and find the engineer and ask him to hold your hand? He's very handsome under all that grease, and I thought he had an eye for you. Or what about the Sleeping Prince?" Across the cabin Ethan Kalloch snored, so utterly relaxed that he stayed on his narrow perch only by some mysterious feat of unconscious balance.

Miranda rose up on one elbow and looked drunkenly across at him in the full glory of black stubble, red flannel shirt, loud braces, work pants, and rubber boots. A stunning aura of stale whiskey and strong tobacco surrounded him in an almost visible cloud.

"If he were ten years younger, and hadn't obviously spent last night on Sea Street," she said, "and was clean, and as good-looking as his cousin, I wouldn't mind." She collapsed. "Go away, Seafair. Just keep holding onto something," she added faintly.

I shut the door behind me with quite a struggle and went forward across the streaming deck to the bow, where I stood hanging on with both hands, proud of my achievement and feeling rather like a bareback rider standing on two horses at once. All at once the deckhand appeared at my elbow. He was a nimble little man who shouted at me over the hiss and wash of the bow wave.

"Cap'n says for you to light somewhere and stay put. You're driving him crazy."

"Where?" I shouted back. "If I go inside with those two, I'll be sick for sure!"

"He says you can come in the pilot house if you keep your mouth shut. He don't gen'rally allow women in there."

"I can keep my mouth shut," I assured him. "It's one of the things I do best." He grinned at that, showing no teeth, and supervised my progress like an officious terrier. The captain had a lumpy and inscrutable face. He looked at me over steel-rimmed glasses, nodded toward a camp stool in a corner, and went back to staring out his open window. Father Emery sat across from me, reading his breviary, or whatever it was priests were supposed to read.

"Will you look in on Miranda now and then?" I asked the deckhand.

"Ayuh. I'll take her a bucket. But don't worry, she's tougher'n tripe."

I can see the pilot house now, the white-painted paneling, the captain's and the vessel's framed papers, the binnacle, the big wheel, the cord for the whistle and the one for signaling the engineer, the thick leathery rim of the captain's ear and the shape of his black peaked cap against the broken sky. I remember the priest's worn face. I can feel the motion of the steamer and hear the creaks, groans, and rattles; my body relives the alternate sways and strains, adjustments and compensations. I can remember the dizzying effect of window sills slanting one way while the horizon slanted in another. I can smell the captain's pipe. I can breathe—no, be possessed and ravished and saturated by—the tremendous cold wild briny breath of that smoky sou'wester.

In my first year teaching music at the Harnden College for Women, Miranda Muir was in her third year there as a pupil. I was given the operetta by my department superior, and that was how Miranda and I became acquainted. For all her poise and grace and a very fine ear, Miranda wasn't much good at the piano, because she was so easily bored by the work involved. But she could sing as naturally and well as if she herself were an instrument in the hands of an expert. She was a perfect operetta heroine, because along with being able to sing she was tall, slender, and fair, with sea-blue eyes. It was she who should have been named "Seafair" instead of me.

Seafair was the name of a Puritan ancestress of my mother's, for whom she had insisted on naming her black-haired and later dark-eyed baby. I understand my father protested and said it sounded like a race horse. Later my stepmother started calling me by my middle name, Helen, in hopes of converting everyone else, but I wore that out by refusing to hear the name. This was my chief act of resistance until the summer when I ran away to Drummond's Island.

It was while I was coaching Miranda for her part in one of those princess-stolen-by-gypsies confections that I heard about her home, Drummond's Island. At the time I was very depressed about the summer ahead of me, and her stories about her island home far beyond the rim of Harnden Hills offered me an escape from the prison of my thoughts. Without actually envying her I often compared her life with mine. I had lost only one parent, she had lost both when she was too young to remember them, but she had been raised by a loving uncle and had three older male cousins whose pet she was. She lived in a granite house called The Eyrie, built on a cliff above the sea; she was a character from a novel, a Gothic heroine, but without some awful secret of terror and madness sleeping behind her innocent eyes. She had no fears, she needed only to move forward in a graceful arrogance through the translucent medium of her life, like the swan in the evening.

I encouraged her to keep her autobiography going as we rested after the coaching sessions or walked in the raw spring afternoons down to the village or on the hills around the campus. Her uncle had died unexpectedly the autumn before, and sometimes her eyes filled with tears when she talked about him. At other times she spoke with a warm, amused affection as if he were still living. She talked about the cousins—Ian and Andrew, the much older ones, and Patrick, closer to her in age so that her stories were full of him, and another boy, Tom, who was as close to them as blood kin. The Drummonds and the Finlays had been together for generations.

The children from The Eyrie had gone to the one-room village school with the fishermen's children, run barefoot in summer, played on the shores, taken to boats as naturally as gulls took wing. I saw them in a series of Winslow Homer paintings as they ranged the fields and forests, fished, boiled periwinkles in a tin can over a driftwood fire and fried mushrooms in butter sneaked out of the house, chewed spruce gum, ate green apples and every berry permitted and some that weren't.

I was twenty-two to her nineteen, but the three years' difference meant little. In a way I had been much more sheltered than she. My life had certainly been narrow to the point of constriction, and at this point I was beginning to think the tightness of it would strangle me. I had two choices. To stay on at the college (with summers at home, of course) and become an institution in time like Dr. Enderby, the head of my department; or go home and teach privately in the little studio that had been my mother's, perhaps making enough to buy my music and my clothes, but never enough to live alone, even in one room. So I would earn my board at home by continuing my governess duties. I wasn't ignorant enough to think I could run away to a city, even one as near as Portland, and support myself. I had no maternal relatives to turn to; my mother had been an only child in a dying-out family.

One rainy May afternoon I told Miranda this over tea in the village; not with self-pity, because I had learned quite a while back that self-pity was a luxury I couldn't afford.

"But there's nothing the matter with you!" she objected. "So why do you talk as if you're condemned to everlasting spinsterhood? Aren't there any eligible men in Fern Grove, for heaven's sake? Somebody who likes music, so you'd have common ground?"

"There's Mr. Adams," I said. "I accompany him at musicales. As they say in the *Register,* he renders selections. Like *I'll Sing Thee Songs of Araby.* He's going bald, and he has a round little belly, not to mention five children. While he sings he unbuttons his waistcoat and then he buttons it up again. Up and down all the time, like playing a clarinet."

Miranda burst into her whooping, robust laugh, which turned heads all around the Fringed Orchis Tearoom.

"He sounds absolutely adorable. Oh listen, Seafair, there just has to be somebody else. They can't all be too old or impossible. Look, the studio's detached from the house, you said. You should have at-homes. You don't know who you'd attract! You might end up establishing a salon of brilliant minds, like some of those old French birds."

"I'm trying to compare Fern Grove with Paris, but I'm not succeeding," I said. "To begin with, there'd be nobody to come to my salon but the organist at the First Baptist Church, if his mother would let him, but she gets nervous if we even play duets together. And there's old Mr. Abbott, who writes verses for the paper to celebrate everything that happens in town. Mr. Adams' wife wouldn't let him come any more than Jack's mother would. The English teacher at the Academy knows Shakespeare by heart, but he drinks."

"He sounds the most promising of all."

"Well, it wouldn't be a proper salon with just one guest, would it?"

"An improper one sounds like more fun."

"What have you been reading, Miss Muir?" I asked severely. "*Not* Marie Corelli, I hope."

"The plays of Oscar Wilde, ma'am," she said, pleating her napkin, and I rolled up my eyes and hissed, "*That* unspeakable beast!"

She rocked back in her chair and her laughter again assaulted the refined ears of the rest of the clientele.

As we sloshed back to school under one huge black umbrella Miranda said all at once, "Come home with me this summer."

"I can't," I said automatically. Then, in anger, "You don't mean it, anyway."

"I do too." We stopped short and glared at each other under the umbrella. "What do you think I *am?*" She took my arm and dragged me off the road into the shelter of some old apple trees leaning over a stone wall. On the other side of the wall three immense Brown Swiss cows stared and chewed. "Come home and work on my music with me," Miranda said. "You can be my tutor for the summer, and that ought to satisfy your family. I'll really work at the piano, to salve our consciences, but we can have some fun too. Come on, say yes."

"I'll sleep on it," I said firmly. But I knew that once I had balanced, however tremblingly, on the brink of freedom, I couldn't step back.

Five weeks later I was balancing on a camp stool in the pilot house of the *Ocean Pearl*. I'd mailed my letter to Papa yesterday, and when he got it I'd be on Drummond's Island. It seemed to me that if I ever reached that mystic isle I'd have outsoared everyone's grasp. Last night I'd treated Miranda to a lobster dinner at the Limerock House, and for my sins I didn't even have a bad dream. What woke me in the morning wasn't my conscience but the bagpipe skirl of gulls over the harbor, a sound that was to haunt my life forever.

I would never be sophisticated; I anticipated, enjoyed, or was disappointed all with the same drowning commitment. When I fall in love, I used to think with complacent pride, it will be the death of me.

And it very nearly was.

*Q*annock was the quarry island. Framed in a pilot house window a mountain top showed dimly like the last scrap of the earth before the Flood drowned it. Then it experienced resurrection and arose from the bubbling deeps as a hill of pink granite capped with green turf and blue-black spruce. The priest closed his book and stood up. I said "Thank you," to the captain, who nodded, and went out on deck. The sea was quieter and there were many gulls about. A warm gust of wind blew the scent of those spruces into my face and I breathed deeply, then hoped I didn't look too foolishly rapt as Miranda joined me at the rail.

The Sleeping Prince came out behind her, yawning loudly and rubbing his eyes, as steady on the slanting deck as if he'd been crossing his own kitchen floor. With an ineffably jaded air he viewed the prospect, then disappeared aft.

Miranda and I stood silently watching the island take on substance. As a child I used to dream of marvelous things happening to me: a door opening before me in a cliff, a sweet voice calling me from a tree trunk, my name written in fire on a still pond. Intrepidly I would respond, and therefore begin a new and enchanted life *far from the haunts of mortal man*, which was a phrase that represented the very peak of romance to me. It can still cause a frisson along my spine, just for old times' sake.

Now it was as if all the imagined beginnings were happening at once. True, I wasn't going into Elfland or through the looking glass, and there'd certainly be mortals, but they'd be different from the other mortals I'd met so far in my life, if Miranda was any example.

Beside me Miranda was so unusually silent that my euphoria became tarnished with uneasiness. I wondered if she was having second thoughts about inviting me home. She loved the place in such a deeply personal way that I could turn out to be an unnecessary and thus irritating third party.

We rounded a drunkenly rolling bellbuoy, leadenly clanging and ridden by a persistent blackback gull, and passed a long point bombarded by surf and crested with madly waving children. The whistle blew, and the children began running back along the point like sandpipers. As the harbor opened before us I decided to tell Miranda at once that I wouldn't get off the steamer when we reached Drummond's; I'd go back to the mainland because my conscience was bothering me about my family. That is, I'd say it if I could manage a cool and final tone, which I doubted. I thought furiously, Damn and blast! I am going to stay at least one week, I don't care whether she likes it or not.

Just outside the harbor mouth, seas broke over a steep ledge with a crash I could hear above the engine. Miranda clutched my arm and said starkly, " 'O Christ! It is the Inchcape Rock!' "

That is why we entered the harbor of Bannock with arms around each other's waist and laughing like fools.

It was a small harbor made smaller by the presence of a five-masted schooner at anchor, the only thing I saw at first as the steamer puffed sedately under the high bow. Then one detail after another sprang into existence as if a great tapestry were coming to life in all its elements, but with its colors muted by the misty air into grayed pastels. Gulls circled overhead or perched on rock and ridgepole. The children who had greeted us from the point were spilling down over a ledgy hillside behind the store and out onto the wharf.

Small houses and lofty rooming houses took up what

level ground surrounded the harbor. Beyond and above the scene the rigging of the quarries stood black against the milky blue of a clearing sky. The steamer, with much swashing, chuffing, and ringing of bells, finally arranged herself beside the long granite wharf. It was high tide and I found myself at once face to face with an interested collection of male watchers of various ages, sizes, and complexions. Miranda greeted them all; she even knew the names of the massive work horses waiting there with wagons for the cases and barrels being hustled ashore.

The cow was ushered across a gangplank and received with Italian blandishments by a stout black-eyed woman and her children, all patting the cow and telling her she was beautiful and adored. Some of the men called jokingly to the woman and she answered back in hoarse, rapid Italian. The Sleeping Prince took an easy long-legged step onto the wharf and began a desultory conversation with a mustached man wearing a derby, who snapped his braces as he talked, and spat tobacco juice overboard at a floating chip with the finesse of someone taking aim with a bow and arrow. The captain took the mailbags up to the store; the sign over the double doors read in faded gold, red, and black, *D. E. Drummond and Sons*. As the harbor shore became more sharply detailed I saw women hanging out washings, and working in little garden patches among granite outcroppings.

Sniffing, staring, listening, I'd even forgotten Miranda until she said softly, "So it wasn't for a wedding or a christening."

I said in astonishment, ready to laugh again, *"What?"*

She didn't answer, and I followed her gaze. The priest was walking up the wharf, and a young woman was coming to meet him, half-running, tall and gaunt in a black dress. Two young boys hurried behind her. One stubbed his bare toe and collapsed over it with a cry, but she didn't look back. Her white face was a grimacing, square-mouthed mask. The priest took her two hands and the mask began to melt like wax in a flame. She wrenched her hands free and covered her face. The priest reached out to the boys. The crying, hobbling one pushed his face against the man's midriff, and the priest gathered the other one in too. I felt the tight response in my own throat that always came whenever I saw a child cry in genuine pain or grief.

"Robert Emmet Dolan must have died," Miranda said in a lifeless voice. "He had the stone-cutter's disease. What will Rosaleen do now, I wonder?" She swung away from the sight. "Why did this have to happen right *now?*" She stood staring out at the harbor, gripping the rail hard.

I sat down on a camp stool, my legs aching all at once from having been braced so long. I didn't want to look again at the little group in black up on the wharf, but I had to, and was relieved to see them going out of sight by one of the sheds. A tall fair-haired man in shirtsleeves walked with them, he and the priest talking. Then a loaded wagon rumbled past them and when it had gone by they had disappeared.

It's a coincidence, I argued with myself. The man must have been sick a long time. He wasn't struck down suddenly just to teach me a lesson . . . After this it was a pleasure to watch the cow in capricious progress up the wharf, tossing horns and tail, stopping short and being coaxed into action again. She reminded me of Phoebe when she was being difficult for a purpose, which was usually to subjugate Papa.

Ah well, toss away, Phoebe, I thought. If Papa has any sense, he'll go into his study and lock the door. Anyway, he can't possibly come after me. He'd never dare make the trip.

A man's voice said, very close, "What in time are *you* doing here?"

I jumped up from the stool, knocking it over, and Miranda laughed. The fair-haired young man on the wharf was the one who'd been talking with the priest. He stood looking at Miranda with annoyance. "It had better be a good story," he said. His eyes were the same bright blue as Miranda's, but set in those sea-faring creases I'd always found so distingué, to use one of Phoebe's favorite words.

"Now, Andrew," Miranda began rapidly, "don't tell me I'm supposed to be on my way to Newport. I've already sent a wire to Mrs. Whitman saying I wouldn't be there because of an unexpected crisis. And it's a crisis when somebody's as homesick as I am, not sleeping, losing my appetite—*you* tell him, Seafair," she appealed to me, almost tearful with sincerity, but went on talking. I was glad I was not called upon, because as far as I knew she had lost neither sleep nor appetite. "So I had to come home, or just fade away," she said, and waited, but apparently didn't get the right response because she became even more fluent and dramatic. "This is a reverse elopement. I'm running home instead of away. I should think you'd appreciate that, instead of standing there looking supercilious. Besides, I might have picked up with the worst elements at Newport, *in spite* of Mrs. Whitman. Some elegant fortune-hunter who'd have to be paid off. Are you coming aboard so I can kiss you, or shall I come there?" She swept up her skirts in preparation, and he jumped aboard.

"Listen, Miranda," he began, but she took his face in her hands and kissed him smackingly on cheeks, forehead, nose, and lips.

"I hate your mustache," she said, "but I suppose Jane loves it." She kissed him again. He took her hands away from his face and said, "Someday you'll run up against opposition that you can't kiss away."

"If you mean Ian, I'll take a reef in that sail when it's time." She reached out to pull me close. "This is my best friend and that perfectly wonderful genius of a music teacher I've raved about in my letters, if you ever read any but Jane's. I've brought her home to help with my music. Seafair, this is Andrew. Andrew, this is Seafair Bell."

"What a pretty name you have," he said. We shook hands. "Do you really think you can teach this girl to play the piano decently, handicapped as the poor creature is with two left hands, and all thumbs at that?"

"Insults, insults," said Miranda. "Or patronizing male

humor. Is it any wonder I've grown up hard and bitter?" She pinched him sharply in the ribs and made him jump and laugh. "How's life in the granite business? Have you got a contract for a bridge across Penobscot Bay yet? Are the Italians still furious with the Norwegians for claiming that Leif got here before Cristoforo?"

"Now the Irish have got into the act by swearing that St. Brendan got here around nine hundred and something, and the Welsh say there's a tribe of blue-eyed Welsh-speaking Indians to prove *their* prior rights. The Scots say they're all insane, and the Finns are too busy talking socialism. Otherwise, all hostilities are suspended until after the July Fourth ball game. The Bannock Buccaneers united against the Drummond Devils."

Miranda gave me a rapturous and agonizing squeeze around the ribs. "I can hardly wait for that ball game!"

"Don't count on your being here," Andrew warned her. "You know what your uncle wanted. Ian will take that very seriously. As I do." He looked it. He had the high-bridged nose and strong jaw of some of Raeburn's Scottish aristocrats, and, while his smile had been charming, his severity made even me feel guilty.

Miranda matched it with cold hauteur. "I'm surprised that you'd allow everything to go on as usual with Robert Emmet Dolan dead. They're not having the band concert and the sports too, I hope. It sounds very disrespectful to me."

"They're having everything. It was Bob's last wish." A teamster called out and another wagon rumbled up the wharf, the big hooves making hollow thunder on the planks. Andrew waited until it had gotten well away from us. "He said if he could possibly manage it, he'd be right there behind home plate taking care that Ole Carlsson didn't give anything away to the Devils in the name of fair play. He said fair play is an invention of the English and he'll fight it from beyond the grave." His mouth twitched. "He will, too . . . The band's to play *The Minstrel Boy* in his honor at the concert."

"With everybody sobbing into their horns and piccolos," said Miranda. She blinked and groped for a handkerchief in all her pockets. I gave her mine. "What about Rosaleen and the boys?"

"Andrew!" someone shouted at him from the wharf, a broad, black-bearded man. "Can you leave the girls long enough to cast your eyes on this invoice? How are you, Miranda?"

"A little sad, Ivor."

"With the Colonel gone and now Bob, it's more than a little sad for us all."

Andrew stepped up onto the wharf. "See you tonight, Seafair. That is, if Miranda gets a chance to step foot on the home island."

"Now what's all this about?" I asked Miranda.

"Nothing that needs to bother you." She gave me a little pat. "It doesn't amount to a hill of beans."

"What he said about your uncle's wishes didn't sound very trivial."

"Now, Seafair, don't go all schoolmarmish on me." Merrily her eyes flashed away from mine and ranged the harbor. She even hummed. Loudly.

"I'm not schoolmarmish," I retorted. "I'm just plain uncomfortable. Whatever you've done or haven't done, they're going to think I've condoned it, or maybe even influenced you."

"Nobody on earth will believe *that*," she said. "And, dear love, you aren't going to Wuthering Heights. Ian isn't the slightest bit like Heathcliffe." She was still watching the harbor. "Look, there's *Eaglet!* Oh, I was hoping for this! Isn't she beautiful? Watch her heel over! It's just like that poem Patrick's always quoting, something about a rapt ship running on her side so low that she drinks water and her keel plows air."

It sounded pretty horrifying to me. I stared obediently at the little sloop flying into the harbor with the speed and grace of a gull skimming the waves, but looking considerably more frail. "He must have known I was coming today," Miranda babbled. "It's mental telepathy. Come on!" She seized my hand and towed me to the *Pearl's* stern deck.

From this distance the man at the tiller could have been Andrew, but Andrew was tied to granite and invoices; this was one of those creatures whom I'd admired from afar, watching them race in Casco Bay, as sure of themselves as if the sea were indeed the great sweet mother in Swinburne's verse. I'd seen them stride up a yacht club pier, windburned, salt-rimed where the spray had drenched their faces, and they walked and spoke differently from other men. I used to think with feverish adolescent passion: the Sea King's Sons. Once I'd tried to write a song about them, drawing heavily on Tennyson and Sir Arthur Sullivan, but the result had been an insult to the splendid subject.

Miranda put her hands to her mouth and let out a long Valkyrie whoop. The man's head turned, and then the sloop came about and whipped insolently under the granite schooner's bowsprit. Boys ran down the wharf, jostling each other dangerously for a chance to catch lines. *Eaglet* made a breathtaking swoop toward us, swept along the steamer's side with her canvas snapping, and without hurrying the man seemed to be everywhere at once. The big sail came slatting and rattling down, a line snaked upward, a bristle-headed boy caught it and made it fast around a spiling.

"Thanks, Mick!" Patrick Drummond called up to him. "You're a good man." He stepped onto *Eaglet's* stern deck, took hold of the steamer's railing, and swung his long body over it like a gymnast. I remember those dirty duck trousers and those wet canvas shoes flying through the air. And then he stood facing Miranda.

"By God," he said softly. "It *is* you. Nobody else can lift my skull like that, not even Erline Pease at her loudest. So you made it."

"Didn't I swear I would? When I found out *you* weren't going away this summer— Oh, Pat!"

She took a step and was in his arms. They hugged each other so violently it was as if they were trying to crush each other into yelping for pity; they rocked back and forth, held each other off, laughed without sense, and hugged again.

I had never felt so lonely in all my poor little niggling poverty-stricken life. I hated it and me with a contempt I'd never had for anyone else, even Phoebe. I was about to turn my back on the scene, before my revulsion was too plainly revealed, when Patrick winked at me past Miranda's ear.

His eyes were the color of the blue roll-necked sweater under his oil jacket, and the wink took me into a secret I couldn't guess but was comforted by; made me at once comrade and co-conspirator. In what, I didn't know. But it was the door in the cliff all over again.

The two were talking in code as far as I was concerned. They didn't have to finish sentences but spoke in fragments. *Patrick's my twin,* she had told me once, *if you ignore such foolish details as our having different parents and his being three years older than me. . . .* They were twinned enough in family resemblance. He was taller, rangy, broad-shouldered, but his hair grew back from his forehead in a widow's peak like hers, and her features, though more delicate, were like his.

Suddenly my name summoned me from the tree, appeared before me in letters of fire. Hand in hand, benignly beautiful in oil jacket and damp mackintosh, they were about to take me into the circle.

"Hello, Seafair Bell," said Patrick. "I'm happy to meet you."

"So am I," I said idiotically. "I mean, I'm glad to be here." In dismay I thought, Is this how it's going to be? Why did I ever think it would be simple to go home with another girl? Well, it would be if I were about ten.

"I'll be back," he said. He sprang up onto the wharf,

carrying a small satchel, and went toward the store, children streaming out behind him like the tail of a comet. I looked after him with a thudding in my chest. Oh, you poor fool, I said in disgust. Stop it.

"We're going home with him," Miranda said. "They'll be ages getting all the freight out. This is the most wonderful luck, to sail home in *Eaglet!*"

"Do you think he got your message?" I asked dryly.

"Oh, he came over for the funeral, but he's got plenty of time to take us home, then come back here and change. Ian's coming over on the *Pearl's* return trip. Come on, let's hurry and get out our dressing cases. Our big luggage can come over from the harbor later."

It speaks for my state of trance that I followed her to the passenger cabin instead of remaining fixed to the deck in terrified anticipation.

"He'll take us right into the Home Cove," Miranda went on. "That way we'll be all settled in by the time Ian even knows we're there. It'll be too late for him to do anything then."

"You mean he's capable of putting you back aboard this boat for the return trip?"

"Yes, except that I'm capable of having a tantrum right there on the steamboat wharf, in the face and eyes of the whole village."

"Pounding your head and drumming your heels and holding your breath, I suppose." I tried to sound amused.

"No," she said seriously. "I shall have to do something far more dramatic, like threatening to commit suicide."

What in heaven's name had Seafair Bell gotten herself into? Just how exotic *were* these Drummonds? Patrick's arrival had knocked the earlier apprehension out of my head until now. "And will he believe you?"

"No, but it might make him laugh. Or he'll ask me how I'm going to do it, and make suggestions. I wish you could see your expression!" She began to laugh. "I told you he's not Heathcliffe, or St. Elmo either. Let's hurry, I can hardly wait. The wind's perfect. She'll run before it like a scared cat."

"You don't make it sound very enticing." Away from Patrick's presence I was rapidly become sane. "Listen, Miranda, I have a right to know what's going on here."

"It's something so silly you wouldn't believe it." She began fooling with the handle of her case, looking down at it a concentration that was far more convincing than tears would have been. "I loved Uncle David. He was the only father I ever knew. And what he planned for me this summer was what he thought was the best for me. I wouldn't have defied him, Seafair." She gave me a quick little smile. "No tantrums *ever* in Uncle David's presence. But I'd have begged him to let me come home, because I just couldn't stand it away from here. I've never spent a summer away from Drummond's Island in my life!"

"And he thought it was time you did."

"Exactly. So these old friends of his were to have me at Newport."

"It sounds deadly," I said.

"You see it!" She was triumphant. "And Ian will too. I'm sure he will. Most girls are supposed to love these things, I know, but I'm not most girls. I'm myself, Miranda."

"Straight out of *The Tempest*," I said, and we both laughed.

he sail to Drummond's Island aboard the sloop *Eaglet* lived up to my expectations. It was frightful. "All I know is how to keep out of the way," I said, smiling with a fierce determination to be the jolly Gibson Girl whom chaps like to be with and call bricks. *I say, you are a brick!* And then it goes on to something far more interesting than good sportsmanship.

I hugged myself into a small ball on the floor of the cockpit, trying not to look sidewise at the white water hissing past my head a few feet away, trying to ignore the pistol shots of canvas and the creak of timbers; trying not to remember that line about the keel plowing air, which it seemed to be doing most of the time.

Miranda and Patrick sat on either side of the tiller. Her hair was pulled loose by the wind and blowing free, and she was exhilarated beyond the peaks of drunkenness. Patrick looked savagely happy.

I found myself staring at him until my eyes were burning from the glare of broken sky behind him, and his head was swallowed in darkness. A following sea rose up like a snow-peaked jade hill behind him, and I turned my head away and gazed up at the taut sail as if transfixed by its beauty, but the tilt of the masthead against the clouds and the demented flapping of the little red pennant began to make me feel seasick. There was a design on the pennant, and I tried to figure out what it was, but that was no help. Things got rapidly worse.

I hugged my knees as hard as I could, bowed my head over them, and waited. Retribution hadn't caught me aboard the steamer, but it would get me aboard *Eaglet*. Once when the boom swung over and the sloop heeled sharply to the other side, I thought we were about to capsize, and it was almost a relief. We were goners anyway; what use to struggle?

All at once she was running with a sweet, smooth freedom, and the sound of the water bubbling along her sides was like the voice of a spring brook in the woods behind Fern Grove. The sun lay hot on my head. I lifted it from my arms. The land rose before us, higher than Bannock, high enough so that I had to tip my head back to see the tops of the uppermost spruces.

Now Miranda and Patrick didn't speak to each other as they worked, and I didn't speak for fear of disturbing the ritual of bringing the sloop to the mooring where a small white dory lay. I knelt where I was, trying to greedily take in everything at once; the dark island above me and its scents, the tourmaline water over white sand, the dazzle of the beach.

I felt the way the long *Romance* of Chopin's First Concerto always made me feel; anguished for something I couldn't name and knew I could never have.

"Seafair!" Miranda stood over me. "What does that expression mean?"

"It's probably prayerful thanksgiving because she got here alive," said Patrick. "You'll notice she's on her knees. Were you scared, Seafair?"

"*Scared* is too small a word to describe it." When I stood up I staggered, and Patrick put out his arm to steady me.

"At least you didn't get hysterical or seasick, so that proves something," he said.

"It proves that I was numb." But I was pleased with the slight praise, and under its influence I stepped down into the dory with a little more nonchalance than I'd shown heretofore. I was placed in the bow seat, where I could admire the back of Patrick's neck. He had shed his oil jacket and blue sweater in the heat, and I contemplated in a haze of pleasure the leisurely rhythm of his shoulders and long back under the thin sweat-dampened shirt. Miranda was talking the whole time and looking all around her, so she didn't catch me at it.

We beached on firm damp sand beside a small spile wharf tucked into the eastern curve of the cove. Far above us the forest looked black in the light pouring down from an almost-noon sky. Westward the woods and the sand beach ran in a long curve to an arm of pink granite like the Bannock stone. Gulls stood on its broad steps and terraces, or paddled in the shallows where rockweed floated, hardly moving.

"I used to run away to this beach," Miranda said. "I can remember once when I was about three. Everyone thought I'd fallen over the cliff, and here I was the whole time, singing *Jesus Loves Me*, and digging away. This was always our beach, wasn't it, Patrick?"

He was pulling on the line that sent the dory out to her own anchorage. She rambled on, "What splendid sandcastles Pat and Tom could build. They'd let me put the gardens in. Even last year we built such a beauty that one of Erline's summer boarders took a photograph of it. Let's do it again this year, Pat. That is, if Ian doesn't exile me."

"He'll exile me if I don't get to that funeral on time. Come on." Patrick picked up our cases and started up the path behind the wharf.

"Is Tom here yet?" Miranda asked.

"Oh, he's been here a couple of weeks." His long legs took him rapidly up the steep path.

"Good," Miranda said, "because I want Seafair to meet him."

Patrick stopped at a turn in the path and looked mischievously down at me. "Why? Do you think Seafair's good material as a minister's wife?"

"Why not? She could play the organ and direct the choir, teach Sunday school, entertain the Ladies' Aid——"

"I don't care if you talk about me as if I weren't here,"

I said. "Because *I* know I'm here, and that's all that counts."

"Profound," said Patrick, tapping his temple. We went on. The steep trail wound among bright young ferns and bay, past clumps of flaming red-violet lambkill, a bank all green and white with bunchberry blossoms. Inside the woods the brown floor of dead spills was stippled finely with sunlight. Crows shouted unseen overhead and flapped to other treetops.

"That reminds me," Miranda said. "How's life in the oaks? Raised any ghosts lately?"

"Ghosts?" I asked. "Is the place haunted? This is even more than I hoped for. I've always wanted to meet a ghost."

"Maybe she'll turn out to be a psychic, Patrick," Miranda said. "She has unplumbed depths. When you hear her play the piano, you'll know."

I've always hated this sort of remark, and was glad that Patrick didn't feel obliged to make a polite comment. We went on climbing in a silence shot through with bird voices as the shadow was shot through with thin arrows of sunlight. I always had a great fondness for the mossy old forests that grow from our granite hillsides, and this felt very ancient; one could almost believe that the broad spread of thick moss thrown like a wrinkled green plush carpet over a slope to our right covered the tumbled remains of buildings at least as old as Troy.

Patrick stopped short suddenly and pointed off to the left. "The eagle's nest, the real eyrie, is up there," he said.

"In those trees?" I demanded, as if I expected to see the eagles standing around in heraldic attitudes like the one on the American seal.

"No, the track leads through them. The nest is in a virgin pine about a hundred and twenty-five feet tall, and the nest itself must be, oh, twenty feet deep at least. It's very old, and it stinks to high heaven." He spoke seriously, almost respectfully. "There's always been a nest there. When William Wallace Drummond was being rowed ashore from his vessel to look the island over, he heard an eagle scream, and he looked up and saw them circling, and he thought it was a good omen. That was what made up his mind for him."

"And as long as the eagles live on Drummond's Island," Miranda said hollowly, "there'll be Drummonds. Anyone who hates us just has to kill off the eagles, and we'll simply disappear."

"Don't be such an idiot," Patrick said.

"Well, almost everybody in the village believes it."

"You mean the ones who believe horsehairs turn into snakes, and tansy bags prevent worms, moonlight will drive you crazy, cats steal your breath, and——"

"All right, you've made your point," said Miranda. She gave me a poke in the back. "Seafair, we're almost there!"

I stepped off the path. "You'd better go first, or you'll be tramping me underfoot." Patrick laughed, but Miranda hurried on and passed him too. Salty puffs of sea wind reached us, and the ancient wood gave way to younger mixed growth with the tender bright leaf of hardwoods among the evergreens, and there were sheltered patches of blueberry and strawberry blossoms.

Then we came out into the open. On our left the open ground twinkling with daisies ran down a long slant to the deep scallops of the rocky shore. On our right a windbreak of spruce marched from the forest to the house.

From a distance the square granite house had been impressive against the sky, but as we approached it grew even more imposing. It had the perfectly proportioned simplicity that becomes elegance. It was gray granite, not pink, but one felt that the gray was the only possible choice. The shutters were white, and the roof was slate. There were four white-painted chimneys. A long clapboarded wing, painted granite gray, had been built onto the back of the house.

Out on this windswept headland no tame shrubs grew around the north and east sides of the house, just dense and cushiony grass spreading like fitted carpet from the walled edge of the cliffs to the foundation of the house. I would have headed, mesmerized, for the wall, but the other two hurried me around the end of the windbreak, past a drying yard and into the wing. We passed through a roomy wood-shed and workshop, a laundry; and finally, beyond a screen door, we came to a wide kitchen with windows open on both sides to counteract the heat from the massive black iron range. The room was still hot and aromatic with the morning's baking.

At our entrance two dogs began to bark, though it sounded at first like six, and a stout black-haired woman straightened up from looking into the oven. Miranda swept her into a hug before she could speak. A Skye terrier flew at Miranda with soprano shrieks of joy. A black Newfoundland boomed and wagged in a stately way.

The floor moved under my feet like the deck of a boat, and the heat was overpowering. I sat down. I had never been so tired in my life, and what was I doing here, any-way? All this hugging and kissing was so exhausting to watch. I'd thought islanders were impassive.

"Give me that mac you're hanging onto like grim death," Patrick said. He pulled it off my arm.

"And this is Seafair," Miranda was saying. "Meg Finlay."

I struggled up again to shake hands. Mrs. Finlay had a good grip, a strong broad face with black eyes and high color. "Welcome, Seafair," she said.

"Thank you, Mrs. Finlay," I said.

"Oh now, it's Meg to everyone. But *you*—" she pointed a finger at Miranda—"have you no more respect for your poor uncle's wishes now that he isn't here?"

"She's already had that today, Meg," Patrick broke in, "and she'll get more when Ian sees her. And you know you can't shame her."

She sighed. "Yes, I know it. But a body keeps trying."

"It's a brand that won't be plucked from the burning, Meg." Patrick took our cases and raincoats and disappeared up a narrow flight of stairs beyond an open door at the right front corner of the kitchen. He was whistling as he ran.

Miranda said righteously, "Uncle David would have let me come home this summer, if he knew I've been homesick enough to die."

"Your uncle had his reasons, and they were good ones." Meg turned back to the oven and brought out a sheet of spicy-scented cookies. "You should have accepted his word without question."

Miranda picked up the frantic terrier. "Oh, my little Charlie, he was so lonesome for his Mum, he was . . . I knew his reasons, Meg, even if he never spelled them out. He was afraid Patrick and I were too close." To me she said, "He had this old-fashioned idea about cousins marrying."

"I don't know if it's so old fashioned," I said. "There's one section of Fern Grove where there's hardly a bright one in the whole bunch, and they all have the same last name."

"Well, they were probably pretty dim to begin with. But we're Drummonds, even if I'm Muir too, and it couldn't *ever* be that way with us. Anyway, it doesn't matter. I could never fall in love with Patrick! It would be practically *incest!*"

Mrs. Finlay flinched as if she'd been slapped, and Miranda put her hand over her mouth and giggled like a six-year-old who's just sworn for the first time.

"My, what big words you've learned in school," said Patrick from the doorway. He was not smiling. "You know all the answers to everything now, don't you?"

"Almost everything," she said flippantly.

"Your modesty overcomes me," said Patrick. "I've got to go back now and clean up for the funeral," he said to Meg. He patted her meaty shoulder, nodded at me, and went out. The black Newfoundland followed him. Miranda looked out through the screen door after they'd gone, still holding the Skye in her arms. "Sometimes I think Patrick can't endure me since I grew up," she said. "He's always cutting me down. That's the negative side of older brothers, Seafair."

"Well, now!" said Meg. "Aren't the two of you starved? I'll get you a mug-up. But first you'd better wash the salt off your faces and tidy your hair. You look like proper gypsies."

Miranda put down the dog. "Meg, you've been saying that to me since I was three, and I expect you'll be saying it when I'm thirty. It makes me know I'm really home." She took Meg by her shoulders and kissed her on each red cheek.

Meg hauled back her head, sputtering, "None of that trying to butter me up now, I know all your tricks, Miss Lady!" But she began to laugh before she'd finished and gave Miranda a sound swat on her bottom. "Get along."

Our mug-up turned out to be a substantial lunch of fish chowder with homemade bread and butter on the side. Meg sat down at the table with us, sipping tea out of a flowered cup constantly replenished from a large brown teapot, which lived under a quilted cozy as big as a beehive. Charlie slept with his chin on Miranda's foot, exhausted with joy. Meg and Miranda talked all through the meal, or rather Miranda asked questions and Meg answered. I think they took everybody in the village, house by house; it became a sleep-inducing jumble of meaningless names. I wondered if Miranda would ever run down. I knew she was glad to get home, but if she maintained this altitude for the whole summer we were both going to be worn out.

When I felt as if I could lay my head on the table and go to sleep, I excused myself and went up the narrow back staircase we had used earlier. It led into a slant-roofed chamber over the kitchen, lighted by dormers, fitted out with a Franklin stove, a made-up cot, and some comfortable old chairs. The walls were lined with shelves and cases in which were arranged and labeled a collection of Indian artifacts, fossils, coins, pottery (in pieces), and what looked to my ignorant eyes like just plain rocks. There were some larger stone objects on the plank mantel over the stove. Four rifles lay across a hand-whittled gunrack on the wall over the mantel. Miranda called the place the Museum, and with an automatic response to intimations of culture I promised the room more attention when I felt more intelligent.

On either side of the stove, doors opened into the upper hall of the main house, and I went through the right hand one. My door was the first one I came to.

There was no unpacking to do, because our heavy luggage hadn't yet arrived from the harbor. I'd worn one of Miranda's summer cottons downstairs to lunch, reefed up around the middle—as she put it—to make up for the difference in height. I undressed and put on the challis wrapper from my dressing case, and walked from window to window brushing my hair. The house stood with its corners to the compass points, and I was in the western corner. From the side windows I looked down into the blossoming shrubs of the walled garden. Southward beyond the garden lay a narrow stretch of field and then the sea blue-green and rough silver. A little way off the western corner of the house there was a small orchard in bloom, then came the farmhouse and barns, surrounded by plowed fields, and pastures in which cows and a few horses grazed. Occasional tall spruces cast dark pools of shade on the turf. A belt of woods beyond the pastures hid the village and harbor.

I moved to the back window then, looking northwest. Between the large plowed and planted area and the windbreak there was an icepond and icehouse. The pond was like a rough circle of sky-blue enamel in its frame of lush grasses until I saw the gulls rising from it or settling on it, breaking its smooth surface.

Then I saw the oak grove lying between the farmlands and the ancient forest through which we had climbed from the cove. Under the afternoon sun and wind it was a rippling lake of fresh new green-gold leaves. *How's life in the oaks?* Miranda had asked. *Raised any ghosts lately?* It would be one of their childhood things, like the sandcastles.

Above the restless glisten of leaves I saw the sea again, and the dark hill of Bannock on the horizon. I thought of the funeral, of the handsome girl in black and the little boys scrubbing at their eyes with their hands, and I felt a personal depression.

I got up from the window seat where I had been kneeling. This was a very quiet house, perhaps because of its granite walls. Though one window was open, the outdoor sounds seemed to come from very far off, filtering through a fine mesh of silence.

I went into Miranda's room. She hadn't come up, and I went on out into the hall, which was more of a broad gallery extending partly over the main hall downstairs. The wide polished boards of the floor were cool to my bare feet. White-paneled doors opened from the gallery into the other rooms across the front of the house and along the northeast side. The wallpaper between the doors had a Chinese landscape design in jewel-like primary colors.

I leaned over the gallery railing and tried to see some of the hall below, and came face to face with a rosy-faced white-wigged gentleman in Colonial blue and buff. His portrait half-filled the landing wall halfway up the stairs. Benevolently he studied me, and I looked back at him with some respect; he looked more substantial than I felt at the moment, moving like a wraith through these alien scenes. I guessed him to be Colonel William Wallace Drummond.

I went along the narrow passage that led past my room toward the Museum, tiptoed with excruciating caution down a few steps, and heard nothing from the kitchen except the loud ticking of the mantel clock. Suddenly it struck one and I jumped. The stroke was echoed melodiously from the main hall. There is something portentous about the way a clock sounds, striking in an empty house. One always expects *something* to be aroused from centuries of sleep before the last vibration trembles away into nothing. At least one did at eight or so, and for an instant I was eight again. I wanted to run back to my room, but walked as decorously as if to a pew in church, resisted an impulse to see if William

Wallace were still watching me, slid into my room, and shut the door. Then I opened all my windows.

Instantly the barrier of silence was breached. I heard the sea breaking below the cliffs, birds in the garden, gulls and crows flying over, and the Newfoundland barking over at the farm.

Tidily I turned back the silk patchwork quilt that was the coverlet on my bed, took off my wrapper, and crawled rejoicing into lavender-scented sheets. The instant I shut my eyes the sound of the sea below the cliff became the bubbling rush of water past *Eaglet's* sides. . . . Into the lee, now . . . Blessed calm. Blessed sunshine. We were safe. If I opened my eyes I would see Patrick watching me, and feel his arm tighten around my shoulders. *Were you scared, Seafair?*

Not with you, I should have answered.

But I was never that quick. Never mind, there was dinner tonight, and the whole summer ahead. *Except for Ian,* one of those mysterious between waking-and-sleeping voices said.

hen I woke up my room was filled with the amber light of a westering sun. Cattle were lowing and for a free-floating moment I was small again, and back on my grandparents' farm in Cornish, waking from an afternoon nap. Then a tern banked past an open window with a piercing cry, and I came back to the world again with a sort of spiritual thump, as if dropped through a cloud. It was almost half-past six by my watch.

Miranda wasn't in her room, and there was no sign that she'd been there. Our luggage stood in the middle of the floor. I took my serviceable but completely undistinguished bags into my room, and took out and hung up only one dress, to wear to dinner tonight. With a delirious sense of freedom from Phoebe I was in no hurry to shake out and hang up the rest. In the bathroom I finished waking myself with the cold soft rainwater piped from the attic cistern, did up my hair, dressed in Miranda's frock again, and went out into the hall. Rested now, I was excited rather than oppressed by the silence within the granite walls.

It was perfectly explainable. The Finlays owned the farm, and Meg came over in the mornings to start breakfast and do what housekeeping chores were necessary. She would prepare dinner and leave it for the family to cook and serve. So she would be back at the farm now, perhaps getting ready to strain the milk and pour it into the customers' cans. Miranda was out somewhere communing with the island, her dog with her. The brothers hadn't yet come back from Bannock, or they were at the harbor. I was absolutely alone in the house, which suited me. Like the cat in a strange garret, I had to take everything in.

I went down my side of the stairs to the landing, and stared boldly back at the Colonel. The blue uniform matched his eyes, but too-good living had thickened the bold features, and the roseate tint probably wasn't all sunburn or the flush of health.

Colonel William Wallace Drummond. Immigrant boy from Scotland, carrying a hero's name. *Scots wha hae for Wallace bled,* Mr. Adams used to sing, back in the world. *Welcome to thy gory bed, Or on to Victory!*

The central staircase descended into a large square hall papered with the same Chinese pattern, but it was carpeted in dark red. Doors stood open into the rooms on either side, there were paintings on the walls, and an immense jug of white and purple lilacs was reflected in a mirror, but I saw all this from the periphery of my vision. I was drawn toward the front door, where strips of small panes on either side framed sea and sky, and a gull drifted as if in one of my dreams past the clear petals of the fanlight.

The heavy oak door opened with hardly a sound and I went out onto a half-moon doorstep of brick. The mast-flag-pole, with a gilded eagle clasping the globe at the top and the flag hanging quiet, stood across the walk, based on a granite outcropping that surfaced from the lawn like a whale's back. Small bright rock plants grew in the seams and crevices.

And beyond all that—ah, the sea. I walked out across the lawn, so as to have nothing else before me. It was as different from Casco Bay as winter from summer. I looked and I looked and thought that I could never grow tired of looking, and that I would always see something different. Today I had the terns screaming and diving below me, some sort of sea ducks riding the surge below the high head to the east, and the deep ocean swells rolling into the big cove, breaking but never really broken on the dark ledges under the cliff.

The air was rich, damp, salty, potent. I breathed deeply, though self-consciously; the physical education teacher at the college was always rounding up the faculty to bully us about our health and put us through lung exercises. "*In*-spire," she would intone, silently count, and then command, "*ex*-pire." Doing Miss Talbot was a standard vaudeville turn in the teachers' sitting room as well as in the dormitories. We considered ourselves lucky that she let us off Indian-club drill and folk-dancing.

I heard a sharp whistle and its answer overhead, and looked up, and saw two big birds rising in great spirals. They were black-winged, and the white heads gleamed in the sun.

The eagles, I thought, and my eyes filled with tears.

I wiped and blinked them away and, sniffling ecstatically, watched until the birds flew off toward a distant southerly point. Then for the first time I realized I was cold in the thin dress, and went toward the house, turning back often to look at the sea.

The hall was dim after the outdoors, and the grandfather clock standing between library and dining-room doors struck seven. Still no one seemed to be about the place. Late sun struck into the hall from the parlor doors, and I went in there. This room ran from the back to the front of the house, and on the long southwest side french doors opened into the garden. Light poured from the sky, glittered like ornaments on the tips of the garden trees, pooled in flames on the Oriental carpets, kindled minute fires in the brass fittings of the two fireplaces; cast itself through ruby, sapphire, and amber glass, flashed like the spark of life in the eyes of portraits, and turned a painted bracelet to warm red-gold on translucent flesh.

The rainbow fire in the breeze-touched prisms hanging from a lamp on the piano called my attention to that. It was a beautiful old square instrument of rosewood. I sat down to it and tried a few notes. The tone was very good. I began to play the *allegro* from one of Mozart's concerti. To play the delicate yet cheerful air now in this strange house tied me to it, however tenuously, as sleep had tied me to the room upstairs. At once *home* became several centuries away, if not actually non-existent. I was sure that even if I put my mind on it I would not be able to summon up the house in Fern Grove, or Fern Grove itself. The northwestern ocean I had seen beyond Bannock went on and on with no mainland to stop it; its tide swept around the world and returned to break against the foot of the seaward cliffs of Drummond's Island, where I sat alone, playing Mozart in a drawing room in a granite house.

Once fairly into the piece, I was absorbed by it until I felt a slight stir of air in the room behind me. There was a long mirror on the wall between the two northwest windows and I caught faint movement in it. But it wasn't there when I looked again. The mirror was like a dark tarn that had been briefly stirred by some unseen presence.

I went on playing to the end, then spun around on the stool expecting to confront Miranda. But as far as I could see, no one was in the room. It had dimmed considerably as I played. The sun had been cut off by the belt of spruce woods beyond the farm. I sat swinging back and forth on the stool, trying to see into the deeper shadows. A small sound caught my ear, and I turned toward the square dark doorway.

Someone was standing there, tall, motionless, faceless. I heard my own gasp, and said sharply, *"Who's there?"*

"I thought Adrienne was walking again," said a male voice, "or playing, rather." The voice was neither Patrick's nor Andrew's. It was like, but deeper and slower. This had to be Ian, the enemy of my summer.

"Who is Adrienne?" I asked. "I thought Miranda had told me about everyone."

"She was the Old Colonel's first wife." He came into the room. A whiff of tobacco fragrance came with him; also a face, indistinct but valid. "When she was a young girl she was a pupil of Mozart's."

I laughed aloud in astonishment. "That concerto was written for one of Mozart's pupils! Your Adrienne might have known her!" I swung back to the keyboard and touched it with reverence. "Someone who knew Mozart, who was taught by him, lived in this house. And played this piano?"

"She lived and died in this house, but I'm sorry to tell you that's a much later piano. However, these granite walls have heard much Mozart. . . . She thought Brawly Bill's Scots favorites were barbaric."

"Oh well, I don't go that far," I said. "I grew up on Robert Burns, and I'm mad about bagpipes."

"They appeal to the savage side of your nature, no doubt." He came and stood by the piano. "How do you do, Miss Bell? I'm Ian Drummond. Welcome to Drummond's Island." It was more perfunctory than hospitable. I was just as brief and didn't put out my hand.

"Thank you, Mr. Drummond. So you have a ghost."

"They used to say so. But she's not one of Patrick's and Miranda's favorites, so she may have left in a fit of temper."

"I'm sorry I disappointed you by being mortal."

"I'm not disappointed. Today I can do without ghosts." I remembered the funeral, and was slightly ashamed of myself for bristling. "Has Miranda left you to yourself all day?" he asked with polite concern.

"I didn't want to go anywhere. I was tired, and this salt air put me to sleep for the afternoon. I came down only a little while ago."

He walked away from me, the whole length of the room, and stood looking out at the sea. I was uncomfortable and felt an urge to justify my presence here; this irritated me into belligerence. In another moment I'd be making myself ridiculous by saying, *I can see I'm in the way here. I'll leave on the next boat, and in the meanwhile I'll stay in my room.*

I got up and left the room, noiseless on the carpet. Just as I reached the foot of the stairs, a door opened at the back of the hall, to lamplight and Miranda's silhouette against it.

"Seafair!" she cried, and came running. "Are you all right? Did you have a good sleep? I've been everywhere, and on the way home I stopped at the farm to see Tom and the new calves and talk to the horses. Can you smell them, or is it my imagination? Come on upstairs and I'll tell you more while I clean up."

I was instantly cured of my pique, and we were starting up the stairs arm in arm when Ian spoke from the parlor doorway.

"Well, Miranda?"

She ran down the stairs and embraced him. "Now Ian, I know all about it," she began. "But I'm not defying Uncle David or being disrespectful to his memory. If you love the island so much that you're making it your life's work, and Andrew's got Bannock, and Patrick turns down all kinds of foreign digs because he thinks he's going to find Norsemen or the Twelve Lost Tribes of Israel or something down in the oak grove—why shouldn't *I* suffer when I'm away from it? After all, it's my home too."

"Yes, it's your home, Miranda," he said quietly. "I can't dispute that." He unloosed her arms, held her by them, and kissed her. "All right. Go along and change. You do smell like the barn."

"Isn't it lovely, though? I don't know which is better, barn or bait or low tide."

"Maybe we could market a blend of all three," Patrick said from the landing, "and call it Drummond Dew."

"That sounds more like a whiskey," Ian said. He lit a lamp on a side table in the hall. As he replaced the white glass shade I saw him really for the first time; the Drummond resemblance was strong, but like the other three he was a complete individual in his own right. For one thing, he seemed much older at that moment.

Patrick came down the stairs. He wore clean flannels and a white shirt and blue tie, and a dark blue blazer. "I've got to lower the flag," he said. "Come on, Miranda, and help fold."

"Take Seafair. I've just stuck dinner in the oven and I'm on my way to wash off the barn."

"Phew, you do stink," he said as he passed her. "Come

along, Seafair." The sound of my name in his voice all but immobilized me.

"Get her a sweater or a shawl or something," Miranda called down from the landing. "Greetings, ancestor," she said to the portrait and ran up our side of the stairs, Charlie ahead of her. Her door banged shut. "You can't call that ever so airy a tread, can you?" Patrick said. "Nothing like the patter of little feet, is there? Especially in number 8's."

Andrew leaned over the railing on the other side of the stairwell and said in mild wonder, "I hadn't thought we were that quiet a bunch around here until she came into the house again."

"We can stand it," Patrick said. "This afternoon was a nightmare. Come on, Seafair." He brought a wrap out from the closet under the stairs and dropped it over my shoulders. It was a hooded cloak in dark brown wool. It was rough but it smelled of heather and peat, or as I imagined heather and peat should smell; and when he opened the front door for me and I stepped out again onto the doorstep I had the sensation of having taken on a different *persona* when I put on the cloak.

The horizon was lost in the beginnings of dusk, and the scattering of dandelions on the lawn had the cold glow of small moons. Atop the flagpole the eagle's silhouette had a miniature reality. I wanted to talk to Patrick but I felt abysmally self-conscious, and in a few moments the opportunity would be gone. As the flag came down into his hands I said, "Will I see the eagles? I mean, do they fly over the island every day?"

"Oh yes, you'll see them. But if you've never seen an eagle before, you'll probably mistake the ospreys for them. They nest over near the Old Quarry."

"Where's that?" I asked, hoping I sounded like a bright, chipper sort—the brick again.

"Oh, to the south'ard," he said with a vague wave of his arm. "The Old Quarry is where the stone for the house was cut. A great deal was shipped out from there too. We'll show you the Quarry Cove, where the vessels could come in and load, and the granite was brought out from the quarry by ox team." It's a wonder I could follow the sense of his words, I was so enamored of the whole situation. He held out one end of the flag to me, and I gathered my wits together enough to remember the ritual, which was strictly observed at school. As we folded he went on, "The Bannock quarry was opened much later. The Old Colonel's grandson, our grandfather, began that, and the pink granite is known in the trade as Beatrice Pink, for his wife."

I tried to think of something less inane than, *Isn't that interesting!* but couldn't, so I settled for what I hoped was an intelligently receptive silence. At least I didn't fumble the flag-folding. He carried a neat tight triangle into the house and laid it on the table beside the lilacs. Andrew's and Ian's voices came from the library. Something crashed in the kitchen.

"I must help Miranda," I said, handed him the cloak, and fled.

chapter 5

When the men were alone, they usually ate in the roomy kitchen. Tonight Miranda and I set the table in the dining room. A hanging lamp with an opalescent glass shade shed a soft effulgence over the long oval table. The room was paneled in mahogany, taking from the light a glow that looked warm enough to be felt. I spoke about it, and Miranda, holding up a decanter to the light and squinting professionally at it, said, "Oh, two of the Old Colonel's brothers brought the mahogany back from Haiti, in logs. They took down a load of barrel staves and dry fish and came back with molasses and mahogany."

How rich she was in relatives, and how nonchalant about such wealth. My forbears were lawyers, accountants, teachers, a couple of farmers; the most adventurous had started West as a missionary to the Indians but met a girl in Philadelphia and never got any farther.

The meal was simple but the setting and hunger made it a banquet. Baked potatoes, baked stuffed halibut, goose-tongue greens from the shore, a salad of beet and onion. The dessert was trifle in a cut-glass compote.

I concentrated on eating, listening, and not looking at Patrick unless everyone else was doing so. Fortunately this was quite often, because Patrick was as effervescent as Miranda. The older brothers seemed content to let them go on, Andrew laughing outright sometimes, Ian smiling now and then. He looked less tired in the lamplight. Sometime during the meal, when Patrick and Miranda were talking in arcane references, I realized that the two older brothers were having a separate conversation.

"The pension'll do her fine, as long as she stays on Bannock," Andrew was saying. "Or over here. She could pack fish for you, couldn't she? Or she could learn to make nets, like some of the other women. Anyway, she can live on Bob's pension, and still save something."

"What does she want to do?" Ian asked.

"She says she doesn't know yet, she can't think. But I have my own ideas. These alleged cousins of her mother's are feeding the flames. I think if she quite dared to defy Father Emery and me she'd be packed up and off with them on the next boat."

"Boston?"

Andrew nodded. "Bob turned her head by running on about her beauty and the Dolans' descent from Irish royalty, and then he kept her prisoner. These two birds who showed up for the funeral are feeding her more of the same—but the jailer's no longer around."

"What does she think she'll do with her beauty in Boston? She's a moral girl, so one profession's out," said Ian. "And she's a proud girl, so I can't see her in service."

"Maybe they're talking up the theater to her. Bob was a great actor when he was properly tuned up. His *Spartacus to the Gladiators* could make my hair stand on end.... Poor Bob. My God, it doesn't seem possible that he's gone." They became silent.

"Listen," Patrick was saying to Miranda, "I'm positive there's another foundation under the French one. And what wouldn't I give to find something so Norse that nobody could deny it! I'd make history!"

"Would you sell your soul to the devil?" Miranda asked.

"Yes, if I knew how to raise him," said Patrick.

"That must be his project for the summer," Andrew said to Ian. "Did you know they taught satanism at Bowdoin? Tom can start saving a soul right here."

"Wait till you see what I've got cooked up for Midsummer's Eve," said Patrick. "But seriously, I'd go out of my mind with joy if I found a Norse site. How are you on digging, Seafair? You look like the tough wiry type."

"Oh, thank you," I said. "It makes me sound like something hard to root out of the garden."

They all laughed. "But I have to recruit my labor where I can," said Patrick, "and the harbor boys won't do it even for pay."

"Because he and Miranda have managed to build up a whole dark mythology around the oak grove," Ian said. "When they were kids they applied to it everything they read, so it's a mad hash of the Sacred Grove at Nemi, Druids, the worship of Mithras and Thor and I don't know what else. Of course they had to impart all the bloodiest legends to their gang, and so the grove has a very bad reputation which it's done nothing to deserve."

"And nobody comes in and messes around my dig," said Patrick. "No youngsters coming there to look for arrowheads and doubloons. It works out well, but I didn't plan it that way. We scared ourselves as much as we scared anybody else. What's really down there, Seafair, besides black flies and mosquitoes, is the site of a number of early settlements up until the time when Castine and his Indians massacred the settlers. The village at the harbor is comparatively modern. The Old Colonel founded that with Revolutionary War veterans."

"I'll dig," I said. At that moment I committed myself to blisters and black flies even to the point of torture; no, I committed myself to Patrick.

"You'll be sorry," Andrew told me. I wondered what he would have said if he'd read my mind. "Oh, by the way, I sent off a quick note to Jane today. With the two girls here there's no reason why she can't come."

"No, there isn't," Ian said. "None at all."

His responses seemed purely mechanical. He excused himself and departed for the library, taking his coffee with him. I hadn't thought Patrick and Miranda were repressed before, but the instant the library door was heard closing behind Ian they became positively untrammeled.

"Lord, this place would be a morgue tonight without you two," Andrew said to me. We were putting the silver away in the butler's pantry between kitchen and dining room.

"*Me?*" I was startled. "What am *I* doing besides being an audience?"

"You're Miranda's excuse for coming home. I don't know if she'd have quite dared to come alone." Out in the kitchen Miranda and Patrick were harmonizing *Green Grow the Lilacs.*

"Would your brother have actually sent her back?"

He looked down thoughtfully at the silver he was wrapping in flannel. "If she'd landed at the steamboat wharf under ordinary circumstances, he might have personally escorted her to Boston to put her in Mrs. Whitman's care."

"Then he's not at all happy about this," I said. "I feel that I shouldn't be here at all."

"*I'm* glad that you're here, and he'll cheer up in spite of himself. We need a houseful of noise. Our father's funeral isn't so far off that the one today wasn't like heat against a burn."

His quiet kindness was reassuring. Odd how the eyes of the same shape and color could be so warm in one person and so glacial in another; though *glacial* was perhaps the wrong word. Ian hadn't been so much cold as remote, like a snowfield at the North Pole.

"If you can give us some good music this summer," Andrew said, "you'll earn your passage for fair. And you can start tonight."

I wasn't quite sure what he meant by good music—if they wanted something quiet tonight because of the funeral—but Patrick put the *Students' Song Book* on the rack, and nobody questioned it. We began working our way through, from the rousing and foolish ones to the slower and sentimental variety. The men had true and passable baritone voices; Miranda's flew above them like a bird above the waves, or like

Eaglet skimming the water that morning, which seemed about a month ago.

After *Beautiful Dreamer* I stopped playing to flex my fingers. Andrew said, "I'm dryer than a cork leg, as Job would say." He left the piano and I heard the gentle clink of glass from somewhere behind me. "Come and have a glass of wine, Seafair," he called.

"Stop plying her with strong drink, Andrew," Miranda said.

"Yes, we don't debauch damsels around this house," said Patrick. "Hello, Ian! Did our warblings wild drag you out?"

Ian was sitting in an armchair beyond the hearth of the nearer fireplace, holding a glass of wine. Charlie lay in his lap. "Not at all," he said. Andrew handed me my glass and I sat down on the sofa facing the fire. Miranda took hers and sat down cross-legged on the hearth rug; Patrick sat beside me, Andrew took the other armchair.

"What would you be doing at home now, Seafair?" Miranda said impishly. "Drinking Madeira before bed?"

"Hot milk," I said. "Or, if we felt really devilish, tea."

"Good God," Patrick said, "maybe we *are* debauching her."

"That word sounds so gorgeously sinful, like private dining rooms in swank restaurants," said Miranda. Charlie jumped down from Ian's lap and into hers. She rocked him, talked nonsense to him, then put him down and reached over and pinched Patrick's ankle. "Come on, bite old Patrick," she said. "*Bite* him."

"Here be dragons," Patrick said lazily. "Don't rile 'em." She moved over and leaned her head against his knees, and yawned. "My, but you're bony, Pat," she said.

"You're a very good pianist," Andrew said to me.

"And she wasn't even trying," said Miranda. "You should hear her *really* play."

"I have," said Ian unexpectedly. "Mozart. I thought it was Adrienne."

"Old Dry Annie?" Patrick said, and laughed.

"I always despised her," Miranda said emotionally. "He saved her from the guillotine, and set her up here like royalty on this beautiful island, and she hated it."

"But think what she was homesick for," said Andrew.

"Her Paris wasn't yours. When you were there they weren't dragging people in tumbrils to have their heads chopped off."

"Well, I'm not up to defending Adrienne at this late date," said Andrew. "It won't do her any good."

"No, and *I* need some defense." Miranda hitched across the hearth rug and knelt before Ian with her hands on his knees. "Tell me you're not mad because I came home. I hate that grim face. It freezes me to the marrow."

He put his finger on her nose. "No, I'm not mad. Do you think you're the only thing that ever gives me a grim face?"

"I know you feel sad about Robert Emmet Dolan, and even more about Uncle David. Don't you think I'm sad too? I've been missing him since the moment I stepped foot on this island today."

She sank back down and stayed by his chair, looking into the fire. He finished his wine and lit his pipe. This act always makes a man seem relaxed, if not actually mellow, so I watched to see what it did for Ian. But I could still sense his preoccupation; he was with us but not of us.

Andrew left the radius of the firelight, and came back surprisingly carrying a mandolin. He tuned it and began playing *Aura Lee;* the thin, fragile thread of melody was appropriate to the time, it went with gazing into the flames and letting our fatigue gradually envelope us in a pleasant narcosis. Almost before I became aware that the tune was becoming something else, Miranda began to sing with it, something simple and minor that I had never heard before.

" 'How often haunting the highest hilltop
    I scan the ocean thy sail to see!
    Wilt come tonight, love, wilt come, tomorrow,
    Or ever come, love, to comfort me?

Fhir a bhata, no horo eile,
Fhir a bhata, no horo eile,
Fhir a bhata, no horo eile,
O fare thee well, love, where'er thou be.' "

Tremors ran delicately cold over my scalp and down my spine.

" 'They call thee fickle, they call thee false one,
And seek to change me, but all in vain.
No! Thou'rt my dream yet, throughout the dark night,
And every morn yet I watch the main.' "

Then the mournful refrain again, and the last words dying into silence, yet the last sound as clear as the first, and each like a drop of water falling in the sun.

O fare thee well, love, where'er thou be.

No one applauded afterward, or even commented, and I was grateful for that. Andrew played nothing more. I stood up, much more abruptly than I'd intended, and said, "If everybody will excuse me——"

The hall clock began to strike. "Midnight," someone said, startled. "I'm going to bed too," Miranda said around a yawn. "But Charlie has to go out first. Come on and look at the stars, Seafair."

"She's falling asleep on her feet," Patrick said. "I'll go with you, Banty, if you're scared something'll git ye. Maybe Dry Annie's waiting for revenge."

"If I feel bony hands on my throat, I'll scream the sky down."

We all trailed out into the hall except Ian, who stayed behind to replace the fire screen and blow out the lamps. Miranda put on the cloak I'd worn, which gave me a small pang, as if she'd usurped something of mine. Andrew lit a candle for me from the row of holders below the mirror. Taking it from him I saw my face in the glass transformed by chiaroscuro into that of a mysterious but alluring changeling. Then Patrick passed behind me on his way out and he too looked into the mirror, caught my gaze, seemed to be momentarily halted as if I'd caught him instead, and then he smiled into my reflected eyes and went on.

In the next instant the front door shut behind him and Miranda. I started up the central staircase toward the Old Colonel. "Good night, Seafair," Andrew said from the foot of the stairs. "Sleep well."

"Good night," I called back. Ian had come out and was standing beside Andrew.

"I enjoyed the music," he said. "Good night."

In the fluttering candlelight the Old Colonel's eyes were disconcertingly alive, but he was never to make me uneasy, even when he was at his most sardonic.

lit my lamp from my candle and undressed. Washing my face and brushing my teeth aroused me somewhat, and when I was in my nightgown I began hanging up the dresses I should have attended to earlier. Presently I heard Miranda shouting good nights as if she couldn't possibly have sung so gently and poignantly with the mandolin. Then Charlie bounced into the room from hers, acting overjoyed to see me, and Miranda followed him, undoing her plackets.

"My clothes are a mess," I said. "I'll have to spend the morning pressing them. Phoebe's right," I said bitterly. "I'm a born slattern."

"Phoebe isn't here, remember? And Erline Pease'll do the pressing. I've already hired her to come tomorrow and do mine and yours both." She stepped out of her dress and began to take pins from her hair.

"You do live like the idle rich, don't you?" Relieved, I bundled myself into bed with a rapturous groan. "Ah, purest bliss."

"That's a good bed," she said. "It was mine. This was my room last year, and Ian was next door; Uncle David had the big bedroom at the front. Ian has that now, and I have his, and so we have a guest room. Before that, one of the boys would give up his room for a guest and go sleep in the Museum."

"I wouldn't mind sleeping there," I said. "I wouldn't mind sleeping anywhere as long as it was on Drummond's Island. Thank you for asking me, Miranda. What does 'Banty' mean?"

"Oh, Meg used to call me her bantam chick." She picked up her dress, and went into the other room, accompanied by thumps and knocks, doors opening and shutting, and remarks to Charlie. I lay studying the painting over the fireplace. I recognized it now as the scene from the northwest window, but in autumn. In the lamplight the October colors took on a gemlike translucence, and the oak grove seemed as alive as it had been this afternoon in the wind. Miranda came back in a blue wrapper. She sat on the foot of my bed and began brushing her hair.

"I love the painting over the mantel," I said.

"My father did it. You can see where he signed it. Matthew Muir. It *is* good, isn't it? He was very talented, and my mother was too, with needlework, things like that. But, as Andrew told you, I've got two left hands and all thumbs at that." Brushing the silvery fall of hair, she continued to gaze at the painting, and I thought she was going to tell me more about her parents, but suddenly she turned those azure eyes on me and said, "Seafair, you like Patrick, don't you? I can tell."

Self-protection was instinctive. "I like them all, though Ian's a bit off-putting."

"Losing Uncle David went harder with Ian than with the rest of us, and that was bad enough. I mean, he has this terrific weight of responsibility for the island ... I worry about him turning into an old bach," she said maternally. "That would be an awful waste of good material."

"What's Andrew's Jane like?"

"Marvelous!" She bounced in emphasis. "They're Philadelphia and Bar Harbor people, insanely rich, but you'd never guess it. No side at all. We met her last year. She and her father and brothers were sailing up the coast, and they put in here during a storm and stayed a week. And at the end of that time"—another bounce and a flourish of the brush—"Andrew and Jane were in love. They've been seeing each other whenever they could, and Andrew spent last Easter with them in Philadelphia and came home engaged."

"What about when they're married? Will he have to go away and be taken into her father's business?"

"Why, his business is *here*," she said in astonishment that I should ask. "He runs the quarry. Ian has the store and the fishery here, Andrew has Bannock, and Patrick—no, Jane's coming here and they've picked the place for their house." She pointed at the back window with her brush. "There's a cove beyond the oaks and already we call it Andrew's Cove."

"And will you marry someone who's willing to come here?"

She leaned her head over, brushing the hair from her crown down over her forehead, veiling her face. "I'll find someone, never fear.... Oh, Patrick was telling me outside about these relatives of Rosaleen Dolan's." She sat up. "They came out yesterday by hired boat, as if money was no object. All dressed up to the nines, flashy clothes, jewelry, scent. Patrick said they look like the owner of a sporting house and the madam. They were quite a sight picking their way to the cemetery in their fancy shoes."

"Is Rosaleen as beautiful as her father told her she was?"

"She looks," said Miranda solemnly, "as Guinevere must have looked. With the kind of bones that'll make her still beautiful when she's ninety. I told Patrick he should marry her and get that blood into the family, and he said he was trying to talk Ian into it."

We both laughed. Miranda got off the bed and said, "Sleep as late as you like in the morning. But if you wake up early and you're hungry, there'll be warm porridge on the stove, and— oh, Godfrey Mighty!" She rushed out into the hall and I sat up in alarm. "Did anyone start the oatmeal?" she shouted. Charlie raced around the balcony, barking wildly. Doors snapped open. "Oh, dear God!" Patrick groaned. "Doesn't she *ever* run down?"

"Her voice was ever soft, gentle, and low," said Andrew. "Yes, I did. But you'd better not forget it next time."

"I won't, darling Andrew," she said. "Is that dulcet enough for you?"

"*Will you go to bed?*" Ian asked, very quietly.

"Goodnight, sweet prince!" Miranda came back through my room. " 'Night, Seafair. See you tomorrow. Come on, Charlie."

After all that I had to read a chapter of Edith Wharton before I blew out my light. Miranda was humming *Evening Voices Softly Sounding*.

I woke early to the call of gulls over the house and roosters crowing at the farm. Drowsily happy I lay listening to an island at dawn, and then fell asleep again. When I woke later the sun was shining on the sort of June-blue morning that is possible nowhere except by the sea. Miranda was humming in her room as if she hadn't stopped since I'd last heard her, except that it was now *Hark, Hark, the Lark* instead of *Evening Voices*. At sight of me she burst into full voice.

"Sing before breakfast, you'll cry before supper," I said, and she said, "They've been telling me that all my life but I think it was just to shut me up. Anyway, I'll take my chances."

Meg Finlay was in the kitchen. Ian and Andrew had already gone, Ian to the harbor, Andrew to Bannock. He went back and forth in a small power launch, with one of the first gasoline engines to come to the islands. Ivor Jenkins, his superintendent at the quarry, also had one, so transportation between the islands didn't have to depend solely on sail or oar power.

I kept anticipating Patrick while we ate breakfast, and that turned my stomach into a fair approximation of a butter churn in action, so it was a relief when Erline Pease arrived and mentioned seeing him at the harbor when he went out to haul his lobster pots.

She put the sadirons to heat on the laundry stove and sat down to drink a cup of tea with Meg. She was a red-headed whip of a woman with foxy features and a surprisingly strong voice. She looked me up and down with frank interest, then said to Miranda, "You lug her home for Patrick or for Ian?"

It was meant to be a joke, because she laughed on the end

of it. You had to laugh with her, the boom of it was so unexpected.

We straightened up our rooms and brought down the clothes for Erline to press, and then went out. "I keep telling myself you don't have to see everything the first day," Miranda said. "After all, we've got all summer. So first I'll show you my cottage."

We took a path from the back door eastward toward the Head, and from out on that high granite prow we could look up the bay toward the heights of Mount Desert and Cadillac, plum-blue in the morning light; east toward invisible Nova Scotia; then across the broad mouth of the great cove toward the uttermost southern point of the island, the Bowsprit. The shore of the cove was diversified, from the height of the Head and the cliffs before The Eyrie, thence descending ledge by ledge to a strip of white sand beach; then there was a small point with a brush-and-pole weir standing off it, rising from the satiny pastel water and crested on almost every pole by a gull, a small sleek medrick, or a cormorant with his wings held open to dry.

Beyond the Weir Cove and out to the Bowsprit, it was the rockbound coast of Maine again, in all shades, shapes, and patterns, from volcanic black to broad bands of white sparkling with mica as the grass sparkled with dew.

"If anybody male asks you to go for a walk out on the Bowsprit," Miranda said, "you'd better refuse unless you want to be engaged."

We went back along the Head to the windburned turf and the tough bay bushes and wild rose thickets that helped to hold the soil to the rock beneath. A steep track led down to a short flight of wooden steps, which ended at the back door of the cottage tucked into the southern lee of the Head. Its shingles had weathered to a bayberry silver, and the bay bushes themselves came crowding up to the railing of the narrow porch that went all around the cottage. Below it there was a short but precipitous slant of rock, and at the foot of that a small stony beach between ledges. In the morning quiet we could hear the stones rattling to the slight, slow rhythm of the water.

We went into a big living room dominated by a massive fieldstone fireplace. The place was warm and dry. Sun poured in through wide uncurtained windows.

"This is where my father and mother lived," Miranda said, very quietly for her. "They began their marriage here. Their pictures are in my room. I'll show you if you haven't noticed. She was Uncle David's younger sister, and my father came here as a summer boarder; he stayed with the Schofields at the harbor. He was an artist and illustrator."

We walked around looking at the water colors, oils, and pencil drawings. Each depicted some facet of the island, people, boats, rocks, a particular tree; a horse running in the wind across a pasture with rough sea beyond him; many sketches of a girl who could have been Miranda. "Jean, my mother," she said.

"And here's a cartoon of himself—learning to sail and getting all fouled up. He adored the island. In the winter they lived in New York, but they came here every spring and stayed until late fall. I was born on the island. I don't think I could bear knowing I was born anywhere else." She looked very earnestly at me. "I really think it would have changed my personality. Warped me, somehow . . . Anyway, it was up at The Eyrie, in the same room where all the boys were born, in the east corner room that's Andrew's now. Meg gave me my first bath and dressed me. Patrick was three and he thought they'd gotten me for him. He screamed his head off when we moved back to the cottage, and Meg had to bring him and Tom down to see me every day."

I wandered around looking at the work, and kept trying to imagine Patrick as a small boy red-faced and screaming with rage and frustration. Tom at that point was nothing more than a name.

"Can't you feel the happiness here?" Miranda demanded

of my back. "They were so much in love, can't you tell? Whenever I come here I feel it. This was always my own special place. My playhouse first, and later I'd come here to read, and write letters, or bring my friends. And I'd always feel so close to my father and mother. I don't even remember them, Seafair; not as voices and clothes. But yet I remember *something*, I must! Because it's as if I'm sharing their happiness and their love whenever I come here. Does that sound silly?"

"No," I said. I had come to the cottage organ by then and I sat down and opened it, and began pumping. "Not silly in the least. In fact, I can almost feel it; it's as if the walls were permeated with it." I played a chord. "Not bad."

"Not bad, when you consider how many fists and boots have pounded and thumped away at that organ over the years. It's a wonder the poor thing holds together." She sat down in a wicker rocker, her hands folded uncharacteristically in her lap, and looked out at the water. "They died in the same diphtheria epidemic that took away so many people on here and on Bannock. Jean swore she'd had it as a child, and she was helping out with the children at the harbor. Uncle David knew she hadn't had it, but he was away until it was too late. Matthew caught it from her." Miranda rocked gently, still gazing at the sea. "It was just pure luck none of us children caught it. Of course we'd been kept isolated at The Eyrie from the time it first struck. I was eighteen months old, and I wouldn't have missed my mother as much as the boys missed her. It was especially awful for the older ones, I guess, because they remembered their mother, and they'd lost her when Patrick was born. Then they lost their Aunt Jeannie. Well, by the time I was old enough to feel cheated by losing both parents, I could come here alone, so I did, and in a way it was like being with them again."

She jumped up from the chair. "There! I've told it and now we can go on to the next thing." She was Miranda again as I had first known her. "I had to get it over with. Let's go to the farm so you can meet Tom. He lived at The Eyrie then too, when Meg had charge of us."

"She still does, doesn't she?" I asked, and Miranda laughed.

"Oh yes, we're her kids all right. We'll never grow out of that."

he first time I saw Tom Finlay he was running across the pasture from Marsh Cove with a newborn Jersey calf in his arms, the Newfoundland trotting ahead, the frantic cow bellowing behind him, so close that I expected any moment to see him gored and tossed. The horses stared, then in one movement wheeled, and cantered to the farther end of the pasture. The other cows also kept their distance.

He was a small figure at the first. All that was definite about him in the distance—except the visible urgency—was the black hair and the long legs. In the heat waves shimmering up from the warm moist earth the little group was unreal, yet our helplessness was very real. I was going to see a man maimed or killed, and I couldn't do a thing about it.

"Where *is* everybody?" I cried out. "Isn't there anybody to help?"

"I don't know," Miranda said in a perfectly indifferent tone. In disbelief I looked at her and saw that she was stunned with fear. "He's too far away."

"We could distract her!" I cried heroically, considering my suspicion of even the most peaceful cow. "Come on." I started for the bars.

"Then he'd have to save one of us," she said. The dog ran at the cow just then, and she turned her rage on him, but he kept out of reach of her horns, and the man seized the advantage and ran faster. Miranda came to life. "Hold Charlie!" she called. She ran down behind the barn, with me behind her, to where we had just been scratching the pigs' backs, and opened the gate into the east pasture. I grabbed the exhilarated Charlie.

The man ran through. The dog, as if knowing his part, veered toward us and lay down, and the cow plunged in past us. Tom laid the calf down on the grass and jumped away from it as nimbly as a dancer, circled the now-oblivious cow, came out through the gate, and swung it shut. The dog went to him, his broad stern wagging in congratulations. I put down Charlie, who rushed to greet the Newfoundland. Tom, wiping his forehead, grinned at us.

"Good teamwork. Thanks." He was soaked with sweat and flushed coppery-red. He had black eyes like his mother's, at once humorous and keen beneath heavy peaked brows. "Hello, Seafair," he said to me. I heard all about you yesterday. Welcome to the island."

"What were you doing out there alone?" Miranda asked severely. "Where's your father?"

"Oh, he and Pearl are cleaning up blowdowns over above Steeple Cove. I saw that Jonquil had disappeared out of the pasture this morning, so I wondered if she'd gone to drop her calf in the woods somewhere. Hero found her." He touched the dog's head. "I wasn't counting on her being so terrified, but I should have known. She's high strung." We looked across the gate to where the cow was now washing her infant from head to foot. "She's new to us," he said to me. "They bought her this spring. I don't know how she was raised, but certainly not like any of ours."

"All yours are raised by hand," I said. "Miranda told me."

"You could call it that. At least they trust us. Maybe Jonquil will do better next year." The three horses had gathered in the corner by the gate, stretching their necks over the fence, nudging at handy elbows and shoulders. The older pair were dignified, the younger one still retained some juvenile quirks that made me shake my head when Tom offered me lump sugar to give them. "I'm not at my best with anything four-legged larger than Hero." The Newfoundland at least appreciated that.

Miranda started to laugh. "Listen to her. She was all ready to run out and wave herself like a red flag in front of Jonquil to save your neck."

"That was before I *thought*," I pointed out. "She who hesitates isn't lost, she saves her own neck."

"I appreciate the impulse," Tom said. "Even if it was rapidly followed by second thoughts. And *you*"—he turned on Miranda—"what were *you* doing? Applauding the Roman holiday?"

"I was in a trance of pure terror," she said, not at all convincingly. But I had seen the truth, whether Tom believed it or not. Anyway, now it wasn't important; the little drama was over and the place was Paradise once more. The young horse suddenly broke into an exuberant canter across the pasture toward the blue rim of sea, and I wanted to do the same thing, though not necessarily neck and neck with him in the same pasture.

Tom's and Miranda's voices had become simply a part of the whole sound of the June morning. Leaning on the pasture bars I didn't care what they were saying. When Miranda jabbed me in the ribs I jumped.

"What are you dreaming about?" she asked.

"I thought maybe Patrick knew a spell to turn that horse into a prince," I said, and she and Tom laughed. We walked up through the buttercups to the house, and under the two big maples to the gate on the road.

We must have talked there at the gate, but I don't remember what about; I recall only that I was mulling in a happy simmer, like a singing tea kettle.

A little way beyond the farm gate, the road left the sight of the sea and entered the spruce woods. When it emerged again we were on the hill above the harbor. At our right stood the small white church, whose steeple rose triumphantly above the tallest of the old spruces sheltering its northern side. The cemetery behind it had been cut out of the woods, and bounded with a low stone wall. Between the wall and the road daisies and buttercups and tawny hawkweed grew thick, and more field flowers had pushed up wherever they could among the granite ledges of the dooryard, trembling and sparkling in the light wind off the sea.

The harbor lay blue and almost empty, except for the Drummond's cutter *Kingfisher* lying at a mooring near the mouth. Waiting for the men's return to the splitting tables, the gulls stood in meditative ranks or shed roofs and harbor ledges, and in single elegance on wharf spilings. Children played around the shore and I thought how my young brothers and sisters would envy the freedom of these. Charlie passed the time of day with a half-dozen dogs and ignored the cats.

The steamboat wharf was deserted right now except for the gulls. A small schooner lay beside the fish wharf, unloading bags of salt, and Ian was out there, but we didn't go near him. Miranda, waiting impishly for my reaction, showed me the hogsheads where the cod livers were kept, their oil being drawn out by the sun.

"Fascinating," I said in a lofty tone. "Even the smells around here are very rich and nourishing." I took a deep breath just to show her I didn't intend to waste any opportunities for self-improvement.

We kept on around the shore almost to the opposite point, and looked inside West India Hall, built in the days of the West India trade for dances and other social events. Coming back we stopped at the school, set well back against the woods. The teacher's little house was beside it, empty for the summer. Then we came down the gentle slope behind the store where the thick meaty salt codfish were drying on racks, and visited the factory, an airy one-story building where a half-dozen girls were cutting and packing the dried fish in small wooden boxes labeled "W. W. Drummond and Sons, Drummond's Island, Maine."

Miranda introduced me all around and told them to come over. "We've just been waitin' for you to git home," one of them said. "Thought for a while you warn't going to make it."

"Well, you know me," Miranda said.

"Ayuh, we know you!"

We made stops in a few houses, where I was welcomed with the unaffected courtesy I'd met everywhere so far. There was no sense here that Miranda was gentry and they the commoners, any more than there'd been with Erline Pease that morning. Miranda cuddled babies, told a four-year-old to stop picking his nose, and gossiped with shameless gusto.

At this rate it took us quite a while to get to the store.

Ian was back from the fish wharf, and his clerk had gone home to dinner. Ian looked at us with amicable amusement; I felt a small shock of surprise to see him thus, separate from the master of The Eyrie and head of the Drummond family.

"What are you going to treat us to?" Miranda asked him. "Besides crackers and cheese?"

"Sarsparilla and Yellow Dock Bitters?" he suggested. "Thins and purifies the blood. Cures chilblains. Clears up the high fantods like a charm."

"Sounds better than nanny-plum tea," Miranda said.

We settled for a couple of bananas. Charlie chose cheese, barking at Ian for it, and stayed inside when we went out.

"Oh, there's Patrick," Miranda said. He was rowing around Northern Harbor Point in a double-ender, standing up facing the bow, and pushing on the oars. I tried to quiet my agitation by methodically peeling my banana. We went across the road and sat down on an old timber at the brow of the beach to wait for him. It was quiet except for the bees in the chicory and buttercups; the children had all vanished home to dinner in roaring hot kitchens. Now and then a gull stretched out his neck to halloo at one flying above him, but it seemed desultory. Slowly, thoughtfully, we ate our bananas, and I watched Patrick row across the harbor to the fish wharf. He put his lobsters in a crate and tied it to the spilings, washed down the peapod, sent it out on a haul-off, shed his oilskins and rubber boots, and began to walk around the shore toward us, carrying a bucket.

"Happy, Seafair?" Miranda asked suddenly.

"Yes," I said, watching Patrick approach.

Patrick boiled the lobsters and we took them out onto the Liberty Knoll, where the flagpole stood, to crack and eat. My few experiences with lobster had been under the most decorous conditions. Now, sitting on a granite ledge and picking out warm lobster with my fingers, I swore that I would never eat lobster any other way.

In the afternoon we went down to the oaks. In mid-June the leaves were newly changed from their first bronze-rose to green and still not full-sized, and when the wind stirred and shook them you moved in neither light nor shadow but in a transparent totality of the two. It was never cold under the oaks then. But later, when the leaves grew thicker and darker, the shade was hardly ever broken, and it never had a chance to warm. Even when the sun burned hotly and light glared up from a motionless, misty sea, when you went into the grove you entered a twilight of cold.

On that first day we still had warm showers of sun, singing birds, and our own giddy sense of well-being.

"There was always an oak grove here," Patrick said, "even though these aren't the originals. Early settlers probably girdled the big trees and felled them, either to clear the place or to get lumber and fuel, or for both reasons. I can show you traces of some gigantic trees."

"I know the lecture by heart," Miranda said. "I'll be back." She drifted off from us down a long avenue among the trunks, her hair changing hues as she moved from light to shadow. Charlie sniffed through the uncurling bracken that was taller than he was. I was delighted to be alone with Patrick and only hoped I could convince him by listening that I was fascinating.

"Now here"—a grassy hollow squared by four short granite posts—"is the site of the first cabin built after the Revolution, by a veteran named Adam Joy, one of the Old Colonel's men. They all were, but Adam came first. He moved to the village at the harbor as soon as there was one, and he lived to a fantastic old age, and used to tell hair-raising stories. My father could just barely remember him."

"He must be one of the grove's more prominent ghosts."

Patrick laughed. "If he roams, it's over at the harbor. . . . My father dug here as a kid. His finds are in a case by themselves in the Museum. Some coins, lots of broken pottery, buttons, utensils, a damn'—darned fine powder horn, a tomahawk—things from before Adam's time, most of them, proving he built his cabin on an existing site. I used to come down and dig in the cellar hole too, alone if I couldn't get Miranda and Tom, determined to find *something*. But my father had been just as determined, so there wasn't anything to find, and I didn't realize then how many levels there could be. So I began looking for a dig of my own. And finally I found something."

We walked on. Miranda was a phantom flickering among the trees at a great distance now, Charlie just the impression of something swiftly moving through the bracken. We came to the ruins of what had once been a huge brick chimney, with fireplaces on two sides. Now it was a pile of bricks with tall grasses and plants growing up around it. The fireplaces were just discernible.

"What's left of Adam's son's place," Patrick said. "He wasn't as tidy or as saving as the old man. Adam salvaged every brick he could to use in his new house."

Then we came to his dig, a neatly squared excavation, in depth about shoulder-height for a man. A primitive hoisting arrangement had been erected on the surface at one corner, and some pails and a couple of bushel baskets stood nearby. There was also a screen nailed to a rigid frame, with a pile of loose dirt under it.

There was nothing wildly provocative or soul-stirring about the scene, yet Patrick stood looking down into the hole as if into Ali Baba's cave. "But how did you know where to dig?" I asked.

"I made plenty of false starts, believe me. But this faintly sunken spot showed up one spring when I was home for

Easter vacation, and nothing had started to grow yet. I knew it would have to be close to the spring that influenced Adam and the others—there where the alder swamp lies now, between the grove and the beach. But I missed the right spot for a long time." He grinned. "Tom and Miranda were so tired of the whole thing that when I did find something they wouldn't believe me. So I started out single-handed. First I found a cabin site for that period when more settlers lived on the islands than on the mainland, roughly from the middle 1600s until the French and Indian wars. This matched some of my father's finds. But I'd been reading about Schliemann digging for Troy, so I went right on down, and found the remains of a French fishing station. Not my conclusion alone, we had some experts down here looking it over, and the coins I found there, and a knife, and they agreed. I'll show you all that stuff... But look, there's a little of the stonework there. The French built with stone in some places."

He jumped down into the pit and pointed out along one side what my ignorance would never have taken for the work of man. "Good job, what?" he said with admiration. "To have lasted this long. I'll be very careful not to disturb or weaken it." He ran his fingers over it and looked up at me with a serious and vulnerable face, wiping away a black fly with his dirty hand. "At other places on the island, and on Bannock too, we've found traces of Basque, Portuguese, and even Italian occupancy. They were crossing the Atlantic to fish long before Jamestown or Plymouth Rock, you know."

"I didn't know," I said. I was dazzled, if not by the tangible traces of the past; I was almost afraid to look him straight in the eye for fear of giving myself away. Luckily I remembered what he'd said at the table last night. "But has anybody found anything Norse?"

His cheeks went red. "That's what I'm going for! The family thought I'd done well enough, finding the French fishing station. But I'm gambling on the chance that they built on something existing, and there's no telling what's under there. Schliemann went down through city after city looking for Troy, I'll give you some of the stuff about him to read . . . Good Lord, we don't know *how early* white men set foot on these shores. I'll settle for proof of the Norse landing, something a lot more than Longfellow's *Skeleton in Armor*, who was probably Lo the poor Indian in a necklace of shell."

"I loved that poem," I said with a sigh.

"So did I!" he said vehemently. "The poem's not a fake. But the original skeleton was no Norseman. Somebody's always turning up a so-called rune stone, or a mooring hole, or a hunk of statuary. It's the great romance of the century, you know. And most of us, if we ever traveled in time back into the year 1000 or so, and landed in the midst of a Viking settlement, would die either from terror or the stench."

He came up the ladder. "We'll find something down there, Seafair. I don't know what, but *something*."

That *we*. "Yes," I said devoutly. "When do we start?"

Miranda was wandering back toward us, and he called, "Don't bother us, Banty, you'll just be in the way. I've got a really dedicated assistant now."

"You mean she's willing—nay, eager—to get down into that hole and do navvy work with a shovel?"

"I'm willing," I said staunchly. Patrick put his hand on my shoulder. "I believe you are. But you don't have to. You can sift through the buckets of dirt. Tedious but necessary."

"I'll do anything," I said.

"Look at her," said Miranda. "That's a glazed eye if I ever saw one. She doesn't even know what she's saying."

"Yes I do," I said. "I'm going to sift and I can hardly wait."

"So you can go fritter somewhere else, Banty, because Seafair and I don't need you."

"Oh, I can occupy myself very well," she assured him. "You'd be surprised how well. But you won't get rid of me that easy. Seafair's lucky, I can feel luck all around her, and you'll probably discover a Norse shield or a brooch or something, and I want to be in on the glory. After all, I've worked hard enough at it all these years. Remember that summer when we dug in the bog over at Marsh Cove in hopes you'd find a preserved body? There, Seafair," she said triumphantly, "you didn't know he was a ghoul too, did you?"

"That's only one of the many facets of my personality," said Patrick. "Turn me any way and I glitter."

We sat down on the ground beside the hole. Patrick lighted a cigarette and gazed into the excavation as if he had Roentgen rays in his eyes and could see through solid earth to unimaginable treasures.

"You needn't think," Miranda told him, "that you're going to keep us working steadily. Seafair's got a lot more things to find out about the island."

"You'll have time to do everything. We've got all summer."

"I've heard that before," said Miranda grumpily. She dug her chin into her fists. "There's never enough time. *Never.*"

Patrick gave her a hard shove that rolled her over onto the grass, jumped up, and ran. She went after him, shouting threats. Charlie ran too, and I sat on the ground watching them go round and round among the oak trees, hearing myself laughing a great deal; I think even if I hadn't been in love I would have laughed with the same irrepressible joy.

om joined us that evening while we were eating dinner. Later we had music, and while we were singing two couples came in from the harbor. I'd met the girls that morning, while they were packing fish. Faustina Pease was Erline's niece, and had the same whippy lean build and fox-red coloring, but she was quieter—at least on the first meeting—and had a long earnest face, with big horsy teeth that her upper lip couldn't quite cover. Prissy Schofield was Rubensesque, abundant in hip and bosom; one felt that if she were free of corsets she would suddenly burgeon out into one great lush cabbage rose. In another few years she'd be blowsy. Now she was exactly ripe. Faustina's young man, Hugh Swenson, was tall and bony, weather-burned to a rich red-brown in which his eyes were an incongruously pale blue. This gave the impression of a chilly, analytical shrewdness until he laughed, which was often.

Whether Dill Kalloch could be described as Prissy's young man or one of her following, I didn't know. He was cousin to the Sleeping Prince of our trip out on the steamer, and he was handsome in a monolithic way, as if one of Patrick's sorcerers had hewn him out of the island's granite. He was huge in shoulder and chest, thick-necked as a bull, and very silent.

When my hands were tired, Hughie produced his concertina, which he'd politely left out of sight, and Andrew took up his mandolin. "I'm the only Drummond since my father who can play an instrument," he said with modest pride.

"Oh, I don't know," said Patrick. "I've never really tried."

"Crazy about yourself, ain't ye?" Prissy gave him a nudge in the ribs that nearly knocked him over.

"Not half as crazy as I am about you, love." He gave her a hard squeeze and she screeched delightedly. Across the hall the library door closed silently. I wondered what Ian did in there by himself: if he sat smoking his pipe and gazing into the fire, or if he wrote letters, or peacefully read. He was quiet at meals, but that was obligatory at the same table with Patrick and Miranda, and he seemed to enjoy their antics.

Around nine Andrew herded us out into the kitchen. "Let's wet our whistles and call it a night. We've all got a day's work tomorrow, or most of us have."

We made coffee and set out a big plate of Meg's chocolate jumbles. "Do you think Ian would like a cup?" I asked Miranda. She was keyed up with the evening, pink-cheeked, eyes brilliant. She floated past me with the cream pitcher, saying, "I don't know. Go ask him." In the middle of the floor Hughie was demonstrating a trick with a kitchen chair, Dill sat on his heels against the wall looking either enigmatic or sleepy, Andrew sat on a corner of the table; Patrick was telling Hughie it couldn't be done. Faustina was setting cups and saucers around, and Prissy was gleefully quizzing Tom on something that didn't make any sense to me. Tom was patiently good-humored as she kept saying, "Now, warn't that so? *You* remember, you ain't that numb!"

"Oh, for heaven's sake, Pris," Miranda said. "Were you vaccinated with a gramophone needle?"

"Gramophones run down, but not that one," Faustina said.

I went out by way of the butler's pantry and down the hall to the library and rapped.

"Yes," Ian answered. "Come in."

He was sitting on the leather sofa before the fire. When he saw me he half-laughed in surprise and got up. An open book fell off his knee to the rug.

"Hello!"

"Did you think it was Adrienne again? Or maybe a stray raven?"

"Too early for that. They come at midnight." He picked up the book. "Come in, come in. If you're looking for something to read, help yourself any time."

"I shall, thank you, but I came now to ask if you'd like some coffee."

"Has Prissy gone?"

I shook my head and he said, "Then I'll pass it up. Prissy's a dear girl and there are times when I appreciate her high spirits, but at other times she has all the charm of a gull discovering a fresh cod head."

"I know what you mean," I said. "I'll bring you a cup here. With a couple of jumbles?"

"Good Lord, no!" he exclaimed. "I don't need waiting on. I'll come out when they're gone."

When I went back to the kitchen I hadn't even been missed. They were all sitting around the table, and everybody was either talking or being talked at, except Dill, who drank and munched with a granitic concentration.

Prissy was still hectoring Tom with crude innuendoes and double-entendres punctuated by gusts of laughter. Then she'd draw a thick hand down over her face pretending to pull it out long and say, "There, I'd ought to be real proper in front of you now, hadn't I, Tom?"

Tom's dark face was set now in a mask of tolerance. One felt that he was keeping back a good deal, knowing that one cold or sarcastic retort would put an unfortunate ending to the evening. As I sat down at the table between Hughie and Miranda, Prissy's sparkling eyes fixed on me.

"Ain't I awful? I don't talk fit to eat, do I? I don't know what you must think of me, you a teacher and from away and all!" And a poor pindling, little thing without an ounce of real woman's blood in her, she might just as well have added. The contempt was there, but I ignored it.

Miranda spoke in a high and cutting voice. "Since Seafair's a lady, she'll never tell you just what she thinks of you, Prissy. But I'm an islander like yourself, and we're a race apart. So I'd be happy to tell you. Shall I start now?"

It cut through the noise like a hot knife through butter. Prissy's already flushed face turned peony red. Tom looked alertly at Miranda, both questioning and warning. I thought his lips started to shape something. Patrick, beyond Miranda, must have touched her foot under the table; I felt her knees jerk irritably toward mine, away from him. Her chin was up. She didn't take her eyes off Prissy, and Prissy stared back with watering gaze, even the whites of her eyes reddening.

In the dramatic silence Dill took a long, contented, gurgling swallow from his coffee cup, Andrew laughed, and in a moment everyone did, loud with relief. Dill glanced up with innocence so mild and bovine that from that time on I ceased to regard him as granite but as a particularly gentle young bull.

Soon Tom got up to go, and that started the others, which was probably his idea. The girls cleared the table first, and Prissy was notably quiet, for her. Miranda left with them, to give Charlie a run.

"Coming, Seafair?" she called back from the entry.

"No, I'll wash the dishes," I answered.

"Go ahead and start, and I'll be back to wipe them! Just as soon as Charlie does his little chore." Her voice was cut off by the slam of the outer screen door.

Andrew had already left the kitchen, saying he was going to write a letter. Patrick leaned against the counter by the sink, yawning and heavy-eyed. "Don't start them," he warned as I reached for the dishpan. "You'll end up by doing the whole thing. That's one of her little tricks. She's likely to go halfway to the harbor."

"I'd like to do them," I said. "I'm too wide-awake yet for bed." The dinner dishes were still there, though we'd scraped and stacked them. They weren't supposed to be left for Meg. I put on my apron, and began ladling hot water from the reservoir at the back of the range, and as Patrick was still watching me I hoped he might volunteer to wipe, and I would ask shrewd questions about archeology, if I could think of any, to show that I was intrigued with the subject and frantic to learn more.

Instead he wandered aimlessly around the kitchen for a few moments and then disappeared up the back stairs. "Oh well," I said aloud, and got to work.

Washing somebody else's dishes when you don't really have to can be a peaceful and relaxing occupation. I was humming scraps of what we'd been singing earlier when Ian came in, looked around like a conspirator, and said, "Peace, perfect peace, with loved ones far away... You don't have to wash those dishes." He poured coffee for himself.

"I know I don't," I said, "but I want to. It makes me feel a part of the life here.... I don't know if that's a good way to describe it."

"You're already a part of the life here, with your music." He stood by the counter where Patrick had stood, drinking his coffee. I washed a few dishes at a time and then dried them. "My father was a fair pianist. More than fair. There were evenings, especially in fall and winter, when he played a good deal, so we grew up with that. Then there's a lot of musical talent of one kind or another around the harbor. In the winter they've always had weekly hymn sings at the church, even though we don't have a regular minister out here now. In earlier days they've had parsons who taught school too." He handed me his cup to wash and began putting the clean dishes away, talking as he walked back and forth between the sink and the pantry. "They've had some great characters out here. My father went to school to a brilliant Irishman who turned out to be an unfrocked Jesuit priest. How and where my grandfather ever picked him up nobody knew, except perhaps my grandmother. At the time there was a Presbyterian minister here. They dueled on every point of theology; called each other heretic every day; and when Rourke dropped dead the parson wept. Their time here was the Golden Age of rhetoric for Drummond's. It's never been so exciting since, unless you count the time the Coast Guard brought the sheriff out to arrest another teacher for murdering his wife back in Bucksport. My father used to say that patriotism wasn't the last refuge of a scoundrel, Drummond's Island was."

"But it feels so far beyond the horizon, as if no one could ever really find you here."

"It's been a great jolt to a number of people to find out that we're attached to the continent by the U.S. Mail and a regular boat schedule."

Patrick came running down the back stairs. "Where's Miranda?" he demanded of me, as if I'd carelessly lost her somewhere. "Isn't she back yet? That nitwit! She could be crawling around somewhere with a sprained ankle, or a broken one! It would be just like her, you know," he said angrily to Ian. "The start of the summer and she'll have to be carted off to be put in a cast, and she'll be ugly as sin about it." He pointed at me. "I *told* you she wouldn't be back until the dishes were all done and put away."

"Then that's what she's doing," Ian said. "Waiting around until she's sure. She's probably sitting out on the Liberty Knoll looking at the stars, or else she's yarning away with Tom down in the orchard——"

"I'm going out," Patrick broke in. "Might as well go now as later. The time somebody doesn't go look for her is just the time she'd pick to break her idiotic neck." He went out, slamming the door.

Ian said, "He's always been that way about her."

"Don't *you* worry?"

"If I worry about Miranda, it's not for that. . . . When she came to live with us, Pat was still the little one, you know, still wholly under Meg's care when Andrew and I could go off and play at the harbor. So he and Tom were used to playing with Miranda either watching them from her pen or falling around in the midst of their things. Even then Patrick would be badly upset if she hurt herself, or if she cried just from temper. If the rest of us had reacted as he did, she'd be spoiled far more than she is."

"I don't think she's spoiled," I objected, "unless that's your term for her being very sure of herself, never in doubt about who she is and what she wants." Then I remembered the circumstances under which I'd come to the island, and said, "I think I'd better keep still."

I wiped out the dishpan and put it away, then removed my apron. He *was* off-putting; he made me feel like a babbling fool. Still leaning against the counter he was meditatively sucking on his pipe stem and gazing at me with the remote stare I'd often observed in pipe-smokers, Papa included.

"Well, I think I'll say good night," I said, sparklingly.

He took his pipe out of his mouth. "Maybe she's not spoiled in the usual sense," he said. "She's generous and kind. Most of the time she's conscious of other people's sensibilities, and when she isn't it's not from callousness, but from a kind of innocence. But believe me, Seafair," and his quiet almost drowsy tone gave the words a chilling significance, "such innocence can be deadly. Which my father very well knew when he wanted to separate her from Pat."

"If I hadn't been so eager to accept her invitation, do you think she would have come home?"

"Yes, I think she would have found a way to be where Pat is." He straightened up. "The last thing I want is for you to feel any responsibility for Miranda's actions. It's good having you here, Seafair. It's good having Miranda home, in spite of everything. We need all this noise in the house, and by noise I don't mean your music, because that's in a class by itself." He nodded at me and went back to the library.

Upstairs, lighting my lamp from my candle, I remembered how, on the *Ocean Pearl*, Miranda had said, "Oh, *Pat!*" and went into his arms. No, I wasn't to blame for what had begun years ago in the nursery. But I was somewhat shaken.

When I turned up my lamp, I saw the books dropped on my bed. Patrick must have brought them in when he was upstairs earlier. I was glad—in fact eager—to read about Heinrich Schliemann, not only to please Patrick but to think about something else besides the Drummonds.

It took me a little while to get my attention completely focused on the print. But I did, finally, by an exercise of will power, and so I was actually startled by an abruptly stifled burst of laughter from outside. I turned down my lamp and got out of bed and went to a back window. Patrick said something in a low voice and Miranda laughed again. Charlie yipped, and was hissed at. Then the shed screen door shut quietly. Silence after that. I went back to bed and blew out my light.

I didn't want to talk to Miranda tonight. I had better be left alone in the dark with my thoughts, oppressive as they had all at once become. I saw now how ludicrous was my attempt to reach Patrick by reading his books and pretending a passion for archeology. Miranda, as I'd told Ian tonight, was extremely sure of herself, and she knew what she wanted. She'd said to him, *When I found out you weren't going away this summer—* Was that what had sent her home?

I pulled my extra pillow over my head so I wouldn't hear their goodnights in the hall, and kept it there until I was pretty sure Miranda had put her light out and settled down.

hen I awoke in the morning to the laughter of mackerel gulls, more than just the night was behind me. The tortuous entwinings of personalities had miraculously straightened out; anything seemed possible, and it was all good.

There was to be a dance on Saturday night, but I couldn't spare the time to anticipate that when each succeeding hour offered me some novel experience, whether in my own company or that of the others.

In the next few days I dug clams for the first time, and went fishing in the harbor for flounder. I watched the tarring of nets in the great kettle bubbling over a fire on the rocks. We sat on the store doorstep eating penny candy and drinking root beer with a flock of children, while across the road the men cleaned codfish on the splitting tables, surrounded by clamoring gulls and a few salt-water crows. We swam in the Home Cove.

We sifted dirt for Patrick in the oak grove; perspiring, grimy, attacked by black flies. "The mosquitoes come later," Miranda said with morbid relish. Patrick, stripped to the waist (I got used to this in one morning by imagining with pleasure how Phoebe would blanch at the sight), dug delicately away with a trowel, muttering, slapping at insects, and educating us. Sometimes Tom was there to help.

Discoveries: One button, which had come off Patrick's shirt several days ago; one fifty-cent piece, which Tom claimed to identify as one given to him by his father to buy firecrackers with on July Fourth, 1886, and which he had lost on that date, and which, he said, Patrick had probably been deceitfully carrying around in his pocket ever since.

One genuine find was an Indian ax. "Now if you could only find a skeleton," Miranda said, "you'd have both victim and weapon, a complete drama. Viking invader slain by Indians."

He was not pleased. "Trouble is, there's not another thing in this layer to go with it." He showed me how it had been shaped from a basaltic rock, grooved and hafted, and probably used.

One morning he turned up a broken mustache cup, decorated with sailing ships. Also a pin tray bearing the words, "Souvenir of New Orleans." In frigid silence he placed the objects on the edge of the excavation. Finally Tom said in a gentle tone, "In all the pictures the Vikings have very long mustaches."

"They're well-traveled, too," I said.

Patrick said quietly, "Seafair, when you first came I thought you were a good, decent, honorable girl."

"A brick," I said.

"Exactly. I never believed—even if anyone had told me— that you could be corrupted enough by these two partners in sin to join in their low humor."

"Please, sir," I said tremblingly, "does this mean I'm discharged without references?"

"Since I can't possibly give you a good reference and still be true to myself, I shall have to keep you on."

"Oh, thank you, sir," I said, bobbing a curtsy.

"I wouldn't trust him as far as I could see him," said Miranda. "He's got a lecherous eye. He'll probably expect to be paid for his kindness."

I refused to go sailing in *Eaglet* one afternoon when the sea was a cold dark blue brushed with silver, and spent the time reading Edith Wharton on a giant's throne of sun-warmed rock below the Head. At least I read when I wasn't watching, listening, or simply *being*. I hoped the other three were madly happy out there, all hanging out over one side of the boat to keep her from rolling onto the other. *I* saw the eagles flying that afternoon, and no mistaking them for ospreys now.

On Saturday morning Miranda got up early to go with Patrick to haul, and I helped Meg to change the beds and tidy the bedrooms. I had a cup of tea with her afterward, and she talked comfortably of the Drummonds and Tom as children.

"I am suffering a sea change," I said solemnly to Miranda on that blazingly bright noon. We were sitting on the hot rocks of the Home Cove, after swimming. "I'm turning into something rich and strange."

"Of your bones are coral made," she said. "These are pearls which were your eyes." She rolled two periwinkle shells toward me. "Are your eyes pearls, Seafair? If they are, they must be the dark ones. The rare ones. Rich and strange is right. Sometimes I don't know you."

"Is that bad?" I asked, wondering what was coming.

"No, it's good! You're blossoming like one of those Japanese paper flowers in water. You're in your own medium, Seafair. This is where you belong."

Kind and generous, as Ian said. But how conscious of my sensibilities where Patrick was concerned? In a way it was a relief to know I wasn't all that obvious. But why couldn't I ask her about herself and Patrick? Or why couldn't I take for granted the mischievous way she'd spoken the day we arrived: *I could never fall in love with Patrick. It would be practically incest.*

We bathed and dressed before dinner for the dance. Miranda wore blue voile, I wore yellow dotted swiss, and we put our hair up for the occasion. It felt tight and almost too heavy after five days of freedom. Miranda daubed me behind the ears with her Roman Violet so our scents wouldn't clash.

"Ah, the Sunbonnet Babies," Patrick greeted us in the

dining room. "They've got their faces washed, their hair combed, and their clean pinnies on, bless their little hearts."

"Darling Little Lord Fauntleroy," Miranda gushed, "where's your velvet suit and lace collar? Not to mention your satin sash?"

"Dearest disowned him when he started to shave," Andrew said. We left the house at sunset, and Tom joined us at the farm gate.

"Where will you get a parish where you can dance, Tom?" Ian asked him.

"I'd *hate* to be a minister's wife!" Miranda said. "No more fun. At least not out in public, anyway. At home it would be a different matter."

"If you were a minister's wife," said Andrew, "he'd be fired from one parish after another. He'd either have to drown you in self-defense, or leave the church altogether."

"Oh, he'd never do away with me," she said smugly. "He'd lose everything for my sake, and then we'd come out here and live on love and periwinkles."

"I keep forgetting Tom's a clergyman," I said to Andrew.

"Oh, he's not hatched yet," Andrew said. "He's still in the sanctified egg of the seminary. It'll be another two years before he's graduated and ordained."

"Aren't the people here scandalized if he goes to dances?"

"Nope," Patrick put in. "He's an island boy, and a Finlay. Finlays were always great dancers. You should see Dougal in a schottische. Too bad they aren't going tonight."

"Seafair," Miranda called to me from behind. "I just told Tom he should marry you. You could be his church organist and choir director, and that way you'd have two salaries coming into the parsonage."

"Marry me, Seafair," said Tom.

"Make it on Midsummer's Eve," Patrick suggested. "You can jump over the fire together."

"You haven't got a chance," I said to Tom. "I want to be chosen for my beauty, not for my utility."

"Spoilsport," Patrick pulled my arm through his. "I shall have to instruct you on the proper cooperative attitude."

"I can hardly wait," I said. "When do you begin?" He laughed and pressed my arm against his side. I felt wonderful. This morning's promises still held good.

As we came down over the hill by the church, a whaleboat full of bachelors from Bannock was just pulling into the harbor. There was a general promenade around the shore toward West India Hall, older people strolling in a genteel way, arm in arm; in front of the store a cluster of young men and girls were in a party mood. Prissy's shrieking reminded me of Ian's greedy gull.

A harassed woman hurried up to him and asked him to open the store. "I hate to, Ian, but the young ones got the summer complaint so bad, there'll be nothin' left of them by morning. I need some of that carminative of blackberry."

Ian was already taking out his key ring. "All right, Sally, we'll get it." He opened the door, and Hugh Swenson sprang up onto the platform. "Might's well git some tobacco."

"Hey, Hughie, pick up some of them breath things for me," a burly young man called after him. His hair was dressed into an enormous Boston curl. "If I take a young woman walkin'," he said, with a wink at us, "I want to be mighty sure my breath's as sweet as a cow been eating violets." "Oh, *Harry*," murmured the girl hanging to his arm.

Patrick, Tom, and Andrew stopped off with the other men outside the hall, and we went inside. We hung up my mackintosh and her cape. The lamps had been lighted in the brackets between the windows, well above the benches that ran the length of the building on either side. Women and girls sat in talkative groups, and children were sliding on the floor, which had been sprinkled with corn meal to make it more slippery.

"Now remember," Miranda advised me, "you can, and *should*, dance with anyone who asks you. You don't have to be formally introduced. Just don't go for a walk with anyone unless I say he's all right." One corner of her mouth took on a mischievous tilt. "And remember what I said about the Bowsprit."

"What about those?" I asked. A couple of stone-cutters were looking in the door. One of them gave me a radiant Roman smile.

"Oh, you can dance with them. After all, they're Andrew's men." She gave them a sharper glance. "Oh! Lovely, isn't he? I've never seen *him* before. He ought to have grapes behind his ears or something. The other's Sophie Filippi, he does beautiful carving."

At the head of the hall a fat gray-headed fisherman was playing runs on a clarinet, and a little dark French-appearing man effortlessly bowed through *The Devil's Dream* as a kind of limbering exercise for hands that had been hauling on a heavy cod line all day.

"Fantastic," I said.

"And he can't read a note of music," said Miranda. "Now let's look at the food."

Across from the musicians' corner a table had been set up on sawhorses and covered with clean white wrapping paper. There were two pails of cold water with dippers beside them and an array of cakes as yet uncut. Miranda looked them over, naming off specialties and their creators. "About half-way through, when everybody's good and dry, they'll bring in buckets of iced lemonade, and the cakes will be cut. . . . Andrew, don't you dare stay up there all evening."

He was going up a steep flight of stairs in the corner.

"Never fear, Banty, I'm taking you on for the first dance." He went on up.

"What's up there?" I asked.

"A pool table. Let's go talk." We sat down with a group and immediately everyone was off on a round of mutual compliments about dresses and hair. They even included me, with a diffident or breezy friendliness, depending on the individual. Then Hugh stalked the length of the room with his concertina, and an Anson twin came in with a snare drum. Hugh sounded a long chord, the girls became palpitatingly alert, men poured in from the outside.

The plump grizzled clarinetist rose, beaming like a lighthouse, and called, "Choose your partners for March and Circle!"

The choosing was fast. Andrew appeared all at once like a genie. "Come on, Banty."

"Where's Patrick?" She rose and took his arm, but kept craning her neck, and then suddenly burst out laughing. "Look at them!" Across the hall Patrick was leading out a coy and dimpling Prissy. "He'll be lucky if he gets through the dance with his virtue in one piece!" Miranda said.

"Seafair?" I'd been so taken up with watching the speedy zigzag traffic I hadn't seen Tom coming. "May I have this dance?"

"I don't know it—I'd only be a nuisance to you——"

"It's not that difficult. We'll show you." He crooked his arm elegantly for me to take.

After the march around the hall, the dance turned into a quadrille in which even the heaviest turned skillfully light of foot. The musicians seemed tireless, but at times during a contredance or a Paul Jones I found myself dancing with one of them, and someone else would have taken his place with the instrument.

They did dances here I'd never learned at Miss Blyton's Saturday Classes, except for the waltz. And Miss Blyton's classes had never prepared me for the sort of affair where everybody comes for the undiluted joy of dancing and where nobody who can move a foot has to be a wallflower. I became acquainted with a variety of styles, grips, breathing (a little wheezy in some of the stouter men, but game), and scents.

Though the ice-clinking buckets of lemonade came in on schedule, there was rather more than lemonade around that night. Some of the quarry workers smelled not unpleasantly of wine, and if Miranda hadn't told me that a bottle of rum was being passed around outside I'd have known it anyway.

But everyone's manners were impeccable. Even Miss Blyton, provided she hadn't fainted early on in the evening, would have approved. One was always asked for a dance and afterward escorted back to her seat and thanked.

Once in a Paul Jones I danced with Ethan Kalloch, the Sleeping Prince of our trip out; he was considerably more lively, he wore rose-scented brilliantine, and he was a graceful dancer with a particularly elegant way of pointing his toe. He didn't attempt conversation; he didn't need to. I saw his cousin Dill lurking in the doorway at one point, quite filling it up, and wondered academically what it would be like to dance with him; as with a statue, perhaps? But he never did come inside, even to go upstairs to the pool table.

chapter 10

As the dance gathered momentum, I saw Miranda only in passing. Once she demanded breathlessly, "Are you having a good time, Seafair?" And I answered, "I never had so much fun in my life."

Otherwise I didn't watch for her; when I had time to look for anyone it was for Patrick's head, as if it were the north star and I a navigator, which in a sense I was. For always, beneath the exhilaration of the music there ran the dark uncertain current of my emotions about him.

So I didn't really miss Miranda until one of the Peases took me back to my seat after *Lady of the Lake*. The girls who'd been near me were up around the refreshment table, joking with the musicians, who were stretching legs and fingers and drinking lemonade.

I was perfectly happy to sit alone, looking at everything as if surrounded by a cycloramic painting, lingering on details here and there. But sooner or later I had to swing to true north, and couldn't find it. Patrick was gone.

Neither Tom nor Andrew were in sight, either. Many of the men had gone out to smoke and cool off, and some had gone upstairs. Ian had been up there most of the evening. So then I looked for Miranda, but she too was absent. Luxuriously I considered my choices. I could go on observing and listening, I could get another piece of cake and refill my folding cup with lemonade, or I could go outside and look at the harbor by night.

Most of the men outside were clustered around the main entrance, but there was a side door out onto the broad wharf.

I went to where we'd hung our wraps, and discovered that my mackintosh was gone. Then I realized the last time I'd seen Miranda was during *Lady of the Lake,* and now it looked as if she'd found herself near the door, been very warm, simply snatched my mac as the first thing that came to hand, and went out that side door. I couldn't remember with whom she'd been dancing. It didn't matter. I took down the heathery cloak and went out onto the wharf and walked to the end.

A melon-slice moon shed a thin light over the rocks and wharves, the sloops at their moorings with furled sails, the dories and peapods like sleeping gulls with their heads tucked under their wings. The air was cold enough after the hall to make me pull the hood over my head. I wondered where Patrick was, I longed to see him, and I felt a sharp, hurtful resurgence of energy at the mere idea of meeting him again. We were living in the same house; but as far as distance went it was more like simply inhabiting the same universe, I an unimportant star and Patrick a planet. And my extremes of ebullience and apathy, hope and despair, were properties of his special ambience, like Saturn's rings or Jupiter's moons.

A waltz began in the hall. I stayed where I was, in this half-tranced state of mind where I could believe anything I wanted. Well out beyond moorings something flashed in the fragile moonlight. I wondered if a seal was swimming out there; we'd seen seals sunning on ledges off Andrew's Cove. But as the flash was rhythmically repeated I realized that I could be watching an oarblade. It was moving steadily across the harbor mouth.

I felt rather than heard the footsteps behind me, a faint vibration through the planks. I had just time to wonder if one of my bachelor partners had come out to further our acquaintance when someone took me by the shoulders, hard, roughly turned me around, and kissed me.

I saw Patrick's head silvered with moonlight in the instant before his face came down to mine. I had never been kissed like this before. I put my arms around him and kissed him back.

It wasn't long; one tends to suffocate after a moment or so. We separated but not quite, holding each other's arms and looking into one another's faces with desperate, blinding stares, trying to read everything at once.

Then he laughed under his breath, and said, "Blame it on the music and the moonlight." He sounded as out of breath as I was.

"I don't want to blame it on anything," I said. More words rushed to be said, but instinct kept my mouth shut. I shivered, and Patrick said at once, "You're cold. Come inside."

I didn't want to. This moment could never be duplicated, but surely there was even better to come. However, his arm was urging me back toward the lights, so I went. *Patrick Patrick Patrick. You feel the same way that I do. . . . What about Miranda? Miranda who?* The name went sailing off, dandelion seed on the wind. Nothing but Patrick now... We met a couple coming around the building, the boy's head bent toward the girl's ducked one; they were finding their way along the wharf purely by feel.

"Watch you don't walk off the end, Pearl," Patrick said, which brought a snorting chuckle from the boy and a theatrical gasp from the girl. Trying to get myself back to earth before we went into the lighted building, I said, "Which one was Pearl? I heard that name over at the farm the other day."

"The boy. Pearl Gillis. His mother waited twelve years for him, so he was her pearl."

"Poor Pearl."

"Poor Pearl nothing. He's a little rooster." He was obviously attempting to find solid ground too, otherwise our faces were going to give us away when we went in. "Where's Miranda got to?"

"I don't know. I think the last dance was too much for her, and she went out for some air. She's probably back by now." Suddenly Miranda became more than dandelion seed. Miranda became my friend, who had brought me here and who was in love with Patrick in defiance of her uncle's wishes. But if many waters couldn't quench love, how could anything else? And if she was not to be blamed, neither was I.

The waltz had finished, and they were choosing partners for the *Portland Fancy*. Patrick twitched the cloak off my shoulders, and flung it at the bench. "Come on, let's go!"

Miranda wasn't on the floor when we lined up, but she was there at the end, and so was her partner from *Lady of the Lake*, the handsome new quarryman. Miranda was incandescent. You scamp, I thought, what have *you* been up to? Tom was back, and Andrew, and so, to my astonishment, was Ian. I'd thought he didn't like to dance or wasn't good at it. He swung me with considerable grace and gallantry, and made me feel we should all be in eighteenth-century costume.

When Patrick left me at my seat, I was going to take the initiative with Miranda by asking her where she'd gone with her partner, but before Patrick and I reached her, she went to the table for a drink. Ian appeared and asked me for the next waltz. I was slightly flustered, as if the Prince of Wales had suddenly singled me out, though Ian was slim, unbearded, and without mistresses as far as I knew. Once I decided that if he didn't start a conversation *I* wouldn't, I relaxed. He was a good dancer, like his brothers. In fact they were all good dancers here, without benefit of Miss Byton's horrible Saturday classes.

Ian returned me to my seat, thanked me, asked if I would like some lemonade, was graciously refused, and went away. "Ain't he some *nice*," Faustina Pease breathed in my ear. "You know I been waiting half my life for Ian Drummond to ask me for a waltz? And then I'd likely fall over my feet and tromp his out of use."

"Who does he usually dance with? Does he have a girl?"

"Him?" She looked as horrified as if we were talking about a priest, then modified it. "Once we thought he was getting sweet on the schoolmarm. She was on *him* all right. Then the Colonel died and it knocked everything galley-west.

Schoolmarm stuck it out till end of school but she won't be back next year."

Hughie Swenson stood over us, and she greeted him with giddy arrogance. "Oh, so it's *you*, is it?" She got up. One of the Anson twins asked me for this dance.

Patrick had disappeared. I expected he had gone somewhere quiet to consider what had happened to us, and I looked forward to being alone in my room tonight to contemplate it. But it didn't seem as if I could sleep unless I saw Patrick first, and some subtle communication could pass between us. I think I floated through that last schottische and must have been surrounded by such an aura of romantic mystery that whichever Awful Anson was my partner asked to walk me home, and he was at least five years younger than I was.

I gave him a kindly yet flattering smile and told him I was already spoken for. The last waltz was *Home Sweet Home* and I danced it with Tom; they could make of it what they would. Like the singer in the old song, I knew my love. Miranda danced with Ian. Andrew danced with one of the older married women. She was very large, really fat, but waltzed with a light-footed poise, and she'd never lacked a partner in the contredances, either.

At the end Patrick hadn't come back. We stood around the hall putting on our wraps, laughing and talking as the musicians put away their instruments and finished up the last of the drinks, and Toby Pease blew out the lamps. Tomorrow some of the women would come in and tidy up. Miranda put an arm around my waist. "How was it, Seafair?"

How was what? I couldn't tell her what was almost bursting in my throat to be said. I said solemnly, "I shall probably never again attend a dance back in the world. Not after this one. Anything else would be as dust and ashes."

Her laugh resounded through the almost empty hall and Andrew said, "Good Lord, she's got her second wind."

He was right. We kept fairly quiet walking through the village, calling out muted goodnights as people dropped off.

But once we passed the church Miranda broke into song, and then we all did; at least she and I and Tom and Andrew did, walking four abreast with arms linked. We did scraps of *Pinafore* and *The Pirates of Penzance,* our voices echoing back from the woods. Ian walked behind us, smoking his pipe. As for Patrick, nobody seemed to think anything of his absence. Perhaps he did this often.

Wind and will ran out eventually, and we leaned on the farm gate saying yawning goodnights to Tom.

"Oh, Tom, come on home with us and have some cocoa or tea or something," Miranda invited.

"My dear girl, I have to help milk in the morning—I told Pearl to sleep late. And also I'm preaching a sermon. Goodnight, everybody."

"Oh, *fudge!*"

"Come on, Banty." Ian pulled her away from the gate. "Goodnight, Tom." As we turned back to the twin ribbons of the road we heard Tom whistling softly on his way toward the house.

"Listen, it's *Stack of Barley,*" said Andrew. "I hate like fury to think they'll clip our Tom's wings."

"They will," said Ian. "And he'll accept, if he wants a church. What he can accomplish from conviction and conscience and pure goodness won't matter a tinker's damn to the deacons if they think he's frivolous in any way."

"I hate it for him," said Miranda, in an abrupt descent from exuberance to bad temper.

"But he chose it, didn't he?" I asked. "Or was he forced into it?"

"No, not forced," said Ian abruptly. "His family's proud of him—so proud Meg thinks she's almost sinful—but they didn't push him. No, Tom made up his own mind. And I think that what's between him and his God is far more important than dancing and the theater. When the time comes he'll shed all that more easily than a lobster sheds his old shell."

"I just can't imagine Tom being God's good man," said

Miranda. Nobody answered her. We had come along the brick walk to the front door. Before us the cliffs stood out over the dark spaces of the sea. Over to the east the thrust of the Head showed as a pale mass. I wondered if Patrick was out there. What if he were inside the house now? How would we greet each other? With eyes, first?

"I'm so tired," Miranda's voice dragged. "I may not get up in time for church tomorrow."

"You will get up," said Ian, "and you will be there. I'll accept no excuses beyond a broken limb or a galloping case of the Black Death. We aren't offending Meg and Dougal—not one of us." He opened the front door and we went into the dark hall scented with lilacs. Andrew lit a candle and touched the other wicks with the flame, until a row of four bloomed delicately wavering under the mirror that gave us back to ourselves like a Rembrandt grouping.

"Does anybody really want anything to drink?" Miranda asked. "Anything that doesn't come out of a decanter, that is?"

"You two go on up," Andrew said. "Ian and I choose the decanter."

"Boozers," said Miranda, dropping her cloak over the newel post and starting up the stairs. Charlie came scurrying down to meet us, stopping on the landing to stretch and yawn. "Oh, fiddle," said Miranda wearily. "You need to go out."

"Let me take him," I said, still in my mackintosh.

"Oh, *would* you?" She smiled down at me. Above her head the Old Colonel watched us, his face alive with the movements of the candle flames. "You don't have to really go out with him, just stand in the doorway. He always sees ghoulies and ghosties at night, so he'll hurry."

"It's no wonder the dog thinks the place is haunted, the way you've brought him up," I said. "Maybe I'll be lucky enough to see a ghost too."

"We'll be expecting a sharp scream," Andrew said to me. "Look, I'll attend to him——"

"No, I'd like to take another look at the stars."

"Then do so, my dear." He went into the library, where Ian was lighting a lamp. I went out with Charlie, across the walk and stood with my back against the flagpole, looking up at the eagle's hunched silhouette against the spangled sky.

Patrick didn't come. Finally Charlie barked from the doorstep, first politely, then impatiently. "Wait a minute," I said to him. Then he became imperious, and I saw a shadow move past the lighted library windows as if someone were coming out to the door.

"Oh, all right," I said. We went in, and he trotted sociably into the library. Ian was pouring from a decanter, Andrew was lighting his pipe, and Patrick stood in front of the fireplace, hands in his pockets, looking bemused. Of the three, he was the one who saw me first. I longed to be frank and bold, to hold his eyes with confident affirmation of what now lay between us, but I could not. I could feel the heat rising in my face, and with it rose my basic disbelief like a flood tide. It couldn't have happened tonight, not to *me*. But it *had* happened. And it was Patrick who looked frankly and boldly at me, and buoyed by this I got my chin up above the tide and said, "Goodnight, everybody!"

"Goodnight, Seafair," Patrick said with a smile. Andrew said it around his pipe, and Ian said it absent-mindedly.

I hung up my mackintosh and Miranda's cape, took my candle, and went upstairs. Charlie raced past, bound for Miranda's room and his nightly biscuit. I was ashamed of hoping that Miranda wouldn't come in to talk. I didn't want to be dishonest with her, yet how could I tell her?

I undressed by candlelight, and called a firm "Goodnight" to Miranda when I came out of the bathroom. She called back around a yawn, "I'm glad you had a good time," and that was that, I thought. But a few minutes later she came to my doorway in her nightgown, and said gleefully, "I swiped Pat's peapod tonight and went rowing."

"So that was you out there."

"Don't you want to know who was with me?"

No, as long as it wasn't Patrick. "Who, then?" I said to humor her. She laughed.

"I'm not telling."

"It was either Dill Kalloch or Romeo."

"Good*night!*" she sang, and withdrew. I forgot her almost at once, alternating between Patrick on the wharf and Patrick in the library.

eg didn't come in on Sunday mornings, so Miranda and I ate alone in the kitchen. She gloomed through breakfast, but her appetite wasn't affected by her bad mood. For someone with a twenty-four inch waist (without lacing) she could put away staggering amounts of food. This morning she made french toast to follow the porridge, and worked her way through a syrup-soaked stack. Being in love, I didn't have quite that much appetite; I kept expecting Patrick to walk in at any moment.

"What are you so mournful about?" I asked her. "Do you hate church so much? You never did at school."

"Maybe it's because I'm the bright and shining star of the choir there. Maybe I'm sulking because nobody asked me to sing today and I just happened to bring my music." She gave Charlie a piece of toast. "Actually Tom did ask me the first day we were here if you and I would do the offertory, but I said I wouldn't barge in on Ada Schofield's plans. She always plays the organ."

"Very commendable of you."

"It isn't at all. I don't want to have anything to do with this service. I don't want to hear Tom preach!" she said. "I don't know why they had to go and ask him, or why he had to accept."

"Well, he's going to be a minister," I pointed out. "He can use the experience."

"Don't you realize that everything is conspiring to break us all up?" she asked passionately. "Patrick adores the island, but once he travels and works in other countries he'll be weaned away. Once Tom's ordained and has a church of his own, he'll go up and up, because he's gifted, inspired, or whatever you want to call it. For them the island will be just a place to bring the children for a week or two now and then, when once it was our whole world and we swore we'd never be parted from it or each other."

"The world of childhood," I began, and her eyes narrowed in humor.

"I don't need the lecture. But you wanted to know what ailed me."

"I know how you feel," I said. "You've known something perfect. But this is life, Miranda. Nothing can stand still."

"Why can't it?" she demanded. Then she grinned at my expression. "I'm not really a spoiled brat, Seafair. But didn't you ever wonder why something perfect *couldn't* last? Didn't you ever feel like screaming and yelling and stamping at the absolute *unfairness* of it all?"

"Yes," I said. "At nine, ten, eleven, and so forth. By the time I'd realized it wouldn't bring my mother back, I was being informed that what had just happened to me without warning one month was going to keep on happening for the rest of my life, or for most of it. I thought dying would be simpler."

"Don't you think Nature has made the most ghastly mixed-up mess of it for women? Meg told me it was God's idea, and for weeks I wouldn't forgive Him. . . . All right, then." She gave me a hard, defiant stare. "I know better now. So who makes the rule that says nothing can stand still?"

"Time," I said.

She made a hideous face. "Time is my enemy, then."

"Miranda Muir," I said. "You're nineteen years old, in good health, in your own home on the coast of Maine in June, and you should be ashamed of yourself for going on like this. You should be thinking of what you're going to *do* and *be* as a woman."

"Oh, I'm growing up, Seafair. Very fast." She took her dishes to the sink. "You've talked me into a stupor and I still have to sit through a sermon this morning." But she came back to me swiftly. "I'm glad we talked, because it was all boiling around in me, and it's not what you can say to the boys, even to Patrick. At least you know what I'm talking about, even if you think it's your duty to brace me up. But I still don't want to sit through that service, because it will be just pointing up the fact that Tom no longer belongs to us. Already he's become something else."

"Oh, no!" I objected. "No matter what, *your* Tom will always exist. Nothing can ever take away the past that belonged to the three of you."

"I suppose you're right," she said with a sigh. "And it's tiresome of you."

Shortly after that the men came back. Ian and Andrew had been over to Andrew's Cove to discuss the layout of Andrew's house. Patrick didn't say where he had been. There was no time for veiled communiqués between us; they all wanted second cups of coffee, and then it was time to dress for church.

Every pew was occupied in the white room, some with Bannock people who had come across on a sea as glassy as that mentioned in the opening hymn. The front rows were filled with children in their Sunday clothes, the boys' heads wetly slick, the girls' hair ribbons trembling like new-fledged butterflies. The pulpit was decorated with vases of weigela, trailing bridal wreath, and purple columbine, and through the open windows puffs of breeze brought the scents of sun-heated spruce woods and the sea.

We sat close behind the children. The Finlays were farther back in the church, refusing to sit smugly under their son's nose. As Ian waited for us to file into the pew, Andrew first, then me, Patrick, Miranda, and then himself, I felt like a character in one of those English novels in which everybody at the Manor attends service to set a good example to the villagers. Settling between Andrew's right shoulder and Patrick's left, unnervingly conscious of the contact, I saw myself as the governess in the novel, mousy on the outside and all ardor within, though I wasn't mousy, and wasn't Patrick's arm pressing against mine while he murmured with Miranda?

I sighed involuntarily, and Andrew whispered, "Too warm in here?"

"No. I think I'm nervous for Tom," I fibbed.

"Tom will do fine."

There was a ripple through the congregation like the turn of the tide or a shift in the wind; Mrs. Schofield came through a door to the right of the pulpit, and seated herself at the organ; she did not simply sit down. She might have been blowsy Rubensesque once like her daughter, but now she was floridly regal, wearing purple silk and a hat piled with velvet pansies. The organ was bigger and more ornate than the one in the cottage. She pumped vigorously with her feet, raised her thick red hands, poised them, and came down in a blast of chord that brought the congregation to its feet. Hymnal pages fluttered as if in a strong wind; and Tom came in at the same door, unembarrassed.

He wore a dark suit and tie, and the white shirt made his skin look brown in contrast. Composedly he went up the steps into the pulpit and opened the hymnal on the lecturn.

"Hello, Tom," called a very small child in the front row, immediately squelched by his shocked elder sisters.

"Hello, Pip," Tom said with a smile. Mrs. Schofield began the first hymn, everybody's favorite, judging from the way they all threw themselves into it. She played well, her flourishes didn't get in the way of her timing. In the second verse I heard Miranda's voice rise strong and sweet, and I was relieved that she had decided to emerge from her depression.

The Responsive Reading was the One Hundredth and Fifteenth Psalm, and Tom spoke the first verse with the quiet ardor of absolute conviction. " 'Not unto us, O Lord, not unto us, but unto thy name give glory, for thy mercy, and for thy truth's sake.' "

I knew that my philosophical maunderings at breakfast

about Tom were nothing more than the rattle of dry beans in a bottle. The reading went on; I took part in it, I remember Andrew's voice on one side of me and Patrick's on the other. But all the time I knew the difference was there. Tom had been called, if I wanted to believe that was how it was done, and this morning I could almost believe it. And because he had heard the voice, he was as far removed from us as if a world lay between us and the pulpit steps. If he had stood there suddenly revealed in the habit of a monk the distance couldn't have been greater.

After that, another rousing hymn, and then the prayer, which was mercifully short. Tom didn't feel obliged to give God a long and wordy account of things He should already know. The scripture reading was the thirty-eighth chapter of *Job,* read with undemonstrative clarity in an almost conversational manner.

Three boys and three girls trained especially for the occasion passed the collection plates, while the rest of the children formed ranks by the organ, little ones held down firmly by older hands on their shoulders, and sang *When He Cometh to Gather His Jewels.* Children singing like this always move me, even though I angrily label myself a sentimentalist.

It was time for the sermon, which I dreaded; I'd sat through so many in Fern Grove that I thought I could write a more than fair sermon myself, with equal measures of threat, exhortation, and promise. Before me the hair ribbons quivered, boys' fingers scratched under collars and along the backs of newly clipped necks.

Behind me there was a stirring and re-settling, a shifting of feet as if to brace for what came next. I wished I could leave, but there was too much fresh air in the church for me to claim that I needed some.

Tom walked to the lectern, put his hands on both sides of it, and looked out at us with that air of serious yet affectionate friendship. "God, speaking to Job out of the whirlwind," he said, "asked him where he was when all the morning stars sang together, and the sons of God shouted for joy. . . . I would like to talk to you this morning about joy."

The service finished with the singing of *God Be with You Till We Meet Again*. The benediction, spoken in Tom's quiet voice, restored to me, at least for those few moments, the pure faith I had possessed as a child. I saw it around me in seamed and weather-burned faces, and my own childhood mirrored in these island children.

There was a little space of respectful quiet as Tom left the pulpit, and then there was a general movement down the center aisle toward him. People surrounded him, shaking his hand, patting his shoulder. Mrs. Schofield stood royally by the organ and received a few compliments herself. I saw the Finlays going out with Ian and being stopped in the front doorway; I didn't believe that they were half as wooden as they looked. The children milled around in an excess of excitement after being quiet for so long. Andrew left by a side aisle, Patrick went off in another direction, and I decided to stay where I was until the front door became unclogged. I was looking out at Steeple Cove, when Miranda gave me an ungentle poke in the ribs.

"Come on, let's get out of here. That way."

There was a door in the left-hand corner beyond the Steeple Cove windows and it opened into the sunny noon silence of the cemetery. Miranda blew out hard and began unpinning her hat. This would have been unheard of in Fern Grove, but we weren't in Fern Grove, so I took off my own hat.

We walked slowly among the stones. The wind brushed through the taller trees, setting the sweeping boughs in drowsy motion. Birds sang, and bees hummed in the flowers and in the wild chokecherry blossoms hanging among the dark firs. Miranda said in a constricted voice, "Don't tell me he was superb."

"No, because he isn't yet. But he can be. He will be."

"Oh, stop it!" She made a violent swing of repudiation with her hat.

"The only trouble with Tom as a clergyman," I said, "is that all the women are going to be madly in love with him. It's a good thing he's not going to be a priest. He'll need a wife to protect him. And *she*, poor thing, will have to be a combination of Caesar's wife, Joan of Arc, Saint Cecilia——"

"Look there." Miranda had stopped short. On a polished slab of pink granite were the names of Jean and Matthew Muir, and under them the words, *They were lovely and pleasant in their lives, and in their death they were not divided.*

"Uncle David chose that for them," Miranda said. "Here's where he and Aunt Myrtis are." There was nothing on this stone but the names and dates. "That was the way he wanted it, but there were always to be johnny jump-ups, because they were Aunt Myrtis's favorites."

The miniature pansies were everywhere, turning bright attentive little faces toward the sun. We stood looking at them until she made that rough, implacable gesture again and said brusquely, "Let's start home. The others can yarn around for hours. Everybody visits like mad after church, as if they hadn't been seeing each other all week."

We took a twisting path through the woods, jumped an ale-brown brook and soaked our Sunday shoes in the thick wet moss on the other bank, went out through ferns under white birches, and finally emerged on the road to The Eyrie.

We didn't mention Tom or the service again.

One of the Sabbath blessings at The Eyrie was the absence of those huge dinners that turned Fern Grove Sunday afternoons into turgid horrors. Miranda put together a salad from ingredients Meg had prepared the day before, and I set the dining room table. There was cold lobster with home-made mayonnaise, Meg's good bread and butter, and a lemon-sponge pudding. During the meal the men discussed Tom's performance. Miranda had nothing to say. Patrick asked mischievously, "Got laryngitis, love?"

"I just don't feel like taking part in an autopsy while I eat," she said.

"Autopsy! It's a paean of praise. He was great," said Andrew. "What did you want, some rousing Calvinist hellfire and brimstone?"

"No sermon at all. Granted, some people might need it, but I prefer to find mine in stones and running brooks."

"That's just to show she knows Shakespeare," said Patrick. "Erudite as all get-out."

She ignored that, haughtily.

We spent the afternoon on the ledges at the Home Cove. Miranda seemed to have gotten her wish; the hours hardly moved. The ocean, blue as the bay of Naples in the painting we had at home, didn't change. It was only by looking back at the beach and seeing how the shadow of the woods gradually flowed pale violet over the sand that you could tell the day was passing by.

We sat barefoot with our feet in tide pools while Miranda wrote letters to favorite classmates. I read, or just sat staring at the sea and wiggling my toes voluptuously in warm salt water. Patrick was spending the afternoon bringing his records up to date, and that suited me. Being within twenty feet of him turned me into a fool, and in order not to sound like one I sat in silence while maintaining a bright expression. I reminded myself of Charlie waiting for someone to mention "walk" or "supper."

Charlie was chasing sandpipers on the beach when suddenly he began to bark, and Patrick came out of the path from the house, carrying a covered jug and a basket. Watching him stride along the beach toward us, I could feel the miasma of idiocy settling over me like fog, though it didn't dim my vision of him. I looked sidewise at Miranda. She was watching him too, with a dreamy half-smile; slowly she kept lifting her hair off her neck and letting it fall again, and she never took her eyes off him. How could he see anybody else but her?

But last night it had happened. It was no dream.

"Is this the gift horse or a Greek bearing gifts?" Miranda said. "I don't know whether we should beware or not look him in the mouth."

"I come from haunts of coot and hern," said Patrick, setting down the jug and basket. "I usually get it 'hoot and cern,' so I practiced all the way out. And don't ask me the next line. Nobody knows it."

" 'I make a sudden sally,' " I said. " 'And sparkle out among the ferns to bicker down the valley.' "

"You must be a genius," said Patrick.

"Not at all," I said modestly. "I learned that poem at my mother's knee. When I was little they used to call me the Brook because I talked so much. You know—'For men may come and men may go, but I go on forever.' "

"Well, you don't talk much now," he said. "You're given to mysterious silences."

"Only because we never give her a chance to talk," said Miranda. She uncovered the jug. "Raspberry shrub, with ice in it. Umm." The basket held enameled tin mugs and a plate of sugar cookies. She gave Patrick her full radiance. "Aren't you a love!"

"Yes, I are. I go around beating my brains out being charming."

"That doesn't sound charming," I said, emboldened by my success with the poem. "It sounds messy."

He shaded his eyes and peered at me from under his hand. "Ah, the Dark Lady of the Sonnets. Are you part gypsy, Seafair? Can you tell fortunes and read palms?" He thrust his hand toward me, palm upward, and I longed for the courage to seize and hold the hand and make up some foolishness about the lines in his palm.

"My coloring is Indian, actually," I said in a superior tone. "It's quite possible one of my ancestors on my mother's side owned this island before your early settlers ever saw the place, and that includes your Vikings."

"Are you going to the Supreme Court and put in a claim?" Patrick asked.

"Marry her quick, dear, so you won't be evicted," said Miranda, handing me a mug.

"I just might," said Patrick.

By a supreme effort I continued my invention. "I didn't want to say so at the time, and steal anybody's thunder, but that ax you found could very well have been made by one of my ancient forefathers. Before he was ancient, of course."

Patrick salaamed, mug in one hand and a cookie in the other. "From now on we'll treat you as your importance deserves. What was Ancient Forefather's name? Something impressive, I presume."

"Not very," I said. "It seems he wasn't a very good marksman, in fact he was a rotten one, so he was known as He-Who-Couldn't-Shoot-Fish-in-a-Barrel."

Patrick and Miranda rolled together in laughter, and Charlie nipped in neatly and stole a cookie. I sipped raspberry shrub as if making a call with Phoebe in a Fern Grove parlor. When the other two had simmered down Miranda asked curiously, "Are you really part Indian, Seafair?"

"Well, I do have an Indian ancestor that I know about," I admitted. "But my coloring's from my father's family, and they were from Devon. On my mother's side, a Francis Faulkingham married an Indian girl, and their son was sent to Boston for a Christian education among the Puritans. He went to Harvard College, and later he married Seafair Weston, the daughter of his guardian and sponsor."

"What became of him?" Miranda asked eagerly.

"Where they started their farm turned out to be Fern Grove. Both Geoffrey and Seafair taught, so they founded Fern Grove Academy. They survived the French and Indian Wars because they'd done so much for the local

Indians. Geoffrey never forgot who his mother's people were."

"What a bunch of Johnny-come-latelies the rest of us are," Patrick said.

"The trouble is," I said, "my Indian blood comes to the boil every time I think of what we've done and still do to the Indians."

"Everybody's blood should boil," said Patrick. "It's a disgrace, and worse. It's criminal."

"Granted, granted," said Miranda, "but do we have to brood about it on an afternoon like this? I mean, why did God give us all this beauty if we weren't meant to enjoy it? Remember the sermon this morning." She folded her hands and lengthened her face sanctimoniously. "I gave it all my attention. I don't know about you two."

"Enough from you, Hortense," said Patrick. They smiled at one another. They didn't need to touch, the smile was enough. I couldn't watch, and began fooling with Charlie. Their closeness was as unexceptional to them as the possession of their five senses; it is only the blind or the deaf who know the agonized yearning for sight or hearing.

And yet as I hugged the little dog and nuzzled my face against his ears I also hugged the indisputable fact that Patrick had kissed me. He could love Miranda—in fact, why shouldn't he? But she could be the one who was *in* love.

I leaned back against my ledge and looked up, and saw the eagles again. Large even at this distance, they swung in wide, deliberate circles without a perceptible motion of their wings.

"They'll do it for hours." Patrick's voice.

Miranda said, "They're watching us. They've watched us all of our lives. Ian used to scare Patrick and me by saying, 'Not only Jesus is watching you, but the eagles are.'" She laughed. "We weren't afraid of Jesus, but we certainly respected those eagles."

"We had visions of being snatched up out of wrongdoing by the scruff of our little necks and dropped out on the

Crumbs for the tide to take," said Patrick. "Therefore we used to sneak out at night for deviltry, thus forming a life-long habit."

"What deviltry could you do at night when you were still small enough to be scared by Ian?"

"Oh, just run around all over the island and feel like hellions with most people in bed and thinking *we* were. Moonlight nights . . . I couldn't sleep then, and I can't sleep now. Sometimes we went rowing in the middle of the night."

"Tom would come with us whenever he could," Miranda said, "and I had a chum from the harbor, Emily Joy, and she made it a couple of times. Then she got caught. Her papa thought she was up to no good, and the rest of us were discovered, and kept in till the alarm wore off."

"Not that the Finlays and Uncle David thought we were having nasty little games." Patrick stretched out full length with his arms folded under his head and his eyes shut against the sun. "But we were always groggy the next day, and, besides, normal human children weren't supposed to be out scampering around when the world's abed. I think they began believing in changelings."

"They'd have believed in worse if they could have seen us in the oaks," Miranda said. "We had the most complicated secret religions, Seafair, you wouldn't believe it. We celebrated the new moon and the full moon, all the solstices, and invoked Diana and Apollo, and, oh yes, Wodin, and plenty of others. Patrick knew *Bulfinch's Mythology* by heart, so sometimes we were Greek, sometimes Roman, Norse, Celtic. We were Druids all one summer. No blood sacrifices, of course, except what the mosquitoes drew." She giggled. "We'd offer food, whatever we'd sneaked out, and then after the ceremonies we'd eat it."

"What a bunch of little maniacs," Patrick said, still with closed eyes. He looked rather like an effigy on a tomb, except for his modern clothes. "Tom was a crackerjack of a pagan priest. He'd heard the call even then, you see. He's just transferred allegiance. I'm sure that if he wandered through the oaks at full moon now he'd hear the old gods calling him."

"Stop it, Pat!" She was laughing but I could see the gooseflesh on her arms as she rubbed them. I felt it on my own. "We used to scare ourselves to death down there, and you know it. It's still with me."

"Not with me. I was never scared. I was always hoping that somehow we'd say the right words to raise something."

"You were lucky you didn't get some early settler," I said, "with his head bashed in by a tomahawk."

"One of your family's victims, I presume." Patrick opened his eyes and grinned at me. "Doesn't it give you a nice cozy feeling of kinship?"

"In a gruesome way, yes," I said.

"You know," Miranda mused, "I always thought Emily allowed herself to be caught. Her father's wrath wasn't half as scary as us parading around the altar in sheets, chanting gibberish, with the moon coming down through the branches, and God knows what about to appear in a flash of fire. Emily's learning to be a nurse, now. I wonder if she ever thinks of the days when we were young."

"You sound like some old lady of a hundred recalling her wild youth." Patrick sat up and grabbed at one of her bare feet, and she planted it against his chest and shoved. Charlie plunged barking into the confusion.

"Where's the altar?" I asked. "What was it?"

"Nothing that could be recognized as such," Patrick said. "It's the remains of the chimney of Daniel Joy's cabin. We didn't dare burn anything in it, even a handful of rockweed, unless there was no wind at all to carry the smell toward The Eyrie or the farm. Anything more in that jug?"

chapter 12

*A*nother thing that made Drummond Sundays stand out as gems of purest ray serene was the lack of a set supper hour. Each person got what he wanted and ate it where he wished. That first Sunday we went back around six and found nobody home. Miranda fed Charlie, and we decided on a nursery tea of bread and butter, tart rhubarb sauce, and cheese.

"Ian's probably walking the shore somewhere," Miranda said. "Out of reach of someone asking him to open up the store for something they forgot on Saturday."

"And Andrew's over at the house site rearranging his plans for the fifteenth time," said Patrick. "He's happy. Maybe this is the happiest time of it for him, right now. To travel hopefully is better than to arrive."

"Stevenson qualifies that," I said.

"But I don't," he said with a charming smile behind Miranda's back. "When I find my Norse relics, and the shouting's all over, what then?"

"You'll go on to something else," I said. "You'll keep on digging in the same hole and come to a standing stone erected by Druids and covered with fifteen hundred years of soil. . . . Seriously, there must be enough lost civilizations in the world to keep you busy for a long time."

"Trouble is, I'm not the only digger. Between us all we can use up the sites pretty fast."

"And then I suppose you'll weep like Alexander with no more worlds to conquer."

His eyes were alight with some sort of calculation, mine

wary; perhaps I'd gone too far, I didn't know yet how tender or how tough the Drummond ego really was. Just as dismay thumped a mailed fist into my midriff, Miranda joined the conversation at some distance back.

"Of course Andrew will be happier with Jane than he is now. He's like all of us in this family, he has a great capacity for happiness. I hope we'll always have it. People like us don't deserve to suffer."

She said it with such a candid lack of arrogance that I didn't protest. But Patrick cornered her. "Don't you think that we've got it all ahead of us, because it's not behind us?"

"It *is* behind us! We've suffered terrible losses, even if we were too young to be consciously aware. They've scarred us. And we certainly suffered consciously, and are still suffering, about losing Uncle David."

"But losses through death come to everyone," he argued. "Especially losing parents. Look at Seafair. Death is a part of life, as Tom can tell you in a better way than I can. What about the agonies private to oneself? The tragedies of disease, and accidents that don't kill but leave anyone half-dead for years? The effects of pure evil, sin, and madness? And what about the simple facts of deprivation—of being eaten with longing your whole life for something you can't have, but can't live without?" He turned to me. "Don't you believe that the Fates balance everything in the end?"

"No," I said, "unless you want to go into the reincarnation theory. Some people have nothing but misery all their lives, and some never seem to be hurt by anything. Nothing bad ever happens to them; they ride like bubbles on a stream. The ministers' favorite explanation is that God never sends more than you can bear. They don't add what we all know, that when it's too much to bear you die or go mad."

"I'd like to hear you confront Tom with that," said Patrick. "But you know what someone, I forget who, says in *Oedipus Rex* about counting no man fortunate in his life until you stand by his grave."

Miranda slammed the breadboard down on the table. "If I may interrupt this pair of ancient Greek philosophers, how about somebody slicing some bread?"

"I am probably," said Patrick, "the world's best bread-slicer." He picked up the knife.

When we'd finished and were washing the dishes, Miranda suggested a sunset row. "We can row out till we have the sunset in the west and the moonrise in the east, won't it be spectacular?"

Patrick, tilted back in a rocker with his feet on the western window sill among Meg's plants, smoking, said ungallantly, "Do I have to do all the rowing?"

"Seafair and I will take turns and shame you."

"And if I row you'll be sorry," I said, "because you can't tell where you'll end up."

"Why, Seafair," he said, "don't you know that's what most men ask of women? A mysterious adventure?"

I *felt* scarlet to my heels; I didn't know how I looked, but I put my head into the cupboard and stacked dishes until I cooled off.

We took sweaters and went back through the cooling, dusky woods to the cove. We couldn't see the sunset from there, but the northeastern sky was pink and amethyst with a few fiery flecks of cloud overhead like floating plumes from a great roseate bird. To the north Cadillac was Mount Olympus in deep purple.

Patrick pulled the dory in and just as the bow beached out on the sand Miranda uttered a sharp little cry. We turned to look at her, and she gave us a pained and bashful smile.

"I'm sorry. I had a pain. It feels like the beginning of summer complaint."

"Gas," said Patrick laconically, untying the painter. "Cheese and rhubarb." Charlie waited, wagging, for somebody to lift him in.

"Thank you, Dr. Drummond. I'd better not go, anyway. You wouldn't want to have to come in especially for me."

Charlie barked at us.

"Then let's not go," I volunteered. "After all, it was your idea, and—" My objection seemed so feeble to me that I stopped before anyone else could think so.

"No, Patrick's going to take you, aren't you, Pat? You do want awfully to go, don't you, Seafair darling?"

Seafair darling resisted an impulse to stare at the sand and dig into it with the toe of one sneaker. How sure of herself Miranda was. And how wretchedly and painfully I wanted to go. If he'd just say something. Or *look* something. But he was grinding out a cigarette stub with his heel.

"Come on, get in," she ordered. "Pat, row out to the Crumbs; that's utterly gorgeous on a night like this."

"Yes, m'lady." He pulled a forelock, and offered me a hand getting aboard. Pushing off the dory and swinging in over the bow he appeared cheerful and happy, and at last I decided that he was, and leaned blissfully back in the stern.

"I'd better run for the house!" Miranda called after us. "Come on, Charlie!" They had disappeared into the woods before we were out of the cove.

Patrick rowed in silence, gazing past me at the shore. I wondered if he was arranging his thoughts and the words with which to express them. I kept trying to pin down my own chaotic ramblings, most of which centered on that blue rollneck sweater. It's not Patrick you're in love with, you dunderhead, I thought, it's the way he looks in that sweater, and his *beaux yeaux*. I mean his *bleux yeux*. Blooks yooks . . . Catastrophic quivers began to shake my tense muscles. Before I could splinter into senseless laughter I buried my face in my handkerchief and faked a hearty sneeze.

"*Gesundheit,*" Patrick said kindly, and I replied with a worldly air, "*Danke schön.*"

Now the spell of silence was broken and surely we could talk. Still Patrick rowed on without speaking, looking around him with an air of quiet enjoyment. We were outside the cove now, sky and sea were melting together in the same bath of liquid rose and lilac, and the gulls going home were tinted to match. I tried to lose myself in sights and sounds, but all I really saw was Patrick, and all I strained to hear was what he wasn't saying.

There had to be a good reason for this. Perhaps he was self-conscious; he didn't know how to begin. The experience could be as shattering for him as for me. I would have to make the first move, or else we should go on and on in this miserable, abject muteness.

"Do you suppose anyone ever tried rowing across the Atlantic?" I asked.

"Andrew and Ian did once," he said. "In this dory."

"How far did they get?"

"About five miles. They'd begun to think it was a poor idea, and they were happy to be picked up by a mackerel seiner and brought home. My father'd been watching them with a telescope. They got walloped."

"I didn't think Ian had ever done anything wrong."

"He wasn't born grown up, you know." Patrick smiled. "He just got there a little quicker than most people do. Maybe the walloping helped."

"Did *you* ever get walloped?"

"Often."

This was good, but it led nowhere except to a vision of small Patrick in a sailor suit or a kilt, being walloped. Furious but never repentant. He and Miranda cut from the same piece of goods.

When was he going to mention the kiss? Should I? How unspeakably bold! But Miranda would have done it. I didn't know how.

The ledges called the Crumbs began to show in wet and shining dark peaks. They looked like the crest of a drowned range of miniature mountains. The dory slid up on a gradual slant of rock, and Patrick handed me out. *Now*, I thought, so sure that his fingers would tighten and hold mine that when he released them I was astonished.

"The tide *is* going, you said." I tried for skeptic humor.

"Oh yes." Hands back in his pockets he looked around as if very pleased with himself. "It's going. I didn't bring you out here to abandon you."

Then what did you bring me out here for? I wanted to ask. Just because Miranda ordered it?

"This is a great place for mussels," he told me. "Those big ones. Look, there's the moon." His hands were still in his pockets. Water slid and splashed gently around us, gurgled in crevasses, and splashed in miniature cascades, flashing in the first moonlight. Afar the island was black against the dull gold of the west, and farther off Bannock was a rounded dark hump.

Last night Patrick Drummond had kissed me as I'd never been kissed before, and that kiss had been burning holes in my memory ever since. It was always there, a third party to everything, a flaming visitant. And now I stood with him as if in a floating shell in the middle of a twilight sea, every familiar landmark of my life vanished. And he kept his hands in his pockets and said, "This is a great place for mussels."

I had been waiting and waiting; I had seized greedily on imagined looks and intonations, and called them secret messages to me. Miranda's attack of summer complaint had come just in time, and I had expected he was as overjoyed as I was. Suddenly I was as wide awake as if someone had tossed a bucket of that cold salt water over me. The deluge also came down on the flaming visitant and reduced it to a heap of rapidly fading embers.

My rage was not with Patrick but with myself. So he'd kissed me in the moonlight at the dance; probably he made a habit of kissing girls he found alone in the moonlight. He'd probably kissed every passable girl on the island, and dozens when he was away at college, and most of them had probably gone through what I'd endured, waiting for the follow-up.

I could only be thankful I hadn't made any expectant move on my own. Outwardly my pride was still intact. The cold was succeeded by an exhilarating heat, and I felt a lovely, if brittle, composure.

"What's that spark of light?" I asked, pointing.

"Mount Desert Rock," he said. He began to name the lights as each became clear through the haze of dusk, some steady, some revolving. "My father used to quote, 'The lights begin to twinkle from the rocks; the long day wanes; the slow moon climbs; The deep moans round with many voices.' Perfect, isn't it?"

"Yes, it is." I was through with worrying about my shortage of repartee.

"Well, I suppose we'd better push off, and sitting well in order smite the sounding furrows."

"To sail beyond the sunset?" I suggested.

"I'd love to, but I guess we'd better go home tonight, or they'll have a posse out."

Now that I had been released we talked all the way home. I got him onto archeology with no difficulty at all. I could do it, now that I expected nothing more of him.

By the time we beached the dory on the dark wet sand, I was rejoicing that I had cut myself free of him so quickly. If I weakened, I had only to remember myself out on the Crumbs waiting for a sign.

Standing on the beach while he sent the dory out on the haul-off, I rejected any view of myself, including my own, of a woman waiting for a man to bring her to life. I was no Sleeping Beauty; I was wide awake. I was not incomplete, I was a whole person with a brain and a life of my own.

Patrick was whistling *Around Her Neck She Wore a Yellow Ribbon*. I saw vistas of unlimited freedom for myself, as broad, clear, and unfrightening as the ocean had been tonight under the rising moon. I had a choice. It might not have been dramatic or exotic, but it was my own, to make the most of it. I could stay on at the college and eventually move on to a bigger school close to concert halls and theaters, continue my own studies, go abroad in vacations, make my life as a professional woman as I could never do at home giving piano lessons, playing Mr. Adams' accompaniments, and waiting for someone acceptable (to Phoebe and Papa) to propose.

If I lived out my life without the love of a man—and at that moment, aware as I was, I wanted no other love *ever* but Patrick's—it was up to me whether or not I became the sour or frantic spinster of the cartoons and jokes. My love would be my work and my music, and *they* would complete me.

Patrick made the line fast, and in a companionable silence we went up the steep path stippled with moonlight. When we came out into the open, the field was bleached and foreign under the moon. Patrick's hair was silver and the blue sweater drained of color, as the ocean was. The house looked a great distance from us. Here and there specks of mica flashed on its walls. It threw a shadow dense as jet, but suddenly a square of yellow light appeared in the black wing and Patrick said prosaically, "Somebody's hungry. So am I."

"Me too," I said.

We went on toward the house past the windbreak and through the damply rising scents of bay and sweetgrass and low tide.

chapter 13

*A*ndrew was in the kitchen making coffee. Charlie greeted us with inordinate fervor, and I picked him up and hugged him.

"Miranda better, or gone to bed?" Patrick asked.

"Better?" Andrew squinted at him. "What do you mean, better? Isn't she with you?"

"No, she thought she was coming down with summer complaint, and lit out for home."

"It must have been the merest thought then, because when I came in Charlie was all alone and lamenting at the top of his voice. Have some coffee?"

"I'd love some," I said. I put the dog down and went to wash my hands at the sink.

"I'll be back shortly," Patrick said, already on his way out. Andrew got out the cups and saucers.

"Look in the cake box, there's a good girl. How about cutting that applesauce cake?"

Andrew sat on a corner of the table smoking his pipe, waiting for the coffee to settle in the big granite-ware pot.

"Enjoying yourself, Seafair?"

"Oh, yes. I hope Jane can come, Andrew."

"Well, her people aren't too stuffy, given their age and circumstances." He got up to attend to the coffee. "At least they haven't fainted away in horror at the thought of their child living a world away from Philadelphia. And in such a world . . . I think that's settled enough."

He poured carefully into three cups, setting the fourth aside. "Patrick won't be back, he can't sit still on a night like this," he said indulgently. "He never could. Well, I shan't when Jane's here. What about you, Seafair? Don't you ever roam in the moonlight?"

"Not in Fern Grove," I said. "And not here, yet."

"You will." He picked up the tray of coffee and I took the one with the cake, cream, and sugar, and followed him. "Does Ian rove too?"

"Oh, yes, he has the family disease. Lunacy in its purest sense. He'll probably go out later tonight, when everybody else is asleep." He led the way into the parlor. "How about some music, or do you call that sneaky of me?"

"Sneaky," I said, "but I'll play, if I can drink my coffee first."

"Finest kind. Ian!" he shouted across the hall.

Before the lamp was lighted the garden lay moon-drenched in grays and silvers outside the glass doors. It was not possible to imagine the pansies and pinks, the opening iris, or how red the roses were, or the color of the lilacs. My reaction was obvious and logical. I sat down and played *Now Sleeps the Crimson Petal,* not with any idea of showing off but because here one could obey impulses, and this was a perfect setting for the song I'd played so often for Mr. Adams in rooms stuffed with overdressed people who had never roamed in the moonlight, or had successfully forgotten that they ever had.

When I finished, Andrew had lighted a lamp, and Ian had come in. He was standing by the fireplace, holding his coffee cup, and he said, "That was very nice."

"It would have been better with someone to sing it," I said.

"Where's Miranda?" Ian asked. "Off with Patrick somewhere?"

It was spoken in the offhand way of someone making idle talk, and Andrew answered as casually. "I doubt it. She had several hours' head start on him. Come and sit down and have your coffee, Seafair."

"Well, Seafair," Ian said in the tone my father used to

take toward my little friends, "where did Patrick take you tonight?"

"Out to the Crumbs. How were they named?"

"Nobody knows," Ian said. "Even Patrick can't dig that out. It was probably derived from some word so different you couldn't trace the connection." Andrew gave cake to Charlie. It was a remarkably sedate gathering, compared to those that included Patrick and Miranda. I felt obliged to describe the beauty of the trip across the water, then thought I was gushing, and was glad to go back to the piano. Andrew wanted something cheerful, so we had popular music. He knew by heart some music hall songs and I worked up the accompaniment. Ian applauded.

"I hope Adrienne's not offended by all this common music," I said.

"Her musical sensitivity should be pretty well worn away by a hundred years of us barbarians," Andrew said. "We used to pound out *Chopsticks* and then yell, 'You hear that, Dry Annie? Hey, was that good, Dry Annie?'"

"You weren't very respectful to your great-great-grand-mother or whatever she was."

"Whatever she was," said Andrew, "she wasn't our great-great-grandmother. The Old Colonel married again, after Adrienne. . . . He'd saved her from the guillotine, and some-times I guess she wished he hadn't, she hated the place so much. So she ran away."

Ian said, "With one of the Colonel's old comrades who'd sailed up from Portland to spend a pleasant summer week here. One afternoon when William Wallace was at the harbor, his old comrade set sail back to Portland with Adrienne tucked away below decks. They left from the Home Cove and went out around Bannock, so the Colonel never even caught a glimpse of the yawl."

"He was greeting the cargo of mahogany logs his brothers brought back from Haiti to panel the dining room and the library," said Andrew. "When he came home, the bird had flown."

"Oh, the poor man!" I exclaimed. "I feel as if I know him, just from the portrait. He has a different expression every time I look at him."

"He does," Andrew said solemnly. "Wait till he winks at you."

"Who knows, maybe it was a relief to lose her," Ian said. "If he married her to take care of her, he might have been upset more by his friend's perfidy—that's the word he used—than by her going. . . . Anyway, it didn't stop him from having the paneling done."

"But here's the really touching part of the story," said Andrew. "In a year or so the man abandoned her, and Brawly Bill found out about it through a business associate. He went to New York by one of his own vessels, found her in wretched surroundings, half-dead, brought her back, and took care of her until she'd coughed and bled her life away like Camille."

"She must have hated him for it," I said.

"Why?" Andrew laughed in surprise.

"Because of what she'd done to him?" Ian asked. "Because he not only forgave her, but heaped coals of fire, and so forth?"

"That, and maybe because he was so resilient," I said. "Impervious. Not wounded into hating *her*. Just calmly moving in and picking her up, and taking her back to the place she despised. Making her feel even more in his debt. And she had no defense left; she was absolutely helpless."

"Seafair, I behold you with new eyes," said Andrew, lifting his cup to me. "You're sure she hasn't been talking to you by Ouija board or table rappings?"

I laughed and shook my head. "Just putting myself in her place, that's all. If all one has left is pride, the unforgiveable sin is to deprive one of it."

"By kindness," Ian said.

"Yes. I always did think heaping coals of fire sounded more like torture than aid and comfort. What was his second wife like?"

"She was Margaret Guild, bless her." Andrew lifted his cup to the lady over the mantel, she whose eyes and bracelet had burned with life on my first visit to the parlor. "She wasn't afraid to take a chance on a forty-year-old widower on an island twenty-five miles out to sea. She came here straight from the parlors of Beacon Hill, and if she ever regretted it she never left word to prove it. She mightn't have been as exciting as Dry Annie, but she was the lady of his house and the mother of his children."

"Does 'Brawly Bill' mean he was quarrelsome?"

"No," said Ian. "It's Scots. *Braw*. It means he was handsome and dashing. Maybe that influenced her. Anyway, she outlived him, and carried on for the islanders as he would have done. She believed in duty. It was the guiding concept of her life."

"Have you ever thought, Ian," Andrew asked mischievously, "what we would have been if Dry Annie had had his family, instead of Margaret?"

"The Drummonds might have died out by now, or the Colonel's blood be wearing different names in different countries. The island itself could belong to someone else——"

"Don't!" I objected.

Ian looked at me with an entirely foreign spark of devilment. "What if it's true, and we're all living in some long, shared, common dream? Or what if somebody's dreaming *us?*"

"And what if you've been going down through the whiskey, pint by pint?" Andrew said. "Come out with any more of those theories and we'll be sending you off for the Keeley Cure."

"I'd rather like being someone's dream," I said, "if it was the right person."

"Oh, but you must already be somebody's dream," Andrew assured me gallantly, "or you will be."

It was so delightful that I decided to go to bed while I was still bounding from crest to crest like *Eaglet*.

When I was very old, I thought, I would recall these

goodnights on the stairs at The Eyrie, how I stopped by the Old Colonel's portrait and looked down at the upturned faces and the fair heads in the candlelight, and I would invest the memory with a drama that was pure creative imagination. At twenty-two, I was still realistic enough to be under no illusions. If I imagined being dressed in something appropriate to the staircase and wearing jewels in my hair, I knew I was in a blue linen skirt and middy blouse, with my hair in a schoolgirl's braids.

I knew also that for all Ian's courtesy and Andrew's easy friendliness I had made no impact upon their lives. So I was no more to these people than the wind or rain beating against The Eyrie's granite walls.

This didn't upset me. At home there was too much attention concentrated on me; here I was neither a cinder in the eye nor a pebble in the shoe. Here I had freedom. Miranda's disappearances and Patrick's conduct contributed to that freedom. I didn't need her at my elbow every moment, and after tonight I didn't need Patrick, if I ever did, and someday the kiss in the moonlight would cease from troubling, like the wicked.

Charlie hustled into my room ahead of me. He had a basket in Miranda's room but he never slept in it if he could help it. He used it as a receptacle for his loot. Tonight when I came in from the bathroom he was nosing around the stand at the head of my bed.

"What are you doing, Charlie?" I asked him, and with no visible guilt he picked up my handkerchief, jumped off the bed, and trotted back into Miranda's room. I followed him and found him sitting in his basket with the handkerchief in his mouth, waiting to be bargained with. I bought my property back with a dog biscuit, and while he ate it I also retrieved a pencil, a small piece of driftwood shaped like a bird, a spool of thread, and a large whelk shell I was saving for my half-brother Julian. I lectured Charlie on the probable fate of light-pawed or light-mouthed dogs. He was charmed with all the attention, and was back on my bed before I'd gotten through the door, virtuously treading out snakes at the foot.

When I was ready for bed I blew out my lamp and walked from window to window looking out at the island. The moonlight lay white as frost on the farm fields and roofs. In the farmhouse under the black maples, did Tom sleep, read, or pray, or lie awake thinking of the years ahead for him?

Perhaps the moonlight confused his sleep so that with the supernatural slipperiness of dreams he could slide back and forth from a man preaching in a great church to small Tom swathed in a sheet, his arms upraised to the full moon shining through a hole in the roof of branches. Tom, a pagan priest at twelve, a man of God at twenty-two. *God's good man,* Miranda had said, mournfully, as if she stood beside the bier of her childhood.

I went into her room and looked out past the flagpole to the sea beyond the cliffs. I couldn't ever go to bed here without a last look at the ocean. Miranda was probably keeping somebody up late at the harbor, over cups of tea and long enthralling gossips. Patrick was a different matter. I could imagine him walking alone, perhaps in the shadow of the oaks, making himself perfectly receptive to capture some message from the past.

I got into bed, rested my feet against Charlie's back, and wondered what secret reservoirs of the past I could draw on. Maybe I'd even pick up a communication from my Indian ancestors, but if their messages should be in the Penobscot language they wouldn't be of much use to me.

Then on the crater-rim of sleep I heard Andrew's voice. *Oh yes, he has the family disease.* What *was* the family disease? Not just the wandering alone, but the *why* of it, in Ian's case? He had said of Margaret Guild that duty was her guiding concept. It was certainly his. But she also had her children; what did *he* have of his own? When he walked alone, was his loneliness so powerful and invincible that it became a personage in itself and thus companioned him wherever he was?

The others were too out-going and out-giving for him to be a dry and passionless stick of a man, unless he was completely different from the rest. I wondered if he had ever been in love and it had ended tragically, if the girl had died or turned to someone else.

I would never know unless Miranda took the fancy to tell me, because I would never ask her what was none of my business. I went to sleep not exactly pitying Ian, which would have been presumptuous with someone like him, but rather sad and off-color.

I didn't know when Miranda came in and Charlie left me.

chapter 14

When I came down for breakfast a little after six in the morning, Charlie came with me. Miranda was still sleeping. The three brothers were just finishing their hearty breakfast, and Meg Finley was having one of her cups of tea. Water was heating on the laundry stove; it was washday.

The older two left for work but Patrick lingered. He had an old wide-awake hat and a scarred, over-stuffed briefcase. "Is that downeast chowderhead still sleeping?" he asked me.

"She was when I got up."

Charlie barked outside the shed door and Patrick went to let him in. When he came back he said, "What time did she get in, anyway?"

I helped myself to oatmeal porridge and Jersey cream. "I haven't the faintest."

"I suppose she *did* get in all right," he said very casually. "You know that for a fact."

"I heard her breathing this morning. How's that? Of course I didn't look closely to see if that was really her head, but I'm reasonably sure it was, and Charlie seemed to think so."

His smile was sheepish. "All right, I'm a worrywart. You don't know—but Meg should—what a fumblefoot she always was, rubbering at a bird or trying to see what somebody was doing a mile away and walking off a doorstep or falling down a ladder."

"She seems very sure-footed now," I said.

"She is, so long as she minds her own business and not

[*127*]

everybody else's. Damn it, I need her this morning."

"Watch your language, Patrick," Meg said.

"Why? I didn't damn anybody, just *it,* and that could be anything. So can you really call that foul language, Meg? Real swearing?"

"This is what I always got from him," Meg said to me, "ever since he was old enough to talk. It was enough to make a body wish she'd never started anything in the first place."

"That was the general idea," said Patrick. "Well, I'm leaving."

"Is there anything I can do to help?" I asked, glad not to be tremulous at the mere thought.

"No, I'm going to bring some notes up to date, that's all, and Miranda knows all the jargon, she can sort my stuff and write it up as well as I can. So thanks just the same, Seafair." He rewarded me with the smile that had shaken the heart out of me on my first day. I felt it shudder now, but I remained true to my liberation. "When she does get up, if it's before noon, tell her I've gone to Weir Point and I can use her. I mean please. And thank you."

On the way out he met Erline Pease. "Good morning, me proud beauty," he said, and swung his hat in a vigorous swat at her derrière.

She yelped. "Oh, blessed be, Pat, I wish I was fifteen years younger. You wouldn't be safe."

"Meg, Tom was just great yesterday," I said.

"Well, he's got a long way to go yet, and there's more to it than fine sermons," she said sternly.

"I know that, but from the way he's starting out he's got everything in his favor."

"Maybe so, but I don't believe in spitting in the face of Providence." She knocked on wood just to be doubly safe, then gave me a diffident smile. "His father," she whispered, "*there's* pride for ye. Couldn't eat his breakfast yesterday for nerves, and gulped and swallowed and blinked his eyes in church. Couldn't get out soon enough. If I'd *wanted* to sniffle a bit, I couldn't give in to it, for having to keep my eye on that man, and hold him together."

"Well, I think there was a lot of sniffling going on."

"Ayuh, there's some around here who love to cry in church," she said acidly. "That wasn't for Tom. That's just to convince God the devil hasn't really got a good holt on their big toe. They likely think Tom's a heretic for telling 'em to make a joyful noise unto the Lord."

Erline came in, still laughing at Patrick. "*That* one!"

She poured tea for herself and had one of the fishcakes from the big iron frying pan. To listen to her one would think the village had been seething with iniquity over the weekend except for the hour when everybody was in church. She never came out with the details, nodding and winking before she quite reached the point. But Meg guessed right every time, shaking her head, sighing profoundly, or sometimes in real shock rolling her eyes toward the ceiling.

It would have been fascinating except that I never could guess just what had happened or who did it. Miranda arrived in the middle of one episode, and said at once, "Who did you say had Prissy Schofield upstairs at West India Hall?"

Meg got up. "It's time we were at the washing."

"At least you didn't say 'little pitchers,' " said Miranda. "Who was it, Erline? Come on, tell me," she teased. Erline shook her head. Miranda gasped dramatically, "Erline! It was never *Patrick!*"

Erline shrieked, "No, no! It was Harry Joy!"

"Who caught them? Were they in *the act?*"

"*Miranda*," said Meg, "I'm not having any more of this. Erline, come along." Erline, sailing behind her out to the woodshed, said over her shoulder, "Nobody saw anything except them two sneaking out. So everybody surmises."

"Well, her father'd better not get out his shotgun on a surmise," said Miranda. "Harry will have him in court for defamation of character." She brought her porridge to the table and sat down opposite me. "How was your row last night?" she asked me.

"Lovely. What did *you* do, after you found out you didn't have summer complaint?"

"Look, here's Drummond's." She shaped oatmeal with her spoon. "And here's Bannock. And here comes the tide." She poured cream carefully. "I used to do this when I was little."

It was this open disregard of a perfectly innocent and normal question that told me she'd faked the warning cramps; she hadn't intended to go with us at all. If she didn't mind throwing Patrick and me together for several hours, she must have known I was no competition. But what was the point of the deception unless she'd expected him to come looking for her when we got back? She knew how he fumed about her wandering around at night and could expect him to come out. She could have been very close by, watching for him.

Yet, the way he spoke this morning, I could have sworn he hadn't seen her at all last night, unless his behavior was a part of the thing too. When they were small they'd lived a secret life. What about now? If she were in love with him, knowing how their elders were concerned about this possibility—and he must have known too, of course—she could have asked him to keep their late-night prowls a secret.

"Patrick's at Weir Point with a lot of paperwork, and he wants you to come," I told her.

"I hope he doesn't hold his breath," she said. There was, I thought, a rather self-satisfied gloss on her.

It was boat day. We rode to the harbor on the wagon with Tom, behind the young horse who showed an interesting inclination to be startled by butterflies. So I concentrated on gripping my side of the seat, while Tom and Miranda carried on a technical conversation about sailing; Miranda never mentioned the service, but when Tom gave me a hand down at the head of the steamboat wharf, I said, "Congratulations, Tom."

He looked startled. "What for? Oh!" He smiled. "Thank you, Seafair."

"I don't know if anybody's supposed to say they enjoyed a sermon, but considering the subject of yours I guess I can say that."

"No fair flirting with the Dominie," said Miranda. The *Ocean Pearl* whistled at the harbor mouth and the children began running down the wharf. A few women followed decorously, making the most of the occasion. Two boys and a girl who'd been going to high school on the mainland came home today, and the first batch of summer boarders arrived. There were two salesmen, and an inter-island peddler named Mr. Lippman. He had a great deal of help from older youngsters, who rounded up wheelbarrows to take his cases of goods around to West India Hall. The inscrutable captain carried the mail sacks up to the store, while the deckhand and engineer got the freight out and helped Tom load barrels of flour and other staples onto the wagon for the farm and The Eyrie.

I had a letter from Papa, and in spite of my resolution to be like Luther—*Here I stand, I can do no other*—I felt queasy in my stomach. I went looking for a quiet place in which to read it.

The front doorstep was cluttered with the new summer boarders writing postcards, women coming to shop, children and Miranda talking to everybody. I went across the road and sat down on the ship's timber where Miranda and I had waited for Patrick one day.

"My dear daughter," Papa wrote. "We were severely shocked by your letter. I could hardly believe that *you* had written it; I could only fear that you had fallen under some pernicious influence." (How could he be so pompous? That was Phoebe's doing. Talk about a pernicious influence!) "But Phoebe soon conquered her own dismay in her wish to reassure *me*. She recollected hearing of this family, the first Colonel Drummond having been one of General Washington's close circle. To be positive that this was the same branch, she went at once by afternoon train to Portland to visit her great-aunt." (For the first time I blessed Great-aunt Carrie, who usually had a congealing effect on my vital juices.) "This lady told her that the Drummond's Island family are in the direct line from Colonel William Wallace Drummond, and that the three unmarried sons are well-known around Bar Harbor."

Unmarried. That was the clue. If anything could make up to Phoebe for the loss of my services this summer, it was the chance of my marrying, and marrying well enough to be useful.

Papa wrote on: "Her great-aunt had assured us that you are in good company. This has put our minds at rest; Phoebe joins me in wishing you a most enjoyable and productive summer, in terms of making new associations and broadening the mind."

Yachting at Bar Harbor, presumably. Or helping to entertain rich yachtsmen at Drummond's. Being taken up by the right people. And with common sense and application on my part (and a lot of luck, Phoebe would add silently), I would end up engaged to somebody. Phoebe would shine at my wedding, if I could time it between her pregnancies. Then, in later years, with Julian, Edith, Hester, Thomas, and Brooks growing up, I would of course do my sisterly duty by introducing the litter into suitable circles.

"Phoebe says that she is packing your summer frocks, and as a little contribution she is having Mrs. Slater make you two new ones. You will have your last month's salary of course, but if you need anything please don't hesitate to write to—Your loving father, Henry Bell."

This was the letter that Phoebe had read and approved. Afterward, before he sealed the envelope, he had written at the bottom of the page, "Have a good time. Love, Papa."

I could be sarcastic about the letter, but not about the postscript.

I decided to write him a good letter and mail it to his

office, and if he had any sense left it wouldn't go home with him to Fern Grove.

I wiped my eyes and blew my nose and hopped up, refreshed, ready for anything. Miranda wasn't in sight. I went around to the Hall to see what Mr. Lippman offered for sale. So I was to have two new dresses to help the cause. Well, they'd be pretty ones, I needn't fault Phoebe's taste. Though she shook her head about my coloring, it was a challenge to her.

I'd wear the dresses to church, and to the occasional dances. The Drummond style of life didn't include lawn parties, charity bazaars, strawberry festivals, driving in carriages, canoe parades, and all the rest which Andrew described as the Bar Harbor rigamarole.

Dream on, Phoebe, I thought kindly. If you could only see me now.

Mr. Lippman had his goods spread out on trestle tables and the benches. Women were talking in low but vivacious voices as they rummaged through a job lot of corsets, and the children were breathing hard over the cheap toys and books. Some of the girls from the fish factory were examining the yard goods, and the cards of braid, lace, and ribbon. They kept holding lengths of goods under their chins and asking each other's advice. I took some crushed-raspberry chambray to a window to get a better light on it. The window looked out on the wharf where I had gone during the dance, and I tried to pick out the exact spot where I'd been standing when Patrick kissed me. A gull stood there, picking at a dead crab. Well, that was as good a marker as any. At least the gull was enjoying himself.

Over to the left of the wharf, beyond the tar kettle and the flat ledges where the men laid the tarred nets to dry, there was a marshy spot where some old boats had been hauled up long ago. Blue flag, swamp candles, and bindweed grew around the rotting hulls. Beyond the boat graveyard the rocks rose toward Southern Point. It was here that I saw Miranda suddenly appear on the skyline, coming from the outer side of the point. She stepped up on a tilted chunk of ledge, walked to its height, and turned to look back the way she had come. Her hair streamed out in the freshening wind.

A strange man joined her. He wore a checked work shirt with rolled sleeves and open neck, work trousers, and knee boots, and he was smiling down at her.

It was Dill Kalloch, who was no stone sculpture of a man when he smiled. He had the amiable magnificence of some of Winslow Homer's life-savers and fishermen; you expected him to speak slowly in some richly incomprehensible dialect. Miranda put her hand on his forearm and pointed out past the harbor mouth. She was enchanted by whatever she saw, she didn't take her eyes from the sight, and Dill didn't take his eyes from her. So they stood against the sky like one of Homer's paintings entitled *Watching for the Fleet* or *Sail Ho*.

It could have been an accidental meeting. Ordinarily Dill would be out fishing like the rest of the men, but for some reason he wasn't out today.

Yet there was that smile down at her, and her hand on his forearm. The night he had been at the house he had said nothing, expressed nothing beyond a mild enjoyment now and then. Instinctive camouflage? There might be more in Dill than met the eye, and there was a good deal of that already.

"Let's ask Miss Bell what she thinks," Jennie Swenson piped behind me. I came quickly away from the window. The girls wanted to know how a green plaid gingham would suit Ethelyn's rather sandy coloring.

It was the first time I'd ever been regarded as the Last Word of fashion, so I advised with enthusiasm and was thanked in the same manner. I decided to take the chambray, and picked out the notions to go with it. Mr. Lippman was joking in a Russian accent with the corset buyers, and I wandered around looking at things until I came to a box of cheap jewelry. I picked out a large brooch cut from thick iridescent shell and decorated with a very curly M in gilt wire. Mr. Lippman congratulated me on my taste, but I suspected a twinkle under his drooping eyelid.

I walked out and met Miranda, who hailed me with joyful surprise. "Where've you *been?* The last I saw of you you were sitting on the log reading your mail, and then you disappeared into thin air. I've been looking for you ever since."

Out beyond Southern Point? "I've been going mad," I said. "Shopping like Emma Bovary, insanely beyond my means. Here." I handed her the pin. "A slight token of my esteem."

"Oh, it's *magnificent.* Something by Tiffany or Cartier's?"

"A little trifle swiped from the Imperial Russian Collection, I think."

"I'll wear it forever. But I'll have to give you a penny for it." She pinned it on the front of her blouse, sticking her finger in the process. "Rubies too," she said, shaking free the drops of blood. They flew across her white duck in a foxglove spatter. "My blood's a beautiful color, don't you think?" She took her purse from her pocket and gave me a penny. "Was that letter from your father? What did he say?"

"That I was to have a good time."

"I'm so glad!" She clasped her hands against her breast. "Is there anything more heavenly than a clear conscience?"

"Who's supposed to have the clear conscience, he or I?" I asked. "Or are you talking about yourself?"

"What have *I* got to worry about?" As devoutly innocent as the Blessed Damozel; even in her eyes. But she hadn't tried to hide Dill. Maybe he was meant to be seen. . . . The Thing began to form nebulously in my mind, like constantly shifting and wreathing cloud, slowly shaping into a bird, a face, an animal—

It had no chance to develop because the children came out of the hall, shepherded by Mr. Lippman. "Hello, Mr. Lippman," Miranda said, putting out her hand. He took it in both of his. "Miranda, you are the morning star. When will I dance at your wedding?"

"Oh, don't hurry me," she said, laughing. "I have a lot of dancing to do for myself before then. But you'll be there when the time comes, I promise you."

"When she was little," the peddler said to me, "she wanted to marry me because I was so rich."

"Mercenary little wretch," I said.

"Were you coming in, Miranda?" he asked her. "I was just going around to Schofields' for dinner."

"I'll be just a minute. You wait there, Seafair." She went in with him. "How are Rachel and Hanna? How's Raphael doing with his store?" Her voice grew faint. I tried to see again the shape in the clouds, if one was to be seen in order that another should not even be guessed at.

She was back again. "Hold out your hand, Seafair," she commanded, smiling. She fastened a bracelet around my wrist, made of multi-colored glass stones. "If your skin turns green it means you have bad blood, because the setting's really 14-carat gold, even if it doesn't say so. I wouldn't choose anything *less*."

chapter 15

When we reached the house the washing was all out, Meg had gone back to the farm, and Charlie was practically hoarse with outrage in the kitchen. We took our lunch on trays out to the garden, and ate at a rustic table in the grape arbor. The stiffening sea wind blew through the tops of the trees, shook and buffeted the fragrance out of the tallest lilacs, but below the wall the sun was hot, full of butterflies and industrious bees.

Miranda yawned throughout lunch, visibly sagging after having been out half the night. I was kept from somnolence by expecting Patrick to show up at any moment and lace into Miranda for not coming to help him. I planned to leave directly he appeared. But he hadn't come by the time we'd finished.

"I'm so sleepy," Miranda groaned," and I've invited everybody over to play Pit tonight."

There was a sagging old couch hammock down by the windbreak and opposite the ice pond, its mattress and cushions protected from dew and rain by a tarpaulin. We spent the afternoon down there with the new *McClure's* and *Leslie's* Magazines that had come in the mail. At least I did. Miranda fell asleep almost at once. Later we went swimming, and that's when we discovered *Eaglet* was gone. Patrick and Tom were also missing. They still hadn't gotten home by the time we were bathed and dinner was ready.

"I know what they're doing, the sneaks," said Miranda malevolently. "They've landed on some island way up in the bay and they're steaming clams and having a high old time without any women around. I sh'd think Tom would be *ashamed.* His poor father out there tilling the soil in this hot sun and Tom acting like a rich man's son just because he preached a sermon yesterday and everybody treated him as if he was Henry Ward Beecher or Phillips Brooks or——"

"You sound exactly the way you did when you were ten and they left you behind. Go ahead, rave," Ian encouraged her. "Better than sulking any time."

"Ian Drummond, I never sulk," she told him grandly. "At least not for long. Just until I think of something to say."

We heard Andrew coming before we saw him. He was whistling *The White Cockade* and slamming screen doors behind him. He came into the kitchen still whistling, swept an arm around Miranda's waist and swung her; released her and took me without losing a step, swung me off my feet, and took on Ian in the fastest and wildest spin of all. Solo, he finished up with a clog step, an imaginary straw hat against his breast, and grinning at us like a happy drunk.

"Jane's coming," Miranda said.

"How'd you ever guess?" He spun the invisible straw hat over our heads. "Yep! She can hardly wait. She's traveling to Bar Harbor with the Strawbridges, and her parents expect me to meet her and escort her here." He gave Ian a slap on the shoulder. "I'm going after her in the cutter. If it's a fair chance I'll be over and back in a day. Take a day off and go with me, old son."

"Why not?" Ian said equably. "Yes. I'd like it."

"Then that's settled. She wants to be here for the Fourth, so we'll go on the second. Allow an extra day. Dinner ready? Smells arregorical. I'll go wash." Whistling again he bounded toward the back stairs.

"What about us?" Miranda called after him. "Aren't you inviting us?"

He stopped in the doorway. "Nope."

"Why?"

"Because this is going to be a vacation for Ian," said Andrew, "far from the clitter-clatter of your little tongue. Absolute silence except for the snap of the sails, the creak of the masts, the musical swash of the wash——"

"And the cooing of the lovebirds," said Miranda nastily.

"That's on the way back, and we'll coo up forward of the mast. Ian will be at the tiller, a man alone with the sea and his trusty pipe——"

"Spare us the poetry," said Miranda. "Seafair's never seen Bar Harbor."

"And I don't care if I never do," I said. "I'm on Drummond's Island and I don't want to get off it till I have to. But you don't have to stay home with me, Miranda, really."

"I didn't think she'd been doing that much," Ian said. She ignored that.

"You see how kind and generous Seafair is?" she asked Andrew. "If she can be that way, why can't you?"

He was smilingly implacable. "No."

She considered him for quite a while. Finally she said, conversationally, "You're a beast. You know that, don't you? Jane's marrying a beast."

"Ay-yup," he agreed. Then they both laughed, and Andrew went on upstairs.

After dinner Ian went to the harbor to play chess with one of the summer boarders. The Pit game was at its noisiest when Tom and Patrick came into the kitchen. Throughout the boisterous greetings. Miranda gazed at them in gelid silence. Patrick kept glancing sidewise at her. Then he winked at me, and yanked her hair ribbon untied. "Miss us, Banty?"

"I was hoping," she said with exquisite precision, "that you were becalmed. In a thunder storm, with hail big as apples."

"Oh, is it mad because we didn't take it along?" Patrick gurgled. "Bless its poor little heart, its feelings was hurt."

"The way you snuck off without telling anybody was pretty childish. I wouldn't have gone even if you'd asked me, if that's what worried you."

"We wouldn't take a chance on it." Patrick picked up his

old Norfolk jacket and began emptying the pockets onto the table. "Guess where we went."

"From the looks of that stuff, Mark Island," Hugh Swenson said. Everybody but Miranda began picking over the collection.

"Look at this perfect adze," Patrick gloated. "Look at the edge on it. It's almost as sharp as it was the time the last man used it. We picked up all this stuff in that little cove that faces southeast. We steamed some mussels for our supper, and finished up with hard-tack and chocolate we had with us. There's a wonderful spring. I never tasted such water."

Dill picked up a thin, elegantly worked knife in dark red jasper. "Handsome," he said. "Some handsome." Miranda reached across and took it off his palm and put it against her cheek, smiling at him:

"It's satin-smooth," she murmured.

"Tom found that," Patrick said. "Dug it out of the bank. Given time, I could make an archeologist out of him yet. Man, that little island's a treasure house, and we've barely scratched the surface. I'd like to buy it."

"Who owns it, anyway?" someone asked.

"Somebody up at Stonington, I heard," said Andrew.

"Ayuh, but he died," Harry Joy said. "But it warn't his. He always claimed it. Heirship property, it is. There's somebody over at Sou'west Harbor——"

Prissy threw herself sulkily back in her chair. "Well, the game's over for the night. Do *you* think this cultch is fascinatin'?" she shot at me. "Or do you make a big towse over it because the boys do?"

"Well, we plain ones have to do something to get attention," I told her. "We can't all be like you."

Faustina gave her a dig in the ribs and hooted like her aunt.

"Oh, come on in the other room," Miranda said impatiently. "They're so wound up now in who left what to who, they'll be going into the begats any time now."

We were working out some really heart-rending harmony for *Whispering Hope* when the men came in.

We sang for a while, but it was a week night and work began early in the morning, so the harbor crowd began to leave soon in two's and three's, successively seen out by Patrick, then by Andrew, and the last group by Miranda. At this point I was left in the parlor with Tom, Patrick, and Andrew. We were all tired, all yawning without restraint, but nobody wanted to make the first move. Finally Patrick stood up and stretched. "I need more than cookies and lemonade to go to bed on," he said. "Those mussels were a long time ago."

"I'll go out and put the kettle on," I offered.

"We'll all go," Andrew said. As we went out through the hall, Tom stopped me by the newel post.

"They've asked me to take another service later, after the Schofields' minister has gone. Would you and Miranda work out something for an offertory?"

"Of course, I'd love to." I said. "Do you have anything special in mind?"

"I was going to leave it to you, and the limitations of the organ, but—well, do you know *By Cool Siloam's Shady Rill?*"

"Yes. It's a lovely hymn. We'll do it." Behind my back I touched wood. *If Miranda doesn't throw a fit.*

"I'll be very grateful. That's a favorite of mine."

Ahead of us Patrick and Andrew were talking about Mark Island. "Just the same, it won't do any harm to start writing letters," Patrick said. "Maybe I could lease the digging rights if nothing else. I could camp out there for a season. There may be a burial ground."

He walked on into the kitchen. Andrew waited to light his pipe, so that I was behind Patrick, and when he stopped short I almost bumped into him. Charlie barked. I heard a rush of movement, the swish of skirts, a quick light step, a feminine gasp. Past Patrick I saw Dill Kalloch standing in the middle of the kitchen, his head just missing the hanging lamp, his big hands out palms upward as if in entreaty. He looked at us with both alarm and bewilderment.

Miranda was still backing off from him, more slowly now, hugging herself with crossed arms, her face flushed, eyes slanting sidewise toward us with a watery glisten.

"What's going on here?" Patrick asked, ominously quiet.

Dill opened his mouth, but Miranda said rapidly, "Nothing. Dill's just going." She loosened the self-hug and made a grab for the doorknob as if for a life line, and swung the door wide open. "Goodnight, Dill," she gabbled. "Thanks for coming, and thanks again for the—uh—chocolate drops."

Dill didn't move. Confusion dug deeper seams into his broad face. Tom said, "I'll light the kerosene stove, Seafair, if you'll put fresh water in the tea kettle."

Patrick walked forward into the kitchen, without taking his eyes off Dill.

"Good*night,* Dill!" Miranda almost shouted. She took his big arm in both her hands pulled him toward the door, and then shoved. Just before she shut the door on him we had a last glimpse of his mutely protesting face. Then she drove the bolt across.

"I'll have a word with him, I think," Patrick said. He strode toward the door but Miranda put her back against it and folded her arms. "Wait up, Pat," Andrew was protesting. "What's going on?"

"That's what I intend to find out. Come away from that door, Miranda."

"Seafair, the kettle?" Tom politely reminded me.

"You'll have to hurl me out of the way, Pat," Miranda warned her cousin, above the clanking of the pump.

"He was mauling you, wasn't he?" I didn't realize one could show white through fresh windburn. Patrick did. Tom straightened up, and Andrew took his pipe out of his mouth.

"He didn't *maul* me," Miranda said scornfully. I handed the kettle to Tom, who nodded at me with no discernible consternation in his dark eyes.

"Then what were *you* doing?" Patrick demanded. "Throwing yourself at him? Leading him on?"

"Oh, Pat," she said with a half-laugh. "Don't be so tiresome. Andrew, can't you gag him or something? Dill and I were just fooling! He bet me I couldn't open his hand and get what he was holding—that red jasper knife of yours, Pat—and, my goodness, you know what a *grip* he has." She was all but trilling, her voice was so high. "Heavens, I hope he doesn't go home with it in his pocket, you scared him so coming out here like the Montagues, or was it the Capulets, I always forget." She ran a jumpy hand over the artifacts on the table. Her fingers pounced on the red knife, picked it up, dropped it. She put her hand in her pocket, and moistened her lips.

"Well, that's simple enough," Andrew said loudly. "How about some strong tea, Tom? I'm awash with lemonade." Tom nodded and began measuring tea from the canister.

Patrick was still watching Miranda. The white pressure around his mouth put years on him. "Fooling, was it? Are you sure it was that knife he had his hand around? You rushed him out of here in a damned guilty hurry."

"Before you could hit him. If he ever struck back, he'd squash you like a mosquito." Miranda laughed.

"*Miranda*," Tom said softly. Her head swung toward him at once. Her flush went deeper, she looked actually abashed. "Why don't you get out the tea cups?" he said. "Come on, Pat, cool down. We've had a great day, and let's keep it that way."

Miranda went to the cupboards without a glance in any other direction. Patrick gripped the back of a chair, his face tormented with indecision. Andrew sat down at the table and began examining the artifacts.

No one spoke to Patrick. I didn't look openly at him, but I knew when he relinquished his rage. The release was palpable. He pulled out a chair and sat down, and said to Andrew, "Look at this one; there's a perfect thumb grip. See? I could skin a fish with this even now, it's that sharp."

A subdued Miranda asked, "Tom, do you and Pat want ham sandwiches?"

"You can ask me directly," Patrick said. "I've never hit you yet except in self-defense. Yes, I want ham sandwiches. *Please*."

By the time we sat down to our tea, the drama might never have happened, except for some residual quivers in my stomach. The Indian things went from hand to hand, and were studied under a magnifying glass. Miranda joined in the discussion about the island and teased Patrick for a chance to give it a new name if he ever acquired it. "There must be hundreds of Mark Islands. We should give it a really distinctive name."

"*We!*" He laughed. "Where'd you ever get *that* idea?"

"All right, then, I shan't attend your Midsummer's Eve thing."

"Good. I'll give Seafair your part and then we'll accomplish something."

Ian came in from his evening at the harbor and sat down to examine the artifacts. The evening ended with comradely goodnights called back and forth, and Miranda planning to go out with Patrick to haul his traps. She came into my room to brush her hair.

"Don't you want to know what happened between Dill and me tonight?" she asked.

"Well, I have as much morbid curiosity as anybody else," I said. "But I wouldn't give you the satisfaction of asking."

She laughed. "Well, nothing happened. There wasn't time. . . . Didn't Patrick *steam!*"

"Was that the idea? To make him steam? I mean, was that your idea of a practical joke, make it look as if you and Dill were guiltily jumping apart? Not that Dill jumped——"

"No, poor Dill just looked thunderstruck. Which he was," she chuckled. "I don't know if he'd have kissed me or not, even with plenty of time."

"But you were trying to find out." I hoped I didn't sound priggish.

"Well, there's something about Dill that intrigues me. He's not stupid, you know. He's not really a dumb ox. Yet

... Well, I've known him all my life, but I *don't* know him. Still waters run deep and that sort of thing." She brushed slowly, her hand as bemused as her face and heavy eyes.

"But what——" I stopped, and made a helpless gesture with my hands.

"What will it get me? Not trouble. I can manage him all right. And I'm not leading him on, for heaven's sake! Didn't Patrick sound *shocked?*"

Which is what you want, isn't it? I thought. To make him look differently at you?

"Pat's so darned officious," she went on. "He'd *like* to be tyrannical, but he takes it all out in words. We've been going at each other hammer and tongs ever since I can remember, but he'd never hit. At least not me, no matter how mad I ever made him. He's not a—a hitter?—a striker? What would you call it? But he's not a coward, either."

She got up. "I'd better get to bed, it'll be five o'clock before I know it. I love going out with Pat when the whole house is asleep, it reminds me of the old days. Night, Seafair."

chapter 16

*M*idsummer's Eve was rained out in a southeast storm. "Now we'll never know what Patrick had planned," I said.

"Nothing, probably," said Miranda. "Oh, maybe a midnight picnic around a fire, something like that."

"On the altar?" I asked. "With incantations?"

"With mosquitoes. *They'd* have the midnight feast. Darling Seafair, don't ever go into the oaks at night, you'll be eaten alive." She looked quizzically at me. "Are you really disappointed?"

"Yes. I wanted to see Patrick in action, calling up spirits from the vasty deep and so forth. Not that I expect any spirits to arrive, but it would be fun anyhow."

"But now that we don't take it seriously any more," she said, "it's no fun, don't you see? The fun was in being half-scared that something would show up. Your heart pounded around in your chest, and your throat got parched, and your eyes felt out on sticks like a lobster's, you were staring so hard into the smoke. It was all you could do not to race for the house, but you were terrified to move from the spot in case an icy skeleton hand was waiting to grab you. But the next day you were always convinced you'd had the best time ever."

I did walk down to the oaks alone that day in the late afternoon, just to taste the atmosphere of the grove in the rain. Nobody knew I went out except Charlie and I left him in the kitchen. It was too early to start dinner, Patrick was working in his room, Miranda reading in hers, Ian at the harbor, and Andrew at Bannock and likely not to start home at all tonight. I put on boots, a long oilskin coat and sou'wester from the collection in the entry, and went down along the outside of the spruce windbreak.

There was at times a brightening, as the clouds thinned passing the invisible sun, and in it the rain came in blowing showers of silver. So I was not prepared for the dusk under the oaks. The deeper I went into the grove the darker it became. There was wind blowing through the top branches with the sound of white water pouring down a distant ravine, but all was a twilight hush underneath.

I passed Adam Joy's cabin site with a respectful if figurative salute, and came to Daniel Joy's chimney, the altar. The open place overhead through which the full moon had shone must be much smaller now than it had been ten years ago. I put the bright yellow sou'wester on the chimney in hope that it would show up later as a guide if the twilight grew darker, and walked on toward the excavation.

Standing by the pit, wondering what lay a foot or more under the soil, I wished again that I would suddenly discover in myself a gift for receiving psychic communications. I knew it was ridiculous. But just suppose I did hear a voice or a message without words, an impulse in the brain, an unbreakable conviction springing suddenly from a mysterious source.

I tried making my mind blank, but it only grew much busier. Imagining black velvet was like imagining space; it had to have an edge somewhere, or I went falling headlong through it forever. . . . Instead of receiving a message from the past, I heard only the needle-fine song of a mosquito hunting for blood. It began to look as if all my grand experiments, including love, were to end with insulting trivialities. I left.

Until now the gloaming under the trees had been wholly enjoyable. But some hundred feet away from the dig I couldn't see the faintest glint of the yellow sou'wester on the altar ahead of me. The darkness had intensified all at once, as if night had come while I wasn't looking. The trunks took on grotesque twists I'd never noticed before, thick roots bore a resemblance to enormous claws, and the noise of wind in the upper branches sounded like the thrashing of some scaly mythical beast.

From the corners of my eyes I seemed to catch odd, flitting movements. *You were terrified to move from the spot, in case an icy skeleton hand was waiting to grab you.*

"Oh, for heaven's sake!" I cried aloud in exasperation, though with an unconvincing quaver in my voice. "Don't be such a *chowderhead.*"

The grove was narrow enough so that I should come out to the alder swamp and Home Cove on one side, pasture on the other; Andrew's Cove at the northwest end, the windbreak at the southeast end. But with no visible landmarks I could keep circling for hours like a lost hunter, and never come out to a boundary. My throat dried and closed up, making it an effort to swallow. Then I recognized primitive hysteria for what it was. This wasn't the Great North Woods. It wasn't winter. I had only to sit down and wait, until morning if necessary.

Except that at the house they didn't know where I was. They knew the sea fascinated me, they'd think I'd gone out to look at the surf and had been swept off the rocks. This did away with any idea of huddling down in a tight bunch against the least hostile tree trunk.

If I could just figure out a way to keep going in a straight line, I'd be bound to come out into the open somewhere. But down here where no wind struck I didn't even have that as a guide. Then, all at once, the gloom lightened and I saw off to my left the pale blob of my sou'wester.

I ran to it before the scene could darken again, looked up at the scrap of pearly sky, and felt I should do obeisance to Something. Low clouds blew over the gap like dark smoke and a rain drop hit my uplifted face. I headed for the first cabin site, and it was here that a wet terrier found me. Someone had let him out, and he'd picked up my trail. We were both terribly and demonstratively glad to see one another.

I didn't tell anyone in the house where I'd been, and they assumed I'd been for a walk down to the Home Cove, especially when I mentioned the birds.

There was nearly a week of wind and rain, with heavy fog in the quiet spells. We spent a great deal of time in the attic. Half of it had once been a playroom which later metamorphosed into a clubroom, decorated according to everyone's taste with anything that could be tacked to the walls, hung from the beams, or stood on the sills of the dormer windows.

A sewing machine and cutting table stood under the window that looked east over the sea, and here I made up my raspberry chambray outfit. Sometimes Patrick or Tom or the two together came up the narrow stairs, and we talked endlessly, sometimes vehemently, often aggressively, occasionally rudely, about politics, social conditions, books and their writers, morals and ethics, philosophy Greek and otherwise. We talked about LIFE, in large letters, while the rain slid down the slates, beat against the windward glass, and gurgled along the gutters and into the cistern.

The *Ocean Pearl* missed two trips, and Andrew was stuck on Bannock for four days. When the storm blew out, he came home. He'd been staying at The Thistle, where the bachelor Scots lived. He said he'd learned the Highland fling, and a good many indecent songs. He'd also been trying to talk to Rosaleen.

"She turned to me when Bob died, but since then she's hardly given me the time of day. Those two are writing and coaxing, I'm sure of it. . . . I think she'd gone now if Father Emery hadn't made her promise to wait out the summer, for the boys' sake. He pointed out all the foul diseases lying in wait in the big cities to grab these island youngsters."

"What about what could be waiting to grab her?" Patrick asked. "Did he play that up?"

"No, because we only suspect. We can't tell her after just one look at that pair that they're Plague and Pestilence. But we want to see some relatives who look a hell of a lot more respectable than these two and who can prove they're what they seem to be." He helped himself to more of the wild strawberries we'd picked that afternoon and went on explaining to the rest of us what Ian already knew. "I wrote right after the funeral to a college friend of mine in Boston. Lawyer, Irish, on his way to being a politician and a dazzler. He knows just about everybody, and has contacts who know anybody he's missed. The Harrigans are supposed to own a lot of property and live high off their rents, but so far he's found no trace of them."

"Maybe that isn't their real name," Miranda suggested. "Maybe they aren't even relatives, but a pair of white-slavers who have done away with the geniune cousins!" She flamed with creative fire. "They've seen Rosaleen's picture in the parlor, on the stand with the potted ferns between the front windows with the fancy curtains ... Can't you see the room, with last Easter's palms tucked over the picture of the Sacred Heart? And they've an order to fill for some sultan's harem or some rich South American. So it's suffocate dear Cousin Kate with a poker-work sofa pillow over her face, and put poison in Cousin Mike's beer, and off to claim this proud Celtic beauty——"

"The trouble with that is," said Patrick, "that sultans and South Americans pay better prices for blonds."

Andrew and Ian listened to the conversation in a sort of cold patience that made them very like. As the chill finally penetrated, the younger two subsided.

"They could be the real cousins, all right," Andrew said. "Once Bob said something about his only kin in America being a bad lot, and he never wanted to see them step foot on his property. He'd never in his life had a house and a bit of land all his own until he came to Bannock, he never would have had it in Ireland. And he wasn't letting it be polluted by the likes of them. . . . His own phrase . . . He didn't tell me their name, so I can only presume that the Harrigans are 'the likes of them.' "

"Then Rosaleen must know all about them," Miranda said. Andrew shook his head.

"Not the way her father raised her. Her beauty was a great cross to him as well as his great pride. He thought the only way to save her was to keep her as ignorant as possible. I know for a fact he never mentioned these relatives to her, because she was so flabbergasted when they showed up and identified themselves."

"But she can't be absolutely ignorant," I objected. "She grew up with other girls and boys, she must have gone to school for a while, she must associate with other women now."

"I think she went as far as the sixth grade before he took her out. After that she barely went outside her own door-yard without lugging her baby brothers along. As I said, her beauty was a great cross to him. He wanted to keep her pure, and Bannock was full of men, even if it was preferable to the great world outside. Nobody was good enough for his dark Rosaleen, and the crime of it is that he's raised her to think the same way. There are two men on Bannock who want to court her as soon as it's decent, but they know they won't get past the front gate."

"Who are they?" Miranda asked eagerly.

"Ivor Jenkins for one," Andrew said. "Pour me some coffee, Banty, please. . . . He's a Protestant, but he'd respect her religion and even raise their children as Catholic, and that's a tremendous concession for a Welshman to make. The other is Rory McNeill, Catholic too, and one of our best artisans. They're both good men and they'd be good to the boys."

"But why does she have to get married?" I asked. "If she's got her father's pension and her own home? I can see why she's crazy for a chance to have her head, after the way she's been kept down."

"Nobody's trying to rush her into it," Andrew explained. "But if she'd be content for a while with her own hearth and garden on Bannock, she could gradually get into the swing of normal existence, mix with people, have some social life. Good Lord, the girl's twenty-one and she's never gone to a dance with a man or even walked to a band concert with one," he said indignantly. "Let alone quilting or sewing in some woman's kitchen. Bob thought they'd fill her head with nonsense, so *that* was out. . . . No, it's what she sees as freedom that scares us foolish. The golden tower of some fairy-tale city that doesn't exist, and some prince who's to be her fit consort and protector."

"It must be what she's dreamed of, all these years," I mused. "Summer evenings when the stars were bright and you could smell the wild roses everywhere, and she was shut in like Rapunzel..." My dreamy tone faded out altogether when I caught Ian's eye. Was he secretly laughing, or not? Thinking I spoke from experience? . . . Anyway, I liked the way he left Andrew's province to Andrew.

"Well," said Andrew briskly, "I've been over talking to Meg, and she can use some extra help especially in summer, with all the canning to do, and so forth. She'll gladly take Rosaleen on—I'll see to the girl's wages—and there's plenty of room for the boys. If she wants to stay on, and let the boys go to school here, we'll work something out."

Ian spoke for the first time. "She can pack fish. Jenny Swenson's going off to high school this fall."

"It sounds perfect to me," Miranda said. "We may not be Boston, but we're bigger than Bannock——"

"Do you supose you can convince her?" Andrew asked.

"*Me?*"

He nodded. "You and Seafair. I'd like you to come over tomorrow and talk to her. You're her age, and she might be willing at least to listen to you. And Seafair's a teacher, she might respect that."

"You *mean*," Miranda said, "that we're supposed to convince her those golden towers and princes don't exist? Andrew, love, if *you* can't do it, you being young and handsome and quite princely in your own right——"

"You know what she called me yesterday, with the most superb insolence? She really put me in my place. 'Squireen.'"

Ian lay back in his chair and began to laugh. The rest of them picked it up. I had never seen such a family for laughing at each other and themselves.

chapter 17

We tried to get Meg to go with us. We both thought that a warm motherly approach would better reach the girl who like us had grown up without a mother. But Meg was afraid of the water. At noon, when we would go over to Bannock on the *Ocean Pearl*'s return trip, the water was so calm that cloud reflections patterned it in lustrous perfection, but Meg wouldn't take a chance on a southwest wind whipping the calm into a smart chop by the time we came home in Andrew's *Toothpick*. She had written a letter for us to take to Rosaleen.

Miranda was uncomfortable and nervous about the whole thing. "I couldn't stand living on this place, it's so noisy," she complained as we walked up the Bannock wharf. The sound of the jackhammers was ruthless, but the residents and the horses seemed unaware of it. We went into the store, where Andrew met us with such good cheer that Miranda glared at him suspiciously. "I don't know why you're so sure this will work," she said.

"I never said I was sure." He gave her a squeeze and kissed her temple. He took my arm. "Come and meet our postmaster." The postmaster was a stout lady, Mattie Bain, whose late husband had been general superintendent before Ivor Jenkins. She had small, sand-colored eyes behind her pince-nez, and a homely mouth with crooked front teeth. But her manner was engagingly breezy. "I'm pleased to meet you. Andrew says you're a teacher. Well, I came to Bannock as a teacher, and ran into the biggest selection of husband material I'd ever seen. It was like going out west in the Gold Rush."

"Seafair's playing the field on Drummond's," Miranda told her. "They're all at her feet."

I maintained an enigmatic silence and a Mona Lisa smile.

"Miranda's giving Seafair the tour," Andrew said to Mrs. Bain. We realized she didn't know what our real errand was. He came out with us, and we went up to watch the work in the quarry for a little while, with Andrew explaining the skills involved in cutting and lifting the stone. Then we visited the stone-carvers' shed, where some men were working on the eagles for a Midwestern postoffice, others on a splendid pair of lions for a library. One man worked alone on the inscription that would identify the building as a memorial to some town's Founding Family. Two more men were doing some exquisite Roman lettering around the rim of a great shallow basin of polished pink granite that would hold a fountain on an estate in Pennsylvania. The words were Latin, and one of the craftsmen translated for us in a Scottish accent.

" 'What shall be tomorrow, think not of asking. Each day that Fortune gives you, be what it may, set down for gain.' It's from Horace."

I was impressed by the work, but Miranda kept sighing and glancing so often at her watch that Andrew asked her if she had a train to catch.

"I just want to get it over with," she said dourly.

"I can see already that you're going to be a great success. You could chin yourself on that lower lip. Well, maybe Seafair's bright face will take the curse off it."

He went back to the store. On the way around the harbor Miranda pointed out the sights in a bored manner; the bandstand, the bowling green, the ballfield, the social hall, the schoolhouse. Every bit of level ground was utilized. Almost every house had at least a scrap of garden, a chicken run, sometimes a pigpen. All yards were fenced to keep chickens and babies in.

Older children played on the beach and ledges. Miranda knew them all by name, and, when the path led by the shore where the whaleboats were hauled up, she pointed out two black-haired young boys in a group of other boys at the end of a long ledge, fishing for cunners.

"Dennis and Michael Dolan," she said. "Isn't the noise *ghastly?* And the *heat?*" She wiped her forehead and upper lip. She looked actually distressed.

"The noise isn't all that bad," I said, "and it doesn't seem hot to me, just right. I didn't know anything could upset you."

"I know it won't work, that's all!"

There wasn't anything to say to that, because I didn't think it would work either. But curiosity and a who-can-tell philosophy have often carried me on in good heart.

There were neither chickens nor babies, not even a cat, in the Dolan dooryard, but a vegetable garden exquisitely ruled and weeded. From the gate to the kitchen door ran a path of crushed blue mussel shell, bordered on each side by young cabbages like huge green roses.

Rosaleen came to the door in black-and-white gingham and greeted us with unsmiling propriety, and invited us into "The Room." She had a very faint, musical brogue.

"Oh, can't we stay out here?" Miranda asked winningly; "I love this kitchen." She took the chair by the harbor window, so Rosaleen had to give in, and somberly waved me to a rocking chair. The bare wood of the floor, table, cupboards, and counter was scrubbed white, the sink and stove lustrously black. Three round loaves were cooling on the counter.

Rosaleen sat down by the table and took up her knitting, a boy's sock in creamy unbleached wool. She did a round with the utmost poise while Miranda prattled on about the view, exclaiming when somebody caught a cunner, and being otherwise artificially gay, as if Rosaleen's silence were driving her to extremes.

I had seen only the girl's gaunt white mask of tragedy the day we came. Now she was rested. Miranda's bearing and her coloring gave an illusion of beauty, but that was what it was. An illusion. Rosaleen had the authentic white-skinned, black-haired, blue-eyed Celtic beauty that goes deep into the bone. Right now her eyes looked more violet than blue beneath the peaked black eyebrows, and there was a delicate flush of heat or anger across her cheekbones. Her mouth had deeply sculptured corners; I found myself hoping she wouldn't smile, for fear we'd see the discolored teeth or gaps that were all too common.

All at once Miranda stopped babbling about the view and took Meg's letter from her pocket, walked across the room and laid it on the table beside Rosaleen. "Would you read this, please?"

Rosaleen gave it an indifferent glance. "I should have known," she said with sardonic humor. "You came on an errand."

Miranda's cheeks pinked. "We were coming to see you as soon as it was all right," she protested. "I was just waiting until you'd gotten rested up and—settled, and so forth. Then Andrew—*Meg* asked me to bring you this." She went rattling on to correct the slip. "Meg wouldn't come herself for fear of its breezing up later. She hasn't been off the island since Tom graduated from college, and she's already dreading crossing the bay when he graduates from the seminary."

Ignoring the envelope Rosaleen said, "So Andrew's up to something. Isn't he the busy one." She smiled in contempt; there were no discolorations or gaps.

"Please read it and say yes." Miranda was at her most winsome.

Rosaleen picked up and opened the envelope. The clock ticked and coughed, the tea kettle breathed a thin thread of song and steam. I longed to go outside. I was oppressed not so much by the heat as by Rosaleen herself, and our pre-destined failure to make any impression on her whatsoever.

"What can you see from that window?" I asked Miranda brightly and went over and leaned on the back of her chair.

We both stared glassily out at the harbor. I don't know what we saw.

A crumpling of paper, a rustle of petticoats. Rosaleen rose and crossed the room and put the letter in the fire.

"Will you have a cup of tea?" she asked. The color had deepened on her cheekbones.

"We'd love it, wouldn't we, Seafair?" Miranda asked me.

Personally there was nothing I wanted less; I ached to be outside, even with the earsplitting racket of the jackhammers, but I smiled and said yes. Rosaleen pushed the heavy iron tea kettle over on the stove. Behind her back Miranda made big eyes at me and pantomimed despair. Rosaleen with stately deliberation laid a starched cloth, brought milk and butter from the cold cellarway, and set the table with white ironstone cups and saucers from the hutch cabinet.

The silence was impossible. Miranda began to talk about the lions and eagles we'd seen in the shed, the beautiful lettering, and how impressed I was . . . I joined in. Thrilling —yes, I heard myself using that despicable word—to watch. What great skill in knowing just how to cut the stone in the quarries! And the horses were beautiful.

I stopped short. Miranda too ran out of steam. Rosaleen measured tea into the pot and poured on boiling water. Her tea cozy was appropriately bright green embroidered with shamrocks. There could be a whole school of art around tea cozies, I thought giddily.

"Will you sit up to the table?" Rosaleen invited. She began slicing one of the loaves.

"Meg could certainly use some help with all the baking she has to do," Miranda said.

Taking her place with a regal air Rosaleen said, "There must be someone on Drummond's who'd be only too happy to work at the farm and The Eyrie."

"If there were, they'd be there," said Miranda. "But they're packing fish, or tending out on summer boarders, or keeping house." She took her cup of tea. "Oh, Rosaleen, we'd love to have you over there! We have such fun singing and dancing. When you're ready for that," she hastily amended.

"And look, you could rent your house here, and add that to Mr. Dolan's pension, and put it all in the bank to earn interest, because you and the boys would get your keep at the farm, and wages in your pocket besides."

Rosaleen listened coldly. Miranda seemed encouraged. "Think what it would mean to the boys! There's the farm itself, and all the island to roam over. They could even have a skiff of their own. And Tom's at the farm now. You don't know him very well, but he's so nice, he'd be like an older brother to them——"

"Oh yes, the little minister," said Rosaleen with a bite in her voice. "I was half forgetting they're all Protestants over there. I couldn't consider it. My poor father would be turning over in his grave."

"Your poor father would do no such thing," said Miranda furiously. "Robert Emmet Dolan was never a bigot, at least not where religion was concerned."

"Oh, he was a bigot in some other way, then?" The lilt was sweet.

"I don't know about any other way. But I can't believe he'd object to you and the boys being over on Drummond's with us. Why don't you ask Father Emery what *he* thinks?" Miranda challenged.

"I don't need to ask Father Emery, and I don't need to be told by anyone, least of all Andrew Drummond, what I should do. Will you have some more tea, Miss Bell?"

"Yes, please," I lied with some mad idea of diverting the conversation. "I haven't tasted such good tea for ages, and I was so thirsty——"

Neither of them heard me. I got my tea but no audience. I drank glumly and wondered if they'd notice if I walked out. Sweat trickled down my back, and my midriff itched all around. I wanted excruciatingly to scratch.

"Andrew hasn't anything to do with this," Miranda said.

"Then why has he been down here persecuting me? Why is he trying to get me out of my house? Who does he want to rent it to?" It flowed out in a stormy torrent. "He wants to get it away from me, that he does. If I'm over to Drummond's, common help in another woman's house, next he can say, 'You'll not be needing your house any more, so why not sell it, we need a man to replace your father.' Not that Robert Emmet Dolan could ever be replaced, God rest his soul."

We understood that the last was her own comment, muttered like a charm just in case his soul wasn't resting but was hovering in the room.

"Oh, for heaven's sake!" Miranda protested. "What makes you so suspicious? Andrew doesn't want to get your house away from you, he just"— I had a feeling she was going to blurt out with *wants to save you from your awful cousins who probably run a house of ill fame*—"he just wants to help," she finished. She was quite red. Rosaleen's cheekbones were red too, her mouth was squared and scornful.

"I'll just thank Andrew Drummond not to try playing Lord of the Manor with me," she said. "Does he think any unprotected woman's fair game for his sport?"

I almost laughed out loud, but I realized all at once that she was serious.

Miranda's eyes were shining with tears of either hurt or anger. I pushed back with a purposeful scrape of my chair across the scrubbed boards.

"Let's leave her to think it over, Miranda," I said cheerily. "After all, Meg didn't expect her to make her mind up all at once. Come on, there are things I haven't seen on Bannock yet."

She got up and went out without another word. "Thank you for the tea," I said, to Rosaleen, "and the plum bread was delicious."

"There is nothing for me to think over," she said. "I am *my own woman*."

"Good for you," I said. "So am I. But remember it when the time comes, don't wait until it's too late."

Miranda was already out through the gate. I followed, leaving silence behind me. I could only hope that she was thinking, if she could think at all beyond her dreams and her suspicions.

I caught up with Miranda by the whaleboats. She was sitting on a gunnel watching the children. She looked around at me with a smile. "I was so *mad*, I didn't thank her for the tea, but she doesn't deserve thanks. Talking like that about Andrew, of all people!"

"How many times did she mention Andrew?" I sat down beside her. "Almost every time she opened her mouth, it seemed to me. Then she made her outrageous statement, which she knew was outrageous, but wished it weren't."

The light broke. "You mean that Andrew's the only man suitable to save her from a fate worse than death?"

"Oh yes," I said. "At least I'm pretty sure of it. It has to be Squireen or nobody; she's got the blood of queens in her, and she can't even see Ivor Jenkins or Rory McNeill. Her father's raised her to think no quarry worker's good enough for her, even a superintendent or a carver. And the Drummonds are the aristocracy around here."

"Well I don't think Andrew would throw over Jane even to save Dark Rosaleen from disaster, do you?"

"He'll just have to hope and pray the college friend in Boston comes up with something bad enough to make a dent even in that beautiful marble skull."

"I guess we'd better not tell Andrew. He'd be so embarrassed."

We laughed and at once felt less depressed. We had done the best we could. At least Miranda had; I'd never had the chance even to attempt to impress Rosaleen with my wisdom as a school teacher.

All we told Andrew was that Rosaleen had resisted us, and that maybe she would think it over and maybe she wouldn't.

"I'd admire her independence if I thought it would hold up," I said.

"She thinks we're trying to take it away from her. Poor Bob thought he was doing the right thing, and maybe he's been her ruin." He put an arm around each of us. "Thank you anyway. What can I treat you with to show my gratitude?"

We chose Malaga grapes and chocolate bars, and climbed the hill behind the store and went out onto the grassy slopes toward the west. Part of this side was securely fenced off as pasturage for the island's cows, so they couldn't meet disaster either in the quarry or off the island's precipitous shores. Relieved by the stoutness of the fencing, I spoke to the cow who had come out on the steamer with us that day. With a mouthful of buttercups she watched us go down the field, and mooed after us in a flattering manner.

We sat on the edge of a miniature cliff to eat our grapes and chocolate, telling each other that the Mediterranean couldn't possibly be more blue than the western sea before us. We watched a group of adult female eiders guiding a flotilla of perhaps a hundred minuscule and whistling ducklings across the shallows.

"Where every prospect pleases and only man is vile," Miranda said, "as Uncle David used to quote when somebody at the harbor made him mad. It had to be something awful to make him mad, so the quotation was justified."

We became aware after a little while that the noise back at the quarry was not only deadened, but gone. "Done for the day," Miranda said. She looked at her watch. "We've got fifteen minutes to meet Andrew."

chapter 18

e walked down to the harbor at sunrise on the morning of the second to see *Kingfisher* leave for Bar Harbor, with all sails set to catch the light southerly breeze. The first sun turned the canvas to gold, and she passed Southern Harbor Point with the silent speed of a ship out of legend.

Miranda and Patrick wouldn't let me watch her out of sight. That was bad luck, they said, and treated me to ghastly tales of ships that never returned simply because they'd been watched out of sight.

We went home through the awakening village. It was a boat day, and Patrick would return later to the store to wait on trade while Ian's clerk, Elmer Myrick, attended to the mail. Miranda offered herself and me as helpers, but Patrick spurned us.

"Not meaning any offense, Seafair," he said to me, "but you don't know where anything is, and as for Emmeline here, she has to spend so much time talking that she'd never get anything done. And she can't even make change. Elmer's Ginnie will be on hand. She knows the stock, can do sums in her head faster than I can, and she's not afraid to fish a slab of salt pork out of the barrel and whack off a junk."

"Now you know what Patrick admires in a female," Miranda said to me.

"That female is all of thirteen," said Patrick, "and small for her age."

"And she adores you," said Miranda. "She'll remember this day all her life. I remember when I was thirteen."

Patrick winked at me. "Who was it? The deckhand on the

Pearl? That writer staying at Schofields'?" A short but calculated pause. "Dill Kalloch?"

"The man who came to fancy up everybody's bowsprits and paint on the names," she said, "I used to sit and watch him by the hour. I was positive I was fated to fall in love with an artist because my father was one."

"Were you in love at thirteen, Seafair?" Patrick asked me.

"With the boy who worked at the livery stable," I said. "What about *you?*"

"I loved my dog, my double-ender, and baseball, in that order."

"*I* can remember when you used to hang maybaskets to the girls," Miranda said. He picked her up, caught her, and tossed her into a wet and bristly clump of juniper. Lying in the midst of it, smiling bravely, she said to me, "He was so *cunning* in his little sailor suit."

I had to give her a hand out of the prickly growth. Patrick was far ahead of us, whistling one of the tunes we'd danced to.

Miranda and I prepared her room for Jane; Miranda was to move in with me. When everything else was done we went out and picked an enormous bouquet of field flowers, and put them in a jug on Miranda's desk.

We were too busy to go to the mail, and Patrick didn't come home that noon because the lobster smack was due. In the afternoon Miranda and I walked all over the eastern field picking wild strawberries. We were to have shortcake that night if the others came. But it was breezing on from the southwest all afternoon. Already I had learned that a certain tone in the rote, as well as a tumbling white smother off the Bowsprit and a boiling froth over the Crumbs, meant it was too rough for either pleasure sailing or work.

"They won't come back today," I said to Miranda, and she nodded as if my opinion was to be perfectly accepted.

Meg had left us a lobster chowder, as something hearty that could be heated up at any time, and the three of us had it that night. We had shortcake too; Miranda could turn out the biscuit with a light quick hand, and there were a lot more strawberries ripening out there for more short-cake later.

Patrick and Miranda discussed the usefulness of the summer boarders in detail. The writer was willing to give lantern slide accounts of his travels; Mr. Clement, the minister, was a regular on the island, and could be depended upon for some good dynamic sermons and had already organized some activities among the children. Today a young couple had arrived to stay with one of the Joy families, and they'd spent last summer in Switzerland. They were both artists.

"Oh, why didn't I go to the mail today?" Miranda wailed. "Artists! And *Switzerland!* Where I've always longed to go!"

"First I knew of it," said Patrick.

"You don't know anything about me, Patrick Guild Drummond. My most sacred thoughts I keep to myself." She began to yodel, which astonished us, and sent Charlie into a keening howl. She stopped, looking pleased with herself. "Anybody want any more shortcake? Any more coffee? Help yourself if you do. . . . What'll we do tonight for excitement? Pat, do you know where Ian put the Ouija board?" He cocked an eyebrow at her and she said delightedly, "You *do* know. What I can't find in this house, you can. Oh, get it out! Ian needn't know."

The mere words seemed to bring Ian's disapproval into the house like a cold fog. I took out the dishpan with a clatter. "If he hid it," I said, "he must have had a good reason."

"Because I had a nightmare when I was about fifteen," Miranda said in disgust. "It had nothing to do with the Ouija board. It was some of that ghastly stuff we'd been reading about the Aztecs and their human sacrifices. Get it, Pat! We'll have some fun!"

Patrick made an ambiguous sound, and she patted his head in passing. "Seafair, you get the dishes into the pan, and I'll be straight back to wipe. But we used up all the cream and we'll want some in the morning, so I'm going to scoot over to the farm and get some." She looked at her watch. "Twenty minutes, no longer. Come on, Charlie. Dig out the board, Pat, *please.*"

She was gone. "Hey, wait a minute!" Patrick called, but all he got was the slam of a screen door. He looked at me and shook his head. "She'll stretch it out just long enough for you to wipe the dishes."

"I don't mind."

"I'll wipe them." He got up, stretching, and lit the bracket lamp over the sink. The afterglow filled the western windows, but shadows were pooling in the corners of the kitchen. We talked without effort as we worked. It was a relief to feel so natural with him; yet, if he should show by one word or gesture that I interested him, would it have all started up again in me? Was it really dead, or simply damped down?

When the kitchen clock struck nine, Miranda had been gone for almost three-quarters of an hour. The dishes were done and put away, the black sink wiped smooth and dry.

We listened to the clock in silence, then looked at each other.

"She's probably trying to get Tom to come over, and he's tired after haying all day," he said. "I know her. Come on into the library. I haven't had a chance to look at the books I got today."

He lighted the reading lamps and built a fire. Then he politely handed me one of his new books and became immersed in another. Print mesmerizes me, even the kind on railway timetables and bottle labels, so I was far away in endless, simmering, desert spaces, discovering one of the lost cities of Alexander, when a small rhythmic sound finally intruded on me.

Patrick, slouched deep in a leather chair, was tapping his fingers on the arm. I watched him. I couldn't see his eyes, he was apparently reading, but in all the time I watched he didn't turn a page. Still the fingers of his left hand tapped out their nervous, persistent code.

The hall clock struck for the half-hour, and we both jumped and exchanged self-conscious smiles. It seemed hours since Miranda had stood in the doorway saying, "Twenty minutes, no longer ... Dig out the Ouija board, Pat, *please*."

"You didn't get the Ouija board," I said.

"I didn't intend to." He got up and stood looking down at the fire. "It's all right for a parlor game, but sometimes it goes beyond a game."

"How?" I asked.

"Occasionally a name comes in that you didn't expect— a real name, of someone you knew—and it buries the whole thing under an ice fall. The fun's gone."

"But where does it come from? I know what the spiritualists believe, but what do you believe? That one of the people is cheating? Pushing the planchette?"

"I know I've never cheated, because then it loses its point. And I've had words come out that the other person couldn't possibly know. So I can't explain it." He turned around to me with a smile. "But I'm pretty positive that disembodied spirits aren't leaning over my shoulder to do the pushing. Which is what Miranda believes, though she won't admit it. Especially when we got Adrienne one night."

"What did she have to say?"

"She said we were a parcel of ill-mannered brats." We both laughed.

"Did she speak in French or English?" I asked.

"Rotten spelling, so maybe it was broken English. . . . Anyway, this happened at a party, and so many of the gang were spooked by it we never used the Ouija board again in a crowd. Then after Miranda dreamed she was about to be sacrificed by a hooded priest on our altar, Ian put it away. I'll tell you this, Seafair, if my father's name was ever spelled out on that board, *I'd* be spooked. For good."

"It would only be your unconscious mind."

"Maybe I don't want to meet up with my unconscious mind. Maybe I want to leave it curled up nose to tail in the dark like a hibernating bear."

"What makes you think it looks like a bear?" We laughed again, but his laugh was cut off by the quarter hour chiming. "She's been gone an hour," he said. "I'll go out and look around. She could have fallen between the farm and here and twisted her ankle."

He was leaving the room as he talked, and I followed him. "No need of your going," he said. "It's cold and windy, and blacker'n the inside of a cow out there." He took down a lantern and lighted it. "Go on back to the fire. I'm sure she's all right, but if I don't go look I'll keep wondering."

I returned to the library and poked up the fire and settled down with my book. The clock struck ten. I listened to the chime tremble away to silence in the empty house.

Over the mantel the white caps in a painting seemed to move as the lamplight quivered slightly. The ship was the *Curlew*, in the setting of some West Indian bay. She had brought back the mahogany logs which had paneled this room.

At the end of a half-hour Patrick hadn't come back. "Now who's gabbling in the farm kitchen?" I said aloud. "I didn't care. For me it was an experience to be here alone at night.

Patrick came in alone, finally. His hair was damp and ruffled, his cheeks reddened. He was angry. "I've been over all the ground between here and the farm. It's dark there. They've gone to bed!"

"She must have gone to the harbor," I said.

"It's the harbor all right." He was grim. "She probably took it into her head to go call on the boarders."

"She was interested in the couple who had been to Switzerland."

"I don't care about that! She's got no business being so damned irresponsible! No thought for anyone else—*ever!*"

"If you say anything to her, please don't bring me into it. I feel free too, and I won't if Miranda's made to resent me."

He nodded moodily at the fire. "All right. I won't mention you. But I've plenty to say otherwise."

I picked up my book again and tried to concentrate on it,

but he exuded unrest. I am always depressed rather than stimulated by other people's anger, even when it has nothing to do with me.

All at once a damp Charlie was with us, smelling now of pitch and now of rockweed, depending upon where you patted him. Panting, he flung himself from one to the other of us, trying to jump up to reach our faces and hands. Patrick ignored these transports and walked out of the room. I heard voices, but not the sense of them through Charlie's noise. Finally I took him up under my arm and went out to the hall. Patrick stood back to me and past his shoulder I saw Miranda, wearing an old plaid coat that usually hung in the entry, her hair loose and wind-blown. She was laughing with mock perplexity.

"I don't know what you're *talking* about! Really, I *don't*, Patrick!" She waggled her fingers coyly at me. "Hello, Seafair!"

"Hello," I said, putting Charlie down. He rushed toward the kitchen.

"When you say twenty minutes and you're gone two hours," Patrick said quietly, "you must know what I'm talking about."

"Are *you* mad with me, Seafair?"

"Not in the least." Coming abreast of Patrick, I took one quick look at him and decided that trying to laugh him out of it was a bad idea. "I'm on my way to get a glass of milk and one of those big sugar cookies, and then to bed."

"A good idea! Seafair, you're so smart. And I'm famished. Come on, Patrick, and sweeten up your disposition." She whirled, whipping off her coat and letting it fly. It sailed halfway across the hall and came to rest in a limp plaid heap on the stairs; it had a weird resemblance to something alive crumpled there. Miranda completed her spin like a ballet dancer and faced us, pointing her toe, her arms in a graceful arch over her head.

"Where's your watch?" Patrick said.

The spirit went out of her face like wine turned out of

a glass. Her right hand went to the empty place on her breast, groped frantically as it found nothing. She looked down at the place then, felt in her skirt pockets, and then began tearing at her belt buckle. Appalled by her panic, I was too numb to help her at first, I kept thinking, Why is she so scared? Then I went forward to help, but she had gotten the belt unbuckled and ripped it out of the loops. No watch fell to the carpet, but she kept looking anyway, behind her and on each side, shifting her feet like a nervous horse.

"The clasp must have come undone, I don't know how." She was short of breath. "I noticed yesterday it was loose—I shouldn't have worn it out."

"Where did you go?" Patrick said. "We'll retrace your route tomorrow morning."

"Everywhere! I can't be sure!"

I'd never seen Miranda so skittish before. She wouldn't look at either of us, she kept searching her pockets, looking down at herself, feeling around her waist as if the watch had been inexplicably overlooked and had been clinging there all the time.

"Charlie was both in the woods and on the shore," Patrick said. His quiet was as unnerving as her state of nerves.

"He missed the pasture, thank heaven," Miranda said with a shaky laugh. "Think what that could produce." She looked at me as if for support, and I said idiotically, "Horrors."

"Speak up, Miranda!" Patrick commanded. "Where'd you go? Can't you give a straight answer? Or did amnesia hit you when you walked out of the kitchen tonight saying you'd be back in twenty minutes?"

"Of course I know where I went, roughly. But I was just walking around enjoying the wind and the night, and I didn't know how the time was going by——"

"Then you lost your watch at the first of it, so it can't be too far away."

"I don't *know!*" she shouted at him. "Stop badgering me! You—you *inquisitor!*"

Patrick took a step toward her and she took a step backward. "Dill Kalloch can help us, can't he, Miranda?"

"What are you talking about?" Panic was gone; she was watchful but somehow exhilarated.

"You went out to meet him tonight," Patrick said. "You knew you wouldn't be back in twenty minutes." He took another step forward, she took another one backward. It was like a dance. "What happened to make your watch fall off? What was Dill Kalloch doing? Or, more to the point, what were you both doing?"

His hand shot out and Miranda flinched. He pulled something from the curling ends of a strand of hair falling over her shoulder. He held it up. It was a spruce twig.

"*Dill Kalloch!*" He spat the name at her. "Running with him! You're no better than Prissy Schofield!"

"If I were you I'd think twice before saying her name," Miranda shot back at him. "Who knows where *you* go when you're out of sight after dark? I'll bet Prissy knows! You'd better look out! You might have to marry her one of these days, and you couldn't even be sure the child was a Drummond." She laughed. "He might even be Dill Kalloch's."

He slapped her. Miranda, after the yelp startled out of her by the blow, didn't even put her hand to her face. She stood erect against the newel post, one side of her face dark red, and laughed.

"Was that for Prissy or Dill?"

"I don't go with Prissy no matter what she claims," he said. He looked white enough to faint. "But can you look me in the eye and swear—yes, you can do that all right, you've been lying all your life. But could you put your hand on the Bible and swear you're not running with Dill Kalloch? Come into the library."

She neither spoke nor moved, but fixed her eyes on his in a kind of glazed blind stare.

"You can't," he said almost in a whisper. "You rotten little trollop. He's had his hands on you, hasn't he? And not just in your hair."

"Listen," I said. I had to clear my throat, which made it rather weak and inane but not ineffectual. Patrick looked at me with astonishment and loathing. He had forgotten me, and now he would hate me forever.

"I know I shouldn't have heard this," I said rapidly, "and I know it's none of my business. Maybe you've fought like this all your lives, but it's a little scary for me, so how about an intermission while I get upstairs and shut my door?"

"Oh, poor Seafair," Miranda exclaimed. "You must think you've stumbled into a rotten performance of *Way Down East*."

Patrick walked into the library and slammed the door.

"Now let's have our milk," Miranda said with a high, unnatural giggle.

"I don't want it now, it would sour the instant it hit my churning stomach."

"Then you'd get butter, lovey." And that foolish giggle again.

I started up the stairs. The crumpled coat was in the way, and I picked it up and shook it out. The watch bounced down two steps and out onto the floor of the hall. We stood staring at it as if it had materialized out of the air. Then Miranda exploded into a raucous laughter, pounced on it, and opened the library door. "Here you are, ducks," she said, and threw the watch at Patrick. She slammed the door and came running across the hall and up the stairs.

I wanted to shut the bedroom door on Miranda, get into bed and drug myself with the harmless opiate of a book, and the desperate silent prayer, *Please, please, make it all right before tomorrow,* the way I used to pray as a child until I found out prayers were no good, they had neither saved my mother nor staved off Phoebe.

But there was always hope, and I had to hope, because I

couldn't bear to believe that The Eyrie had been ruined for me. In the meantime, we had to sleep together.

We didn't talk getting ready for bed, but silently stayed out of each other's way. When I was washed up and in bed, trying to read, Miranda came in her nightgown, hair brushed and braided, her face shiny with washing and innocence. She looked about fifteen.

"You're owed quite a bunch of apologies, Seafair," she said.

"Maybe it's the other way around," I said. "I shouldn't have been in on a family row. But I didn't know it was going to happen."

"Neither did I. Or I'd have gone up the back stairs and straight to bed. You'd have known I was in because of Charlie, and Patrick would have waited for tomorrow morning to read me the riot act, and the watch wouldn't have been lost, either."

She was both rueful and tired; the combination made her sound and act more mature than usual. "Don't let the summer be spoiled for you, please, Seafair." She knelt on the foot of the bed. "I told you Patrick and I have had wild rows all our lives, and we don't think how they sound to someone else. Uncle David used to spank us for them, and Ian has too, and we were always being sent to our rooms. He never did hit me before, but he's been on edge lately. Nothing you'd notice; but I do, so I shouldn't have goaded him. And then he rattled me." She made a face. "Patrick is going to feel just awful to think you're taking this so seriously."

"Patrick already feels awful to think I watched the whole thing. He'd probably like it if I'd left The Eyrie for good before he gets up tomorrow morning."

"Don't you talk like that, or I'll go down and get him now."

She looked perfectly capable of it. "Forget it," I said.

"Anyway, I couldn't bear to have you go away. Summer's just begun. And what would you do?" she asked slyly.

"School's closed, so you can't go back there. All that remains is Fern Grove."

"Which is either hemlock or the asp. All right . . . Where did you think the watch was, Miranda?"

"Dropped somewhere between here and the harbor, naturally." She gave me the steady gaze of innocent surprise. "Why, did *you* think— No, of course you didn't."

Could you look me in the eye? Patrick had asked. *Yes, you could.* "I didn't know whether he was more worked up about the watch or Dill Kalloch."

"I forgot to tell you that in addition to having a temper, Patrick is naturally suspicious and also a skinflint. So the infant cousin must have been running wild, and while she was sinfully engaged she lost the watch that he paid for with his own money. Not only is she careless with her virtue but with his gifts. And she's too big to spank. . . . That's the truth about Patrick, the Drummond Monster. I love him dearly."

"I think that compared to you I must have been raised in a bell jar," I said. "No pun intended." But you panicked, Miranda, I thought. You certainly did.

he next morning the wind had gone, and Patrick asked me if I'd like to go with him while he hauled enough pots to get lobsters for a picnic on the shore tonight. Like Miranda, he had the faculty of complete erasure. In his attitude and hers there was no trace of last night. It could have all been hallucinations on my part.

I'd grown used to the dory, but the peapod felt as light as an actual one, and when he hauled his first trap I sat rigid in the bow seat, gripping both gunnels hard enough, it seemed, to put my fingers through the thin wood. But she scarcely ducked sidewise with the weight of the wet trap, and by the time he'd hauled three I let go my passionate grasp and was daring to move my eyes, turn my head, even twist around on the seat to see the sloops and other peapods at work.

There wasn't much conversation. He seemed perfectly happy and contented. From time to time a vision of the lamplit hall with its glowing red floor and the staircase rising to the Colonel's portrait clicked into my mind's vision like a lantern slide at a lecture; I saw Miranda in panic and this man in a gray and throttling rage. Then it would snap out again and Patrick was rowing us toward the next trap, intoning in a hollow voice, "I go to seek the white whale."

He put into Home Cove to take the lobsters up to the house. Meg was baking and Miranda was helping her. Patrick and I had a mug-up, then he left to take the peapod around to the harbor and I went upstairs to change my clothes and be sure our bathroom was tidy. Miranda being a great splasher.

I anticipated Jane's arrival with a blend of curiosity and worry. At the idea of a third girl in the house I became jealously anxious about my prerogatives. And what about the things Miranda and I did together with a spur-of-the moment craziness that a Philadelphian might consider improper or, even worse, juvenile? Would good manners smother us under a wet blanket?

We intended to be dressed up and at the wharf with flowers for Jane when they arrived. "After all, a future Drummond lady ought to be met with some ceremony," Miranda informed us at lunch. "No matter how we act after she gets here."

"When the disillusionment sets in," said Patrick, "and she discovers she's really moving into an annex of the Booby Hatch."

Meg made reproachful sounds. "What time will they get here?" I asked.

Patrick shrugged. "There's not much wind today. They won't be too fast. Mid-afternoon, I'd say. You've plenty of time to come down and give me a hand."

We went down to the grove after lunch, and Tom and the Newfoundland walked across to the grove during the noon break from haying. While the two men hoisted up buckets of loose soil, Miranda and I knelt on the cool damp earth and scraped away with our trowels at what might turn out to be the central hearth of a Norse house.

"You know something?" Miranda said to me, slapping at a mosquito and leaving dirt in the part of her hair—her forehead was already smeared, and I know there was quite an overlay around my ears, which the mosquitoes found very rich in whatever it was they wanted. "In Greece and Egypt and those places they hire local people to dig. They have to pay them."

"We're doing this for love," I said.

"Really?" She sat back on her heels, beaming. "Have you got to that at last, Seafair?"

"Got to what?" Tom said, leaning on his shovel. "What have you found?"

Miranda looked up at him and laughed. "The subject is love."

I said with bored dignity, "I mean love of the *work*."

"Ah yes." She put a finger under her chin. "The work. Speak for yourself, Seafair. When he starts having us make bricks without straw, then you'll lose your idealism." She slapped herself hard on the cheek and looked with satisfaction at the squashed mosquito on her dirty palm. "That makes five."

I went back to scraping. "If you're just going to sit there counting corpses, Banty," Patrick said, "you might as well get out. You're only taking up space."

She cowered. "Don't whip me, master, I'm working." She picked up her trowel. "Abraham Lincoln didn't know about the Drummonds. He was just thinking about *Southern* slaveholders. But Patrick can be saved by the love of a good woman, Seafair," she said loudly. "Just think of that. You wouldn't want the loss of his soul on your conscience, would you?"

Patrick said, "Tom, what culture was it where they buried women alive?"

Charlie, who'd been rolling voluptuously in a pile of dirt, suddenly flipped onto his feet and ran off through the oaks toward the house, barking. Hero stayed where he was, but his heavy warnings echoed in the grove. We all stood up, looking in the direction of Charlie's flight.

"I knew it would happen some day, Pat," Tom said. "You've gone and raised a ghost in broad daylight."

"That must be why we can't see it," Patrick said. "Sunlight, and a poor quality of ectoplasm. Everything's shoddy these days."

This is how we were discovered, grimy, sweaty, and bitten, clustered in a shoulder-deep hole. Andrew stood on the brink in his sailing clothes, laughing at the astonished faces tipped up to him. Jane was a green-eyed Gibson girl in denim skirt and middy, and she was laughing too.

We went back to the house and cleaned up, and all fixed their lunch. We milled around in the kitchen getting out the leftovers, bumping into each other, and laughing for no reason whatever. The doubts were gone, she wasn't going to be a wet blanket.

Sometime during that hilarious meal I thought of Ian, who had stopped off at the store. I had a pinching little discomfort about our having such a good time while he ate lunch at the store because he was too busy to come home. I had seen that long look of his often enough not to forget it easily. It was neither gloomy or self-pitying; but to me, remembering it now while Patrick was reciting, "Jane, Jane, she never was the same," it was the steady, undeceived, perfectly contained contemplation of a lonely life.

"What are you thinking about?" Tom asked me.

Startled, I said, "Why?"

"True Yankee, answer one question with another ... You and I aren't Drummonds or Drummond kin. I wondered if you were thinking about that. Feeling out of it, maybe."

It's Ian that's out of it, I thought, and it can't always be from choice. "You couldn't be much closer to them," I said.

He nodded. "Patrick and I are genuine foster brothers, did you know that? My mother nursed him along with me. It makes a close bond, but our families have always been bound together." At the other end of the table they were coming out with a rash of "Jane" verses and limericks. "But the chances are that my children won't grow up with Patrick's the way we grew up. We've already set out on divergent paths. We'll see each other often, I hope, but in two or three years it's inevitable that our lives will divide forever." He said temperately what Miranda had said once on the edge of tears.

"It reminds me of something," I said.

" 'Before our lives divide forever, While time is with us and hands are free.' Yes."

"I've never known a place as beautiful as this island," I said. "But I'm beginning to think I'm more of a free soul for not belonging to it. I love it, and sometimes I feel as if I'm living in a romantic painting, I want to stay in it forever. But I know I can't, just as I know it's not always summer here. And if I had a choice, it would be very hard. The island could be a millstone around my neck."

"You're very perceptive," he said.

"Well, I didn't think that clearly about it until just now," I told him, "so it must have been your lucid scholarly influence."

He laughed out loud at that. "What are you two doing down there?" Miranda called. "Making an assignation right under our noses?"

"I could have courted her, proposed, and been accepted," said Tom, "all under cover of the unseemly racket up there. Well, I'm going haying. Excuse me, everyone."

"We'll be over to help tramp hay," Miranda called after him.

"Poor Tom," said Patrick. "That kind of help he needs as much as two broken arms."

Jane was sleepy from arising at four that morning. She went to bed for a nap so as to be fresh for our picnic and the bonfire at the harbor. Andrew was going across to Bannock for the rest of the day. Patrick announced that he was going down to the couch hammock to read a scientific article, and wanted no interruptions. Miranda and I, leaving Charlie in the house, went to the farm.

"He *says* he'll be reading," Miranda said. "But he'll sneak right back to the dig again. If there's anything good *he* wants to find it. You'll notice he only invites us down when there's a lot of manual labor to be done."

"Well, I don't blame him," I said reasonably. "Everybody

has a ruling passion. What's yours? Besides the island, that is."

"My family would tell me it's getting my own way. And maybe they're right. But I think I'm really quite nice in spite of it all, don't you?"

"Like the little girl with the little curl," I said.

Tennyson was right about the days when there is a livelier emerald in the grass, a brighter sapphire in the sea. That was such a day. We stood in the hay rick drawn by Prince and Jim, tramping down the sweet-scented loads Tom and Pearl pitched up to us. We rested in the pool of shade at the end of the field, and drank cold switchel from tin mugs dipped into the bucket. On the other side of the wall the cows and the young horse were obsessed with our presence. Major kept nudging Tom who playfully pushed the big head away, but it kept coming back. Dougal watched them. His brown skin looked too stiff with weathering to smile, so when he did the effect was surprising and contagious.

"When Tom was little," he said, "he smelled of horses half the time, and the other half it was fish and rockweed."

"A seahorse," said Miranda. The boy Pearl, lying on his back on the grass, thought this was ineffably funny and rolled over laughing.

chapter 20

We had the picnic out on the Head, beginning with a swim off the rocks. Tom was with us. His parents had been asked, but Dougal said that after a day's work he liked to sit in a proper chair at a proper table, preferably his own. They were going to the harbor later to watch the bonfire with the Gillises.

At sunset we carried back to the house everything we hadn't been able to burn, except for what could be left for the expectant gulls. We shut Charlie in, and walked to the harbor.

Over our heads the sky was still blue, but the afterglow was the color of apricots, the boats and houses were all washed in the rose-orange light. The harbor was deep pink, crisscrossed by ripples and ruffles of blue from the oars and wakes of rowboats; it reminded me of some hair-ribbons I'd had, salmon-pink on one side and blue on the other, that had always filled me with a gluttonous rapture, as if I could have eaten them and they wouldn't have tasted of thread but of the food of fairy tales, the kind served by invisible hands at midnight feasts.

Except for the older people on porches and doorsteps, everyone seemed to be on the move. Children who weren't out in boats chased each other among the strollers, threatening with cap pistols. Strings of lady-fingers crackled. The store was open with Elmer in charge, selling home-made ice cream.

Andrew took Jane off to meet people, and Ian went into the store to help Elmer. Tom, Patrick, Miranda, and I were loosely together among the interweaving crowd, talking here

and there, separating briefly, two or three of us coming together now and then in varying combinations. The pastel
wash of color dulled into the translucent mauves and blues
of twilight. Out on the end of Northern Point the pyre rose
like a primitive monument, and the skiffs and dories were
converging on it. Beached children were rushing off to be
out there for the climactic moment when the fire was lighted.

"*Not* by a Drummond?" I asked Tom.

"No, always by a Joy, because Adam Joy built the first
bonfire to celebrate the anniversary of the Declaration of
Independence."

"Tom!" someone called, and he turned away. Patrick had
disappeared, and I didn't know when we'd lost him. I
couldn't see Miranda for the moment. I was all at once surrounded by four with linked arms, Faustina, Hugh, Prissy,
and a young man named Clem Dyer. "We're going to get up
a dance at my house after the bonfire," Prissy said. "You
comin'?"

"I'll find out what the rest are doing—" I twisted around
to look for them and I thought I saw Miranda's head gleam-
ing in the odd light some distance away.

"You come anyway," Hugh Swenson said. "There'll be
somebody to walk ye home."

"Land of love, yes," Prissy agreed. "Any number of 'em is
just pantin' to!" She and Faustina thought this was tremen-
dously funny, and the two boys looked tolerantly amused.

Suddenly the church bell began to ring from the hill, and
the silencing effect was almost instantaneous. Then the war-
whoops and rebel yells began. The others left me as if swept
away, and out on the point there flame swept up the pyre. It
became a tower of flame spraying fountains of sparks, and in
the darkening waters of the harbor another fire blazed with
its own weird beauty.

"Superb!" a man said behind me. "I can see why they wor-
shipped it. I must be a savage at heart." It was Mr. Clement,
the minister staying at Schofields'.

"We all must be," I said. We talked for a few moments, without looking away from the fire that lighted our faces even at this distance. Well around the beach toward West India Hall a giant salute exploded and laughter went up like a skyrocket; I thought I heard Miranda's voice in the confusion, and wondered if Dill Kalloch were there too, and Patrick watch-dogging. The minister's wife joined us. "Mrs. Swenson has asked us in for tea when the fire's over," she said to him. She sighed. "They never last long enough."

I wandered back toward the store where the light shone out brighter as the flames diminished. Ian was silhouetted in the doorway, and sooner or later the rest should gather there. But Prissy and Faustina and their beaux were sitting in a row on the steps, and I veered off before they could see me. A kitchen dance would be fun, but as the bonfire died something damped and dulled down in me. I felt less consequential than a bubble in the wake of a dory. Though a bubble couldn't be sad, and I was.

Once away from the lighted store I walked faster past the houses, slipping like a shadow around people. I knew the cure for what ailed me: a session alone at the piano in an empty house. There were times when my music was what filled the empty shell of me with substance; it was as much my own as my blood and brain and flesh. My music, that was to be my life, if it were not already that.

At the top of the hill, by the silent church, I looked back at the huge red glowing heart of the bonfire, and then turned back to the two pale parallel tracks of the road. Here I am, I thought, walking alone at night through woods on an island twenty-five miles out to sea, and only the fire-flies know it . . . Against the velvety dark of the woods they were vagrant sparks of light. The turn had cut off all sound from the harbor, and there was no rote on the shores tonight. Except for the inescapable scent of the sea, I could have been far inland.

Then I heard footsteps rounding the turn, and smelled tobacco smoke. *Patrick?* I'd been alone with him many times lately, and had barely felt a qualm. But *barely* wasn't the same as no qualm at all.

"Is that you, Seafair?" It was Ian.

"Is the celebration over?" I asked.

"Until tomorrow, yes. Some of the youngsters are roasting potatoes in the embers." We began walking. "Where's Miranda?"

"I don't know where anyone is and they don't know where I am. It's like walking around wearing a cloak of invisibility."

"Do you like that?" he asked. "Or do you feel you're being neglected or ignored?"

"Never that," I said emphatically. "No, I always thought a cloak of invisibility would be pretty nice to have. At times," I added for the sake of honesty.

"I'm glad you qualified it. Sometimes I feel as if you're too self-contained to be true." I could tell he was smiling, it changed the quality of his voice. "Look, were you by any chance enjoying yourself when I came along and ruined it?"

"Yes," I said truthfully, "I was enjoying myself, but you didn't ruin it. If it weren't for you, I wouldn't be here to enjoy it. . . . I was smelling the woods, and watching the fireflies, and feeling like the old lady who said, 'This be none of I.' "

"Do you often have trouble recognizing yourself?" he asked.

"Doesn't everybody?"

He didn't answer. We walked on a bit in silence, and then I said, "That was a foolish question, because you've never had a bit of trouble recognizing who you are on this island. There was never any doubt about your place in life from the moment you were born."

"Which makes me out to be a monster of smugness from the cradle on."

"No," I protested. "But you seem much older than you really are, as if you were born to responsibility and you've never questioned it."

I sometimes wonder if we would ever have talked like this in a lighted room, instead of under the shield of night, out of doors.

"And what makes you so sure of that?" he asked. "That I've never questioned?"

"I apologize. I hate people who take one look at me and give me a case history of myself. I always rise to the bait and begin protesting and asserting, and end up hot and fussed and furious. But you don't do that. I know you're looking enigmatic even in the dark."

"Is that what you'd call it? Miranda says that's the expression of a judge trying to decide whether the criminal shall be drawn and quartered, or simply hanged. The fact is, it's just the way my face is. —We're a bunch of passionate patriots around here," he said dryly. "We forgot to take in the flag." He opened the front door to let Charlie out, and we walked across to the Liberty Knoll. The white-painted pole seemed topless, its eagle lost in the night sky. The flag hung limp in the stillness with a glimmer of white stripes. It came down with a soft whirring of the block and slither of line, and I caught it. We went into the hall, where Ian lit a lamp and we folded the flag. Charlie watched through his silky bangs, waiting for a move toward the kitchen.

"He's a great little chap," Ian said. "When Miranda's not here I take him to the harbor every day. He's the unofficial harbor master."

Animals were always a safe subject. Fluently I discussed cairns and pugs and collies I had known until Ian suggested coffee, perhaps just to shut me up. The fact was that when I saw him and felt that he was seeing me—beyond the skin, you might say—he disconcerted me. It had been far different out there in the starlight.

Out in the kitchen, busy with the stove, he said, "Where did you say Miranda was?"

"I didn't say. Because I don't know. Prissy and Faustina were getting up a dance, maybe she's there. Where are Andrew and Jane, for that matter? Tom? Patrick?"

"And where are the snows of yesteryear? Patrick rang the church bell, I know that much. I don't like their all melting away and leaving you standing."

"How do you know I wasn't the one who melted away?"

"Shall I escort you back to where I ran you down, and leave you to yourself?"

"To tell you the truth," I said, "I was sneaking back to play the piano. And you were probably looking for some peace and quiet."

"What you want and what I want aren't necessarily incompatible," he said.

"Well, then, if I shut the doors and keep my foot on the soft pedal——"

"You needn't do that."

Carrying our coffee cups, we went to the parlor. I said I didn't need a lamp, and he lit two candles in hurricane shades on the mantel, and went off and left me. Charlie got up in the wing chair by the nearer fireplace. At first I was fretfully, even guiltily conscious of someone across the hall. With an effort I put him out of mind and limbered up with a few short things which required only never to be rattled off as if they were of no importance.

But the *Well-Tempered Klavier* was something else. One sat straighter, arched one's wrists higher, tightened the spring in each finger. One was on one's mettle, the wire walker in ballet skirt and parasol; a single misstep and the whole lovely exercise ended in disaster.

I made no misstep. When I had finished my back was wet, but I was triumphant. I was restored to myself. Of this whole day and its events, for me the playing of the Prelude and Fugue in C Sharp Major was its *raison d'être*.

I blew out the candles and crossed the room. Ian was standing in the library doorway. I had just a glimpse, only enough to let me know he was there, but he turned away and disappeared in the next moment.

Charlie ran upstairs ahead of me, and when I lit my lamp he was already nosing around the pillow. I got him one of his biscuits and ordered him down to the foot of the bed. I hurried to get through with the bathroom before the other girls came, and was just in time. As I got into bed I heard Andrew and Jane in the upstairs hall, her low laugh, and her warning, "Look out for the candle."

It had been a long day and the bed felt good to me. I stretched out and pressed my feet against Charlie's back. I didn't know where Miranda was, and I didn't care. Beside the intricate glories of Bach her games with Dill and Patrick seemed about on a level with London Bridge or Steal Eggs. I loved her for her gaiety and her generosity, and for bringing me here. But to concern myself in the least with what went on in her head, or any Drummond head, when I could spend that time with Bach—never again.

chapter 21

e went to the harbor at noon to watch the dory races both with oar and sprit sail. Then came the ball game between the Bannock Buccaneers and the Drummond Devils. A good crowd had come down from Bannock for it. The game was played in the field between the village and the Old Quarry woods. Mr. Clement was chosen as umpire, and made a pleasant clerical joke about the ease of being partial to neither devils nor buccaneers.

In the shade behind the store, at a table improvised of planks on sawhorses, Ian, Elmer, and other volunteers slashed off slices of watermelon for all comers. Miranda, Jane, and I each collected a wedge and joined a crowd of children.

We sat on the grass with watermelon juice dripping on our dresses, spitting seeds with professional accuracy. We applauded everyone in action, including Mr. Clement, who was unflappable even when assailed by a variety of accents and temperaments.

Practically every able-bodied young man on Drummond's played at some time in the game. Tom was an easy, graceful batter and fast runner. The Awful Ansons decorated outfield and infield. Dill Kalloch was an effortless catcher. Ivor Jenkins of the black beard was another one. I don't know if I watched Patrick more than I watched anyone else, but it seemed as if he were before my eyes constantly. He was intensely involved in the game; like Miranda, he never did anything by halves.

Andrew went in as catcher for the Buccaneers, and instantly Jane forgot everyone but him. Tom came off, and was replaced by Hugh Swenson, who warmed up with an air of careless power in the best Sockalexis style. Tom got a slice of watermelon and came around the edge of the field and sat down in the shade behind us, his sweater draped over his damp shirt. His cheekbones were as red as the watermelon, and his black hair was soaked where he'd just turned a dipper of cold water over his head. We all greeted him as a hero, and the smaller children looked at him with shy reverence.

Miranda moved back until she was sitting beside him and began scolding him about dousing his head in cold water. "Don't you know that's how De Quincy became an opium eater?" Beside me Jane leaned forward tensely as the Buccaneer pitcher wound up. Hugh made a wide swing at the ball and missed. As Andrew caught the ball all the children yelled and whistled, and Jane sat back with a small smile of satisfaction.

"I just missed Pat last night," Miranda said in a low voice. "I think he was waiting for me. I scooted upstairs and got into Seafair's room just as he came out of his. He couldn't come after me without waking up the other girls."

"Miranda, I don't like this," Tom said.

Should I let them know I could hear them, or should I get up and leave? I looked sidewise at Jane. If I could hear it, so could she in the intervals between the children's chatter, but there was nothing to guess from that Gibson girl profile except that she was so entranced by Andrew she was conscious of nothing else.

"It's my own business," Miranda was protesting. Her voice was hushed but very clear. "You're an only child. You don't know what it is to have older ones wanting to know everything you do, discussing it, passing opinions, handing it around——"

"Because they love you. They're concerned."

"I know they love me, and I love them. But I just want to keep something to myself. For a while, anyway . . . Please, Tom?" She took on a wheedling note. "Pat suspects, but he can't prove anything." A childish snicker. "He's about ready to call Dill out."

"Which will end with Patrick getting the beating of his life," said Tom. "Dill is gentle, up to a point, but so is the ocean. Promise me something, Miranda. That you won't let it happen. If you think it's likely to, then you've got to face the music."

"I'll promise you anything, Tom," she said, and laughed.

"I don't like the way you say that. How much are your promises worth?"

"Can't you guess, Tom? You've known me nineteen years. . . . Look at Dill. Isn't he beautiful?"

"You're not being fair to Dill, either."

"I can manage him, I tell you."

There was another outburst of cheers as Hugh Swenson hit a home run; around me the children jumped and screamed. When the outcry began to die down I heard Tom say very softly, "If you don't put an end to the situation, I will."

I felt an almost insuperable relief. Tom knew what was going on. He knew the principals and their breaking points; if Miranda liked teetering on the thin edge of danger, using one man to maneuver another, at least someone was watching, someone who knew to what extent the danger existed.

The Bannock Buccaneers won, but it was a close game. The ovation was tremendous and they were anything but modest about it, clasping their hands over their heads like champion prizefighters; the Italians threw kisses at the crowd. The Devils treated them to beef sandwiches and cold ale, and then they sailed home for their band-concert that night, and fireworks.

We went back to The Eyrie for a light supper, and returned to the harbor at dusk for our own fireworks. I was prepared for Miranda to disappear sometime during the confusion, but she stayed with us all evening, and was in high spirits. I wondered if she'd taken Tom's advice in spite of her bravado. It wasn't in Miranda to be submissive, but she wasn't a fool. Perhaps she'd already discovered what Tom had warned her about: that Dill couldn't and wouldn't be used indefinitely.

After the last Roman candle had died out, the last Catherine wheel spun, the final sky rocket gone to glory among the stars, we straggled home. We sang for a while in the parlor. Jane was a competent pianist, and took over from me to play some of the latest show tunes from New York. It was a good finish to a perfect two days of holiday.

Andrew began taking Jane to Bannock with him every day. She was a good amateur photographer, and with her Kodak she explored the island, and made acquaintances among the women and children. Miranda and I worked at the dig when Patrick wanted us, we picked strawberries for shortcake and for Meg to make jam. We swam whenever the wind permitted, we went rowing, at which I was becoming almost expert; we clammed, fished for cunners and pan-broiled them for dinner at night. We watched the mailboat come, and the salters unloading. One big black-hulled smack sailed down from Boston regularly with barrels of supplies for the store and took away fish and lobsters. This required our closest supervision. There was some sailing, but I occupied myself on shore.

The mackerel hit, and the men seined them to be shipped in ice to Portland and Boston. Patrick, Tom, Andrew and we three girls frequently went out at sunset in the dory and double-ender to jig. I was sorry for the gallant blue and silver fish, but stimulated by the beauty of the hour and the companionship. We'd come home gloriously fishy and damp. If we hadn't already had dinner, we sometimes broiled or fried a mess of fresh fish then and ate hungrily at the kitchen table. Ian salted some away in crocks for the winter, and Meg pickled a batch according to an ancient recipe. We ate spiced tinkers, baked in a beanpot in the oven; we complained about growing fins but kept on eating until we were well and truly tired of mackerel.

If no one came to The Eyrie in the evening, we went out. Andrew and Jane might separate from us, but occasionally stayed with the group, which could end up at the harbor playing cards or boisterous juvenile games in someone's kitchen, or at an impromptu fire on a beach.

There were times when Miranda disappeared again, but since Tom knew what was going on I felt he was never very far from her and Dill. Patrick also vanished at times, either innocently in quest of his own company for a while, or trying to keep an eye on Miranda; whenever he and Tom came in together I had the suspicion that Tom had distracted and circumvented him somehow. They would usually be involved in vehement but good-natured argument about some abstruse subject. There was something about Tom; you believed that he could, and would, take care of things.

Ian went to Rockland on business on the *Ocean Pearl* one day, and that night we had a party at The Eyrie best described as a wing-ding. Not that the harbor crowd stayed away when he was there, but this time more of them came, those who were a little in awe of him.

"Ian's wonderful," Miranda said earnestly when we were getting ready, "but he casts a shadow. He can't help it."

"You make him sound grim," I objected.

"You said yourself he was off-putting."

"But I don't find him that way any more," I said.

"Neither do I," said Jane. "I think people are trying to force him too soon into his father's shoes."

"Don't look at *me*!" Miranda protested. "I'd *love* to turn him into a *boulevardier* type. But he resists like some tough old Calvinist."

That night Jane taught us the rowdy Kitchen Lancers which the Bar Harbor girls had learned from some young British officers, and Hugh Swenson and his sister Jenny taught us a Swedish *hambo*. The dancing took place in the kitchen, which was certainly big enough, but later we moved inevitably to the parlor and the piano, and a fireplace for making popcorn. Some of the girls stayed afterward to help with the dishes, but the next morning Miranda and I had to pick popcorn out of the carpets, scrape up candle wax, and wash smoked lamp chimneys. Jane had gone off early to Bannock with Andrew.

"This is just too much," said Miranda. "The next party's going to be at the cottage. That's mine, and if we want to leave it in a mess until we get ready to clean it up we can."

Jane told us at dinner one night that she had met Rosaleen. She was photographing rocks and surf on the southern slopes of Bannock when Rosaleen and some other women came down the hill to pick strawberries. Jane had met most of them already, and one of them asked them all back to her kitchen afterward for a cup of tea. Rosaleen was disdainfully silent while the others were friendly, but at least she stayed with the group.

Jane had been impressed by her. "She looks as if she'd been invented by the Irish poets to show the way their queens ought to have looked."

"Her beauty's her undoing," Ian said.

"John Knox is among us," said Patrick. Ian gave him a good-humored sidewise glance without moving his head.

"I wish to God I'd hear something from Boston!" Andrew said. "Come the end of summer she'll be gone and there's nothing we can do about it. It's the boys I'm worried about. What'll happen to them? I feel like telling her, Damn it, *go*, but leave the kids to me."

Ian said, "And then you'd hear the speech about her poor father turning over in his grave at the very thought of it."

"Whirling like a dervish at the thought of their living with Protestants. We got that one," said Miranda. "Still, she wants a Drummond, you know. If she can't have Andrew, she'd likely settle for Ian or Patrick."

"I'm wedded to my career," said Patrick, "and Rosaleen would be a profession in herself. Come on, Ian you're settling down too early to be an old bach. Think of Dark Rosaleen descending the front stairs. The Old Colonel would come right out of his frame."

"And think of those fabulous kids you'd have," said Miranda. "Half Puritan Drummond and half Irish tiger."

Ian rose and bowed. "I can't tell you how much I appreciate your efforts on my behalf. All I ask of you is one simple favor: please let me do my own proposing." He sat down again to loud applause.

A few days later Jane actually went to the Dolan house. She had gone to promise Rosaleen prints of some photographs she'd made of the boys down on the rocks, cleaning flounder. Rosaleen was anything but gracious. She couldn't see why Jane had wanted to "take" the boys without shoes. Why hadn't she sent them home to dress in their good clothes and shoes?

"We're not bog-trotters, you know. You needn't think that of us."

"I didn't think anything," Jane said. "All I saw was children having fun. Great painters have always painted barefoot children. Maybe because young bare feet are a lot more attractive than shoes."

That attempt at humor got nowhere with the absolutely humorless Rosaleen. Anyway, her final reason for not wanting the prints was that she'd soon be moving, and the pictures might be lost in the mail.

"Oh, where are you going?" Jane asked.

"The city!" Rosaleen's smoulder blazed into life. "I've known nothing but this rock ever since I was too small to remember anything else. This rock—I hate it—it broke my mother's heart and it killed my poor dad."

Before she could have Robert Emmet spinning in his grave Jane tried to pin her down to a specific city and specific plans, but the girl was either shrewd or naturally elusive. Or perhaps not yet sure of anything, except that she was going.

"If it's city life you want," Jane said, "I could get you a place in Philadelphia."

"In service?" said Rosaleen in the same tone in which she had said "without shoes."

"It would be something to support you and the boys for the time being," Jane said. "But you could get more education if that's what you want, and perhaps get into clerical work; stenographers and typists will always be in demand. I have an aunt who's started evening classes for girls who want to have a high school education."

"I'm educated enough," said Rosaleen, "and, as for working in a shop or an office, I'd not do that any more than I'd go into service. Thank you very much, Miss Greenleaf, but I know what I'm going to do. I'm only waiting till the fall season begins." She drew herself up, which was the only way to describe it. "I'm going on the stage in Boston."

Miranda said, "Like Maxine Elliot!"

"Oh, shut up," said Patrick. "Go on, Jane."

"I was struck dumb," she said solemnly. "Oh, I recovered enough to ask her if she was joining a repertory company, and at what theater, and so forth, but she was magnificently vague about that. It was none of my business and she suspected me of welfare schemes that were as bad as white slavery, if not a form of the same, and if Andrew Drummond had sent me I could just tell him— But I never found out what, because I made a graceful departure, and the lady in the next house called over the fence that was a headstrong young one on her way to destruction and that poor Robert Emmet Dolan was——"

"Turning over in his grave," we chanted.

"I wish you'd waited to hear what you were supposed to tell Andrew," said Patrick.

"I was afraid I wouldn't be able to repeat it," said Jane demurely.

chapter 22

We had our first cottage party the next week. It was a roaring (literally) success. Around midnight the guests departed singing by the light of the full moon. The six of us from The Eyrie—this included Tom—made a few futile gestures toward straightening things up, blew out the lamps, closed the windows in case of fog, and went up the steps too winded to sing. We were hoarse, wilted, and pleasantly exhausted. At the top Andrew took Jane out onto the Head to find a favorite nook of his own among the rocks. Patrick and Miranda sent a few flippancies flying after them, but without much conviction.

Part way across the lawn Miranda said hurriedly, "Excuse me, and don't ask why . . . 'Night, Tom." She went off over the grass toward the front door.

"Hope you make it!" Patrick called after her.

"Don't be vulgar," she retorted, and went in. The library and parlor were dark, but Ian's windows overhead were lighted.

At the Liberty Knoll Tom said goodnight and left us. We went into the dimly lit hall, where Patrick lit candles for us both. He was wearing the blue rollneck sweater tonight, and the sight of it earlier that evening had brought back all the exquisite agony of our first meeting. In the moonlight the color had been dulled. But now the blue glowed forth suddenly with the candlelight, and so did the color of his eyes.

"What's the matter, Seafair?" he asked teasingly. "Seeing ghosts behind my shoulder?" He pretended to try to see too.

"The place is teeming with them," I said. I took my candle. "Now for the sleep-walking scene from Macbeth. *Good-*

night, Patrick!" And then I laughed. I saw the shift to perplexity in his eyes just as I turned and went up the stairs.

"Hey, wait a minute!" he called after me. "What does that laugh mean?"

"What laugh?" I riposted brilliantly, and continued on my way. At the head of the stairs my heart was beating harder than my swift upward passage could account for. If he had been perplexed and intrigued by my conduct, so was I.

Ian's door was ajar, letting a narrow band of light out into the hall. The door of my dark room stood all the way open, as I'd seen it last. Miranda wasn't in the bathroom, either. I had the strongest certainty that she'd invented her urgency as she'd invented the summer complaint, and had gone straight through the house and out the back door, taking Charlie with her.

Dill had been one of the last ones to leave before us. I wondered if she had expected Patrick to see through the excuse. What was the point of her meeting Dill if Patrick didn't *know*? As for Tom, who knew what was in his mind when he said goodnight at the Liberty Knoll? Tomorrow he might put his ultimatum into effect. That would be interesting, I thought, but I was still preoccupied with the instant at the foot of the stairs, my own inexplicable laugh, and Patrick's reaction. Was it possible that I had deep within me the true tendency to flirt?

I knelt on my window seat and looked out. It seemed a hideous waste not to be out in the fine mild night, and according to my code I didn't need male company to make the moonlight perfect. It already was. I went silently into the hall. Across the stairs well Patrick's door was just as it had been when I came upstairs, and Ian's door still let out a slash of amber light. I went down the back way.

Long windrows of luminous cloud fanned up over the zenith as if from some central core far down in the west. Stars glittered in the clear dark blue spaces between. There was a strong fragrance of nicotiana from the other side of the garden wall, and I sniffed it with satisfaction, reminding myself of Charlie when he couldn't take his nose away from some delectable spot. Then I walked down the farm side of the windbreak to the couch hammock. Here I sat contemplating the whitened fields and the steel-blue ice pond, and the line of ocean beyond Marsh Cove. It was warm, it was lovely in a spellbound fashion until I became gradually conscious of something to my right, looming like a wall or a black cloud.

It was the oak grove. I couldn't see it because of the windbreak, but I could feel its silent mass. I seemed to be falling prey to its mythology. I wished I had Charlie with me to cuddle. Miranda certainly didn't need him while she was driving Dill into a state of inarticulate frustration. Poor Dill, the doomed middleman.

Damn that blue sweater ... What if Patrick was down in the oak grove now, instead of trying to keep an eye on Miranda? Perhaps he didn't even know she'd gone out. But if I want seriously to compete for his attention, I'd have a fairer chance against his watch-dogging than against the spirits of the dead past. And why did *that* phrase give me a touch of cold grue?

I decided finally that it wasn't Patrick's ghosts but the dewy damp of the couch hammock. I could hear Phoebe. *Don't sit on damp seats. Don't sit on a stone wall, don't sit on the ground. Don't get your feet wet, you can get an undercold.* The last word whispered in the tone which she used for "baby" (unborn), "bathroom," or "bowels."

I was furious for having introduced Phoebe into the entranced night scene, and as for an undercold I'd been sitting where I pleased all my life, as much as was possible, and I despised people who worried about wet feet and cold bottoms. But I still wished I had Charlie.

There was a soft crunch of grass underfoot. Someone was coming, Andrew and Jane perhaps. "Hello," I called, to warn them I was there.

"Hello!" It was Ian who came up to the hammock. "I thought you'd gone to bed."

"I came out again. It was so beautiful."

"Yes." This was followed by a hush that made my ears ring. He was apparently not at all overjoyed by the meeting.

"Well, I said, unfolding my drawn-up legs, "at least I've dried off the hammock for you."

"Now that's a womanly little touch I'd hardly expected. Don't go." He sat down beside me.

"If you came out to be alone——"

"Did I say that? Relax. Unless *you* happen to be alone from choice, as you're always telling me whenever I find you by yourself. Do you mind if I smoke?" This positive spate from Ian almost unnerved me.

I said meekly, "Please do. I like a pipe better than cigars." *You must draw men out,* Phoebe said. "Do you have a special mixture made up?" I asked. "It's an unusual fragrance."

"Prince Albert," he said.

Quenched, I sat silently in my corner of the hammock until he got his pipe going. "There are two matters I want to take up with you," he said. "One of them is this: weren't you and Miranda supposed to be working on her music this summer? I haven't heard her touch the piano except one night in a very halting accompaniment to her own singing, full of wrong notes."

"You're away all day," I said feebly.

"From what I heard that night I'm willing to bet that you two don't spend an hour a week at the piano. I don't think she could get through *The Happy Farmer* without stumbling."

"Well, does she have to? At her age she'd look pretty silly sitting down to play that for the guests. As for accompanying herself, she should do better. I'll start working with her tomorrow."

"If you can pin her down. Look, Seafair, I'm sure you'd have worked with her before if you could have managed it, so don't blame yourself."

"But I wouldn't have worked with her," I said unhappily,

"because I've hardly thought of it. I'm as bad as she is, if that's the word."

"That's not the word." The kind tone made me feel even worse.

"It's as if I came here under false pretenses. But I did have the intention to coach her. Then everything turned out to be so much more than I'd expected—and heaven knows I expected something wonderful enough from Miranda's description."

"And it's more than wonderful?"

"So much more that I've gone back about twelve years. I wake up in the morning thinking, What will I see and hear and discover for the first time?"

"Then go on like that, and don't worry about Miranda. Even with your help she'll never be an even mediocre pianist, because she won't work at it on her own. I don't suppose she needs to. There'll always be someone somewhere who can play for her. Go ahead and have fun, Seafair. The summers grow shorter and shorter the older you grow."

"You sounded incredibly ancient," I said. "It reminds me of something our dean likes to quote when we junior teachers get too sure of ourselves. 'The oldest hath borne most; we that are young shall never see so much, nor live so long.' "

"Lear," he said. "We did it in school."

"You weren't Lear, by any chance?"

"As a matter of fact, I was a tremendous success as the Fool. You can't imagine that, can you? . . . I don't know why I didn't go tonight. I wanted to. But did you ever have the feeling that you'd cast a heavy shadow?"

"I think I know what you mean. Yes. I do know."

"I don't feel old, Seafair. It's something quite different. Rather like feeling very young but loaded with millstones. Summer becomes just another burden then." It was said without self-pity. He got up briskly. "Look, they're all out. Come back and play something. Do you know *Solveig's Song?*"

"Yes." I rose.

"My father used to play that. It's the first thing I recognized by name as an entity, and I always associate it with my mother for some reason."

As we strolled toward the house he talked matter-of-factly about his mother. He remembered many things about her in sharp detail, but there was only blankness surrounding the circumstances of her death.

"Because it didn't happen here, I suppose, and I didn't see her when they brought her back. My father must have tried to explain, he was like that, but I must have not wanted to know."

"I remember when my mother died," I said, "because my father was so utterly distraught. I remember his old aunts whispering that Henry was losing his mind with grief, and I was terrified by the picture the words presented, and afraid to ask anybody about it."

"And I suppose nobody thought you needed explanations. Some people see quiet children as vegetables. Did your father ever make any attempt to talk with you about your mother's death?"

"No. But I know now that he didn't know how to begin, and he was truly in a dreadful state. . . . When he brought Phoebe home, and for a long time afterward, I couldn't forgive him for being so unfaithful after all his terrible grief. Now I know why it had to be."

"Why?" asked Ian.

"When you're small your parents seem so old. Now I know my mother was about your age, and he wasn't much older. I'm almost their contemporary!" I laughed at the strangeness of finding it out, just now, like this. "A man like my father couldn't have gone on without a woman's love, he needed it like air to breathe and water to drink."

Ian didn't comment. We walked slowly toward the house. I reflected on my own words. *A man like my father.* What about a man like Ian? Could this be one of the things that weighed on him? *Summer becomes just another burden.*

Watching Andrew with Jane, listening to the piano in the dusk; at thirty, bound hand and foot and dragged down with weights, not all of them named responsibility.

When he spoke again he began telling me about the days when the house abounded in small boys and a just-walking Miranda. I heard of a bathtub turned into an aquarium for a baby seal, duels with lath swords up and down the front stairs. Trying to climb to the eagle's nest. Hunting for ambergris.

It all sounded like E. Nesbit's stories come to life and I was sorry when we reached the house. Andrew and Jane were in the kitchen making hot chocolate, and we sat down at the table with them. Miranda came soon, and Charlie hurtled past her and over to his water dish.

"Look at all the lights!" Miranda said. "The Drummonds are really on the road to ruin. Three lamps burning and no ship at sea!"

"We have to do something reckless around here," Andrew said, "to make up for what Jane's missing at Bar Harbor."

A screen door slammed in the shed, something was kicked out of the way, and Patrick stalked into the kitchen. He looked only at Miranda. He was very flushed, but spoke in a flat tone.

"Are you going to haul with me tomorrow or not? You'd better."

"Yes, I'm going!" She shouted at him. "You'd better dig out some earmuffs if you don't want your ears ripped right off your skull."

"Five o'clock!" He slapped the words at her and ran up the backstairs. Miranda poured hot chocolate for herself. I said vapidly to Jane, "We really must work up some duets." I hate duets.

She looked at me solemnly in the eye and said, "I get the parts with the crossed hands. I'm ever so graceful at it."

In just the time it would take for Patrick to get up to his room and close the door, Ian said to Miranda, "What was that all about?"

She ran her hands under her hair at the back and flipped it out as if to cool her neck. "Has Patrick been officially appointed my *dueña,* or did he just take on the job out of a sense of duty?"

"I thought *dueñas* wore lace things with tall combs," said Andrew.

"I was never so humiliated in my life! What does he think I'm going to do, for heaven's sake? Be seduced under a spruce tree?"

"Calm down," said Ian. "What happened?"

"I simply went out with Charlie and decided to walk a bit, and get calmed down after all the singing and dancing. Patrick decided I was going astray in a cranberry bog somewhere, and spent the last hour beating the bushes for me like the Watch and Ward Society in person."

"Where did he finally run you to earth?" Andrew asked.

"On the way home. By *myself.*" She threw a venomous glance at the stairs. "And began putting me through an inquisition. I informed him that Rosaleen might be in danger of a fate worse than death, but that we didn't have any vicious fiends on this island, just a poor unfortunate maniac named Patrick Drummond."

Andrew laughed and Jane's mouth was twitching, but I remembered Patrick's gray face and the blow in the hall that night. Miranda could assure me again that such a flaming row was normal, but it could still shake me up.

Ian wore the same slightly inquiring expression. "Why are you going with him tomorrow morning, then?"

"To have it out once and for all. To put an end to this. He's been simply awful this summer, Ian. You have no idea. When you and Andrew went to Bar Harbor, we had a fearful do, and Seafair was ready to leave the next day."

"Why keep this one going then? He'll probably be over it in the morning."

"Well, *I* won't be. He needn't think he can start something and then walk away from it when *he's* tired of it. No, I'm going to have my say."

"Let me have a talk with him," Ian said. "You know he's always been over-protective about you since you came into the house. In some ways he's never outgrown that."

"He's never outgrown a lot of things. He's very young for his years, if you ask me."

"And I suppose you're very mature," said Andrew.

"Go ahead and laugh!"

Andrew pulled her down onto his lap and kissed her cheek. "I loved you too, but you were a lot more of a nuisance around here than my dog was."

"Thank you, dear Andrew . . . I *think*. I'm going to tell Pat tomorrow he'd better get himself a girl and stop making a career out of being Big Brother. Here's Seafair——"

"Leave me out of it," I said, sick of the whole puerile deception.

Ian said with finality, "I don't think we should be discussing him anyway. Stay away from him tomorrow morning and let me talk with him."

"I wish you wouldn't," she said rapidly. "Look, Ian dear, it *is* between him and me after all, it's not the first time we've quarreled and it won't be the last . . . I mean we have to finish it, don't you see? And then everything will be fine for a while. That's how Patrick is, and how I am too. I may have tormented him into this just a little, made him suspect something that wasn't true. You know how I can do, even though I hate to admit I'm not absolutely an angel." She laughed, but it was shaky. "I suppose I'm almost as possessive about him as he is about me; after all I was always his army, his shadow, henchman, whatever you want to call it . . . *no*," she said ringingly, "it would be very unfair and disloyal of me to expect you to deal with our quarrel. So can't we consider it all unsaid, and have some nice music?"

She smiled enchantingly around at us all.

"I should think after that long and impassioned address to the court you'd be hoarse," said Ian. "Sit down and drink your chocolate, and then we'd all better get to bed."

We went up the front staircase more or less in a group.

On the landing we paused at the portrait, holding up our candles and Andrew said, "Good night, Colonel, sir."

"I'd like to have known him," said Jane.

"Then I wouldn't have had a chance," said Andrew.

Miranda put an arm around Ian's waist and leaned against him. "Ian, promise me you'll leave Patrick to me."

"On condition there'll be no more of these nursery squabbles."

"All right." She reached up and kissed him.

"Buttering up," he said, and she laughed.

During the goodnights in the upstairs hall, I was as conscious of Patrick's door as if he were standing there with his face closed and locked against us. I felt an ache of sympathy for him; I knew what it was to go to bed in a rage, convinced that I was right no matter what the cause was, while everyone else went callously on as usual. I wished for the courage to call "Goodnight, Patrick," through the panels but I was too self-conscious. Miranda might decide to call something too, and he would think we were laughing at him.

We gave Jane first turn at the bathroom, and I expected that Miranda would say something about the quarrel, but it was as if her outburst downstairs had never taken place. She yawned voluptuously. "It seems about a year since this morning. Wasn't it a terrific party, Seafair?"

"Mm," I said, as if I were too drowsy to make an effort. I remembered that I hadn't played *Solveig's Song* for Ian. And he'd said he wanted to take up two matters with me, but we'd only discussed one, and I went to sleep wondering what the other one could be.

woke in the first light with a gull banking past our open windows and calling. I felt as if I had hardly slept all night.

It was nearly half-past four by my watch. As usual, Miranda slept as soundly as Charlie did at her feet. "Are you going with Patrick this morning?" I asked her, softly. "It's nearly five o'clock. More or less," I added, to temper the lie.

She flopped over in bed with an upheaval of bedding that nearly dumped Charlie onto the floor and was out of bed at once, rummaging frantically through the clothes she'd thrown onto a chair last night. She took an armful into the bathroom and I settled comfortably back into bed. Charlie turned round and round treading out a new nest, and curled up in it. When Miranda came back, dressed after a fashion and trying to brush snarls out of her hair, wincing and muttering, I murmured, "Did Pat really find you going astray under a spruce tree or in a cranberry bog?"

"Oh, for heaven's *sake!*" she hissed at me, and left.

I went back to sleep, and slept better than I had all night. When Charlie and I got up, the sun was well up also, and everybody had gone. Meg sat down with me while I ate breakfast, and had one of her large cups of tea. I made the beds, and then went down to Drummond Cove to write letters.

For the children I described the things the island children did for fun. The "halfs" were nice enough youngsters, and I really loved them: the first time I held Julian in my arms, when I was fourteen, I wished that Phoebe would go away and leave me to raise the baby and keep house for my father. I liked each baby as it came along, in spite of my resolve *not* to. I was making a collection of seashore things for them.

For Papa and Phoebe I wrote up a scintillating social season. Jane's coming from Bar Harbor casually linked the two places. Our dancing last night sounded like a decorous delight shared by a throng of post-debutantes. Actually it had reminded me of what I'd read about high old times out West in Gold Rush days.

With that happy aura of virtuous accomplishment which is like no other, I was sealing my letters when Miranda and Charlie came down the path by the cottage. She had two Banbury tarts in a napkin, and we ate them with Charlie staring at us and drooling. Miranda looked as if she'd never had a worry and never expected to have one.

"Well, and did you get it straightened out?" I asked.

"Well, and I did," she said merrily.

"Then he won't tell Ian about Dill."

She grinned like a malicious urchin. "Ian wouldn't fuss about anybody I ran around with, as long as we didn't elope. But Patrick thinks all men but the chivalrous Drummonds, and Tom of course, are out to debauch girls in the finest tradition of the dirty novels we used to pass around at school. Well, he hauled, and we argued, and a crab bit him and he swore, but I finally convinced him that Dill was a lamb with me, so gentle and kind and respectful as if I were a porcelain figurine. And *then*," she said with a dramatic pause, "and *then* he said that I was leading Dill on, and that was dishonorable, a woman's low trick and so forth and so on ad infinitum, or at least until we came into the harbor."

"It doesn't sound very straightened out to me."

"Oh, I'm not going to see Dill any more," she said casually, playing with some shells. "It's not worth all the fuss.

He's not that much of a lamb, at least he's rapidly getting not to be, so it's not so much fun now."

"You mean the donkey's making grabs for the carrot?"

"Seafair, don't be vulgar! Also, Patrick threatened to talk to Dill, which means somebody will be hurt, because Dill's enormously strong."

And you think Patrick's beginning to react properly, I added silently. She was trying to juggle three shells. "Tom and I have it fixed up to go sailing, and so when we were washing down the peapod I asked Pat very sarcastically if he had any objections to my being out of sight with Tom. He gave me a disgusted look and said be sure we left *Eaglet* shipshape. Too bad Tom and I don't want to cut up, isn't it?" She cackled like Prissy. "We could have loads of fun, and all with Saint Patrick's blessing. . . . Come on with us, Seafair. Tom likes you."

"I like Tom too, but not enough to spend the afternoon being scared out of my skin. Go ahead. You can have my blessings as well as Pat's."

"He's going to dig all afternoon. Don't go near him or you'll have to work."

We had one of the best afternoons ever. We worked separately for a while, Patrick down in the pit and I sifting dirt. Of course I didn't find a thing, though I prayed to Patrick's heathen gods for an ancient button or coin or needle. But I enjoyed myself. Patrick whistled erratically, and I hummed something else. The breeze blew through the oak leaves like an echo of the surf on the outer shores.

"You've a feeling for this sort of thing," he said once. "Which is more than I can say for Miranda . . . Schliemann's wife was a tremendous help to him."

I had a vision of myself as an archeologist's wife, dashing in sun helmet, divided skirt, boots; keeping scientific records, paying the native workers, sleeping at night in a tent on the desert.

"I'm a free agent now," Patrick was saying, "the way I won't be if I get into an expedition to Greece or Egypt or Mesopotamia. This is my project completely, so I can keep at it until I have something or until I decide there's nothing. If there *is* something—" He jumped to his feet with a wild yell that rang through the grove, and stretched his arms toward the hidden sky. "I don't know what I'd do. I can't imagine—all I can think of is up to that moment——"

"To travel hopefully is better than to arrive," I quoted, and he laughed.

"All right, rub it in. I guess maybe nothing could be better than the actual moment of arrival. When you're *certain*. Then after that——"

"Anti-climax."

"I'll risk it," he said. "And who knows what else is on here? You joked about digging deep enough to find a standing stone. It doesn't have to be a joke." He sat down beside me. "You know, this oak grove was always my runaway place. And *why?*" He pointed a finger at me. "This is where inherited memory comes in. Why shouldn't anyone inherit memories as well as physical characteristics, like the color of eyes or a predisposition to tuberculosis? . . . I know my Scottish background well. But each of us, as small children, knowing nothing yet about the Drummonds, experienced the same reaction the first time we heard bagpipes. They called to something inherent in us. Our mother's parents were English. Their roots were deep in the Wessex soil. They were proud of how little Norman blood was in them, and how they'd been in the same place for hundreds of years. I never knew my mother, and I didn't hear what I've just told you about her family until I was ten or so. But there was always something about this grove that drew me, from the time I could walk alone. As if something waited for me here, and wouldn't let me off."

I rubbed my arms and he said, "Do I give you gooseflesh?"

"Never mind. Go on."

"Who knows what was passed down in my mother's

family from generation to generation? Who knows what some of the earlier ones might have been and done, that could only be whispered about? Deeds so secret, so mystic, so bloody, that after a while the inheritors refused to acknowledge them? But the knowledge was still there. They had *happened*. Forgetting them didn't wipe them out. Who knows what lay in my innocent mother's unconscious mind, that she passed on to me but not to my brothers? —Do you think I'm talking sheer rot?"

"No! Who would have believed once in the telephone, the telegraph, the gramophone? Why not a human instrument?"

"Thanks, Seafair," he said almost fervently. "Your eyes are shining? You look as if you've seen the god."

"Which one?"

"Take your pick. I think Pan's the tutelary god of Drummond's, especially on a moonlit summer night."

"*I* haven't seen him, and, besides, who was it said Great Pan is dead?"

"He's not dead around here. You'd be surprised who's secretly wearing hoof and horns." He was lighting a cigarette, and looked over at me with a mischievous cant of the head and said, "For all you know, it could be me."

The island was enjoyably shaken up for a week by the Elder. He was a self-ordained preacher representing some splinter sect that had found the Hardshell Baptists too liberal. He sailed the coast all summer long in his small sloop *Jerusalem*, putting in at the islands to conduct revival services. He was a Newfoundlander and had been a fisherman since he was old enough to pull his weight on an oar; the men respected him for this. Some people went to the nightly services because they were great entertainment. Some went to be saved, and were; every year.

We went to the Sunday service. The man was blisteringly severe, enough to take the comic edge off his pulpit gymnastics. Meg and Dougal went to the evening services, and

Meg reported to Miranda and me each morning on the rate of salvation.

"That Prissy Schofield. Farming right up front and kneeling as if she wasn't the worst besom on the island."

"It's sinners he wants, Meg," Miranda said.

"That's what he's got in that one. Every year she goes through it, bawling like a calf and the tears running like the alser swamp in spring, and she'll worry about hellfire and damnation till the *Jerusalem*'s hull down on the horizon, and then she'll be out in the bushes again."

"Let's just be grateful," said Miranda piously, "that she waits until he's gone. She could be trying to get *him* out into the bushes."

"That'll be enough of *that*."

"He knows his Bible backward and forward," Tom said. "He's read nothing else since he was converted, and he succeeded in making me feel as if I had gone into the ministry for the money. If you didn't hear the call when your hands were frozen to the oars in a lost dory off Banquereau, then you just never heard the call."

"Where did you hear the call, Tom?" Miranda asked. "You never told me."

Tom just grinned.

The effect of the Elder had scarcely worn off when the FitzRoy Players came, after a week on Bannock. They were a shabby group who looked as if they'd lived hard, but they came off the steamer with an air, and we were willing to be spellbound.

They set up camp upstairs in West India Hall, and turned downstairs into a theater. First we saw pirated versions of *Shore Acres* and *Little Lord Fauntleroy*. The star of this was the youngest FitzRoy son, small for his age and with curly blond hair to his shoulders. The first afternoon, drawn to the shore like any boy, he was called upon to defend his masculinity, and did so with professional speed and skill. After that he spent his spare time with the harbor boys. Generously they admired his performances and didn't even jeer when he played serving maids in the *Scenes from Shakespeare*.

These were the real meat of the banquet. The kerosene footlights transformed cheap and practical material into opulent velvets and silks. Mr. FitzRoy was genuinely moving as the Moor, and the audience hated Iago and said so. Desdemona's death caused gasps and a couple of hysterical yelps. When, too late, he discovered her innocence, there was some uninhibited sobbing here and there.

FitzRoy's daughter, niece, or young second wife—we never did get it straight—was a touching Cleopatra. I wasn't very experienced in theater arts, and for all I knew her performance was pure melodrama, as shoddy as the costumes. But my throat was aching when she received the news of Antony's death, and when she died I was afraid I'd be joining the weepers. I sat rigidly between Tom and Ian, and stared at the stage with glazed eyes.

"Now boast thee, death, in thy possession lies a lass unparallel'd," Charmian said, and the glaze melted. I saw the finish through a watery blur.

After the last performance we gave them a party at The Eyrie. There were great amounts of food and drink, music, recitations, and impromptu performances by the Players ranging from the balcony scene in *Romeo and Juliet* to music hall turns.

After they left for Matinicus, their next engagement, we went in for Shakespearian evenings. *Othello* and *Antony and Cleopatra* were naturally the first choices, because they were so fresh in our minds. Everybody played several parts, and we took turns at the leads. Jane wouldn't do either Desdemona or Cleopatra, but was convincing as Emilia and Charmian. Ian surprised us one night by playing a silkily horrid Iago to Tom's Othello, with Miranda saintly in a white peignoir for the murder scene, her hair streaming loose. Andrew and Patrick and I did our version the next night. Andrew was a villain without the courage of his convictions, but Patrick outdid the whole Booth clan, according to Jane.

" 'It is the cause, it is the cause, my soul, Let me not name it to you, you chaste stars,' " he muttered over my couch, and the fact that he had a book in his hand didn't take away from the drama. The kisses brushing my cheek were rather a waste, since I knew they weren't meant for me personally, but I surrendered all selfish ambition to the performance.

" 'One more, and this the last; So sweet was ne'er so fatal.' "

" 'Kill me tomorrow; let me live tonight!' " I begged, was refused, and strenuously smothered to death.

" 'She's like a liar gone to burning hell: 'Twas I that kill'd her,' " he whispered searingly across my corpse, and I had a horrifying sense of being dead indeed, but able to hear. And I dreamed of it that night.

We went on to *Hamlet, Macbeth,* and *The Merchant of Venice* before we wore it out. Those who came over from the harbor didn't have to worry about reading Elizabethan English; they could be ambassadors, courtiers, soldiers, or ladies-in-waiting, and make up their own speeches as long as they knew what the scene was about. The opinion was that we should form our own company and go barnstorming like the FitzRoys, and we had plenty of volunteers.

We played in the garden, and out on the Liberty Knoll. Hamlet and Laertes dueled up and down the stairs, with Jane and Andrew sitting under the Old Colonel's portrait as Gertrude and Claudius.

We went to bed with the lines ringing in our heads like chimes, and woke up with ideas for improvements on the way one team had played the night before.

At that point it seemed as if summer would go on forever.

e had the first glimpse of the end of summer, like the first landfall on a voyage you wished would go on indefinitely, when Jane said she would be leaving in a week. She had to be back in Bar Harbor by the middle of August, when her family would be collecting. Miranda and I had the whole of August ahead of us, and two weeks in September. But there was something about Jane's date for leaving that broke the once-solid block of summer into units all too quickly used up.

We had to make her last week count. We had supper picnics and late-evening fires on the beach, there was a dance at West India Hall, and one day we went deep-sea fishing in *Kingfisher*. It wasn't rough, but where we anchored to fish we rode a monotonous swell and I got seasick, and I had to be held humiliatingly by my belt—by Ian—so I wouldn't pitch overboard. Everyone else went on hauling in fish with repulsive enthusiasm. But I was able to eat hot fish chowder when the time came.

The night before Jane left we had the party in the cottage which Sam Baldwin photographed. The next day Jane and Andrew went to the mainland aboard the *Ocean Pearl*, to travel overland to Bar Harbor. Andrew would stay with the Greenleafs for a week.

The early goldenrod and first brown-eyed susans edged the road, and the reticent blue of asters appeared. We picked raspberries around the Old Quarry, and blueberries on the open slopes. I remember us gathering highland cranberries among lichened granite outcroppings on the high ground overlooking the weir, and seeing the shags sitting on the weir poles with their wings spread out to dry. Brown infant seagulls whistled after their mothers, and overhead an osprey family were excitedly piping. Over us all, far higher than the fishhawks, so high we kept losing sight of them, the eagles flew.

Andrew sent us postcards from Bar Harbor, like a traveler in a foreign country. We hoped nobody in the postoffice there had read his comments on the quaint customs. Then he wrote Ian that he had met a millionaire who had bought two hundred acres on a point above Mount Desert and fancied an Italian palace of Beatrice Pink. "Sounds awful," he wrote, "but the price doesn't. I'm staying on for a week to meet his architect. I've written Ivor."

On Bannock, walking pneumonia broke out. A doctor came from Rockland to stay through the worst of it, getting in some fishing and sailing on the side. No one got pneumonia on Drummond's, but a form of summer complaint hit the village, with chills and fever and aching bones. None of us at the farm of The Eyrie caught it except Ian, who was unable to get up one Saturday morning.

Miranda went in to see him, and was ordered out. "I don't choose to be the victim of your delusion that you're Florence Nightingale," he told her wearily.

"Miranda in a sickroom is purely ornamental, like flowers," Patrick told me, "except that flowers can't keep asking you how you feel, and keep shaking your pillows when you've finally got them just right."

It wasn't a boat day, so Elmer wouldn't need any extra help at the store. Patrick went out to haul his traps, and Meg told Miranda and me to stay out of the house so Ian could sleep. We took some peaches in a basket and walked all the way around the outer shore to the uttermost point of the Bowsprit.

Most Drummond mornings were memorable for me, but this one stands out because of its low-keyed, almost somber mood. Not because of the weather, which was August's brightest and best, but because of Miranda herself. I thought she was already nostalgic for the summer before it had gone by, because I was, and I tried to buck us both up by talking about the autumn activities at the college. But she was only half-hearing. She didn't seem so much depressed as preoccupied, and somehow much older.

Suddenly she interrupted my ramblings. "Come sailing with Tom and me this afternoon, you coward. If you go back to school without once taking the tiller of *Eaglet,* you'll hate yourself for ever and ever."

"No, I won't."

"Don't be so smug! I hate these people who are so proud of their ignorance. Look, if you learn something this year, you'll be all ready for next, you see?"

Next. I had never realized the transcendent beauty of the word. "You mean I'm really invited back?"

She began to laugh. "Well, we've got to work on the piano sometime, haven't we?" She brought out the peaches. "Here, we'll have a toast to it in peach juice."

To this day the taste of ripe peaches brings back with the immediacy of pain that morning on the Bowsprit, the heat of the sun and the cool saltiness of the wind, the red and white trawl kegs bobbing amid spangles of light, Miranda mopping peach juice off her chin, and from the Old Quarry woods behind us the weirdly echoing cries of children playing some game of hiding and pursuit.

That afternoon I went down to the dig with Patrick while the other two went sailing. I was willing to learn as the price of returning, but not today. Anyway, Miranda didn't mention it again after we left the Bowsprit.

Patrick and I didn't talk as much as we did the last time, but his mood was positive, as if he knew something was there and he would reach it in time. As I sieved dirt I imagined Patrick's forebears, wreathed in mistletoe, greeting the summer solstice under a Sacred Oak in some little English valley deep in the folds of forested hills. Maybe it was still inviolable in its secrecy, sealed off by the centuries as flies were sealed and preserved in Baltic amber.

The four of us were together in the evening. We went for a walk to the harbor and bought ice cream, which we ate out on the store doorstep. Across the way some men were baiting a hake trawl. Pipe smoke and voices rose leisurely in the fine still evening. The summer boarders were rowing in the sunset. This place was so remote, its life so engrossing, it was almost impossible to believe that anything else existed; that cities steamed and screamed and stunk in the heat.

Tom was the quietest that night. Miranda was herself as far as I could tell, sparring with Patrick, talking with everyone who was inclined to talk. We walked slowly home, and sat for a long time on the wall at the edge of the cliff to watch the moon rise out of the sea. The air was warm, with just enough breeze to keep the mosquitoes off, and the sound of the water breaking all around the arc of the great cove was a constant soft shushing. The color of the moonpath lightened from gold to white, and the surf flashed in sudden erratic bursts of light as if it were tumbling diamonds in its foam.

"It's after *eleven!*" Miranda said suddenly. "And nobody's even *thought* of Ian."

"Which he's probably finding very refreshing," Patrick said. "I'll look in on him while you get out some grub." We walked back across the lawn toward The Eyrie, and around the garden side. Tom said goodnight at the spot where the path branched off to the orchard. "No mug-up tonight," he said when Patrick protested. "I've had a long day."

"I keep forgetting you've been with Babbling Banty since noon. Your ears must need a rest."

Miranda conspicuously ignored this. "Goodnight, Tom," she said. "It was a wonderful sail."

"It was, wasn't it? ... Goodnight, Seafair. ... 'Night, Pat." He went down the path into the dappled pattern of light and shadow under the apple trees.

"See you at the dig tomorrow?" Patrick called after him.

"No, you won't," Miranda said. "Tom believes in remembering the Sabbath and keeping it holy."

"Don't mock him!" Patrick said angrily. "That sort of thing isn't funny, it simply marks you as a fool."

Miranda laughed at him and took my arm. "Come on, Seafair, let's have some devil's-food cake. You'd think Meg would make just angel-food nowadays, wouldn't you, in honor of Tom?"

Patrick followed us without speaking. He went up the back way to look in on Ian, and when he came down the quick flare of rage had been quenched along the way. "Sleeping like an innocent child," he said.

We ate cake and milk, cleaned up our dishes, and tiptoed up the back stairs into the Museum by the light of one candle. "I've never spent half enough time in here," I said guiltily. "I promise myself that starting tomorrow I'll really study things. That's a good Sunday project, isn't it? Do you suppose Elsie Dinsmore would approve?" There was a complete set of the Elsie books in the attic, and Miranda and I both despised the heroine.

"I don't know," said Miranda. "Any little idiot who sits at the piano until she faints because she refuses to play *Annie Laurie* on Sunday would probably call looking at fossils and arrowheads on the Sabbath licentious living."

"Speaking of licentiousness," said Patrick, "Ian was almost smiling in his sleep. He's probably dreaming of a woman. I think our Ian cuts loose in his dreams and lives a life of wild revelry."

"He could afford to go to London or Paris and kick up his heels," Miranda said.

"Drummond's isn't so bad." Patrick gave me that faunish glint I'd seen before. "Remember what I told you about hoof and horn."

"What's that all about?" demanded Miranda.

"He's trying to tell me that nymphs are racing through the island underbrush with the local satyrs after them."

"How lovely," said Miranda dreamily. "Like one of those painted baroque ceilings, except that our nymphs wear corsets and open drawers."

"And the satyrs wear fish scales instead of goatskins," said Patrick.

I whispered goodnight and went firmly into my room. Miranda and Patrick murmured something outside her door, began to laugh but throttled it, and then I heard her moving around, talking softly to Charlie between such audible yawns that she set me to yawning too. We swapped a few words when we met in the bathroom doorway, and separated for the night. I tried to read but I couldn't make sense of the words, so I blew out my lamp and lay gazing at the moonlit windows, lulled by the perfume of night-scented stocks from the garden below and the sound of crickets. Above, beyond, and below everything was the muted swash on the shore. What an absolutely perfect way to go to sleep, I thought, and went to sleep.

Something woke me, not all the way; I had gone too deep for that. But I sensed movement around the edge of my pillow and my lamp stand, and remembered as if from another decade that I'd taken a wrapped penny sweet from my pocket that day and laid it on the stand. A little girl at the harbor had given it to me on the store doorstep in the evening.

"Charlie, stop that and settle down," I said, trying not to wake myself completely. He climbed over my feet and began circling, then flopped. For a small dog, he made quite a flop, and jarred me wide awake. I wondered how long I'd been asleep. Far off the grandfather clock chimed a quarter-hour, but which one? I sat up and tried to see my watch by moonlight,

Quarter of one. I lay back and concentrated again on the fragrance, the crickets, and the musical murmurings of tide around the big cove. The day's scenes and faces and voices sparkled, changed color and key in my head. Patrick was in everything.

The next thing I knew I was at the bottom of a cliff, and someone was calling me from the top. *Seafair, Seafair!* I tried to tell them I was all right and would be up there as soon as I found the trail, but I could barely move my tongue or force sound from my sleep-drugged throat. Charlie was with me. I knew he was jumping off my bed even though I could see him ahead of me on the trail that climbed diagonally toward the top of the cliff.

Seafair, hurry!

I woke up in a light that was too dull and cold for moonlight. Dawn.

Patrick's voice. "Seafair, *wake up!*"

"I'm coming, I'm coming," I said thickly, got out of bed and bumped dizzily against my lamp stand, picked up my wrapper and struggled into it on the way to the door. When I opened it Patrick was holding something against his chest which to my fogged eyes appeared first as simply a white bundle. He said in a calm voice, "I was chopping kindling and I had an accident. I've cut my finger off."

The bundle was his left hand, wrapped up in towels. I was too stunned for a dramatic reaction. I said in the same expressionless manner, "Keep your hand up like that. Have you lost much blood?"

"I sprayed the shed and kitchen before I got to a towel, but I didn't hit an artery." He leaned against the doorframe. His color was bad even allowing for the bleak gray light, and he was sweating and beginning to shiver. I guided him into my room and made him sit down, and wrapped blankets around him.

"I'll get Ian," I said. "It's lucky the doctor's still on Bannock."

"I always time my accidents perfectly." His teeth were starting to chatter. "But Ian's sick. If he hurries he's likely to keel over." He had a hard time talking, it was as if he were too cold even to breathe. "Go to the harbor and get

somebody to take me across to Bannock in the *Toothpick*.
Either Anson is good with gasoline engines. So is Hugh." He
leaned back, exhausted. I swung his legs up onto the bed,
put more pillows behind him, and doubled one under his
left elbow to help hold his arm up.

"What about Tom?" I asked. "He's nearest."

"He may be a great preacher but he's no good with
engines. Don't rouse them up, Meg will come tearing over
here like a broody hen. Do as I tell you, Seafair," he said
with authority.

I put my sneakers on. I'd wear my mackintosh over my
nightdress and wrapper. "I'll call Miranda to fix hot water
bottles——"

"*No*. We don't need her in this. She can't stand blood."
He looked exasperated with himself and with me too. "It's
beginning to hurt. It was numb before. Hurry up."

"Don't move," I warned him. I went into the hall, and
Charlie nearly tripped me up getting out first. My own
teeth wanted to chatter now. I almost cried out as a dim
figure confronted me in the dusky hall. It was Ian in a
dressing gown. "What's going on? I heard Patrick calling
you."

"He was cutting kindling, and either the hatchet or his
hand slipped, and he cut off his left forefinger."

"Oh, good God," said Ian. "What in hell was he cutting
kindling for? And at this hour of the morning?" He brushed
past me into my room. I ignored Miranda's closed door as
I passed it. I knew how deeply she could sleep, and if the
sight of blood made her sick we were better off without her.
Downstairs Charlie was scratching at the front door and
barking. I ran down and let him out. The sun was up from
the sea, a scarlet globe suspended in a bank of fog. I went
out on the walk, grateful to Charlie for giving me the excuse, and took long reviving breaths of morning air. The first
sounds of the birds were comforting ordinary.

I had a vision of Charlie getting into the blood in the
kitchen and tracking it around, so I gave him some biscuits

from the tin kept in the dining room, and shut him in there. When I finally went upstairs by the back way, I met Ian coming through the Museum on his way down. He was dressed, and except for being pale he looked quite well.

"I'm going to Bannock for the doctor," he said. "I've got him into his own bed. Will you be all right?"

"Yes, of course. I'll make him drink something hot."

"Good girl." He went on downstairs.

"Seafair," Patrick called from his room. I went to the door. He was well covered, and his arm was raised on pillows. Against the white linen his tan had become an ugly yellowish gray, his eyes seemed to have lost their natural blue and were a curious no-color, as I had once fancied blind eyes to be. He was still shivering.

"Stay with me." He spoke with more difficulty than he'd shown earlier.

"In a few minutes. First I'm going to get a hot water bottle for you, and some tea to warm you up."

His grin was ghastly. "I couldn't clean up the blood, but I threw the finger into the stove so it wouldn't upset you."

"By gorry, that's great of you." I left him.

I ignored the trailing spatters and blotches of blood as much as I could. I lighted the three-burner kerosene stove with a minimum of difficulty, considering my shaky hands, and set the tea kettle over one burner and two saucepans of water over the others. To use the time until the water heated, and to warm myself up, I revived the banked fire in the range, being careful not to look for the finger. There was always plenty of kindling in a basket beside the woodbox, and why Patrick had chosen to cut some at that hour I couldn't imagine, unless he wanted to do something active and useful because he was awake so early and it was too dark to work in the grove.

When the fire was going nicely, dampers adjusted, and more water heating, I filled the hot water bottle from the first saucepan to get hot, wrapped it in a towel, and ran upstairs to put it at Patrick's feet. The bed shook with his tremors. Back in the kitchen I made tea in a small pot, set it on a tray with a sugar bowl and two cups and spoons, and returned to him. He couldn't hold a cup, and I put my arm around him and held the cup to his lips. His hair was wet and darkened with sweat. When he was ready to rest, I took a few swallows from my own cup; too big and too hasty, and they burned all the way down.

When he wouldn't drink any more but was shaking less, I said, "I want to get dressed before the doctor comes. All right?"

"Yes, but hurry back. I feel so damned awful. I know I'm not going to die, but I feel like it."

"I'll hurry."

Charlie's muffled barking reached a crescendo of rage or hysteria. I ran down to look at the fire, transferred all the vessels of water to one kettle on the big range, and turned out the kerosene burners. I gave Charlie more dog biscuits and left him crunching. I didn't want him up digging at Miranda's door. If we were lucky, she'd go on sleeping until the doctor had dressed Patrick's hand and was being given breakfast.

I dressed and did my hair and went back to Patrick's room. He was drowsing, and I warmed up my tea from the pot and sat there sipping it. His half-sleep was broken by erratic bouts of trembling. Bruises were beginning to darken on his forehead and left side of his face. The towel didn't seem any bloodier than before. Losing a finger was bad enough, but it shouldn't interfere with his work, and the loss was on the left hand. He could have cut off his hand, or mangled it beyond help, fainted, and bled to death before we ever knew.

The thought almost brought up my tea.

Was it just me that he wanted with him, or would he have begged anyone to stay? No, he certainly didn't want Miranda, he always said she talked too much, and there was this business about hating blood ... While we were alone now I could imagine that I was the only person who could help him at this particular time. He had come to *me;* I had been his first thought.

He stirred, and moaned as if in deep grief or utter desolation. I spoke to him and he looked at me without recognition. Then I spoke again, and saw his eyes clear. Without answering, he dropped off again. Sunlight grew in the room. I looked around at the work table at a window, the shelves of books, a scattering of photographs and drawings. Over the fireplace there was a framed painting representing the landing of Norsemen on a wild coast. Below it on the mantel stood a beautifully rigged sailboat, and a company of kilted iron soldiers.

Charlie was quiet downstairs. Only the clock broke the silence, and Patrick's sleep now seemed very deep. With the hot tea and the chance to rest, I sank into a sort of waking dream, so that when Ian and a short bearded man appeared in the doorway I was like one waked roughly from sleep.

"I'm sorry we startled you, Seafair," Ian said softly. He had more color in his face now. He was carrying a basin of steaming water. "This is Dr. Porter. Miss Bell."

The doctor nodded brusquely when I told him about the tea and the hot water bottles. "Very good. Excellent. We won't need you now, however."

"No, I can help out on this part," Ian said, setting the basin down on the work table. "Maybe you'd get breakfast for us, afterward?"

"Yes, certainly." I went out feeling dismissed, though to be truthful I wasn't quite sure how well I'd do when confronted with the place where the finger had been lopped off.

But I could clean up the blood in the kitchen. In the light of full morning I saw a great deal more than I had before. When he came in from the shed he must have swung his hand around somehow because the drops were sprayed far and wide. The table hadn't escaped a shower, and it was on the counter beside the sink and splattered on some of the cupboard doors. I could trace his frantic race for a towel.

Out in the shed there was blood on the chopping block, the dropped hatchet, and spots on the dry pine kindling. Well, that could wait, but not the kitchen. I went to work with cleaning rags, strong soap, and an abrasive cleaner where the stains were most persistent on the white wood.

All this while Charlie was scratching and whining on the dining room side of the butler's pantry. When I had done what I could, I let him into the kitchen. He took a long splashy drink to prove that he'd been really in distress, and then went smelling around the kitchen.

I ground the beans for coffee, and as usual the aroma was restorative. I put a fresh cloth on the table and set it, got out the big iron skillet, and began cracking eggs into a bowl. Charlie went to the screen door into the shed, but I wouldn't let him go out there. Suddenly he drew back from the screen, ears flattened, and crawled under the stove.

he doctor ate a hearty breakfast and complimented me on the scrambled eggs. Ian ate a small bowl of oatmeal and refused coffee afterward. He sat tapping his fingers on the table and gazing at nothing, while Dr. Porter told me with what I considered a gruesome enthusiasm how he had treated the injury.

"Simple kind of thing. Happens all the time. Lot cleaner and healthier than blowing a finger off with a giant salute." He buttered more toast. "Nothing better than home-churned butter. . . . I just sewed it up with black silk sutures, not that there was much to get hold of to run a puckering string through. I've got it bandaged loosely to keep it clean, but it must have the air to it. There's to be *no salve* on it." He pointed his knife at me. "Don't let anyone come up with his great-grandmother's remedy for everything from cancer to the rum horrors. Reason my patients don't develop gangrene every time they slice something off is I don't seal the thing up away from the air."

I looked with distaste at my coffee. Ian said severely, "Good Lord, that won't give you any strength." He cut a thick slice from the fresh loaf, took a lid off the stove, and toasted the bread on a fork over the flames. I started to protest that I couldn't eat it, but there was something about him that kept my mouth shut. When the bread was golden, he slathered it with butter and put the plate before me as if delivering an ultimatum.

"Thank you," I said meekly. The toast was good, and I began to feel better at once. Even the coffee improved. The men talked in unhurried voices, and Charlie lay under the table with his chin on my foot. The Ansonia clock struck half-past seven; I had to look twice at it because the wakening had been so long ago it felt like noontime now.

"Jenkins tells me Andrew's run onto some millionaire who wants a granite palace," the doctor said.

"Yes, they're talking it over with the architect next week."

"Jenkins is a capable man to leave in charge," the doctor said. "I don't know whether it's because he's not married, or because he *is*, to the business."

"He'd like to be married to flesh and blood," said Ian.

"Ah, the Dolan girl. Rather him than me!"

"He'd be good for the boys."

"That's not what she's looking for," said the doctor dryly. "She dreamt she dwelt in marble halls," he half-sang in a humorous, creaky voice, and winked at me. "They tell me that she's been muttering about the gentry treading on the faces of the poor peasantry. I didn't know she considered herself a peasant."

"For the purposes of drama she does," said Ian, "all the while knowing that the blood of queens flows in her veins."

"Well, she does look royal," I said. "At least what I used to think of as royal when I was younger."

"She's certainly a handsome young woman," the doctor agreed.

"Maybe she's not wrong," I said, "to believe there's something else beyond Bannock and marrying a quarryman who may die as her father did."

Both men looked at me, the doctor with indulgent amusement and Ian with surprise lightening the tired planes of his face. "You say that with great feeling," he said.

"Because I'm sorry for her," I said. "And I can feel a little bit of what she must feel, even though I can make my own living and I'm not handicapped by beauty. She thinks she was meant for something wonderful in life, and she can't accept anything else any more than she could put a rope around her neck and hang herself."

"Which sometimes happens," the doctor said, "to these haunted beauties when they're fifty."

When they left to go back to Bannock, Ian told me not to touch the shed. "I'll clean up out there."

Upstairs Patrick's door stood open, and I looked in. The shades were drawn against the glare of day, so the room was filled with a sort of twilight. Patrick's face was turned away from me, and he was sleeping. The bandaged hand lay on his breast, the arm held up by a sling. There was a strong faint antiseptic scent, and Charlie sniffed suspiciously.

While I was making my bed he went to the door between my room and Miranda's, nosed it open, and went into her room. He had ways of getting people up and I listened for their results, while planning how to tell her about the accident.

First, I want to tell you that Patrick's all right. Last two words heavily emphasized.

Such is the perversity of human nature that this opening is almost guaranteed to convince the listener that somebody isn't all right at all, is in fact on his way to the undertaker. My father tried it on Phoebe when Julian fell off the carriage house roof and broke his leg, and it sent her into hysterics. He now found it expedient to simply announce that Brooks had stepped on a rusty nail or Edith had gone head first down the cellar stairs.

So I'd tell her the way Patrick had told me, and the way I'd told Ian. But first, I would stand in front of the door so she couldn't dash across the hall and wake Patrick up to see if he was all right.

It then dawned on me that Charlie was back underfoot, and I hadn't heard any of what Miranda called "scrummaging," a game in which he tried to dig her out of the bedclothes and she resisted.

I opened wide the door. She wasn't in the room. Her nightdress hung from one of the pineapple-topped bedposts, the covers were thrown back in their usual upheaval.

"Now when did she accomplish *that?*" I whispered. She'd have had to get up and go out sometime in between the other comings and goings, so that she didn't know what was going on. Perhaps she'd been up ahead of any of us. At *dawn?* She wasn't usually that early a riser, unless she was going to haul with Patrick. But this time could be a whim, and she'd come home presently, starved, shoes soaked, and either very exhilarated about where she'd been, or very silent.

The Eyrie had the ensheathed stillness that had affected me so unpleasantly on my first day. But then I had been an alien, an immigrant kindly allowed in but knowing she could never become a citizen. Two months later I was treated as one of the household by Ian and as a necessity by Patrick.

When I had finished the dishes, neither Ian nor Miranda had come. I knew that to chug across the three miles to Bannock and back in the *Toothpick* would take quite a while, but whatever Miranda was doing should be limited by the approach of churchtime.

I returned to Patrick's room. He was awake and watching the door. "Hello!" he said strongly. "I'm glad to see you. I thought everybody else was dead, or I was."

"Ian's not back yet and neither is Miranda. I wonder what she's doing."

"Come and sit down," he said. "Put up the shades first." When I did, the windows were filled with the blues of sea and sky.

"Would you like something to eat?" I asked.

He shook his head. "No. Sit down, Seafair. Please. I have to tell you something."

I'd thought I was calm by now, but the way he spoke caused my stomach to curvet into a wild and independent life of its own. I didn't know what he wanted to tell me, I only knew I didn't want to hear it. "Do you suppose she's gone rowing or fishing all by herself?" I asked, nervously vivacious. "I should go down and see if the dory's gone. Of course it's almost flat calm, she shouldn't be in any trouble——"

"*Sit down*, Seafair," he said. He sounded like Ian. He seemed to have added ten years to his age since early this morning.

I sat.

"Miranda's gone," he said. "She and Tom."

"What do you mean—gone? Gone out fishing? Out for a morning sail?"

"Gone for good," he said. "Or at least for as long as it suits them. It's a long way to California. It might as well be China."

I thought that he was delirious, or that whatever the doctor had given him for pain had caused wild dreams. With relief I sat back in my chair and said, "Tell me the rest of it."

"You're humoring me," he said quietly, "but I swear to you it's the truth. Why do you suppose I could make such a damn' fool slip with the hatchet? I was so mad I could hardly see straight. That's why I was cutting kindling—trying to keep occupied till I could decently wake Ian, sick as he's been." The corners of his mouth turned down. "Got him up all right, didn't I? What an awakening! And for you too." His voice softened, and he reached his good hand toward me. I took the fingers in mine.

"Start at the beginning," I said.

"It wasn't Dill." It was as if he didn't trust himself to raise his voice. "They were just using him. She gave that up when she thought I might tangle with him and find out the truth. No, it was Tom all along and I never guessed."

"It was Tom *what?*" I was desperately trying to sort it out.

"In love." He got the words out with obvious difficulty, he stirred his legs under the covers as if they oppressed him, and turned his face away from me toward the wall. "Talk about incest! But maybe she didn't see him as a brother just because I did. That's why she had to get home this summer, come hell or high water. To see *him*." He turned back to me.

"She used you, Seafair. She used you just as she did Dill. She used him, and you, and Tom never had a chance."

"But I thought," I began in my astonishment, and he raised himself up, looking hard into my face.

"You thought what?"

"I don't know!" I cried to cover my confusion and embarrassment. It was a much worse moment than that in which he'd waked me a few hours ago. "I just can't believe it, that's all," I protested. "I never saw anything—she never gave me a hint!"

"Look, I don't think this elopement has been planned for a long time," he said. "I think it happened all at once. You've heard her moaning about Tom going into the ministry, as if he was becoming a monk and renouncing the world. If Tom did want to hold off marriage till he was out of the seminary, she could scythe that idea down like someone lopping off a daisy. The way I lopped off my finger." He winced and looked down at the bandaged hand. "And if she could get him out of the ministry altogether, she would . . . and she has."

His voice went hoarse, and I got him a drink of water.

"While they were sailing yesterday they must have been talking things over, and they went up alongside one of those mackerel seiners that was going to the main last night, and made arrangements to go in with them. Somewhere to the west'ard, dammit, I can't remember where, Tenant's Harbor, Herring Gut, Friendship—" He shrugged impatiently and winced again. "You see, I walked in on this. I thought everybody was in bed. I'd been reading for an hour or so and couldn't drop off, it was the damned moonlight again, so I dressed and went downstairs to go out. I thought everybody was in bed. There they were in the kitchen."

His eyes gazed past me at the memory, and I almost turned around to look myself. "They were at the table, getting ready to write their notes, hers for us, his for his parents, to be left propped up against the sugar bowl in the best traditions of melodrama. Miranda looked at me with eyes like blue glass in a doll's head, and never said a word. It was Tom who talked. Said there was no way to come out in the open with it without upsetting everyone, but once it was an accomplished fact it would be easier to accept. They were going in on the *Lorna Doone*—she was leaving about two—and they'd take the train from Rockland to New York, and then leave for California. His seminary funds would pay the way and look after them, and once there he could teach. They need teachers out there. His heart wasn't really in the ministry anyway, he said, it was more to please his parents, but the time comes when you have to choose your own way."

"But somehow it makes Tom sound so cold-blooded," I said. "He couldn't have been acting in the pulpit that day—could he?" I heard the appeal in my voice. Patrick's mouth pulled up on one corner.

"They've been acting all summer, the pair of them."

"But I never took him for a coward." I remembered his telling Miranda she'd have to be honest, or he would take over. It hadn't meant what I'd taken it for. "How could he *not* face his parents? How could he insult them like this? *Tom?*"

"This garbage some call love makes fools and cowards out of the best of us," he said savagely. "If Miranda'd done as she should have this year, Tom would be doing as *he* should. Because he really wants the ministry; I don't believe he was acting that Sunday, no. But she's turned his wits, trying to get him away from God. Can you see them staying together? Oh yes, they'll *have* to stay together, they'll be babes in the woods out there, but she'll destroy him, and he'll end up as nothing. She'll destroy herself at the same time. My poor foolish self-centered Banty." His laughter took on an odd note, as if tears had thickened his throat. "Last night the process of destruction began before my eyes."

"You—you must have argued with them," I said. "You didn't just stand back and let them go, did you?"

"Where do you think I got these?" He touched the bruises on his jaw and forehead. "Ian asked me, but I pretended not to hear. Right then I couldn't be sure it had happened at all. Shock, I guess. But I know now. I tried to get in their way to keep them from going out, and Tom knocked me down. Yes, *Tom!* I hit a corner of the table and went unconscious. When I came to, they were gone. They hadn't stopped to write their notes—why bother, with me around to give the news?" he said ironically. "It was after three. I went to the harbor and the *Lorna Doone* was gone. Well, Ian was sick and I thought at daylight we'd decide what to do. The Sunday train doesn't leave Rockland till late in the day, so we'd have us plenty of time to get there."

He shut his eyes. His breathing was slack.

"All right," I said, "you've told me. Now save your strength. This isn't the end of the world, Patrick, no matter what anybody else does. Just be thankful you didn't slash an artery."

"Then poor Tom really would have blood on his conscience, wouldn't he? But it's the end of the world for Meg and Dougal. When I think of telling them I wish I *had* slashed an artery."

"Meg loves Miranda." I tried for what sparse comfort there was.

"The same way she loves me, with all my shortcomings and whims and weaknesses. Yes, she loves Miranda, her banty chick. But as a wife for Tom? Crumpling him up and playing him like a hand puppet? Wrecking his life two years away from ordination, after all their hard work and his? Oh, God, Seafair," he said in anguish. "I can't make them wait for him to write. They'll be missing him by now. I've got to tell them, and I don't know how."

"I'll tell them," Ian said behind me. I jumped. Patrick said with a dim humor, "Have you learned to materialize between Bannock and here?"

"I stood out in the hall until the end of the story," Ian said. "I wanted to hear it all without breaking in on the account." He came into the room, coldly self-possessed. "I'll tell Meg and Dougal and then I'll go to the mainland. I should be able to stop them in Rockland."

"And put Miranda in a convent?" Patrick asked. "Teach Tom his duty?"

"Tom knows his duty. He's got to face his parents now or he'll never be able to face them later. I'd be proud to have Miranda marry Tom. But she's too young to marry anybody right now. They've got to be sure, and it must be done right."

"They sounded very sure last night," said Patrick. "They'd had all summer to make sure. All those times when nobody knew where Miranda was."

Ian glanced at me, and I flushed with indignation. "Believe me, I had absolutely no idea about this."

"I didn't say that you had," Ian said gently. "Patrick, you rest. I'll take care of this."

"What's happened?" We heard Meg in the hall, breathless with hurrying upstairs. She came into the room and stared at Patrick with color leaving her face except for red blotches on her cheeks like the marks of slaps. "What have you done to yourself?"

Patrick grinned at her. "I'm a gorm, Meg, that's all. I thought I'd cut you some nice fine fancy kindling, and I gashed my finger."

"You look like death," she said grimly.

"I feel like death, but I've been assured I'll live."

Ian put his hand on her arm. "I went to Bannock for the doctor, Meg, and took him back again."

"And *you*," she scolded. "After what you went through yesterday! You'd better get to bed yourself! Now where's Tom? His bed's not been slept in, and I thought he stayed here last night to go out sailing early with Patrick. But he must have gone with Miranda instead, as if they didn't get enough of it yesterday."

Patrick turned his face away. Ian said, "Come on down to the kitchen, Meg, you must be ready for a cup of tea."

"What about Patrick?" She was militant.

"He needs his rest, that's all. You can come up later and fuss over him all you want. Come on down and make a pot of tea for the two of us." He eased her away from the foot of the bed. I started to follow, and without opening his eyes Patrick murmured, "Stay with me, Seafair."

Ian looked back at me and nodded. I sat down again. "I'll take along these clothes," Meg said. "What a mess! It gave me a turn," she was saying as they went into the Museum, "to see Tom's bed like that. I thought, supposing they were climbing around the rocks in the moonlight, you know how they do, and fell, and we slept all night, never dreaming . . . You have seen them this morning, haven't you, Ian?"

And Ian's voice, deep and calm, "No, but Patrick has."

Patrick sighed and whispered, "Oh Christ."

$\mathcal{S}$tanding in Miranda's room, I heard the church bell begin to ring. Ian and Dougal should be leaving the harbor by now. I wondered what Ian would have said to the inveterate standers-around-the-shore; something simple and brief, I imagined, that would imply a business trip without actually saying so.

Miranda's toilet articles were gone from her dresser, and I didn't look to see what else she had taken. Patrick said they hadn't much luggage, just a small bag apiece; they hadn't wanted to make any obvious preparations. Charlie followed Miranda's passage around the room as if at the heels of a spectral presence. When I heard him whining softly I picked him up, hugging him and blowing in his neck until he began happily squirming and trying to lick my face. I carried him into my own room.

Tonight they would be back, or tomorrow morning, and nothing would ever be the same again. This might be the row that Miranda and Patrick could never make up; he was far too bitter about her deceit, and I suspected that his genuine respect and admiration for Tom had taken a bashing. As for Meg and Dougal, there must always be a wound; he'd been willing to sneak off in the night, he'd never wanted to go into the ministry but had only done it to please them.

But maybe Ian had omitted that. The more I thought about it, and him, the more I became convinced that he wouldn't have told them.

I went across the hall and looked at Patrick. He was sleeping deeply now, with the information passed on and somebody else taking charge. I went downstairs without my usual salutation to the Old Colonel. The quality of the house's silence had changed again, because Miranda was not simply out in the woods, on the shore, or sailing. She was gone. It didn't matter if she were fetched back; the intent was there, almost the same as the deed.

Grateful for Charlie's busy company I went out into the garden and began cutting dead stuff out of the beds. I could understand the force which dominated Miranda. What I could not understand was how she could have gone for good without a word to me, even if it hadn't come until the last minute; a waking and a whispering when she was ready to go.

I stood by the sundial listening to the wind and the surf beyond the garden walls and watching the clouds blowing from south to north, and saw one of the eagles tracing his great circle against them. In a way my angry hurt was assuaged by the sight.

The next time I went upstairs Patrick was in his dressing gown, and sitting in a chair by the window. He had combed his hair and looked a little more natural, though his eyes were shadowed.

"I was going to surprise you in the garden," he said, "but at the head of the stairs I felt as if I were teetering at the top of a glass mountain, so I retreated. Can you bring us up something to eat?"

We ate at his work table by the window with a view up the bay toward the north and east. Neither of us mentioned Tom and Miranda. Patrick talked entertainingly about the recent discovery of some cave paintings in Spain, thousands of years old, and we discussed what it would be like to find something like that on the North American continent. After we ate he wanted to get out and stretch his legs. He felt less weak than before, so we made a cautious progress down the stairs and went out the front door into the rough southwest wind. When we had pushed out to the edge of the cliff, spray flew up to our faces. Patrick put his right arm through my left, and clasped my hand, palm to palm and fingers laced.

"Isn't this wonderful?" he shouted at me over the roar

from below. The wind blew his hair back from his forehead and slapped color into his face. "Tell me it's wonderful!"

"It's wonderful!" I shouted back, and he laughed, and tightened his fingers.

"You're supposed to keep quiet," I reminded him after a while. "You don't want to start it bleeding again."

"No, I don't," he said. "I'm not staying away from the dig one hour longer than I have to. I know there's something there, Seafair. I know it just as surely as I know the sun will rise tomorrow."

We went back to the house and he decided to work at the garden table if I would get his materials for him. I did, and prepared to read, but he asked me to play instead. "Even if you just do scales. It sounds like life."

It was his only reference, oblique as it was, to what had happened.

I didn't do scales, but went to work on Bach again. Whenever I stopped to rest I would swing around on the stool and see him out there in the arbor at the end of the grassy path beyond the sundial, writing steadily from one line to the next, totally lost, or rather totally oriented, in what he was doing. Then I would swing back to the keyboard and find myself. There was a curious detached beauty about that afternoon, all the more so because I knew that such an afternoon would never happen again. It was a hiatus between what had been and what was to be.

We knew by late afternoon that it would be too rough for *Kingfisher* to come back tonight. Meg came across from the farm at sundown to sleep at The Eyrie. The proprieties must be observed, no matter what. The Gillis father and son had done the milking, and the last of the harbor children had gone with their milk cans.

"I've sent word to Erline not to come tomorrow because you're all down with the epizootic," she said. "And they think Ian took Dougal in because that wisdom tooth was half killing him. I'll find it hard to forgive these two for all the lies we've had to tell."

She never met my eyes, and suddenly it hit me—really struck hard—that she believed I'd known all about the plans from the first. She bustled around, telling Patrick he should be in bed and making me feel as if I'd kept him up; he shrugged and went, not only to indulge her but because he had gotten very pale and tired all at once. She took up a hot drink to him after he was in bed.

While she was upstairs, I lighted the fire in the library. I was determined to tell her that I hadn't known anything of what was going on, hoping it would remove the strain while we waited for the return. Perhaps we could talk freely, and feel better for it. I had a pretty picture of our sipping tea by the fire, but she didn't give me a chance even to suggest it. She came into the kitchen when I was putting the kettle on and said, "I'm fair scunnered. I'm going to bed."

She went upstairs to Miranda's room and Hero went with her. That left me with Charlie in a house in which three human beings were locked hopelessly apart from one another, not by walls but by their thoughts. I sat stubbornly using up the library fire, my feet on the fender, Charlie on the leather sofa with me, and tried to read *Bleak House* as a hedge against apprehension.

But even Dickens was no help tonight. I put the fire screen in place and blew out the lamp, and took Charlie through the parlor and out into the garden. He made the most of it while I watched the moon disappear and reappear through the whipped and ragged clouds. I'd seen such skies in illustrations of tales of horror, and in a superstitious regression to childhood I shuddered at the thought of wandering alone in the open under such an ominous ceiling, like one of those heroines lost on a moor crowded with ghosts or quicksands or both.

In bed I realized how physically exhausted I was, and three pages of *Bleak House* did their work. I stirred enough to blow out my lamp, and fell asleep until Patrick roused the rest of us by shouting. Hero's deep bark so close bewildered me at first, and Charlie's yips went off like a string of firecrackers. I was out of bed before I was fully conscious, while Patrick kept shouting unintelligible words of fear or warning. The house is on fire! I thought. I got out into the hall, almost falling flat over Charlie, and bumped into the solid bulk of the Newfoundland in the dark. There were no flames coming up the stairs, no smell of smoke. Patrick's hoarse, strained cries went on.

I ran around the gallery but Meg was already there beside his bed, talking as if he were six or even younger. The shouting stopped.

"There, there. Everything's all right. You had a dream, that's all. No call to raise a ruction." She lit a candle, and I backed off from the door and out of reach of its small glow. She looked twice her natural bulk in the full nightdress and thus hid him from me, but I could see the restless twisting of his legs under the covers, and sometimes an outflung arm, including the one with the bandaged hand, pulled out of its sling. I could hear his hard breathing.

"Let me get that hand back where it belongs," she said. He muttered something about Miranda, and she said in a strong, jovial voice, "She'll be back tomorrow, mad as a wet hen. Her and Tom both. I'll have something to say to that young man, if his father hasn't already put a flea in his ear." She laughed, a comfortable sound. "And he likely has. Now go back to sleep. . . . Just think of Dougal trying to help Ian sail. Reg'lar cow-yard tar, that one is. I'll bet he was feather-white by the time they got there, don't you?"

I was back in my own room before she turned to leave his. Charlie was already curled up in my place. I was shivering, and not just because the house had an autumnal chill. The dog's little body felt so warm that I simply moved him over enough to give me my place back, and pulled the covers up over us both. I went over and over the scene in which Patrick told me about the elopement.

This was now so vivid to me it was as if I'd seen it myself, their faces stricken, guilty, then defiant in the lamplit kitchen, the struggle, Patrick's fall, and the other two hurrying away on the twin white tracks of the road. I knew how the church was whitely glistening, the houses washed in light. The wharves would look snow-covered; it was a village entranced, held forever in a silver sleep, with only these two alive in it. No, these two and their rushing black shadows. It made four to go down the ladder to a skiff, and the oars stirring whirlpools of dead light, out to the black schooner at the mouth of the harbor. The scene was locked into an atmosphere so nightmarish, so macabre, that in my overtired brain the imagined fishermen helping them aboard had bare skulls for heads, and when they raised the sails the canvas was black.

It was hideous; it was also hysterical. I identified my fantasy as derived from another of those old woodcuts or engravings like the one with the girl on the haunted moor. So I began practicing Bach on an imaginary piano, choosing a magnificent Steinway, and since my music was entirely on a spiritual plane I could play as well as I chose. Naturally I played magnificently, to suit the piano; and so I put myself to sleep.

eg went back to the farm before I got up. At least I was to be trusted with serving breakfast to Patrick. While I was setting a tray he appeared in the kitchen, dressed. He had managed everything but tying his shoes, and I did that for him. He patted me on the head and said, "Thou'rt a good lass. I'll speak to Squire about thee."

"Thankee kindly, young Master," I said, bobbing several curtsies in a row. "Happen he'll let you buy out my indenture."

"I thought all the time those were your own teeth." Our laughter was all out of proportion to this juvenile wit. Then he sat down in his place like a hungry man.

"They've been successful," he announced. "We'll hear good news today, I'm sure of it. Maybe I'm psychic after all." He looked rather smug about it. "The instant I remembered what's happened, I knew they'd be back today, with Miranda good and mad." He chuckled. "Mad as a wet hen."

Meg's words. He didn't remember his nightmare, only her reassurance.

"Well, I hope you're right," I said, "and you probably are." I began to eat my own porridge.

"I know I am! They'd have to hire a rig to get from Tenant's Harbor or wherever it was, and they might have hung around there half the day, getting to Rockland just in time to take the train. But they'd still have to go to the station." He stopped eating and looked thoughtfully at me. "They were pretty stupid to have told it, don't you think? But Tom was rattled and Miranda's a rattle to begin with." He started to eat again.

"How's your hand?" I asked.

"Throbs if I move it around too much, but not when I'm still. I don't think it's infected." He looked at his bandaged hand with a whimsical curiosity. "The damnedest thing, I could swear my finger's there. I keep trying to wiggle it, and crook it, and I can feel it obeying me. You don't suppose it can haunt me, do you? You did decently cremate it, didn't you?"

I pushed my plate away. "I didn't look closely into the stove yesterday, when I built the fire."

"Poor Seafair, I've ruined her breakfast. I'm sorry, love. It's just that I feel so good this morning, after yesterday. Forgive me?"

I looked into his eyes, accepted his humorous entreaty at face value, and said boldly, "If you feel good, I feel good."

He cupped my chin and cheek in his hand and said with the greatest tenderness, "What would I do without you now?"

"That's a good question," I said. "Who'd tie your shoes?" I realized that I was quite wildly happy.

"Let's go down to the Home Cove and wait for them," he proposed when we'd finished eating. "Ian'll come in there so nobody at the harbor will know those two have been gone. We'll whistle and cheer like mad for the return of Lord Ullin's Daughter, and give them bouquets of bracken and goldenrod."

"Let's not," I said. "It'll be awful enough for them."

He pinned my hand down with his and said as if surprised, "Are you *sorry* for them, Seafair?"

"Yes. Not because they're being stopped. But if they thought it over after they left the island, and decided it was wrong, and came back of their own free will, with dignity, then it would have saved face all around. But to be fetched back against their will, like bad children by the truant officer—I don't want to watch *that!*" I said with revulsion.

"How do you know they're being dragged back like captives or truants? Maybe while they hung around for a yearlong day in a Sunday-killed town, waiting for train time, they came to their senses. Though from the looks of them that night they're so far separated from their senses they'll never find them again," he said disgustedly. "The fact is, they *are* bad children. Unfortunately they're too big to spank, so they'll have to suffer embarrassment instead. Tom will have one kind to endure, and Miranda's just lucky that Ian doesn't believe in keeping her under lock and key. That's what I'd do."

"I can't decide whether you sound like a prig or Savonarola," I said.

He burst out laughing. "What scorching eyes you have, Grandma! 'All the better to burn you to a crisp with, my dear,' " he quavered. "Well, I'm seared, my love, but only slightly, and I intend to get something out of this homecoming, even if it's only a chance to make it memorable for them."

"But they're coming back to eat crow! Isn't that punishment enough? Can't you be generous?"

He tipped back in his chair and kept on laughing. There was a kind of harsh luminosity about him that both angered and alarmed me. He almost hurt my eyes. "My dear girl, I only want to thank them for this"— he touched the flamboyantly discoloring bruises—"and this." He moved the arm in the black silk sling.

Now I could see his mood as a natural result of the emotional and physical disasters that had befallen him. I said more easily, "If you can't act as if nothing's happened, I don't blame you. But rage or even refusing to speak to them would be a lot more honest than ridicule. And they deserve anger. After all, you took a great deal from them."

"Yes, I took everything." He was so quiet that he was almost inaudible. "And I wish to God I'd slept through the whole night and never caught them. But I didn't sleep, and I did catch them." He put his hand to his face again. "So everyone must suffer the consequences. There's no escape from the immutable law."

"I hope you mean a general law, not one enacted *for* or *by* you personally."

"Because otherwise it makes me a monster of self-centeredness?" He swung high a rigidly extended arm, a clenched fist. "Like this, an egomaniac?" He lowered the arm. "But each of us is the center of a separate universe, you must know by now. Admit that you've been thinking, Oh, dear, why did all this have to happen to spoil things for *me?* And—How could Miranda keep such a secret from *me?* And—Now I suppose I ought to leave, because who wants a stranger around in a family crisis?"

Considering humiliation as fire, I was being roasted at the stake. Rescued only by a good healthy cold splash of righteous indignation. "Now that you've given me such a subtle hint, I guess I'll go pack. I can leave on the mailboat this morning."

I started to get up, and he seized my wrist in a punishing grip. "Don't be such a little jackass! Or should I say a jenny?" That hard light was all about him again, and he seemed to be watching for me to wince at the pain. I would not; but I was wild behind my stolidity, not with pain but with a sense of helpless degradation. No one had ever hurt me like this before, smiling, and I loathed him and myself for it. A half-hour ago I'd been wild in another way, with sycophantic rapture because he'd patted my cheek and said he needed me.

Charlie growled uneasily, crawled out from under the stove, and pawed at me. Patrick loosened his grip and lifted my wrist and kissed it. The familiar teasing and affectionate expression began around his eyes. "I'm sorry as hell, Seafair. Don't go. We'll all need you."

His mouth against my skin; astonishing. I could feel nothing but the returning circulation but I was still amazed. In an odd way it was more intimate than the kiss had been.

"After all, Miranda and I have to have somebody to talk

through. The fact is, we may never speak directly to each other again."

"For about twenty-four hours," I scoffed. Danger had gone from the room, if it had ever been there. Maybe danger wasn't the word, but something— "You two couldn't stand it that long."

"Don't be so sure, Miss. You don't know a thing about it. We may have to keep you as a permanent buffer state around here."

"And when we're all tottering with age, people will refer to me as the Old Buffer."

He groaned. We were safe again, almost as before. I cleaned up the dishes, and he went upstairs for his journal. We went out to the Liberty Knoll and put the flag up; then Patrick, wearing the wide-awake for shade, sat with his back against a boulder and wrote. I played with Charlie, throwing his tennis ball for him or running with it so he'd chase me, which he liked better. I was anxious to get the return over with, and kept going past the eastern corner of the house so I could look down toward the place where the path came out of the woods.

The mail boat whistled in the harbor. I went back to Patrick, tired of the game with Charlie, tired of anticipating. If I turned my back, they would come.

"I should go over to get the mail."

"Don't." He didn't look up, though the pen stopped. "I like to have you here. Besides, they think we're all down with the distemper, remember?"

"I could have recovered first." I stood up by the flagpole and watched the sky for the eagles, but I saw only the family of ravens who inhabited the Old Quarry woods.

"Sister Ann, Sister Ann, what do you see?" Patrick asked.

"I see a cloud of dust upon the road," I began, and stopped. I did see a flicker of motion where the harbor road came into the open. "Someone's really coming, Pat. Maybe they're bringing a message."

He got up to look. "Is it a kid?" We both stared at the distant figure moving like a mirage through the mid-morning glare and the heat ripples rising from the ground.

"It's Dougal," Patrick said in a dead tone. "Now what?" As if mesmerized we watched the tall, thin shadow stop at the farm gate; we heard Hero's booming welcome, and at our feet Charlie yipped eagerly.

Still gazing at the now-empty road Patrick slid the journal into his jacket pocket. "Come over to the farm with me, Seafair."

"I'll walk to the gate with you but no farther." He started to protest, but I shook my head. "Whatever it is, they'll feel better talking to you alone. You're family and I'm not."

He took my hand. "I want you with me, can't you see?"

And I wanted to be with him. But I couldn't forget how Meg's eyes had avoided mine. To walk into her home without invitation would have been an intolerable impertinence on my part.

Patrick looked almost forlorn when I left him at the gate, but he made no more protests. I went back to The Eyrie, taking Charlie. I argued with myself that Dougal's return alone could have a perfectly normal and reasonable explanation. But I was shaky with suspense. I went into the parlor and tried the piano as diversion and sedative. It wasn't very successful, there was too much interference. Incontrollable thoughts invaded my head like a runaway team racing down a village street and scattering everything and everyone. The disturbing conversation with Patrick at the table this morning could kick Bach away as if he were no more than a crumpled page of newspaper blown into the roadway.

Obstinately I stayed at the piano, irritated beyond common sense at my mistakes and in consequence making more. I thought Patrick would never come. And when he did come, how would he be? No one in my life so far had ever made me feel so inadequate; to keep going at all with him, to try to be prepared for what came next, to have an answer for anything he might say, was like walking the railway trestle outside Fern Grove and wondering if you felt the vibration of an approaching express that you hadn't known about. But if you had a head for heights there was something exhilarating and irresistible about walking that trestle.

He was back. He stood by the piano, looking at me as if I were responsible for everything. "You should have gone in with me, to take the curse off it. Dougal's a walking woe."

If I answered quietly it was because I couldn't do otherwise. "What's happened?"

"Why did they have to have only *one?*" he demanded. "So it's as if Jesus himself has turned his back on them? Seafair, did you ever see someone so ground down and crushed with despair that the only way you can stand the sight is to despise them? Almost *hate* them?"

"Will you tell me *what happened?*"

"Of course they never showed up at the railroad station! They never intended to, and we were the fools to have swallowed it. And of course the seiner never put in at Tenant's Harbor or Friendship or Herring Gut. Ian called the buyers there."

"You look awful," I said. "Come and sit down." He obeyed, still talking.

"He had the station master telegraph the other stations along the line between Rockland and Portland, in case they were waiting at some other point, but they weren't. Then he began calling fish buyers east of Rockland, but that was a damn faint hope, because they could have left the *Lorna Doone* somewhere in the bay for a smack heading for Boston."

"Has Ian gone to Boston?"

"No, because he'd still be too far behind to catch up with them. He called Andrew and got him to wire his so-called useful friend in Boston, to hire private inquiry men to watch the terminals in Boston, New York, and Chicago. The theory is that once Ian knows where they are, he can have them detained until he gets there, because he's Miranda's guardian, and so forth. I hope to God this politician does better than he's done in locating Rosaleen's shady relatives," Patrick said, "but I doubt it. I have this rotten, roiling sensation that tells me the next word will be from California. *If* they bother to write."

"How do we know they're going to California?" I asked. "That could have been misdirection too."

"Why don't you come right out and call it lying?" he asked brutally.

"All right!" I said. "Lying, then. Why spell out California? They can be followed there too, you know. It's not the days of the wagon trains and Indian attacks. They have Pinkerton men and police there, too. They could lose themselves right here in Maine, on the principle of *The Purloined Letter*."

"You could be right," Patrick said. He sounded almost dazed. "I never thought of that. Then what in God's name do we do to stop them?"

I shrugged. He got up and walked over to the open garden door. "I always knew Miranda could lie like Ananias, but I never knew it about Tom. How can you grow up with somebody like a twin, and never really know them?"

"Miranda said you and she were the twins. In spirit, anyway."

"Oh, we've traits in common, no denying that. And there's the special cachet of being the youngest, and motherless; everyone wants to make it up to you, and you're conscious of your own dramatic importance. Miranda and I made the most of that, I'm afraid." We went out into the garden and paced slowly toward the sundial. Charlie stalked a goldfinch. "But Tom—well, in some ways Tom's more my brother than my own are. He's only a few months older than I am. Meg mothered me as she did him, and once I thought she really was my mother and everybody was lying to me about it." He looked around at me with a slight grimace. "Tom was always the steady one. Old Slow-but-Sure. When we had to memorize in school, and Tom recited, 'I am as constant as the northern star,' I thought that was perfect for him. —Turns out he's constant to Miranda, and she's constant to what she wants, so the two of them are turning everybody else's world upside down to achieve what Miranda desires."

"You sound like some sour old codger," I said. "I agree they shouldn't be doing it this way. But you and I are young like them. We should be on their side. A little, anyway."

He slapped his good hand hard down on the sundial. "You're hedging! Putting a good face on it. Why don't you show some honest-to-God hurt because she never breathed a word of this to you? Or are you too *ladylike?*" He bore down venomously on the word.

"Of course I'm hurt! But more than that I'm sad, oh, almost bereft, because if they do get to California I may never see her again and she's been a blazing star in my life."

He listened with a strained expression as if concentrating on some secret code message hidden in my words.

"Well, that's what you wanted to hear, isn't it?" I asked angrily.

"That's enough, isn't it? It says it all." Then he smiled, and the glassy, gaunt effect was wiped out. "The fact is, they'll be caught up with, reasoned with, forgiven, and come back here for a September wedding, and you'll be the maid of honor and catch the bride's bouquet. Let's get something to eat, and then do something strenuous. It's like a wake around here without the corpse."

"You can't do anything strenuous," I reminded him. "But I can. Let's go down to the dig. You could sit quiet and rest your hand, and give me directions."

"The dig's the last place I want to go, until Miranda's back again. For God's sake don't accuse me of sentimentality. But some of the happiest times of my life have been when we were all down there." He shook his head like a horse bothered by flies. "Come on, Seafair, it's time you learned how to sail."

"That's what Miranda said. If I'd gone with them that day, maybe none of this would have happened." I looked woefully at him, and he said, "What do you bet? They had their minds all made up, so forget it. Now you're going to sail. There's just a light breeze, and you can't sink *Eaglet*, unless you're some kind of diabolical genius. Let's go."

One thing about the present crisis, it made learning to sail seem a very small crisis indeed.

When we passed the pines marking the way to the eagle's nest he said over his shoulder, "I climbed up to it once. Unbeknownst to my elders."

"Weren't you scared?"

"Ay-*yup!* I didn't know which was going to grab me first, my father, one of the eagles, or the ghost of some Indian whose totem the eagle was."

"Or one of your own ghosts," I suggested.

"No, mine stayed down in the oak grove where they belonged. They all have great territorial integrity, you know. Well, I kept on climbing, and found out for myself just what I'd been told, there was no way of getting around that twenty-foot-deep mess of sticks and up to where I could look in at the eaglets."

"You were relieved, of course."

"I was relieved. Because if there'd been a way, I'd have had to try it, and I had visions of myself being plucked up in talons and taken out over the sea and dropped. I thought the eagles were much bigger than they really are." He laughed. "Later I found out that Ian and Andrew had tried the same thing. And so had Father, and probably every other male Drummond at the age of ten or twelve." He assumed an imaginary monocle, and said with a gargling accent, "A strange puberty rite, *nicht wahr?*"

"*Ja, ja, gewiss, Herr Doktor,*" I said. He reached out his good arm and hugged me to him. "My God, Seafair, I'm glad you're here. Did I tell you that before?"

"Yes, but I like it," I said candidly.

"Do you indeed?" He gave me a brief hard kiss on the mouth.

wouldn't build up a card castle on that one quick kiss in the woods the way I'd done on the kiss at the dance. There was nothing wrong with enjoying a kiss and not considering it a committal for life. One does not become engaged to a sunset, or betrothed to a field of wild flowers. One does not fall in love with a rainbow. Consider such a kiss as a natural phenomenon, and it becomes considerably less complicated . . . if one is strong-minded enough.

Anyway, this one cheered us both up, and I approached the sailing lesson with a more positive attitude, even if it was something less than devil-may-care.

Patrick laughed at my clumsiness and scoffed at my apprehensions. "Anybody who can play a Chopin étude can certainly sail," he said.

"Then anybody who can sail can certainly play a Chopin étude, so when we get back—if we ever do—?"

He laughed as he hadn't laughed since the night before Miranda ran away. It was as if once he'd cast off from the land he'd cast off all its woes and burdens. He was like that bird which must be on the sea before it can take wing.

I began to feel friendly toward *Eaglet,* if not on terms of actual familiarity. I became so confident I suggested a little turn out by the Head, and when we came up into the wind I had too much to handle. Patrick called me a landlubber and a farmer, and wouldn't take over until I was on the edge of panic.

It was almost sundown when we landed back on the beach of the Home Cove. I had rowed us ashore and put the skiff on the haul-off; out at her mooring *Eaglet* lay with sails furled, the sea-going knots retied, after several unsuccessful tries. My hands were tired, my shoulders ached. But I had sailed. I had become a distant cousin, many times removed, of the salt-water aristocracy.

Patrick was fastening the haul-off line with one-handed half-hitches around the stake, and I was trying to rub the sore muscles between my neck and shoulders and gazing off along the shaded beach, empty except for Charlie and some unflustered sandpipers. I would have given anything to see Miranda coming, shouting something like, "I see the White Whale bit Captain Ahab's hand off, and it serves him right."

"Let me do that," Patrick said behind me, and with his good hand began strongly kneading one shoulder and then the other. I held back the ouches; I liked too much the rough familiarity. He pushed me around as if I were Miranda. Between his touch and Miranda's absence I didn't know whether to rejoice or to weep. There was always the blatant truth that all these hours together wouldn't be happening if Miranda hadn't run away.

"Seafair? Are you sleeping standing up?" Patrick's hand gently shook me. "We'd better get back to the house while you can still walk. Maybe I could manage to lug you over my shoulder in a fireman's lift, but I'm not sure."

Meg had been back to The Eyrie and had washed our lunch dishes, which she wasn't supposed to do. I felt reproached. "She must think I'm a slattern," I said.

"The black-headed slattern," he recited. "A rare shy bird whose habitat is in deepest Pianoforte ... That's out in the Spice Islands. *Awfully* nice place to be."

I wouldn't laugh. "I'm already in her bad books. She thinks I knew."

"Never mind. Anyway, she had to start the oatmeal, because if we don't have porridge every morning the world will drop off its axis like a baked apple."

She had left us a beef pie, still bubbling hot under a

biscuit crust. We were hungry, and we had a tacit agreement not to mention Miranda and Tom as we ate. I washed up our dishes, determined that Meg shouldn't.

"And then I'm going to teach you chess," said Patrick.

"Women can't learn chess. It's a well-known fact."

"It's well-known rot," he said. "You've learned how to sail, haven't you?"

There was no arguing with him. Besides, it didn't matter whether I was stupid or not; it would take up time, and that was the idea. We used up a good two hours over the chessboard in front of the library fire, until we were both groggy. He looked ashy and half-sick when we left off.

He'd been too active, but I knew better than to mention it. I went to bed before it was really dark, hoping he'd do the same. I left my door just barely ajar, and read, fighting to keep my eyes open. The stair carpet muffled footsteps, but after a while Charlie pricked up his ears and looked toward the hall, and in a few moments I heard the soft closing of a door across the stair well.

I blew my light out after that. We were unchaperoned, something Meg would never have allowed under ordinary circumstances, and I hoped that she wouldn't remember it all at once and leave her bed and husband to trudge over from the farm and attend to the proprieties. She might even insist on my going back to the farm with her, if she didn't want to leave Dougal.

The next thing I knew it was morning; the third morning of Miranda's absence. Incredible that I should be used to it so soon. Yet I wasn't used to it at all.

Patrick's door was still shut and I hoped he would sleep for hours. My hands and arms were lame this morning, and the mere effort to recall anything I'd learned about chess brought back the memory of an almost nauseating fatigue. When I went into the Museum I met the fragrance of coffee coming up the back stairs and like a coward I was ready to go out the front door without breakfast rather than meet Meg. But Charlie was going downstairs so fast he was in danger of falling on his head, and skidded into the kitchen with such hysterical ecstasy that I could only think, *Miranda!*

It was Ian. He had pushed back from the table to hold and calm the dog. "It's all right, all right," he was murmuring, his big hand smoothing and stroking.

"How did you get here?" I asked stupidly.

"Sailed. Fair wind this morning. I left Rockland an hour and a half ago." In his newly sunburned face his eyes looked deepset; normal thinness had become near-gauntness. "Get yourself something to eat and sit down. I want to talk to you."

I poured coffee and obeyed. "Is there any news?"

"None yet from points west, and *Lorna Doone* seems to have dropped out of sight. I'm beginning to wonder if she ever existed. Oh, she's real enough, but was she *here?*"

"Didn't people at the harbor see her?"

"I don't know, I haven't talked with anyone about it yet. But I won't be surprised if nobody did see her. All we really know is what Tom and Miranda told Patrick." As he spoke their names, there was only a slight flicker across tired and reddened eyes. "There was a boat all right, because they're gone. No skiff's missing, so the schooner's tender could have come in and taken them off Northern Harbor Point, for a guess. But her name could be another piece of fiction on their part. . . . Aren't you going to have more than coffee?"

"I'm not hungry," I said.

"Very well." He pushed his plate to one side and folded his arms along the edge of the table. "All along we've been ignoring the one person who could probably tell us about this. Who must have been in on it."

"Who?" I asked in honest curiosity. "Dill?"

He shook his head slowly, not taking his eyes off me. "Come on now, Seafair. Loyalty is admirable only to the point before it becomes callous stupidity, or worse."

I was too astounded to be angry. "They've got to come

back," he went on, as patronizingly logical as if he were dealing with a recalcitrant child. "If they're determined to be married, all right. Dougal and I have agreed on that. But not this way, as runaways, and Tom's future tossed to the four winds like a pan of orts to the gulls. Miranda's future is involved too, because some day she'll feel guilty about him, and he'll blame her even if he doesn't say so. What about love then?"

He repeated the question, "What about love then, Seafair? . . . Tom can be moody, morose, eaten away inside. And I've known Miranda for nineteen years, I know what's in her background too. . . . This could be complete catastrophe for them both. Do you want that for them, Seafair? Can you honestly say so?"

"I can honestly say *no*, and I'd have told them if I'd had a chance. But I didn't know what was going on."

"I find that hard to believe."

"Then you'll just have to go on believing what you want to."

"I don't want to. I've liked you all summer, Seafair. I liked you that first day, when I told you about Adrienne. But all at once nobody is what they seem. I don't know Tom and Miranda any more. They've become strangers, plotting this all out while looking me straight in the eye. The way you're looking at me now."

I was so enraged now I was very quiet. I just wanted to be quit of this place and never lay eyes on a Drummond again.

"I'm looking at you like *that*," I said, "because I'm not plotting anything, and I know nothing of a plot. Miranda let me think she was flirting with Dill, and then after the last scrap with Patrick she said the flirtation wasn't fun any more. Once, earlier, I heard Tom tell her that something should be brought out into the open, but I thought it was all to do with Dill. Any time Miranda mentioned the future, it was always something to do with school next fall, or with next summer here."

He was silent a few moments, without looking away from my face. Then he said, "So she used and deceived you again. I can only apologize. Eat your breakfast. How about some porridge?"

I didn't want it, but I had to do something. I helped myself. "Meg's right about it," I said.

"That it's a solid poultice laid against the wounds of the world?" he asked dryly.

"Something like that."

He arose. "I'm going over to the store and attend to a few things, then I'll be back for some clothes and I'll see Patrick then. How's his hand?"

"It was all right last night. Are you going to stop at the farm?"

"I'll have to give them the latest lack of news, I suppose. I'd rather be shot," he said flatly.

"Then will you tell Meg I wasn't involved in this elopement?" I asked. "I can't get around to it with her, she won't let me. But she'll believe you, Ian."

"I'll do the best I can."

She came a little while later. "Good morning, Seafair," she said. Yesterday she hadn't spoken my name once. "Is Patrick up yet?"

"Not yet."

"I'd better look in on him." Turning at the foot of the back stairs she said with an unusual diffidence, "I forgot all about you last night, Dougal being under the weather and all. But there, what folks at the harbor don't know can't hurt 'em, can it?"

"I guess not," I agreed. I went on washing Ian's and my breakfast dishes. She came back very soon.

"Sleeping hard, and he doesn't look feverish. Sleep's what he needs." What you need too, I thought, ashamed of my own heavy, unbroken sleep. She didn't mention Ian, but as usual took refuge in being busy. As she got out the mixing bowl and bread board, I said, "Is there anything you'd like me to do?"

"Nothing comes to mind except if you'd like to pick some blackberries. They're that ripe they're falling off the vines, and it's a sin to waste them. Patrick's real partial to blackberry fool." She gave me a two-quart pail and told me where there should be good picking at the edge of the field among the alders, at the edge of the oak grove.

I was uncommonly cheerful as I picked. For Ian to believe me, and to have convinced Meg, made up in some degree for the hurt Miranda had done me. Yet the hurt was fading rapidly as the distance widened between us, not only in geographical miles. By seeing her not as a friend but as a sovereign personality, I could understand that if Miranda was passionately in love with Tom, and afraid of losing him if anyone knew about it, then she had deceived me simply because she believed it was a matter of her own survival.

Come back, Miranda! I entreated among the blackberry vines and the goldfinches swinging in the seeded thistle heads. *Come back!*

The August heat rising up from the dry ground almost equaled the strength of the sun. I walked a little distance into the fringe of the oaks, where Charlie lay sprawled on his belly, his hind legs stretched out behind him. The susurrus of the leaves overhead gave an illusion of coolness to the shade. I sat absent-mindedly eating warm berries from the pail. Then I saw Patrick just passing the couch hammock. He looked as he had always looked, coming along with his loose, easy stride, in a hurry with so much to do and think about that he'd need several lifetimes for it.

When he came nearer I could see that his face was stiff under the brim of the wide-awake. I wouldn't have called him and broken his train of thought, but Charlie barked, and Patrick's head swung up and around. He was like a deer sniffing the wind. "Over here!" I called, waving from the shadow to catch his eye.

He came toward me fast. Charlie ran to meet him. He ignored the dog and said curtly, "Have you been down to the dig? *Have* you? Because I told you——"

"I wouldn't go without you! I'm afraid of the ghosts. Are *you* going down there?" I asked. "Remember, I said I was ready to do all the work in the cause of science."

He made a nervous, jerky gesture with his bandaged hand. "Another week ought to do it. I'll have to wear a glove, but I'll be able to work. In the meantime I try not to think about it; it's driving me crazy. I said I wouldn't go there till they came, but I don't know if I can wait."

"They should be here by then," I said, "unless they do slip by the cordon and get to California."

"Sometimes I don't give a damn if they do," he said, "if they'd just be quick about it so we can all settle back one way or another. If they're bent on chaos, let 'em get on with it. The rest of us'll survive."

"Meg and Dougal?" I asked softly.

"They're the ones to suffer the most. If it weren't for them, I'd say the other two could go to hell.... Coming home?" It was said so naturally, as if I belonged there.

Ian was in the kitchen with Meg when we came in. I went up to my room to leave them alone, washed up, made my bed, and went across to Patrick's room. But Meg had already been there.

In about a half hour I went tentatively downstairs again, intending to busy myself in the garden, but Patrick came to the door of the library and beckoned me in. Ian stood with his elbow on the mantel. "I was telling Pat that Elmer's all squared away for the next few days," he said. "I told him about the accident, and he thinks he can get Mr. Clement to lend him a hand at mailtime. Incidentally, they know about the elopement now. If any bad jokes are being made, I wouldn't hear them, naturally. I think everyone's more stunned than anything else. You'd better go over to the farm to sleep at night, Seafair."

"*No!*" Patrick said explosively. "I'm more bothered by this damned hand than I wanted to admit. Seafair distracts me. We sit up a lot later than they do at the farm, and we talk about all kinds of things. . . . And if I wake up in the night with one of these nightmares, I know someone's here." He gave me one of those quick and beguiling smiles. "I woke myself up at quarter of one last night, and I came across the hall and stood by your door till I heard your breathing. Then I could go back to sleep. Good God, Ian, I'm not going to seduce her!"

"I wasn't worried about your attacking her honor," Ian said. "But gossip can do that, and I'm responsible for her as long as she's in this house." He looked both thoughtful and harassed. Finally he nodded. "There'll have to be someone else here in the house then, if she doesn't go over to the farm. You can get one of the girls from the harbor."

"Not Prissy," Patrick said. "*My* honor'd be threatened then. I'd have to lock my door."

"Conceited young ass, aren't you?"

"I can't help it if I was born beautiful," said Patrick. "We'll get Faustina. She's courting, and she won't be sitting around under our noses all evening expecting to be entertained."

Ian turned to me with raised eyebrows. "I'll see her this afternoon," I said.

"Good."

We all went out to the kitchen with him. He put his arm around Meg's solid shoulders and kissed her cheek. "They'll get Faustina to come in."

Meg sniffed, whether from disapproval or recently peeling onions I couldn't say. "Don't worry any more than you can help, Meg," Ian said.

From the way she looked up at him, I realized that there was a special relationship between him and her, as between two adults. She treated the rest of us as children.

"After three days of not knowing where they are, I've given up worrying about what pulpit he'll fill. To see them alive is what I want."

"Of course they're alive, Meg!" Patrick said angrily, but she didn't look away from Ian.

"They're alive, Meg," he repeated, but quietly. "Why shouldn't they be? The *Lorna Doone* didn't go where she was expected to go, that's all. It's a matter of finding out where she went."

"I never would have believed Tom could ever be so deceitful," she said, and set her lips together in a narrow colorless seam. She didn't look at any of us after that. We left her and walked down to the Home Cove where *Kingfisher* lay.

chapter 29

*P*atrick said after lunch that we were to have another sailing lesson. The wind had risen, and he was
figuratively rubbing his hands and looking gleeful.
"I have to see Faustina," I announced smugly.

"We'll sail around." He was just as smug. And sail we did.
He was kind enough to take the tiller for most of the way
and allow me to be the crew. I was no longer terrified when
Eaglet heeled, and now I knew what his orders meant; I
was learning the language fast.

I went up to the factory to speak to Faustina, who would
be pleased to come to The Eyrie that night. Patrick waited
around in the store, wearing his sling with the careless elegance of a soldier of fortune home from fighting in somebody else's wars. As usual he attracted children, and he
treated them all and me to ice cream cones. Of the three
brothers he was the only one who, consciously or uncon-
sciously, could assume like a different shirt the feudal grace
of the young lord of the manor.

We sailed back home up the northwest side of the island,
and it was close to six o'clock when we returned to the
house. I fed Charlie and went upstairs to make my bed for
Faustina, and Miranda's bed for me. When I opened her
closet to hang up my nightgown and robe, the faint scent
of Roman Violet came out to me, and after the elation of
sailing I was overwhelmed by a homesickness for Miranda
that was almost a physical malaise.

Suddenly the door from the hall was pushed open, not by
Charlie, but by Patrick. He stood staring at me as if he didn't

quite recognize me. "I heard something," he said. "I thought —" He made a futile motion. "I don't know what I thought."

"Me too," I said. "When I opened the closet—" We were silent, not knowing what to say, and then Charlie ran in and jumped up on the bed. "Charlie, you're still all wet and sandy!" I scolded gladly, grabbing him up. Patrick laughed. The sound was forced but so was my vehemence, and we both knew it. Keeping Charlie under my arm I said, "I'm going down now and set the table."

He stood back to let me pass, but instead of following he stayed there in the room. I don't know for how long. When he did come down, our supper was ready on the table. He had on a clean shirt and his hair was damp from the comb. He wore an alert, optimistic expression, far different from what I had seen upstairs.

"Did I ever tell you about the lions of the Processional Way at Babylon?" he asked. "And the great Gate of Ishtar?" He was graphically entertaining about this all through the meal.

We had the lamps lit and I was washing the dishes when we heard Hughie's distinctive bray in the woodshed, and Faustina's shriek.

"I wonder where he grabbed her," said Patrick.

Heads came around the door. Hughie's face was mostly grin, Faustina's was red and delighted. "We're goin' knoll-in'," Hughie said. "Be back sooner or later."

"I should hope so," said Patrick severely. "At dawn I'll lock the doors."

They withdrew, convulsed. "I didn't tell her where she's supposed to sleep," I said.

"We can leave a note on the table and the lamp turned down, but she's likely to get back just in time for breakfast."

I had another chess lesson that night. I worked at it conscientiously and showed a faint glimmer of understanding, for which Patrick congratulated me. This time I had the firmness to terminate the evening before exhaustion could set in.

Patrick woke me by having another nightmare. I knew what the shouting meant before I was conscious, and had rushed across the hall and into his room by the time I was fully awake.

"What's that?" he snapped. "Who's there?" His voice was high and breathless.

"It's me," I said. "Wake up."

He didn't hear me. "Who is it?" he kept asking. Outside, the dull light of the waning moon lay over the world, and inside the house it was not exactly dark, but something worse than that. My nightgown must have had a spectral glimmer. "Don't come any nearer," he warned me. I could tell his right hand was groping around on the lamp stand. "Whatever you are, I can deal with you!"

"Patrick! Patrick!" I called, trying to keep my voice down and yet get through to wherever he was imprisoned. Charlie had followed me into the room, and suddenly his elbow began rhythmically hitting the floor as he scratched.

"Who's that knocking?" Patrick whispered. "Do you hear it? Don't let them in, Miranda. They've come up from the grove." My scalp was tightening. "They shouldn't. They know better. They're just trying to scare us."

"And they've succeeded," I said in a normal voice. If Faustina woke up, I couldn't help it. "Wake up, Patrick! It's only Charlie chasing a flea." I went to the foot of the bed.

"*Miranda!*" He laughed incredulously. "It's really you, isn't it? When did you get back?"

"It's Seafair," I said. "Miranda's not back yet, but she will be."

There was silence. The anxious, defensive hand became quiet. I could make out the shape of his head against the pillows but only a blur for his face. He seemed to be holding his breath and listening. "Seafair," I repeated. The clock struck two.

After a moment he said, "Good God, did I wake the house again? I don't know what's wrong with me. I should sleep in the library, or the Museum. Or even in the loft of the woodshed; that would be best."

"You didn't wake the house, you woke only me," I said, "and that's why I'm here—for the nightmares. Remember?"

"Still makes me feel like a damn fool, anyway. I'm sorry, Seafair."

"Would you like a hot drink?"

"No, no. Go on back to bed. Oh, light the lamp, will you? I'll read a while." He sounded perfectly ordinary again. I groped around for his box of matches and lighted the lamp. Illumination sprang up in the room and caught him gazing at the lamp with a kind of fascination. "It was the damndest thing," he said. "I was lost in the dark somewhere and I knew there'd never be light anymore . . . and here it is. I'll never take it for granted again."

His hair was dark with sweat around his forehead, but his face was changing with every instant, as radically as the room had changed from dim to bright. I was allowed to put an extra pillow behind him while he reached for his book. Almost with relish he said, "Back to those lions, and with any luck I'll dream about them."

"Yes, dream of them and Babylon," I said. "Goodnight, Patrick."

"Goodnight, Seafair. Thanks very much." He didn't look up from the pages.

Across the hall I glanced into my room. I could make out the bed, the coverings undisturbed since I'd turned them back. Faustina's satchel was like a crouching cat on the floor where I'd set it. . . . I wondered with mild curiosity where they avoided the drenching dews of these nights, not to mention the mosquitoes.

I got back into bed in Miranda's room, Charlie snuggled up to my legs, and for an exercise in enticing sleep I tried to remember the whole of *How Far Is It to Babylon?* I couldn't get past *Could I get there by candlelight? Aye, and back again.*

But I slept. Charlie growled very softly once and I half-woke, and heard surreptitious movements in the next room. Faustina was in.

Wednesday was gray, and the scent of rain to come blew in the windows. Faustina's bed was neatly made and she had already gone when I got up, a little past seven. Across the hall Patrick slept slumped against his pillows, the book slid off his knees, the lamp flame tiny and lost in daylight.

It would be a day for fires, for me to work at the piano, for Patrick to write up his records and journal. I could almost wish that it weren't a boat day. There'd be something from Ian, to tell us what he'd found out when he got back to Rockland yesterday, and whatever it was it would disrupt the fragile peace we'd spun for ourselves. —Didn't I *want* to know that Miranda was coming back? Was I actually resenting her?

It was rather horrifying. I ran down the backstairs and said, "*Good* morning, Meg!" I thought I could almost read her bleak contempt for my callousness. "I'm trying to cheer myself up," I explained.

"When did that Faustina finally get in last night?"

"I don't know. I went to bed early and right to sleep."

She made an ambiguous sound which would have amused me under other circumstances. She had lost weight in the last three days, there were scooped-out dark circles under her eyes, and her firm cheeks seemed to sag slightly. I couldn't think of anything to say as I ate, and decided she would prefer my silence to well-meant silliness. She brightened when Patrick came down, and after a few moments I left them.

I ignored tidying my room, and went straight to the parlor, shut the double doors, and lighted a fire. Puffs of wind struck hard at the tops of the garden trees, and the sky was darker than it had been when I got up. The first spatters of rain hit the seaward windows. I settled down at the piano, and the familiar motions brought the sense of being in my rightful place, of *belonging,* that nothing else—or no person —could ever bring me.

I worked until I was tired. No one had come to open the doors and I thought that Patrick and Meg were still talking in the kitchen, as they'd been when I left. To stretch I walked to the seaward end of the parlor, where rain was now running steadily down the panes. Beyond the glass, sea and sky were a gray blur. The white flagpole and the gaudy geraniums around its base showed up through the shimmering screen of water in an abstract design; the lawn had the unreal green of a plush parlor set in a certain house in Fern Grove, loathed by me since a childhood in which its owner was always inquiring with saccharine greed, "Do you miss your mother, dearie?"

I went back to the piano and took it all out in a stormier-than-called-for performance of the *Grande Polonaise in E-flat*. I didn't hear the doors open, but saw Charlie out of the corner of my eye, and knew I'd left him in the kitchen waiting for dishes to lick out. I went through to a literally bang-up finish, swung around on the stool, and there was Patrick.

"I'd applaud if I knew how to do it with one hand," he said.

"You could throw roses," I said, "and for money I'd do a gypsy dance."

"The boat's in," he said. "Young Ginnie brought the mail over. . . . Poor kid looked half-drowned, but she wouldn't stay and dry off."

I could hardly get the question out. "Any news?"

"There's a letter from Ian, but I haven't opened it yet. She said there was one for Meg and Dougal too."

"Hadn't you better read yours?" We were both so unnaturally low-keyed it was almost ludicrous.

"I want you to read it with me," he said, holding out the envelope.

"All right. Let's sit in front of the fire." I took the letter with synthetic gaiety, and had quite a struggle to open it, my fingers were so clammy.

It was dated yesterday afternoon, and began, "Dear Seafair and Patrick," which gave me a geniune shock of pleasure, "*Good news.*"

We sagged against each other. "You read it," I said. "My voice feels all wobbly."

"I don't know about mine." He cleared his throat and began to read. The *Lorna Doone* had been at Thomaston before daylight Sunday morning. No one had seen her come upriver and dock, so no one knew if any passengers had disembarked. At first light a boy in her crew had been sent upstreet to rouse up some local merchants who had contracted to take her next trip of mackerel. After these men had seen to the transporting and fresh icing, one of them had opened his store long enough for the seiner to stock up. She'd gone downriver as soon as there was enough water to take her. The crew hadn't said anything about bringing someone in from Drummond's.

Patrick stopped here and I said, "But how——"

"There's more," he said.

Across the basin that Sunday morning the four-master *Marjorie Montrose* was waiting for the flood tide to start her on the first leg of her voyage around Cape Horn to San Francisco. Those friends who went aboard after church to bid the Captain and his wife goodbye saw two passengers very briefly; at the arrival of the visitors, they went quickly to their cabin. They were a young couple, a dark man and a tall, fair girl. The Captain's wife didn't name them. She said only that it was a last-minute arrangement, they'd approached the captain early in the morning, they had good references, were married, and could pay well for the privilege of making the voyage to California.

Patrick stopped reading. His face was without expression.

"What is it?" I asked hoarsely.

"I was sure they were dead," he said. "I kept dreaming. I kept seeing the seiner quietly sinking in the bay in the moonlight, without a trace. I'd wake up convinced they were fathoms deep out there—her hair streaming in the tide—the crabs—" His voice cracked. He was crying and trying not to. I put my arms around him and he put his good arm tightly around me. "Read the rest of it," he said thickly.

"She was to stop at Boston, New York, and then Norfolk, and take on cargo at each port," Ian had written. "She's just left Boston. I'm taking the night train out, and if I can't catch her in New York, I'll be there to meet her in Norfolk.... I've called Andrew."

He ended with hopes that Patrick's hand was still healing well, and with thanking me for keeping Patrick company. "I thank you too," said Patrick solemnly, his nose almost touching mine. We laughed foolishly, and kissed. Then we looked into each other's eyes and he said, "You've got three eyes, you know it?"

"You've got one on the bridge of your nose," I said.

He kissed me again, longer than before. Charlie scratched at my knee, wanting to get in on the fun. Patrick broke off with a sigh and put his face against my neck, and I laid my cheek against his hair; it seemed as natural a succession as a scale. Charlie jumped into my lap.

"It has to be them," I said. "It's too perfect a coincidence. Even Ian's convinced."

"And if Ian's convinced, he must have received the word directly from Above," Patrick mocked me. He hugged me harder. "My comforter."

"Miranda will be furious as being cheated out of a Cape Horn trip," I said. "A long sea voyage was her idea of a perfect honeymoon, she told me once."

"Poor Tom, she'll probably blame him for everything."

"The Captain's wife said they were married. When could they have?"

"What weird grammar you speak. They don't need to have. What's one more lie?"

"But the same cabin——"

"If they're in love," he said, "why shouldn't they share the same bed?"

We were motionless and silent for a moment, in which his fingers tapped against my ribs and my thinking was unpleasantly chaotic, with one thin tough strand of reality sharp as a scarlet wire. *I envied them.* I might never admit it aloud, but I admitted it to myself. Then I moved out of Patrick's arm, or attempted to. He still held on.

"What are you going to do now?"

"Isn't it lunch time? Doesn't this make you hungry?"

"No, it isn't lunch time," he said resignedly. "But if you're dying of famine, by all means let's find some food."

"And think about how happy Meg and Dougal must be," I said, remembering them for the first time.

"And we'll think about them too," he said. "But why we can't think of them in front of the fire here, I'll never know." He sighed, and I said, "Poor, martyred Patrick."

The storm worsened. It would have been a frightful afternoon if we hadn't had good news in the morning. But it was one of the best, of a class with those long attic hours with Miranda. We spent it in the library. Charlie lay on the leather sofa with me while I read about Babylon, and Patrick went back to writing at the Old Colonel's desk.

We drew the curtains early and lit the lamps. I made hot chocolate and we toasted bread over the fire and talked archeology. It was an innocent and happy time. If like a shadow presence the other Seafair was present, the one who got seasick on camelback and could catalogue artifacts with the best of them, it was a harmless indulgence of my own, and Patrick didn't know. The one he did know kept priming him with questions. *You must draw men out.* Well, I was doing it, and perhaps in the future the shadow Seafair would become substance. Meanwhile, one had to start somewhere.

After all the toast and hot chocolate, we hadn't bothered to heat up our dinner when Hughie and Faustina came. They stripped off oilskins and sou'westers in the shed, and came in with their faces beaten red and shining with rain. "Real old combustible, ain't it?" Hughie said. "Apple-shaker, this one. Like to swept us across the farm and out over Marsh Cove."

"Ain't it some *good* about Tom and Miranda?" asked Faustina. "I was so glad, I cried."

Patrick hadn't been alone in worrying about the seiner going down; there'd been a number of guesses around the harbor as to what reef or shoal had finished her.

"Or she could've started taking in water and just sank," Hughie said. "Likely she's some old basket, held together with spit and a prayer." He had brought a bottle of rum. "I figgered we ought to celebrate. You want it straight, Pat, or hot buttered?"

"Hot buttered rum sounds better than it is," said Patrick. "We'll have it straight. What about you girls?"

Faustina tittered in pleased indignation at being asked. I said I didn't like hard liquor (I'd never tasted any). Patrick took a lantern down cellar and brought up some cold and dusty bottles of Meg's wine, currant, grape, rhubarb, and dandelion, which I chose for its sunny color. There were more sophisticated wines in the house, but these home-made vintages carried the flavor of my Drummond's Island summer.

We sang at the piano. "I hope that Captain's wife has got a piano on board," Faustina said. "I bet Miranda's singing for 'em right now. My, they'll hate to lose her at Norfolk."

We finished the evening with our dinner at midnight. That is, Patrick, Faustina, and I ate. Hughie had been his own best customer for the rum, and was snoring on the library sofa. Faustina insisted we should wash the dishes, even though I said I'd be willing to get up early in the morning and do them. Hughie looked settled for the night, and I'd counted on Faustina's going up to bed and giving Patrick and me a little time to ourselves. Behind her back we grimaced in humorous dismay, then he blew me a kiss, and winked.

"I'm going to bed," he said. "I'll pitch down some blankets for the sleeping beauty. I'd take off his boots if I could manage with one hand."

"*I* can manage!" said Faustina with spirit.

"I have no doubt that you can manage a lot more than his boots."

Faustina sputtered in not very convincing outrage. "Goodnight, ladies," Patrick said, and went yawning up the back stairs.

austina and Hughie must have left at daybreak. Meg was over at sun-up, ready to do the delayed washing. She had already sent word to Erline to come and help her. Today was like the first day of the world, and the first day of our lives. We all moved quickly, radiantly, without effort; Meg was as light as a dancer about the kitchen, up and down the stairs. When I went out to hang up the dishtowels, the wind brought me a hitherto unknown music—Dougal whistling as he dug early potatoes.

Meg changed the dressing on Patrick's hand and told him to stay out from underfoot while she did his room.

"I'll be a long distance from underfoot, love," he said. "I'm taking Seafair to the Bowsprit to see the surf. It'll be shooting up off there like Old Faithful. And then this afternoon"— he leered at me— "I'll give you a sailing lesson. We've got just the wind for it."

"You will not," I said.

"That's right, girl, you stick to your guns," Meg said. "Get you out there in that cockleshell and drown the both of you, and give the rest of us heart failure. I know him and his sailing."

"Why can't I dig?" I demanded. "You've got your own Crete or Troy, or Sumer and Babylon, right here, and——"

"You're getting altogether too well-educated," said Patrick. "We'll all go down to the dig when the elopers come back. I expect to get a lot of work out of them if they're contrite enough, which they should be." He held up his bandaged hand. Meg's face darkened and saddened, and he saw it, and said caressingly, "Don't, Meg. It was my own fault. A couple of years from now, when you see Tom ordained, I won't even be missing that finger."

"I don't know about being ordained." She went to the sink. Her back to us, she said in a low voice, "If he never wanted to be a minister he doesn't have to be one."

"Anybody can make a mistake in himself, Meg." Patrick put his arm around her. "Tom might have found out in college that he wasn't cut out for the ministry, but he shrank from hurting you and Dougal. But now he's made the break, and you're so thankful he's alive that you wouldn't care if he said he wanted to be a wagon painter or a pack-peddler."

"Well, maybe," she said gruffly. He laughed and kissed her forehead.

At the Bowsprit the surf was indeed spectacular. We had to shout to be heard above the sustained roar and the separate crashes, so we gave up trying to talk. On the outer side of the point the rock ran down to the water in a long slope where once it had flowed as a broad stream of lava, and we walked part way down it toward the surf. I stopped when spray flew into my face, but Patrick went on. Not far beyond him the rock was wet. When the next sea broke, foaming scallops of water rushed up the slope and darkened a fresh area. Patrick kept on walking.

"Charlie, come!" I called, afraid the little dog would get caught by a breaker. He came to me, but Patrick didn't look around. I had the curious feeling that he was defying the water, looking it in the eye, trying to control it as a lion tamer controls his beasts. A fresh sea crashed home; water flew up in a green-and-white wall and arched over him. I tasted salt on my mouth, and saw the sliding lace at his feet.

"Patrick!" It broke from me. "Who do you think you are, King Canute?"

He kept on walking as if he were beyond hearing or even remembering me. "I think your sense of humor is absolutely rotten!" I shouted, and turned my head so sharply my neck hurt. "Come on, Charlie, we'll leave this maniac."

The next sea was so loud it sounded at my very back. I swung around, expecting to see Patrick trapped and swept off his feet, already tumbling over and over to death among the ledges.

But he was still standing. It was washing around his ankles. As it withdrew, he turned slowly—reluctantly, it seemed—and walked up the slope toward me. His face was leached of life. Behind him a new sea broke over the place where he had stood, and I felt an answering saltiness in my mouth like the start of nausea.

"Are you terrified?" he said. The somnambulist had disappeared somewhere between me and the print of the last wave. "Listen, I have that distance calculated to the nth degree."

"Said by how many before the seventh wave swept them to their doom? And there's something about 'the great third wave, that never a swimmer shall cross or climb.' Do you know that one?" Talking helped. It made things ordinary again. Blessed word, *ordinary*.

"Tom would know. Save it till he gets here."

"Well, as I screamed to you back there, I don't think much of your sense of humor."

"But you adore me anyway."

"Doesn't *everyone?*" I asked. "You're lucky I don't consider us engaged. Miranda told me what a walk to the Bowsprit means."

"Naturally we're engaged!" He laughed, and squeezed my fingers painfully. "Let's *us* elope, Seafair! What do you say?"

Faustina woke me early Saturday morning, being sick in the bathroom. I went to see if I could help her, and she said weakly, "It's that cussid summer complaint."

She wouldn't eat anything, she'd have breakfast at home, if

her stomach felt better. "But I doubt it will," she said morosely. She left, and I was wide awake in the dawn. At least it was a fair one, with a nacreous pink sky, the trees rising romantically from lakes of mist, and bird songs preternaturally loud. I dressed and went downstairs, leaving Charlie burrowed deeper into the bed. I had made a pot of coffee, and was toasting bread over the flames when someone came through the woodshed. It was Patrick. Just before he realized I was there I caught one glimpse of his face, fatigued, even desolate. Then recognition, and the smile flared up like a match flame in the dark. "What got *you* up?"

"Faustina being sick. What's your reason?"

He came over to the stove in squelching sneakers and damp trouser legs and backed up to the open oven door. He gave me an abashed look, as if he'd been caught in something ridiculous. "I never got to sleep. I read till all hours, got up around two, read in the library for a while and made some notes, then went out around four. The stars were so bright and thick, and it seemed warm, so I've been rowing. Rowed around the island as a matter of fact." He held up his bad hand. "No worse for wear. It did it good, I think."

"Filthy bandage. Meg will have a fit. How about breakfast?"

"No, thanks. Food doesn't appeal to me right now."

"You haven't got what Faustina's got, have you?" I asked.

"My love, if I've got what Faustina has, I'll make medical history."

It took me a moment, such was my innocence. Then I said, "Oh, no! Oh, poor Faustina!"

"Poor Faustina nothing. Now she can get Hughie before a preacher. She's as determined in her way as Miranda is. Their methods may be different, but they're both unscrupulous as hell, and they get results." He pointed his finger at me. "Hughie and Tom have now joined the ranks of the hollow men. Empty inside. Emptied of life. They think they're getting what they want, and they walk wide-eyed to their execution." His smile was almost tender. "What about you, Seafair?"

"What about me what?" I turned my toast.

"Are you that kind of predatory female? Should you be named Arachne too?"

"Do we have to be scientific at six in the morning? I know Arachne is a name for a spider, and no, I've never seen myself as the female who devours her mate. In fact, I've never thought of a mate. I *think*"— delicately I replaced the stove lid—"that I'll devote myself to my career. I can now understand why that's what some women prefer."

"And why, if you can explain in fifty words or less? Neatness counts."

"Men asking hostile questions at the crack of dawn."

"Who's being hostile *now?*" His smile didn't change. So it had all been a sadistic little joke, the entreaties, and saying he needed me, and all the little ways of touching and holding; he'd been watching my predictable reactions from the very first day—that wink aboard the *Ocean Pearl*—and waiting for this moment. I could have thrown the toast at him and rushed from the house.

Instead, I put the toast on a plate, buttered it, cut it in two neat triangles, and carried it to the table. And now I offered silent homage to all the maiden ladies of Fern Grove who were so desperately or so graciously proper, chins held up by more than the boning in the necks of their shirtwaists, balancing pride on their heads like an invisible water jug.

Patrick sat astride a chair and watched me over the back of it. "And after all those damned dull books you read, too," he said. "And all the blisters you raised at the dig. It's a shame. Poor Seafair."

"Don't pity Seafair," I said. "She's the lucky one. She's off on the Monday boat." Not to Fern Grove, I had already decided. Back to the college, perhaps, for a few weeks of almost-isolation, in which to get my face straightened out before fall term.

I carried my half-drunk coffee and half-eaten toast to the sink and walked out of the room balancing the invisible jug on my head. But I won't carry it in Fern Grove, I thought. I wouldn't become one of *those*. . . . I saw the whole thing as I went upstairs. Retirement at seventy after a busy professional life; perhaps a little apartment in Boston, hard by the museums and the symphony. If nature never did betray the heart that loved her, neither did music.

In my room, where Faustina had left the bed tightly made, I began going through bureau drawers. Charlie kept me company, very inquisitive and concerned. "Miranda will be back in a few days," I said to him. Would I have a dog in my dignified old age? No, I would get too attached to it, and people would smile tolerantly and tap their heads at the sight of my grief when it died. Not that I gave a damn about people, but never more should anyone have the opportunity to laugh at me.

When my bed was heaped with things to pack, Charlie and I went up the narrow flight behind the Old Colonel's portrait to the top floor. The luggage was all at one end of the attic, and I had to pass through the clubroom where we'd spent so much time on foggy days. Our apple cores were still in a flower pot, and our books left where Patrick had interrupted us the last time we were there.

I hurried to get my bags and escape before any more memories came to life. Well, the Drummonds couldn't be perfect, I thought as I went downstairs. They just *are*. I'm the one who made them into some sort of supernatural beings. I mistook that good grace of theirs for something else. Of course they're charming, of course they're kind. That costs them nothing. When it begins to be expensive they have ways of shutting off the account.

When I reached the foot of the attic stairs, Patrick was just going away from my door. I didn't need apologies, or want them; I had already begun my withdrawal from this unnatural world. I stood still, waiting for him to go away to his own room without seeing me. But he didn't go. He stood back to me, the good hand clenching and unclenching by his side.

Charlie, whom I'd left upstairs looking hopefully for mice behind the trunks, now came hurrying down behind me, saw the figure in the hall, and rushed out, barking, until he knew who it was.

Patrick turned toward us. "Seafair," he said. It was a grunt of agony. He came and took me in his arms, and I thought he was going to crack my ribs. "Oh, my God, Seafair. They're dead. They're *dead!*"

"No," I said. "No, no, *no*. You dreamed it. You fell asleep in the kitchen and you dreamed it."

"Ian's home." His voice broke and became a shaking half-whisper. "I didn't dream that. He came for Meg and Dougal. He's gone to the farm now, to tell them."

"Tell them *what?*" As long as I wouldn't believe, it wasn't possible, it hadn't happened. *This* wasn't happening.

"The ship was rammed by a steamer in fog off Delaware or Maryland somewhere. The night of the storm here, when we were drinking the rum and Meg's wine and making fools of ourselves . . . They couldn't reach her till the seas went down, and she broke up. No survivors. Some bodies but no survivors." His embrace crushed even harder.

"I won't believe it," I said furiously. "Ian hasn't seen the—" I couldn't say bodies. "He hasn't been there, he can't *know*."

"No, but he and Andrew are going there. Some little village where they took them. Ian got as far as Boston, then he heard about it and came back to tell us. He wouldn't write it. He's taking Meg and Dougal with him if they want to go. Andrew's gone on."

"We don't even know if they were on that vessel," I argued. "There could be another couple light and dark like that." At this point neither my body nor my brain accepted Ian's facts. While I stroked Patrick's back I was sure that his tortured, wrenching, male weeping was for something that simply could not be. Otherwise I could not have been this collected, this cold.

Finally he released me, and pulled out a handkerchief

and wiped his eyes and blew his nose. "It's only just begun," he said. "It'll get much worse. It's terrible to have your dreams come true, did you know it?"

"She will be back," I said meticulously, as if teaching him a foreign language. I propelled him toward his bathroom. "Wash your face."

I left him in there and ran downstairs. Charlie thought it was one of our races, and easily won. Ian stood by the stove drinking a mug of coffee, and Charlie threw himself at him. Ian leaned down and scratched the dog's head, murmuring, "Hello, Charlie." Then he looked across at me. My first impression was of an aged and awful tiredness.

"How can you be positive it's true?" I demanded.

"We'll know for sure when we get to the town," he said. "But there seems little doubt. The *Lorna Doone* landing her fish there, the couple asking passage early the next morning —nobody in Thomaston could guess who they might be."

"But as long as you're not *absolutely* sure," I began, and didn't know where to go from there. We heard Patrick on the back stairs and both watched tensely for him to appear. He was carrying himself very straight, with the effect of almost leaning backward. His hair was damply brushed, and cold water had taken away some of the marks on his face, though his eyes were still bloodshot. The bruises were in the green-to-yellow stage.

"You'd better come in with us," Ian said to him. "You won't want to be here alone. The dog can stay over at the farm with the Gillises. They're moving in while Meg and Dougal are gone."

"I don't want to go ashore," Patrick said evenly. "I'd go out of my mind over there. No, I'll wait here till you come back. All of you." He snapped off the last phrase as if biting off some abhorrence. "I won't be alone. Seafair's here."

"It's time for Seafair to be going." Ian turned courteously to me. "We appreciate all you've done, Seafair. I'm glad you were here while Patrick's been recovering from his accident. But he's better now, and—well"—for the first time his poise slipped out of focus—"there's no point in waiting now, is there?"

Patrick slammed his good fist down on the table and walked out of the room.

"I have a responsibility to your father, Seafair," Ian said to me. "We just don't have any legitimate reason for keeping you here any longer."

"I know that," I said, "but Patrick shouldn't be alone."

He nodded. "Whatever he thinks, it would be better for him to go with us than to stay here. However, I have neither the time nor the inclination to deal with him. If that sounds cold, it's just that I know Patrick, and right now I have to think about the Finlays as well as the Drummonds." He walked around the kitchen with his hands in his pockets. It was the first time I had ever seen him fidgety. "I suppose you couldn't be ready to go in with us now in the cutter, and you probably wouldn't want to. What about Monday, and the mail boat?"

"Monday," I said. The anesthesia was beginning to wear off and my voice sounded peculiar to me.

"Good. See if you can persuade Patrick to come in too. We'll be gone, but we've got old friends in Rockland he could stay with."

And could they deal with his nightmares? I asked resentfully. Can he find solace in cobblestones and city buildings? I didn't say anything but I must have shown it.

"Seafair," he began. Then he shook his head. "I have to leave now. They'll be at the cove waiting for me. We all have to make this wretched journey to Fenwick Island, in Delaware. If Patrick would come ashore and be with us, that's what I want. If he won't come, I can't do anything about his condition."

I saw the weariness and the grief in him, and was ashamed of my resentment. I said, "I wish there was something I could do for you and for the Finlays."

"That's what we always wish," he said, "and there's never anything. Nobody can be helped to bear anything like this, it has to be done alone. . . . Look, will you see that Elmer gets this note?" He laid the envelope on the table. "Good-bye, Seafair. I've enjoyed your music." He went out. I stood there in the kitchen listening to his footsteps through the shed, the final shutting of a door, and then I went looking for Patrick.

ow the residual silence of the house had taken on the texture of finality. The polished woods, the carpets, the portraits, the flowers, were like the funerary furnishings surrounding a dead Egyptian ruler. Almost overcome by it, as if the air itself were dead, I ran upstairs looking for Patrick; I started in the attic and came down, room by room. He wasn't in his own or in either brother's room. With a new timidity I looked into Miranda's room, and was relieved not to find him there. He was not in mine, not in the Museum, and I couldn't locate him anywhere on the first floor.

He wasn't in sight along the edge of the cliff or out on the Head. "Find Patrick!" I said to Charlie, but though he was willing he could only pick up the old track out to the Liberty Knoll where Patrick and I had taken the flag down last night. We'd believed then that Miranda and Tom were alive. We'd been arguing and enjoying it while we folded the flag. I was trying to get out of the chess game while he told me it would help me to discipline my brain, which was extremely untidy.

"But they *are* still alive," I said fiercely to Charlie. I didn't believe myself, but to admit anything else would be to lose the last handhold over the abyss. "They are alive. *They are alive.*" I willed them to be alive.

I ran back into the house and got the flag, and raised it. As the folds fluttered in the breeze and then snapped out handsomely, I could hardly see the colors through the moisture in my eyes. "They are alive," I said once more.

It occurred to me that Patrick might have at last gone down to the dig, to be alone with, or to come to terms with, Miranda and Tom. Now the place really had ghosts, for him, anyway; he hadn't questioned their deaths, he had accepted them without a fight.

I knew better than to join him there. My position as an outsider had never been more clear. In the grief of this place I had no existence. But I could do Ian's errand, and I took the note over to the harbor for Elmer. He was busy cutting off salt pork and I waved the note at him, left it on the counter, and hurried away like a coward. Afterward I walked for a long time with Charlie. We went down onto the beach of Drummond Cove and around to Weir Cove, where the men were taking out herring.

I sat on the rocks watching them. The thistles and Queen Anne's lace, the drying tangles of beach peas, the shore-birds that Charlie chased, Charlie himself in his happy ignorance—everything said that nothing had changed.

Miranda was away but alive; otherwise how could everything be as it always was? She was alive, in love, defiant, excited. I saw her as if she were there before me. She was not dead. Not drowned. Tom, too, spoke and smiled in my mind, he came half-running across the field carrying a calf, he was Laertes to Patrick's Hamlet, dueling on the stairs; he was hauling in a codfish that looked as long as he was; he was waltzing with Miranda, solemnly and gracefully, round and round in West India Hall.

The men out there straining and sweating to seine their silvery harvest couldn't know yet what had happened, so that made it easier for me to suspend reality. When finally they rowed away their doryloads of herring, the gulls following them, I had to go back to the house, where the news would lurk like a monster that had taken possession of the place.

Mrs. Gillis was in the kitchen. She was a big woman with a lumpy but pleasant face. She had been crying, and spoke thickly. "Meg said I should cook dinner for you."

"You don't have to," I said. "I can get us some meals over the weekend, and we won't be wanting much anyway."

"You have to keep your strength up," she chided, but kindly.

"After I leave on Monday you'll have Patrick to look after, unless he goes ashore too. Then it'll just be Charlie."

"He's a good little tyke." She seemed faintly relieved. "Well, you just let me know, now. Maybe I better send over some of what I fix for my crowd, just in case. What about milk and cream and eggs?"

"We've got plenty, I think. But I can come for some."

"It's a blessing you're here with him," she said to me solemnly, from the doorway. "Those three, always together. He'll be taking it awful hard."

I did not see Patrick all that day. The hours went by somehow, but I have always preferred not to remember what a desert it was. In the late afternoon I remembered once catching him napping in the couch hammock, with the wide-awake hat tilted over his face. So I walked down there. It was empty, I was very tired, and my defenses were weakening of themselves. I wanted to cry, but when the tears were finished, the facts would still be there. I sat down for a few minutes in the shade and gazed across at the farm with eyes that felt seared as if with constant staring or lack of sleep. The place looked as tranquil in the late afternoon light as a George Inness painting. I could not bear to look at it for long.

Northwest of me the oaks kept up their rich dark green rustling, they always seemed to catch a breeze no matter how still it was. If Patrick was there, I could not go to him, and it was not simply a sensitivity to his private sorrow.

Charlie and I started back toward The Eyrie. I fed the dog and made tea for myself. There was only one way to occupy myself without pacing back and forth trying not to wring my hands, trying not to go from window to window. I went into the parlor to play the piano.

I took the easy way out, playing whatever came into my

head from the classics, light opera, popular music, folk music. One phrase suggested another, and I would move into another song hardly knowing it. This was how I began improvising my own version of the song Miranda had sung to Andrew's mandolin, *Fhir a Bhata*. At that moment it had no personal significance as I worked out chords and harmony, it was simply a problem I'd set myself. I half-sang, half-talked the words.

" 'How often haunting the highest hilltop,
    I scan the ocean thy sail to see!
    Wilt come tonight, love, wilt come tomorrow,
    Or ever come, love—' "

Hands came down over my shoulders and crushed my fingers flat on the keys and held them there. The discord was hideous. In spite of my contempt for females who screamed, I screamed. Charlie was in a frenzy. I was held in a vise, I couldn't move one way or the other. Then in the last of the sunset light I recognized Patrick's bandaged hand and the blue sweater sleeves. Charlie pawed at both of us, crying with anxiety.

"Patrick, for heaven's sake!" I said. "You're breaking my wrists!"

"I don't ever want to hear that song again!"

My head was forced against his chest, and I could feel his voice begin there. "I thought I was alone in the house," I began to apologize, but he released my hands, took me around the waist with his good arm and lifted me off the stool, then slammed down the piano lid.

"I don't ever want to hear that piano again, either," he said. He stood looking down at it, with its unfortunate resemblance to a coffin, as if he would have murdered the piano if he could.

Such a mood was not to be approached, or even spoken to. I left him there and went back to the kitchen, rubbing my wrists. The tea kettle was steaming on the stove, and a strange kettle was beside it. Mrs. Gillis must have come in while I was in the parlor. I lifted the lid and smelled clam chowder. My stomach contracted convulsively, but I needed food, I'd survived on tea all day. I lit a lamp, set the table for two, and ladled out a small bowl of chowder for myself. With the first hot swallow I knew I was hungry in spite of everything. I was so tired from struggling to keep Tom and Miranda alive that both my mind and body ached.

I was astonishingly glad to see Faustina. She had been crying on the way from the harbor and was still sniffling. Her nose was very red.

"Where's Patrick?" she asked in a hushed voice.

"Somewhere in the house. Have some chowder."

"I couldn't swaller it." She poured a cup of tea for herself and said at once, "I'm going to be married. Hughie and me, we're going off to the main on the Monday boat. If Ian was here we wouldn't have to. He's a justice of the peace."

"Congratulations," I said. "I mean it. I think Hughie's a peach."

Her eyes filled up. "It's what I been wanting. I been filling my hope chest for years, it feels like, but Hughie's half-gull and half something else that don't want to settle down. Well, now I got him and he warn't a bit ugly about it. My folks are some pleased too." Her tears overcame her completely, she scrabbled around for a handkerchief and said brokenly from it, "But this happening to Miranda and Tom, it's took all the joy out of everything."

"I know," I said. "But in time you'll be happier."

"We already decided if it's a boy it'll be Tom, and if it's a girl—" She couldn't finish. *Why?* she cried. "People like that, it shouldn't happen to them! Turned over to the crabs and the fish——"

"Stop that, Faustina!" I very nearly shouted it. "I don't want to hear it! We don't know that they were drowned. Everybody's taken it for granted but me. But nobody knows for sure they were even on that vessel."

"No," said Patrick's voice from the shadows of the back stairs. He came into the room and said pleasantly, "Hello, Faussie, dear. Dry your tears, they may all be for nothing. What do we have to eat here?"

He sat down at the table, seeming at ease. He had shed the sweater, he wore a clean white shirt open at the neck, he looked and smelled just washed. I got a bowl of chowder for him, and our eyes met; there was nothing in his look that referred to the scene in the parlor. All that was left of it was a burning tenderness in my wrists and fingers.

I finished my meal and said, "I can hardly keep my eyes open. I'm going up to bed."

"So'm I, pretty quick," Faustina said. "Seems like this day was a year long."

"Oh, let's have a game of crib first, Faussie," Patrick said winningly. She couldn't resist his manner. I left them playing at the kitchen table and went upstairs with Charlie, to be met at the head of the stairs with a powerful slap of recollection; I was sleeping in Miranda's room.

I couldn't. Not any more.

I went into my own room, where I had started packing after the words with Patrick, and chucked everything back into the drawers. I got a fresh nightdress and wrapper rather than take those in Miranda's closet, and went across the hall to Ian's room. Meg had thoroughly aired and cleaned it after his sick spell, and it smelled of fresh sheets.

Charlie seemed at ease here, but for me to climb into the Old Colonel's four poster felt rather like lèse-majesté, and the other militarily austere furniture seemed to stare in disapproval, but at least it didn't have an air of piteous bereavement, like Miranda's things. I left the shades undrawn and lay staring at the stars over the ocean until they hypnotized me into sleep.

When I woke up the room was full of sunshine, and I didn't know where I was at first. Charlie, squirming on his back and kicking energetically, oriented me, and at once I wondered if Patrick had had nightmares, and I had been too deeply asleep to hear. Remorsefully I got up in the chilly room, and went to my bathroom to wash and dress. Faustina had gone.

Patrick's door was ajar but he wasn't in it. From his windows I looked across lawn and field toward the water, but there were no fishing boats out; it was Sunday. He could be out rowing somewhere, or even sailing. There was a good little breeze. Or he could be in the oak grove again. I sighed, resigned him to his own fancies, and went back downstairs.

He hadn't made coffee, so I wondered just when he'd gotten up. I got breakfast for myself. I'll tell you one thing, Patrick Drummond, I said silently, I'm not staying in the house all day *today* in case you decide to come back.

I spent most of the morning walking around the shore from the Home Cove to Andrew's Cove and back again, and when I came back to the house to get a drink and rest before starting out again, I saw the first callers coming along the road, direct from church. I had just time to wash my face and hands, and put on a fresh dress and shoes, and then meet them at the front door—remembering through greetings that I had raised the flag yesterday morning to signify No Surrender and had forgotten to take it down last night.

The morning callers were Mr. and Mrs. Clement and a few of the summer boarders who, like them, were regulars and had known the family a long time. Thanking them for their kindness and saying that Patrick preferred to be by himself for a while, I began to have the sensation of existing in a dream within a dream. Presently I'd be narrating the whole thing to some receptive audience like Miranda, saying, "And it seemed so *real!* Not awful, but fantastic. One couldn't possibly take it seriously."

In the afternoon the village people began coming. Most of these brought food of some sort. Over and over I said, "Thank you. You're so good. Yes, Patrick's very upset. He doesn't want to see anybody right now. You understand...."

But he's grateful to you." Over and over I said, "But we're not really *sure*. We don't know yet if Tom and Miranda were on the vessel."

The younger ones accepted it with pathetic eagerness, the older ones nodded kindly—but I could see that it was just kindness. Someone had seen a shipwreck in tea leaves; someone had dreamed of a birth, which meant a funeral; a bird had flown into a house, another bad omen. Omens were everywhere, like a flock of crows. I didn't contribute Patrick's nightmares about drowning. Across the parlor the closed piano looked more and more like a coffin. I'd put books on it, flowers, and a ship model from the library, but it wasn't much help.

The food would keep coming until the funerals were over with. *Funerals.* Obscene word. I wasn't admitting there'd be any. I put the food away in refrigerator, cupboard, or bread-box. In the late afternoon the tide retreated. I had a scrapy throat, and aches in my bones for no reason at all. Good, I thought drearily, I'm coming down with their damned old epizootic.

I went up to my room and began to pack for departure tomorrow. The scrapy throat was from having to talk so much, the aches from keeping myself braced. Outside the windows the late afternoon light at the end of August was far different from that of June with all its promises. I found that I was weeping as I packed. The tears ran and ran. Charlie lay on my bed and watched with distressed dark amber eyes through his bangs, and I told him between sobs that he was a good boy, everything was all right, don't worry.

He wasn't convinced. He followed me into the bathroom where I went to lower my face into a basin of cold water. I held it there as long as I could, lifted it, took a breath, and dipped it again. When I thought I had the weeping conquered, I dried my face. When I went back into my room, wiping my wet temples with the towel, Patrick was leaning in my doorway. "I'm so damned tired," he said draggingly, "but I can't stop moving."

"We'll see to that," I said, trying to sound as authoritative as Meg. "Come on across to your room." He was oddly docile, as if there was not much left of the original Patrick. He sat on the edge of the bed and I took his shoes off. "Now lie down," I ordered, and he protested, "I don't want to sleep. I don't want to dream." He swayed groggily toward his pillows as he spoke.

"You won't dream," I promised rashly. "And I'll be right back."

I went down and made him a cup of cocoa, dropping in the prescribed dose of the pain-killer the doctor had left. Patrick had refused it up till now, and this he wouldn't know about.

He was still sitting on the edge of the bed, his chin on his chest. "Have you had anything at all to eat today?" I asked, and he responded slowly, as if from a long way off, blinking and frowning at me.

"What?"

"Where have you been, anyway?"

"Oh, here awa', there awa', Wandering Wullie," he said with a ghostly creasing of humor around his blood-shot eyes.

"Well, drink this and then take a nap," I said.

"You guarantee I won't dream? Because I always believe you, Seafair, you know that." Smiling to himself he took the cup and drank, then lay back and swung his legs up. His eye-lids dropped, he said something which I couldn't understand, and nothing more. I covered him and went back to my packing. When I would have had to light a lamp, I went back down to the kitchen. I hated that room now, and the parlor was impossible since the piano was closed; the dining room was too full of the family dinners there. But the library was different. I could look past the long-drawn-out torture of the chess lessons, when we were tying to make the hours pass, to the stable presences of Ian and Andrew.

I was there, reading the Old Colonel's privately printed account of his years with Washington, when Hughie and Faustina came, still in their Sunday clothes. Hughie was subdued and decorous, as if his stiff collar had a death grip on his throat. I sent him upstairs to help Patrick undress, and he brightened considerably at that thought of being useful. When he came back he said that Patrick hadn't waked even while having his trousers skinned off him, and his sweater pulled off over his head.

I was shamelessly glad of their company. We moved to the kitchen after a while; their presence neutralized the woe which had sunk into its walls as the blood had sunk into the floor. I set out a rich spread of the day's offerings, and we ate.

Faustina was happy about tomorrow when she was not sad about Tom and Miranda. Several times I was tempted to tell her I would be going too, but I couldn't face the fresh spate of conversation about it. Finally Hughie left, after a prolonged goodnight to Faustina in the shed, and we went to bed.

I returned to Ian's room, and Faustina didn't need an explanation of this. "I don't blame you," she said. She wanted to be sure the door was tightly closed between my room and Miranda's. "If I heard a sound in there I'd die," she said. Suddenly she burst into noisy tears. "When I think why I'm *here*," she tried to explain but could go no further.

"I know, I know," I kept saying, "we just have to do the best we can, that's all." I left her when she'd quieted and went to listen outside Patrick's door. His breathing was deep and slow. Thankful that he was having peace for this little while at least, I went back to bed carrying my own peace very carefully.

J didn't sleep soundly until near daylight. Consequently I didn't see Faustina when she got up and left, and I imagined her astonishment when I appeared to go aboard the boat. I wondered if she'd thought it strange I hadn't wished her well last night.

The morning was gray and close, with fog disappearing to reveal a monotonous world of flat water and no-color sky, then drifting and dripping back. Entirely suitable weather for my last day on Drummond's. The halcyon days, the poet's days of wine and roses, were so long gone that I could scarcely remember that the sun had shone only yesterday and the seas were blue.

Patrick had slept all night under the influence of exhaustion and the drug. I couldn't bear to go and leave him sleeping, to have him wake up in the empty house, so I went to his room at last with a cup of coffee, and tried to wake him up. It was difficult, but I accomplished it by washing his face with an icy cold wet cloth. He stared at me in bemused astonishment, looking very young.

"Listen, Patrick, I'm going in on the boat today, remember?"

"What for?"

"Sit up and have some coffee. It's very good. . . . I'm going because Ian told me to. You remember that, don't you? And Faustina and Hughie are going in today to see about getting married."

"High time, too," he mumbled. "What's this about Ian's orders? Can't you make sense?"

His sleep had been too deep; he'd forgotten everything. I

felt sick to my stomach with dismay. "Come on down to breakfast and we'll talk about it more then. Drink your coffee and it'll wake you up."

When he hadn't appeared in a half hour, I went upstairs and found that he had fallen asleep again. I stood by the bed watching him. He had wiped me out of his life yesterday with a malicious jibe about man-eating spiders. As for the embrace later, if Meg had been there she would have gotten it, it was simply his blind groping for comfort. Yet, looking objectively at him as a man—a boy—isolated in a wilderness of sorrow, I hated to leave him. What would he do alone in this house, with no one to come back to from his wanderings? To wake up in the night and knew he was alone? Even Charlie would be gone, over to the farm to be looked after.

He was stirring, and I left the room quickly. In a little while he appeared in the kitchen. By his face, no longer blurred and innocent with sleep, I knew he had remembered. He sat down at the table and rested his head in his hands. Without speaking I set a fresh cup of coffee before him, and he roused himself to drink. I waited until he'd drunk most of it, staring all the while at a far corner of the room.

"Ian's right, you know," I said gently. "There's no real reason for my staying here now. I'd have to be leaving in a few weeks anyway." He didn't look around. I waited a moment and began again. "It's over. Whatever Ian and Andrew find down there at Fenwick Island, it's over. If they *weren't* on the ship, if they're halfway to California or all the way there by train, they'll come back when they're ready, or you can go to them. If they—if nobody ever finds them, well—" I stopped. I wished I had never to think or explain again in my life.

"I'm still here, Seafair," he said in a low voice, still gazing at that corner.

"Come ashore with me," I urged. "You know people in Rockland, but if you want to stay in a hotel I'll stay there too, while we're waiting." This wasn't quite how I'd planned it, but there I was saying it. "It would be better for you out of this house."

"No place is *better* for me," he said coldly. "No place is good, or even fair to middlin'. I'm staying here."

"Then you could keep busy at the store all day and sleep nights at the farm." It was a feeble suggestion and was ignored. I said, "I'd better put a fresh dressing on your hand before I go."

That too was ignored. Rather than hover indecisively, I went upstairs and put the last of my toilet articles into my dressing case. I had only to collect my mackintosh and I would be ready. A wind was rising, making a chilly little whistle around the screen. I didn't care how rough the bay would be, I only wanted to be away from here, and wished the whole thing would be automatically erased from my mind the instant I stepped on the mainland.

Lastly I went into Miranda's room to strip her bed, but I lost my courage. A bare mattress would make it look too much like the room of someone who had just died. The people in the photographs had suddenly taken on life; they were watching me with either unbearable knowledge or unanswerable questions. I avoided all the eyes, and turned to hurry out.

Patrick stood in the entrance from the hall. He came in and glanced around him in the same swift, elusive, perhaps cowardly way I'd done, and then before I could go across to my room he stepped into my way.

"Don't go, Seafair," he said. Simply, not humbly. "Please."

"I have to go."

"Not on Ian's orders. What the hell does that have to do with us? Who cares about Mrs. Grundy right now, for God's sake? Do *you?*" His right hand took my chin in a hard pinch. "*Do* you? Are you that kind?"

"It's not that, Patrick," I protested. "Believe me."

"Then what is it? Is it because you're tired of being sorry for someone? In a hurry to get on with your own life? To close the door on Miranda and me?" He let go my chin and said softly, "If you're not here to hear my voice, I'll go mad. I have no pride. I'm begging. Don't make me lose everything at once."

It wasn't *me*, it was because I was the only one left. But my objective view of him was superimposed on the more intimate one, and pity was such a wrenching cramp in me I thought for an instant I was about to disgrace myself by throwing up.

He took hold of my shoulder. "You can spare me another week, can't you? Until they come back? Please. You've become almost a part of me, Seafair. If you go now it'll be another amputation."

"All right," I said. I could hardly say it out loud.

He drew me to him and rocked me in his arms as he had rocked Miranda. "Thanks, thanks!"

I got my face away from his shoulder and struggled out of the bear hug. "I'll have to write a letter and get it to the boat," I said.

"Write it where I can watch you." He was almost exuberant.

I wrote it at the kitchen table while he ate a fair breakfast. I told Papa there was sickness at the Drummond house and I was staying on to help out; if I didn't get to Fern Grove before school opened, I'd be home the first weekend possible.

Patrick insisted on taking it to the harbor to mail. "I'm afraid you'll change your mind," he said candidly, "and get aboard the boat."

"Since it won't be here for an hour or more, I'd have to fly out over the bay to do that, wouldn't I?"

"I wouldn't put it past you. You have hidden gifts."

"Ayuh," I said, like Faustina. "But levitation isn't one of them. Not on a physical plane, anyway."

He shaved and allowed me to put the clean dressing on his hand before he went to the harbor with the letter. "Give my love to Faustina if you see her," I called after him. When I was alone I was nearly jubilant one moment, because this was what I really wanted; in the next I was beset by suspicion of my own motives, dread of losing Ian's good opinion of me, worry of how to handle Mrs. Gillis. That was the least of it, falling into the Mrs. Grundy category. Everyone was too upset by the supposed tragedy to be concerned with superficialities. I say "supposed" because I was constantly washed over with disbelief, so strong it was as if Miranda herself had called to me from the next room.

Ian and the Finlays had taken the late train out of Rockland Thursday night. There was no knowing how long it would take them to get to Fenwick Island, how involved or difficult the journey might be. But Ian was to telegraph a friend in Rockland as soon as they had made the identifications, and this man would get word to us.

When Patrick came back with no mail besides the usual, and a dozen ears of sweet corn he'd stopped to pick at the farm, I felt reassurance like cold water blowing over a burn. Wasn't it true that no news was good news? He behaved as if he believed it.

"Well, we sail this afternoon," he announced, and as usual I recoiled.

"It's miserable! It's a day for fires. It's a day for *chess*," I compromised. "I feel like chess today."

"Liar." He pulled my ear as he used to pull Miranda's. "It's warm out, and it's time you learned how to handle *Eaglet* in a northeast breeze. There's a nice little one springing up." I thought of bargaining with him for a chance at the piano, but decided to wait until we were aboard *Eaglet*.

We tacked most of the way to Bannock, and I took the sloop into the harbor myself, remembering the first time I'd seen her and Patrick. A five-master was being loaded at the wharf. Light from a just-invisible sun touched the blocks of pink granite and made them glow as if from within themselves.

"She'll be leaving on the tide, as soon as she's loaded," Patrick said. We made fast near the head of the wharf, almost opposite the store. "Come on ashore and I'll treat you," he said handsomely.

"Wait," I said. A woman walked past the store and down toward the vessel, alone, straight as a mast, exaggeratedly tall from where we sat in *Eaglet*'s cockpit. Rosaleen Dolan, unaware of us. She wore a long coat-sweater over her dress, and her hands were pushed hard into the pockets. She stopped beside the schooner's bow, staring the length of the vessel. It was like watching a leopard in a zoo staring out past the bars and the faces to where Africa must lie; it was the reason I hated zoos. If by some fluke the beast became free it would never find Africa but would die miserably, victim of humanity.

"She's trying to get up her courage," Patrick said. "If she thought there was a way to hide on board, she'd be gone like a puff of smoke. She's got money in her pocket, you can bet."

"And it's the end of summer," I said. "They made her promise to wait, because of the boys."

"To hell with the boys. She'd go without them this instant, if she could. She's past thinking straight."

"We shouldn't watch her. It's...indecent." I tried to look at the village hanging to the slopes and the quarry rigging against the sky. What I saw instead, my vision drawn like a compass needle to true north, were the two little boys hovering around the corner of the store, watching her as if they were afraid she might disappear, but were also afraid to approach her.

The donkey engine stopped, men wiped their sweating faces and took out pipes or cigarettes. There was some laughing. Big hooves shifted on the planks, tails swished at flies. Ivor Jenkins looked around, his smile white in his black beard, saw Rosaleen, and his smile disappeared. He went toward her. When he had almost reached her, she turned abruptly around and began her swift long pace back up the wharf.

Patrick stepped onto the bow deck of *Eaglet* and spoke her name but she walked by with no change in her face or even a sidewise flicker of her eyes. Ivor stood looking after her. She went on past the store and the boys fell in behind her, but they kept their distance.

"Poor little devils," Patrick muttered. "They don't know whether they're afoot or on horseback."

I wished we hadn't come; I had enough to nag at me without the memory of those two.

In the store several people came up to Patrick to offer condolences. He turned them off gracefully, shaking hands or patting a shoulder. "But we're not a bit sure yet, you see," he said. "In fact, we're pretty furious with them for sending everybody all around Robin Hood's barn, aren't we, Seafair?" This with a luminous smile at me, and mutely I nodded, taken aback by this new phase of Patrick. "They're probably honeymooning up on the Allegash," he continued merrily. "With the moose and the bears."

This made everybody laugh, and Patrick put his arm around me and hurried me out. "Always leave them laughing," he said. "I learned this when I was in vaudeville, in a previous incarnation."

On the way back to Drummond's he took the tiller and sang most of the way, poking me with a foot until I had to join in. I'd never felt less like singing. Still, I coöperated in hopes of getting a fair exchange. When we had *Eaglet* snugged down for the night and were rowing ashore across the silent green and silver cove, I said, "How about my having the piano for an hour?"

"What for?" He sounded honestly surprised.

"To practice. After all, it's my work——"

He grinned. "Right now your work is *me*. Look, let's eat in the dining room tonight, with candles and so forth. Have we got something more than left-over clam chowder or fish hash? Or can you make something mysterious in a chafing dish?"

"If you call Welsh Rabbit mysterious, yes. But I seem to remember a putting pan of baked stuffed lobster on ice yesterday Somebody or other brought it."

"Perfect!"

We were very talkative and gay, but once during the candlelit meal, watching Patrick pouring wine, I suddenly saw Ian's face, soberly intent like this, in another place, and it was like icewater poured over my head and down my back, freezing me until my teeth chattered.

Patrick heard my teeth on the glass. "What's the matter?"

"A sudden chill," I said. "I hope I'm not getting that summer complaint."

"Oh God, I hope not too. I'm no good as a nurse and I refuse to have Ma Gillis charging around in here."

"I'll just go out and jump over the cliff," I said with dignity. The chill passed, and would stay away as long as I held off that vision of Ian looking down at something by lamplight, something which dreadfully held all his attention.

fter the afternoon sailing, the combination of wine and chess did me in and even Patrick conceded I was of no earthly good to him. He waved me off to bed, exasperated.

"You're going to be a crotchety old man," I told him. "Goodnight."

The Old Colonel watched me coming up with my candle and the Skye terrier. I wish you were here now, I told him. In the flesh, that is. To take hold and tell us that we'll survive this.

Stoutly packed into his buff and blue, one broad thick hand on his knee, the other doubled on his hip, he had been watching his descendants for a hundred years or so with sardonic composure, humor, a kindly twinkle, or the impersonal scrutiny of one who simply waits to see what happens next; however the Old Colonel regarded you, it depended on what you were looking for, as well as the way the light fell. Tonight I found nothing but the painted face of a man who had probably been listening to the artist's reminiscences of other subjects, or his troubles with his wife.

I had forgotten to make my bed, which I'd stripped that morning. Putting on fresh sheets roused me again. Nothing I read helped, either. I found myself listening hard, grateful for Charlie's breathing, envious of his deep and innocent sleep. I will never have a granite house, I thought, I want wood that breathes and creaks and settles. I want mice in my house to scamper around between floors. The farm cats must have been very efficient, one never thought of mice at The Eyrie.

I hadn't even heard the clock for a long time, and suddenly I realized Ian must have forgotten to wind it this week, as we were forgetting to take in the flag.

I shut my eyes on the pale rectangles of the windows and imagined myself back aboard *Eaglet*.

My hand shaped to grip the tiller, and I felt Patrick's arm behind me, his hand guiding mine. This might well be all I had of him. Who had a right to cheat me out of it? Ian, or my father, or anybody else? *Miranda?*

It brought her into the room with me. Either she had evoked her name or it had evoked her, and I wanted to speak to her and hear her answer; I wept for losing her and for the whole askew business of my being here like this.

"Seafair."

Charlie, who had slept through Miranda's visitation, sat up bristling. "Seafair." It was Patrick in the hall. "Wake up."

I came upright, trembling, expecting that he'd seen her. "What's the matter?"

"Let me in." He came in anyway. I scrabbled around trying to find matches, and he said, "Never mind a light." He sat down on the edge of the bed. Charlie greeted him and went back to the foot and began washing. I could just dimly make out the tartan of Patrick's dressing gown.

"Have you been dreaming?" I asked. "Or haven't you been asleep? Let's go down and make hot chocolate or something."

"Don't talk like a nanny," he said irritably. "I don't know if I've been asleep or awake. I know I can't stand my own thoughts. I keep thinking I'm to blame if they're dead. You could say I killed them."

"How? Why?" I demanded.

"I should have been able to hold them back somehow that night." He sat hunched over his folded arms. "Made a big touse. Got Ian up no matter how sick he was."

"Tom hit you, remember?"

"Why didn't I do something after that?" he demanded. "No, I acted like a lunatic or a mental defective. Where was my *brain?* How anybody could be so damned *stupid.*" His groan seemed to come from his toes. I leaned forward and took his arm between my hands.

"You were dazed from hitting your head. You didn't quite remember what had happened at first. Remember? You might even have had a slight concussion."

"Did I say that?" he asked with a pitiful earnestness. "Did I really say that?"

"Yes, you did."

He slumped with a sigh. "See how crazy I am? I didn't remember that. I kept thinking, Why didn't I stop them?"

"You would have if you could," I assured him.

"Oh God, what a relief, *what* a relief!" His laughter was shaky. "I was ready to go hang myself in the attic." He reached for me in the dark, took me clumsily into his arms, and cuddled me against him. "You're my lucky stone, you know that?" he murmured.

"The kind you find on the beach, with a ring around it?" I felt light-headed and was getting rapidly more so, with his lips going over my ear and temple and cheekbones.

"With two rings around it," he said. "Couldn't be luckier. Don't ever leave me, Seafair. Promise." He put his mouth over mine before I could answer, and tightened his embrace. Without words but with a mutual agreement, as if we both knew the steps of the same dance, we shifted around to be comfortable and easy-fitting in the embrace. The kisses grew more ardent and greedy, as if the more we had the more we wanted.

"Let me stay here tonight," he whispered. "Don't make me go back to that room."

"Yes," I said. "Stay." I said it strongly. Martin Luther again. *Sin boldly*. But I couldn't believe it was sin. Not this, any more than Wagner's love music was sinful. It was outside all the judgments, scales, and values that I had known until now. It was two people grasping life in a granite house that would otherwise have been a mausoleum. It was two people and a cheerfully oblivious small dog in a room like an ark, surviving a flood that had killed their world. When I turned back the covers for Patrick I knew what I was doing, and I did it with a fierce and frightened joy.

"I love you," I said to him during the night, because this was not a thing that should happen without love, and I was no more ashamed to admit it than I was to get rid of my nightdress. "I love you."

"I can't live without you," he said. "This puts a seal on it. You're mine now, no matter what. I'm sorry if I hurt you."

"You didn't. I mean, I don't care. I wanted you to. It's part of it."

"Next time it won't hurt." He caught up my tears delicately with his tongue and gathered me closer to him. "Sleep now. We're Wynken and Blynken, and Charlie is Nod, and we're adrift in a wooden shoe out among the stars." He laughed softly. "Charlie's been riding the billows like an old salt."

Cradled and proud, I slept. Sometime later in the night, when we had separated in our sleep, he reached for me to draw me back to him and I rolled gladly over to him. Settling me against his chest, putting a leg over me to hold me securely to him, he said a name.

"Miranda."

So that's it, said the voice inside my head. It offered neither malice nor quarter. It simply stated a fact.

I couldn't get free of his unconscious embrace and I lay there wondering how long before I would have to explode into the convulsive motions of one fighting for life. He slept on serenely, dreaming that it was Miranda he held in his arms. How totally I had been fooled, yet no one had done it to me but myself. Miranda had deceived me only about Tom, and I had long since forgiven it. Ian must have known about Patrick, or suspected, when he was displeased about Miranda's coming home and spoke of the havoc created by the innocent. But naturally he wouldn't have told me, a stranger.

The reaction was pure hell. In fact, lying there waiting for a chance to break loose, I thought quite coherently that this must be my particular hell. I might move physically from his arms, but never again in any other sense. Always now I would be a prisoner of shame, disappointment, rage—anything bad. I knew it all now, I looked it in the face while I lay there. I even remembered the kiss at the dance, that had been meant for Miranda, because I'd worn her cloak and her perfume.

With the first rooster crowing at the farm and the first gulls flying in, he released me, lay over on his back, and went on sleeping. The bruises were almost gone now, and he looked happy because he thought Miranda had returned. When he woke it would be a different matter, but I had no room for pity except for myself.

I slid out of bed and went into the bathroom to dress. I knew I wouldn't look any different, but I avoided the mirror anyway. I went out through Miranda's room. Charlie slept on with Patrick, so I moved alone through the tomblike silence and the gloomy light of the hall and stairs. I went out the front door and took what seemed like my first long breath in hours. I'll never go back in there, I thought wildly, knowing it was an empty threat. I'd have to wait until tomorrow's boat, and there was nowhere to stay in the meantime.

It was chilly, still gray, and very wet. I walked out onto the Head, down onto the northeastern shore and all along the rocks close to the water, around the base of the promontory where the eagle's nest was, into Home Cove, around the next point and into Andrew's Cove; along Marsh Cove; up over the rocks and across the field of juniper above Steeple Cove, through the woods behind the church, and then back along the road to The Eyrie.

Sunrise flushed the whole sky with pink and gold. The long and strenuous walk had beaten some of the fire out of my system, so when I saw smoke rising from the kitchen chimney, blue in the sunrise, I merely wondered dully how I would greet Patrick. Or how he would greet me. Perhaps he would want to avoid *me*. I felt a little surge of hope, proving I wasn't entirely benumbed.

Charlie met me outside the woodshed and escorted me in. Patrick wasn't there. There was coffee, and my place set at the table. Squishing in my wet shoes, my damp hem dragging at me, I went straight to the stove and cupped my cold hands around the hot coffee pot.

"Where have you been?" Patrick shouted from the head of the back stairs. He came running down. "In another ten minutes I was going to get a search party out." His glare was familiar; usually Miranda was the recipient. *Miranda.* I felt like sagging where I stood.

"I've been for a walk," I said, turning away. He took me by the arm and yanked me around to face him. "Don't you ever do such a thing again, do you *hear* me? I thought you were dead. That you'd slipped off the rocks somewhere, or killed yourself because I'd ruined you."

"It would take more than that," I said, "to make me kill myself." I stood passively in his grip, looking at him, and it was there in my mouth, the truth I wanted to tell him. But suddenly he smiled and wrapped his arms tightly around me, which pressed my face into his shoulder; it was as if he wanted to stop me from speaking. "I missed you," he said. "You don't know how I missed you. Don't ever run away from me again. Because I need you!"

Not *Because I love you,* I reflected with a curious lack of bitterness. He can't say that because he is faithful to Miranda. I suppose I can respect him for it. What had he thought when he woke in my bed this morning, and knew how false his dreams had been?

"Could I have some coffee, do you think?" I asked.

"Sit down and I'll wait on you," he said eagerly, pushing me toward a chair. "Look at you. Soaked feet, wet clothes—how far have you been, anyway?"

I told him. It was an extraordinary situation, to find myself talking in such an ordinary way; extraordinary too that the ultimate intimacy had driven us apart. I sat there eating the food he served me and inventing details to compensate for the fact that I'd taken in practically nothing on my long walk.

"Well, you're back now," he said contentedly, "and that's what matters. You'd better change into something dry. I'm going to haul a few traps and we'll have some lobsters to eat. How's that?" He grinned at me. "I'll wear a mitten over that hand. It won't be very handy, but I can manage. I'll have to, with Hughie gone. Hey, want to come?"

"Not really," I said. It would probably be bad for his hand, but no use to object, he wouldn't listen anyway, and I was anxious to have him away from me. I'd thought I couldn't feel worse than I'd felt in the night and early morning, but this was a different sort of misery. He tilted up my face and kissed me before he went. It was affectionate, but not like last night's kisses. "If you weren't here waiting for me," he said quietly, "I don't think I'd bother to come back."

Alone, I was not alone; the moral dilemma was left to bedevil me, and by "moral" it didn't mean the world's interpretation. (Or Fern Grove's, to narrow it down a bit.) If I could get through the promised week—and I didn't know how I could, unless by stated agreement we went back to the *status quo ante*—wouldn't that be the duty of friendship, distinct from anything else? Could I run from him in abhorrence because of something he didn't even know he had done? Just how deep did my fine theories of compassion go?

It tormented me all the while I changed into dry clothes and made a fresh bed for myself. Between these sheets which I was bundling out of the way I had been ruined, Patrick said, half-joking; Fern Grove and most of the rest of society wouldn't have been joking. They'd have seen to it that I knew I was well and truly ruined.

I didn't feel ruined, seduced, tainted, or corrupted, except in a way none of them could have possibly understood. And I had done it myself. I was the one who had turned back the covers and said, "Yes. Stay." And I was the one who had told myself that I knew exactly what I was doing.

I didn't weep for my virginity, but I did weep for the deluded joy of the night. Afterward I went downstairs and into the parlor, where morning sunlight showed the dust that hadn't been removed for a week, and went to the piano, to begin again.

The piano was locked.

chapter 34

If Patrick had walked in then, he would have heard something. I almost ran from the room, and out the front door. Charlie shot ahead of me.

By the time I reached the wall I realized that the locked piano was nothing compared to the waking to someone else's name. I sat on the wall for a while, watching the medricks dart and dive. Ducklings paddled after their mothers. The cycle of life went on as I would go on. Last night couldn't kill me if I refused to allow it to kill me.

After a time, I was no longer furious with Patrick. After all, we had something in common; we had each lost a love. *Never seek to tell thy love/ Love that never told can be.* Blake had it right. *For the gentle wind does move/ Silently, invisibly.*

It blew on my shoulders and the back of my neck as I walked toward the house, the Drummond sea wind which after a week I would never feel again. Patrick would be dead to me, and if Miranda should return, or at least be found alive, she would be dead to Patrick. Losing her to Tom must be worse than losing her to literal death. At least if she were dead, Tom wouldn't have her, and Patrick could dream that she might have been his eventually, given time.

I felt ancient with experience because I'd already lived that dream out and waked from it. I went to Meg's cupboard of cleaning materials and got what I needed and began to clean the parlor. I started at the seaward end and washed the windows, the mirrors, everything else that was glass. I dusted. I pushed the carpet sweeper. I would do the same in the hall, and then in the library. I observed to Charlie that dusting every book, whether it needed it or not, would probably use up a good deal of my week. I would vary dusting—which I had always loathed—with waxing and oiling where it was necessary. I could launder the bedroom curtains and linens, and Meg would return to an Eyrie as spotless as I could make it. In years to come she might remember me with admiration as a good housekeeper, I thought cynically. Then again, she might prefer never to remember me at all, and, if the Drummonds did, it would be as somebody who was there when their world disintegrated. My name would be forever associated with tragedy, like the messenger who brought bad news and must be killed for it.

When Patrick came in it was almost noon, and I was polishing one of the brass fenders in the parlor. He strode forward, swearing, and hauled me up roughly from my knees. "What do you think you're doing?"

"Well, I have to do something!" I said with spirit.

"I should have taken you with me." He gave me a hard, angry kiss, and shoved me away. "Go wash your hands. We'll cook up the lobsters and then go sailing."

Last night was an insuperable barrier between us, but I didn't know how to breach it without losing my own poise. I might even cry, which would be terrible. I kept hoping, all the time we were cooking the lobsters and eating them out on the Liberty Knoll, that he'd notice some restraint about me, and demand an explanation. But there was a kind of hectic, self-centered gaiety about him, as if he were keeping up a clatter to frighten off thought itself. Perhaps when we were aboard *Eaglet* we could both calm down. Out there, borne along by the sea and the wind, I could talk and he could listen. Perhaps we could have honesty, if nothing else.

Mrs. Gillis came in while we were carrying our debris into the kitchen. She exuded mournful disapproval of my continued presence, but Patrick was watching her with the springy anticipation of a blue-eyed cat waiting for the moment to pounce, so she offered no opinions. "I've brought a baked stuffed haddock for your supper," she said to the pump. "And some fresh cukes and tomatoes. Apple cobbler."

"Thank you, my gillyflower," said Patrick. "A sumptuous repast." She nodded stonily at the pump and left.

"She won't be back nosing around," he said in satisfaction. "She's shocked to the ears. She couldn't look at either of us for fear of reading the marks of sin all over us."

When we left the house to go down to the sloop, the wind had freshened and cooled, and the fog was twisting and billowing over the sea like lilac smoke.

"Look at *that!*" I wailed.

Patrick looked, and shook his head. "Well, well." He smiled at me, drowsily.

"I guess if we can't sail I'll walk over to the harbor."

"We'll take a nap," he said softly. "The fog will shut in thick all around and we'll take a nap."

"Somebody will be sure to come to call. Somebody who hasn't come already." I wanted to go to the harbor more and more with each moment. But if I got there, could I make myself come back?

"We'll lock the doors. No, that would make them suspicious. We won't make a sound, and they'll think we're at the dig. Nobody would follow us there."

"*Patrick,*" I began; I think I would have told him then, if he'd given me the chance.

Instead he reached over and touched my face, and gave me that sleepy smile again. "I want to see you, Seafair. I want to see if you're that pretty brown all over, or creamy where you aren't tanned."

"I'm *red* all over right now," I objected. I felt scorched.

"So you are." His fingers tapped my cheek, walked down to my throat. "What's the matter, Seafair? Don't you want me to see you? Don't you want to see *me?* There should be no shame and no secrets between lovers."

"There are other secrets," I said, "and there are other ways of seeing."

" 'It adds a precious seeing to the eye; a lover's eyes will stare an eagle blind.' "

"*Are* we lovers, Patrick? Of each other, I mean? You never told me."

"Of course I love you, you funny little twit." He burst out laughing. "Come to bed and let me prove it all over again."

Perhaps he won't sleep this time, I thought, and dream it's Miranda. If he didn't say *I love you* the way I wanted him to, at least he had said it in another way. And Miranda was not here; but I was. Perhaps something would happen today to change everything, so I would never have to tell him whose name he had spoken in the night. Perhaps consciously he had already given her up. I had only to be here, and the rest would take care of itself.

His hand fondled my ear, delicately fingered the lobe, stroked, caressed. I pushed my head against his palm. "Yes," I said.

Charlie slept curled up in a corner of the room, on Patrick's dressing gown. This time there was none of the compulsive, desperate haste, but an afternoon seemingly without end. No shame, no secrets.

"I love you, Seafair," he said to me at last. The words came in a heavy, drugged sequence, and then he fell asleep. This time his hold was loose, and I got away before he could remember in his sleep and erase what he had said. Carrying my clothes I walked naked around the stairwell to my room. Charlie frisked around me with obvious thoughts of his supper.

I washed, and did up my hair for almost the first time since I'd come to the island and begun wearing it down. I put on one of the dresses Phoebe had sent me, smiling at the irony of it. Of all the occasions Phoebe could imagine, this certainly wasn't one of them.

I went downstairs and fed Charlie and let him out. He disappeared into the fog, which was thinning to a yellowish luminescence as the sun set.

It was still too early to begin heating our dinner. I was about to go into the garden to get fresh flowers for the table when I noticed the pan of lobster shells by the back door. We'd intended to throw them onto the rocks for the gulls when we went out to sail. This reminded me of something, very indistinctly, but by gazing at the shells as if at a crystal ball, and concentrating, I remembered.

When Patrick and I had gone upstairs a few hours ago, arms around each other, amorously bemused after a period of intense kisses in the kitchen, Charlie had run up ahead of us with something in his mouth and into my room, and I had a hazy recollection of bright red-orange legs hanging from his mouth and of thinking in vague dismay, He's got a lobster body. God knew how much shell he'd crunched down while Patrick and I leaned against the counter in each other's arms.

Gently I fingered my lips. Seafair Bell's mouth would never be the same again. Neither would the rest of her. I laughed, and went up to find the lobster body, hoping he'd left it in his bed and not mine.

It wasn't in my room. The door was ajar into Miranda's, and when I swung it wide the curtains stirred at an open window, and the light breeze picked up that phantom scent of Roman Violet, which always made me acutely homesick for her. I wanted to see her head flung back in that boisterous laugh, I wanted to feel her hard hug and hear her say *Seafair, I'm so happy for us both, I can't stand it.*

But I will know all those things, I argued on the brink of weeping, because she isn't dead. We'll hear by tomorrow's boat.

The lobster body was in Charlie's bed, along with various other finds which would shortly be replacing the scent of Roman Violet with something far more pungent. I hadn't thought of airing his bedding for so long that I was ashamed. I knelt beside the basket to pick out an old-rose hair ribbon of Miranda's, another of my handkerchiefs, a little booklet of inspirational verse and insipid water colors which he must have found in the attic, a chewed pencil. The richer finds were a partially dried starfish that I'd been saving for the children, the lobster body, a codfish tail, and a ham bone he must have brought home from the farm. Distastefully I shook the blanket, and a crumpled slip of blue paper fell out. With a little pain I recognized Miranda's dashing script on it—she liked to use a soft, black drawing pencil—and straightened it out to read, knowing it would make me even more lonely for her and whatever picnic she'd been planning out. She was always making lists—

My own name came at me with the exigency of a shout.

"Dearest Seafair, They all say I'd make a perfectly horrible minister's wife. (I don't mean Tom will be a perfectly horrible minister) and now we'll find out. We'll be back in five days at the most, married, and moving into the cottage, and then nobody can do anything about it, which is why I never told *you* anything, darling, so you can be perfectly innocent and blameless when they ask you. You'll find this when you wake up in the morning, and it will be too late then to stop us. I'm also leaving one downstairs for Ian, and Tom's leaving one for Meg to find when she comes over. (He doesn't want to take a chance on her getting up in the night and finding it.) We both love our families dearly, but we want to be together and we've wanted it for a long time. It's no fly-by-night love even if we are flying by night! We just can't be apart any longer.

"They allow married students at the seminary, and I can find something to do to help our finances. See you before the week is out. With as much of my love as Tom can spare —M."

Kneeling there in a kind of trance, reading the note over and over, I remembered the slight movements around my pillow that night, and I'd thought sleepily that it was Charlie looking for candy. Now I realized it could have been Miranda leaving the note, and that Charlie had come in to me when she left. He must have stolen the note later, at some point between the moment when Patrick woke me with his bloody hand and my first chance to return to my room.

I stood up with infinite care, like one trying to balance on a point of rock above a precipice. I was very light-headed. At the same time I knew enough to hide the note. I wrapped it in my handkerchief and pushed it down between my breasts.

Until now I had never had the genuine conviction that this was the room of one dead; there had been sadness, even dread in it for me, but never this absolute certainty. But now I *knew*. I believed Miranda's note; she had intended to be back in five days, she had not come, therefore she was dead. Not aboard the *Lorna Doone,* because the seiner had safely reached Thomaston, and if some dreadful accident had overtaken Tom and Miranda on the mainland later that day we would have known very quickly.

We would hear tomorrow that the couple aboard the *Marjorie Osborne* were strangers. Ian would come back to start another search, not knowing yet that it should begin on Drummond's, where the blood spattered far and wide. And no notes left anywhere except this one, because Charlie stole and hid it.

You must be very quiet about this, Seafair, I thought. Go down the back stairs and out of the house. Don't panic. If you run you could fall. Don't even run going through the orchard, but don't look back either. You must go to the farm and tell them to—tell them— I put my hand across my mouth as if to hold back vomit, and turned to go through my own room.

The door from the hall opened with the click of the thumb latch like a pistol shot. Patrick stood there.

"You're *back*," he said in amazement.

"I haven't been very far."

"Yes, you have. As far as anyone can go. The ultimate journey, but there and back by candlelight. How was it in Babylon?" His laughter was hushed and unsteady. "It *was* all a dream, then. That's what I've been praying, but I was running out of hope. And here you are."

He took me in his arms. "Don't ever go away again. If you do, it will be the death of me. Why are you shivering?" He tightened his embrace.

"It's damp, we need a fire. Let's go downstairs and build one." I tried to sound both whimsical and petulant, somebody's spoiled darling. "Please, Patrick?"

"All right," he said agreeably. He swung me toward the stairs with an arm like an iron cinch around my waist. "We've got a lot to talk about, and promises to make, and vows to swear. Because you're never going to run away from me again."

We went down, step by step. The Old Colonel was just so much paint and canvas now, his rosy face and buff waistcoat pale blurs in the dusk of the hall. I thought, If I could make myself throw up right now he'd have to let go. But I couldn't retch, though salt water ran in my mouth, and we continued our dreadful descent. Mrs. Gillis, I prayed, Please come over, please interfere, please be nosy, please please *please*.

"Let's unlock the piano!" I exclaimed with artificial gaiety at the foot of the stairs; I all but clapped my hands. "Let me play a bit. If I'm to stay, you can't keep me away from the piano."

His laughter was entirely natural. "What? *You* and the piano? You with your two left hands, all thumbs?"

I could not move a foot farther, literally. At least I felt I couldn't, yet my thinking was as rational as if I'd gone past the end of terror into a passionless limbo. Should I be Miranda and keep him in this mood, or try to make it clear that I was Seafair?

"You'll trust me as far as the kitchen to make us some coffee, I hope?" I asked brightly.

"If I let go of you, you'll be gone again."

"But I came back. I *am* back. Pat," I whispered, "it was always you I wanted, but they all tried to prevent it. Tom was just a blind, like poor old Dill. Darling, believe me. Tonight I'll prove it to you in the only way. But first I've got to eat. I've come such a long way, Pat, and I'm so tired."

Listening, he still held me, trying to read my face in the gloom. Here where we stood in the hall Cleopatra had died, and Othello had whispered over Desdemona's body, *She's like a liar gone to burning hell; 'twas I that killed her.* The place was clamorous with echoes; if I listened I would go as mad as Patrick was.

"Please, Pat?" I begged. "Something to eat, and then—just us. Everyone else is gone. The night belongs to us."

"All right," he said. "Come along." He headed us toward the kitchen. We heard Charlie barking at the shed door, and I said, "I'll let him in," but he pushed me aside and went himself. While I was measuring my chances of getting to the front door, he came back, and Charlie was all over me. Patrick began lighting lamps. For an instant or two his back was toward me, but I couldn't run then, I was too far from the door to the hall, and in any case I'd have fallen over the dog.

The set of his shoulders and the way his fair hair was ruffled up on the crown had a dear familiarity that drove into my stomach like a dull blade. When he turned, he squinted at me with the old half-amused exasperation.

"What's all *this?* A disguise? What for?"

"I'm Seafair, Patrick," I said quite tranquilly. "You've been dreaming again."

"Come on, I'm fed up with that joke! I want that yellow hair of yours falling free, and the long throat, and the blue eyes. Or isn't it for me after all?" The sarcasm was violent. "Tom had it, didn't he? He had it all. You conspired against me, and now you keep coming back to torture me like a damned vampire. I should have buried you with a stake driven through your heart."

"*I—am—Seafair.*" It was low and slow because I was too numb to be otherwise. "I'll show you, if you'll let me go to the piano."

"Oh, no! *Oh,* no!" He was almost hilarious. "You don't get away this time! You're going back to the grove where you belong. You'll be mine all right, forever and ever, because nobody else will know where you are." He walked toward me, laughing till the tears ran. "How could you forget? They *never* come up from the grove. You know that!"

"I'm sorry," I whispered meekly. "I forgot the rules. I'll go back." I stepped sidewise to get behind the table, calculating a dash for the shed, but with that ghastly, merry grin he seized the table and slid it the width of the kitchen to crash against the door. Charlie barked and jumped up against his legs. I ran for the front hall, heard his swearing and Charlie barking behind me; then the dog's high yelp of pain stopped me, but for barely a second.

I reached the front door with Patrick so close that when I slammed it behind me I could hardly believe I'd done it; every instant I kept expecting his hand to fasten on the back of my dress or in my hair. The door was torn open behind me before I was fairly past the Liberty Knoll, but I escaped into a low drift of fog.

I was afraid to stop and listen for him, equally afraid to circle blindly and crash into him. But as long as I kept my face toward the sound of surf I was heading toward the edge of the cliff. There I turned and ran along the wall toward the south.

I had to stop for a moment, my throat was burning and I had a stitch in my side, and I crouched against the wall trying to hear him above the heavy swash below and the clamor in my own ears. It seemed to me I could hear him calling, but I couldn't tell how close; the fog was blowing in deceptively thick and thin streamers as it began to clear.

The wall wasn't flush with the brink of the cliff, and I climbed over it and crawled along close to its base on my hands and knees until I collided with wet bayleaves that showered cold drops over me. Then I started my cautious descent to the shore.

Almost directly over my head, he shouted.

"*Miranda!* It's no use! You can't drown because you're already dead! You'll have to come back to me in the end!"

I let go of the tough bay stem, and slid and rolled to the

bottom, breaking my momentum by grabbing at anything along the way. Some plants pulled loose in my grasp, juniper stabbed like thousands of needles but held fast to the slope, rose bushes scratched but also held. The last ten feet or so, nothing stopped me. I landed in a bed of beach peas, and crept into a place where the water had sucked turf out from under an immense clump of rugosa rose bushes, making a kind of cavern around their roots. Muddy, shoes gone, hair streaming, dress ripped, scratches and scrapes on most of me, I huddled there trying to get my breath.

Perhaps ten feet away from me the surf broke, and spray reached in my cave. I wasn't afraid of the water; I'd take my chances with it anytime. The surf could drown me, but if I ran away it wouldn't follow, and as soon as I thought my lungs weren't going to explode I crawled out and along the base of the slope, always southerly. I ran into thistles, more rose bushes, and trailing blackberry vines that grabbed my ankles. Several times I had to wade through places where the water ran up on little pebbly breaks between the ledges, but the cold surge around my legs was reviving, not frightening.

I couldn't tell how far I'd gone; it seemed as if the tortuous journey had been going on for hours. If I reached Weir Cove I could get to the harbor—if I could find my way through the woods. But it was almost dark now and everything looked alike; I could scarcely recognize marks on the shore on which I'd walked so often. Still, I could huddle somewhere until daylight, if I were sure Patrick couldn't find me.

At that point I vomited, and, when it was over and I'd washed my face with cold sea water, I felt a little better. It seemed to have cleared my head, and suddenly I came to something I recognized, a broad white band of quartz in undulating folds across a dark, flat face of rock. It shone up at me through the dusk.

It occurred just past the end of the diagonal path that led up the cliff to the field across the road from the pasture. I went back and found the opening between a stand of thistles and an old lobster trap. The track was damp, and the smooth turf was slippery in places. I went on all fours where I had to, and again clutched at anything that would give me help, blessing the tough bay. About halfway I was sure that Patrick was waiting at the top. But the vision of lights and safety at the farm was stronger.

He wasn't up there, and a fresh northwest wind blew into my face. The fog was gone, the dark had come, and I could see the lights of the farmhouse. I would not look further, as if to dare to glance toward The Eyrie would reveal God knew what.

He could still be waiting for me. He could have guessed by now that I'd try for the farm. I waited a few moments, hunched into a compact and unobtrusive bundle in the tall grass, trying to decide whether to run for the harbor or the farm. I'd made so many fatal wrong guesses, I was sure now that whichever way I chose would be the wrong one.

But in the end I picked the farm. I climbed the pasture fence rather than run up the road to the gate where Patrick might be standing in the shadow of the maples. If there were beasts in the pasture that night I didn't know it and I didn't care. They, like the surf, had no desire to murder me. I approached the farm from the rear corner of the barn where Miranda and I had stood kneedeep in buttercups that day, and had seen Tom running with the calf in his arms. As I came up to the back of the house, under the clotheslines, Hero began to bark. I didn't dare call him by name, but stood still waiting for him to come up and recognize me; and as I waited, and his heavy bark shook the night quiet, Mr. Gillis came out through the shed with a lamp in his hand.

chapter 35

*A*ll I told the Gillises was that Patrick's mind had been affected, that he had been having bad nightmares for some time and now he was having them in daylight. It had frightened me, so I had run. He would probably be all right in the morning.

I must have been a pretty weird apparition with my tattered eyelet embroidery and bloody scratches. The two boys silently stared. Mr. Gillis's adam's apple went wildly up and down. Mrs. Gillis was divided between concern for my condition and a fear of madness.

"He could murder us all in our beds!" she said. "Burn the house down over us!"

"Should I go find him, I wonder," Mr. Gillis pondered, ruthlessly squeezing his lower lip. Mrs. Gillis cried out at this and I said again, "I'm sure he'll come to his senses by morning, if he hasn't already. Could you put me up somewhere? Or I'll go to the harbor."

They wouldn't hear of that. I could have Tom's room and the boys could go into the open chamber. "I'd just as soon stay *there*," I said, but I couldn't tell her why the very thought of Tom's room made me flinch. She could only see that it was far more suitable for a young lady than the unfinished ell chamber. She brought me a basin of warm water, soap, cloths, iodine for the worst scratches, and one of her own nightdresses, Meg's being tent-size. Mr. Gillis, going out around the barn with a lantern, met Charlie, who must have followed my tortuous route. He was frantic with relief to see me, and he was unhurt.

When I was in bed, Mrs. Gillis brought me a cup of tea.

She offered food but I couldn't take it. She talked for a while as I sipped the tea, if you could call it talk; lamentations, sighs, repetitions of "I never!" and occasional fits and starts of terror if someone even stirred downstairs. I wanted her to go away, but then I was left alone to contemplate Tom's room by lamplight. It was as bad as being in Miranda's room.

For so long I had obstinately maintained that the two were alive, and now I wondered quite objectively if I could hold together under the knowledge that they were dead.

And Patrick was out there in the dark. If he hadn't remembered what had happened to Tom and Miranda, if his mind had blocked it out, that surely wasn't sanity; but if he'd known all this time and had been playing a part with us, that was more terrible than the delusions.

I tried to read, but couldn't bear to handle Tom's books. I turned to the Bible, but I couldn't separate that from Tom, I kept coming across notations that brought his voice into the room. So I lay there, unwilling to blow out the lamp for fear that in the dark I should start reliving the whole business, from the discovery of the note. This I had thrust into a pigeon hole in Tom's desk, so Charlie couldn't find it again. The dog lay where I could keep my hand on him, and slept deeply. I listened to the muted activity downstairs, as the family tried to be quiet but discussed the situation in whispers. In a little while the boys were sent to bed, and I shut my door and blew out my lamp, so Mrs. Gillis wouldn't feel obliged to look in on me when she came up.

Listening to the small natural sounds of a house at night, and for some outside noise that could mean Patrick was nearby, or rather this demon who had taken on Patrick's body, I thought how grotesquely comforting the idea of demonic possession could be. It left the person himself untouched and innocent.

Unbelievingly, I woke in full daylight, and I couldn't remember falling asleep or even growing drowsy. I knew exactly what had happened and where I was. The farm was wide awake, with roosters crowing, a cacophony of quacking and honking around the duckpond, milk pails clattering under my window, calves bawling, a boy's voice calling and a horse whinnying in reply. Charlie was sitting up, quivering and staring at the door. He let out a frustrated little yip.

There were men's voices in the kitchen, and I thought I heard Patrick's. I sat up then, shaking like Charlie. If he was lucid this morning, what was I going to tell him? That he'd murdered Tom and Miranda and tried to kill me? How could I drive that thunderbolt into his face? I couldn't. I couldn't do anything; I was at the end. I folded my arms on my knees and put my head down on them.

Someone tapped at the door and said, "Seafair, are you awake?" While I was trying to make it true that it was Ian, Charlie jumped off the bed and attacked the door in an ecstasy of welcome.

"Yes, come in," I called. I was so relieved I could have cried, but now I had to tell him the truth. One fact canceled out the other. He said, "Go on downstairs, Charlie," and came into the bedroom. He looked more tired and was thinner, worn down to bone, but neither ill nor too shaken to cope. He stood at the foot of the bed without speaking, just waiting.

I said at once, "I disobeyed you. I was all ready to go, but he begged me to stay. I wanted to, so I did. I brought this all on my own head. But I know where they are."

"I'm afraid I do too," he said. "At least I know they're somewhere on the island. Maybe in the cellar somewhere."

"In the grove," I said. "I'm sure of it. How did you know?"

He sat down on the foot of the bed. "There was a wire waiting for us in Washington when we stopped there. The couple on the vessel had been identified beyond a doubt. They were from Waldoboro. Elopers, too." His mouth twitched, but it couldn't have been a smile. "However, they'd been married, and he had a job in San Francisco. The Cape Horn trip was a spur of the moment idea when they heard there was room on the vessel." He rubbed his hand hard over the side of his face. "I don't think I've slept since then, and I hadn't slept much up *till* then. We had to stay two days in Washington because Dougal came down with some sort of distemper from heat, exhaustion, nerves, the whole works. Andrew came back to Rockland, and when we arrived yesterday he met us with the news that the *Lorna Doone* was in port with a fresh trip of mackerel."

He stopped, and sat looking at his loose, open hands. In the wait I heard Hero's bark outside and Charlie piping up with him. Children were coming from the harbor for milk, and Mrs. Gillis sounded both hurried and harried. A youngster sang out, "Hello, Andrew!" and he answered from out by the barn, pleasant as he always was.

"She'd brought no passengers in from Drummond's that night," Ian said. "They told Andrew the young couple had come up alongside in a little sloop that afternoon and asked for a chance in. The time was set, but they never showed up. The seiner waited a half hour, then hoisted sail. But there was no other way for Tom and Miranda to leave unnoticed. —So we started out at three this morning, and just got into the Home Cove a few minutes ago."

"Dougal and Meg too?" I asked.

"No. He was determined to come, so we had a little conspiracy with Meg not to let him know we'd gone until it was too late. With any luck, he's still sleeping right now.... Tell me about yesterday."

First I told him where the note was in Tom's desk, and he found it. He must have wept inwardly as he read it. It was so much Miranda, it brought her into the room, voice and all, as the notes in Tom's hand had evoked *him*. When Ian had finished reading, I told him that Patrick had taken me for Miranda come back to haunt him, and that I had run away.

He stood up. "Andrew and I will find him," he said tonelessly. At the door he stopped and stared straight ahead at the panels; at least by the set of his head and rigid shoulders I thought that was it, but he might not have even seen them.

He made a short, anguished sound, like a harshly caught breath or a strangled cry, but when he looked back his face was nearly blank. "He must have deliberately cut off his finger," he said in that same voice. "To explain the blood. I hope he's dead. I hope he's killed himself." He walked out quickly and I got out of bed to run after him, nearly tripping myself up in Mrs. Gillis's nightgown. I caught hold of his sleeve on the landing. "Let me go with you to the house," I begged. "I don't think he'll be dangerous now, when he sees you. This morning he may not even know what it's all about. I can't forget how happy he was when you wrote that it was good news. I'd swear he hadn't any idea then what he'd done. But it must have all come back to him yesterday, and it was too hideous to bear. But now he may have driven it off again."

"That's why I hope he's dead," he said. "For all our sakes, including his. Very well, Andrew and Sam Gillis can go down to the grove and look around, and you can go to The Eyrie with me."

"I'll be down in five minutes," I said. He went downstairs and I hurried into my clothes, such as they were after last night. The eyelet embroidery was almost in rags, and I had no shoes. There was no one in the kitchen when I went down; Mrs. Gillis was washing milk pails in the shed, the boys were about their chores, I knew where Andrew and Mr. Gillis had gone, and Ian was sitting on the chopping block in the sun waiting for me. Charlie was with him.

We didn't speak as we walked up through the dew-soaked orchard. Charlie picked up a windfall and ran with it. It seemed incongruous that dogs should play, birds could still sing, and the apples go on reddening; everything should have stopped. When we came out of the orchard I looked instinctively up at the sky and saw an eagle, circling a mile high (it seemed) in balanced, effortless flight. The usual thrill of awe was missing. Simply, I envied him.

Nothing had changed in the kitchen since last night, so Pat hadn't had anything to eat. The room smelled of the lamps, and Ian blew them out. Charlie hurried to his dish, as if he'd expected the brownies might have left him something good overnight.

"I'd better get into some decent clothes," I said, "and start to pack. The last thing you need around here now is an outsider."

"I'll go upstairs with you," he said. He looked in my room first, into the bathroom and Miranda's room, and then went to inspect the others. Charlie accompanied him, importantly enjoying the unusual activity.

The first thing I did was to draw the curtains on the northwest windows so I would not see the grove. In a few moments Ian came back and said outside my door, "Nothing. Look, don't bother to pack now. I don't want to wait around, and I won't leave you here alone. If you don't go today, it doesn't matter." He waited a moment and then said dryly, "After what you've been through with us you're not all that much of an outsider."

Just the same, I thought, I'll bet you wish I'd never been born. When I joined him in the hall he gave me a preoccupied nod. It wasn't until we got downstairs that he said, "One of the rifles is missing from the Museum. I'll deliver you back to the farm and then I'll go down to the grove." He whistled to Charlie, who hadn't chased us downstairs. In response the terrier began barking sharply, like a dog sighting a squirrel in a tree, and we both called and whistled. Finally he came in a headlong, scrabbling plunge, and we turned to leave the house.

"So now I've caught you," Patrick said from the foot of the back stairs, "and this time you won't get away."

"*Pat!*" Ian went toward him with open arms. "Where were you? I've been all through the house."

"You forgot the attic. But Charlie didn't." He motioned Ian back with the rifle. "Don't come any closer. And don't remind me again that we're foster brothers. Foster brothers don't steal from one another, or let themselves be stolen, I might add."

"I'm not Tom. I'm Ian, and I don't wish you any harm. I want to help you."

Patrick laughed. "I suppose you've got another name for that one." He swung the rifle toward me. "Something besides slut, trollop, whore, I mean."

"That's Seafair, Patrick," Ian said quietly, "and you know it. It's not Miranda. You know where Miranda is, don't you?"

"Right there," said Patrick. The moment was totally without fear for me. This was the end, and knowing it I was far past such a flimsy consideration as fright. So this is how they could do it, I thought with a detached wonder; the women going to the block, and even making speeches first. But I couldn't have made a speech. I couldn't even swallow, let alone move my tongue.

Patrick looked terrible, face smudged with dirt, his eyes far back in his head, his clothes muddy, his hands almost black. He spoke to me with lazy amusement. "How can you be in two places at once? Why can't you stay dead? I watched all night to be sure you stayed put, but the minute I turn my back you're up again."

"Pat, go back to the grove and see for yourself," Ian said. "We'll all go. We won't run away."

"Oh, no!" His smile was a caricature of the real Patrick's. "You think you can work something on me. You think I'm mad. You're the mad ones, to think you could ever get away with it. You've both betrayed me once, but never again. Now we're going to take a walk."

The word *walk* electrified Charlie, who began jumping around. Patrick herded us out of the house by way of the front door. "We're going to the cottage," he said. "That is where you're going to die again. Don't touch her!" he shouted as Ian took my arm. "How can you be so indecently possessive in front of me? What does it take to burn shame out of you?"

Crossing the lawn with the sun in my eyes, Charlie dancing about as if it were all in fun, I wished he had shot us back there in the kitchen in that moment when I was ready for it. Now I was so frightened I could have collapsed in the wet grass. But I kept on walking and Ian suited his stride to mine, so at least we were side by side, if not allowed to touch. I kept hoping somebody would see us from a boat, and come ashore. Going down the steps to the cottage our backs were to the sun, and I tried to see out across the cove, but the only sail I saw was well off the Bowsprit. Ian was ahead of me and I kept thinking he must have some move planned for when we reached the cottage; but I realized that one doesn't argue with the mouth of a rifle, which must always have the last word.

Once we were in the cottage we were securely tucked away out of everybody's sight and hearing. Patrick motioned us to sit down in the chilly living room, where the sun hadn't yet reached. The place smelled of dry wood, a knot of sweetgrass on the wall, and very faintly of soot from the chimney. I sat huddled on the organ stool, hugging myself to keep from shivering too openly. Ian sat down on the couch.

"May I give Seafair my coat?" he asked.

"*Miranda* doesn't need a coat," Patrick replied with a grin. "She's like a liar gone to burning hell. Or going. Shortly."

Charlie went sniffling around in the bedrooms, looking for mice. Patrick took a straight chair, keeping the rifle aimed at us. Silence. Flies buzzing against glass, gulls walking on the roof, crying a warning as another flew over.

"You're owed an explanation, Seafair," Ian said conversationally. "I don't know if it will make anything easier to bear, but you should know the facts."

Patrick lifted an eyebrow. "Go ahead and talk," he said in a weary, dragging voice. "A few minutes won't hurt, since you'll be silent for eternity. No more secrets behind old Pat's back. No more touching and kissing, no more—" He yawned loudly and withdrew to his silence again.

"Miranda told you her parents lived in this cottage," Ian

said. "She thought they both died of diphtheria; it was the only thing to tell her. The inscription on their stone was chosen for her benefit, but my father told Andrew and me the truth when we became adults, so we would understand why Miranda and Patrick must never be allowed to marry. Patrick was so possessive of her from the start, and the two were always so close, it was a thing he was afraid of."

"Fascinating, isn't it, Miranda?" Patrick interrupted. "To find out how weird your inheritance really is. Talk about inherited memory; if it existed in your case you'd never have been able to endure this cottage all these years."

"When did you find out about it, Pat?" Ian asked. He sounded merely curious.

"Oh, I always knew how the old man felt about cousins marrying—he preached it at us all the time we were growing up. But one night I listened outside the library door and heard him tell my brothers just why he was opposed to these particular cousins marrying. He'd have done anything to separate us, short of banishing one of us forever. That was something I kept from you, dear foster brother."

"And wasn't it any warning to you?" Ian asked with friendly interest.

"Why should it be? If dear Aunt Jeannie wanted to push her husband off the cliff in a tantrum because he'd made some sketches of Ada Schofield, and then say he'd committed suicide, that was her problem. Not mine. Miranda there"—the gun barrel moved toward me—"and I were as sound as dollars. She's a rotten little liar, but I don't call that insanity."

Ian said to me in that leisurely way, "It's true about Jeannie. When Matthew died, my father thought at once she'd married a man tainted with insanity, but in the delirium of her diphtheria,—which she really did catch—he found out the truth. She had been psychopathically jealous of her husband. She was always the gay, incandescent type, great fun to be with, much like Miranda, only more so; *dangerously* high-spirited, which Miranda never was. Jeannie plunged from the heights to terrible depths. —It wasn't Miranda who reminded my father of Jeannie."

Patrick yawned again, and the rifle barrel wavered. He had a sleepy, unfocused look.

"What happened with Jeannie," Ian went on, "was a shock my father never really got over. We'd had what are kindly called 'eccentrics' in every generation, but nothing to this extent. So you can see why his normal aversion to the marriage of cousins became a stringent prohibition."

"Talks like a professor, doesn't he?" Patrick said to me. "He should have been one, not a storekeeper. I'm not mad," he said to Ian with great dignity. "I know you're Ian."

"If you're not mad," said Ian, "you'll let us walk safely out of here."

"Not *her*. Not again. Tom's waiting, you know."

"I'm not Miranda," I said in a low voice. "I'm Seafair."

"Who's Seafair? Oh, she was here earlier. I don't even remember what she looked like."

It was no longer a blow. "I play. Remember, Patrick? Miranda was no good. Two left hands and all thumbs." I spun around on the stool and began to play *The Spanish Cavalier* with all the frills I could squeeze out of the old organ. While I played I knew nothing of what went on in the room behind me, but I could see Ian from the corner of my eye. He was perfectly motionless. Charlie jumped up beside him and lay half across his leg. I went through the song once more, with fresh variations, stopped, folded my hands in my lap, and stared at the yellowing keys."

"All right, you've made your point, Seafair," Patrick said with an utterly normal boredom tinged with familiar mischief, and I burst into tears over the keyboard. The rifle crashed to the floor and he said, "Oh, listen, love, what have I done *now?*" He took me by the shoulders and twirled me around on the stool until his guant and dirty face could look into mine. The blue eyes red-rimmed with sleeplessness strained with a heart-breaking anxiety to read an answer.

"Don't cry, Seafair," he begged. "I can't stand it."

"And I can't help it," I wept.

Patrick said ruefully, "I have the distinct impression that I've done something unforgiveable. Tell me what it is, Seafair love."

That was to be his last lightning-glimpse of sanity. Almost in the next instant he *knew*, and he could not bear the knowledge. It was a raving stranger whom Ian clubbed with the rifle stock, and then held in his arms, looking down into the suddenly empty face as if he had just killed the sun.

The bright day fades, and we are for the dark.

chapter 36

Kingfisher left from the Home Cove, so no one at the harbor knew who and what sailed with her. They would know soon enough, when the Gillis boys got over to the harbor. Later there'd be no hope of keeping the story out of the newspapers. The privacy now was only a short respite, which would end when *Kingfisher* tied up at a Rockland wharf.

Of the three living who sailed on the cutter, one didn't know that Tom and Miranda sailed with them. Patrick was restrained as humanely as possible on one of the bunks. He had gone far beyond reach of the brothers. The last contact had been in the cottage.

I wanted to stay at The Eyrie rather than at the farm, what with the Gillises' nerves and having to sleep, or not sleep, in Tom's room. But Ian told me what I should have known, that the nights alone in the granite house would be far worse. While Andrew and Mr. Gillis knocked together two long boxes, Ian went to the Schofields', and spoke privately with Mr. Clement. The minister and his wife came to The Eyrie to stay, and they were tactful enough neither to ask me questions nor to pretend that nothing had happened.

As soon as *Kingfisher* left, I wrote to my father, saying there had been two deaths here and I was staying on to help out. I was hoping without much conviction that when the news broke in the papers he wouldn't brave the bay to fetch me home. I wouldn't go back with him, and I wished there were a way to forestall him. I gave the letter to young Pearl Gillis to mail so it would go out on that day's boat.

Horror heaped on horror has a nullifying effect on the emotions, I discovered as we went through the next three days. There were no formal callers now as there'd been after the news of the *Marjorie Osborne* disaster. Children coming to the farm for milk sometimes brought messages from parents. *If there's anything I can do . . .* But they were either too stunned or too sensitive to come in person. They had a great fear of being suspected of "nosing around."

I went back to house-cleaning. Mrs. Clement wrote letters, read, worked in the walled garden. We took walks on the shore and talked safely of botany, birds, children, and teaching. Mr. Clement went daily to help Elmer in the store. After dinner at night he asked me to play, and that was therapeutic. I had believed for a time that I would never be able to play again. I had accidentally found the key in a vase in the dining room while I was cleaning.

On Saturday morning the *Ocean Pearl* came out on a special trip to bring the caskets, Ian and Andrew, Meg and Dougal, and a crowd of Drummond friends and business associates, some friends and relatives of the Finlays, and most of Tom's class from the seminary. Mr. Lippman also came. He had wanted to dance at Miranda's wedding.

Jane returned with Andrew, and we embraced like old friends. The hot September noon when we were getting ready for the funeral she said, "Seafair, I won't ask you anything, but if you ever want to talk, I'm willing to listen."

"Thanks," I said. "The time may come." But you'll never hear about it, I thought. Not about what I have to live with.

I thought I had gotten myself into a suitably numb condition for the services. I spoke with, or nodded to, people who were too mannerly to stare at me as almost the third victim. Faustina and Hughie, who had come home yesterday, were still dazed with the news. The Awful Ansons were so quenched they looked ten years older. Prissy was almost unrecognizable from weeping, and Dill Kalloch's broad handsome face was set in patient, uncomprehending pain.

The front of the church was filled with all the flowers

the island gardens could produce, beside the expensive tributes from the mainland. The closed caskets were nearly hidden. Tom and Miranda are not there, I told myself. If you believe as you should, you know they are not there in those boxes. Miranda's hair and Tom's black eyes mean nothing. The essence of Tom and Miranda *is not there.* The essence is in all the things you remember, that you laughed about or that made you very happy. . . . Only, how long before you can stand to remember them without a bayonet stab each time? How long before you can be satisfied with only the essence?

Ada Schofield broke down on the first hymn, and one of the seminary students took her place at the organ. I thought with restful objectivity, So Matthew Muir painted her and his wife objected. She must have been in full bloom then. . . . If only I could have remained so detached. . . . Then a group of Tom's classmates arose to sing Tom's and Miranda's favorite hymns. It was hard enough to listen to *Still, Still with Thee* and remember Miranda singing it in chapel; but when they began *By Cool Siloam's Shady Rill* I bit on the insides of my cheeks until I tasted blood. I could see Tom holding me back at the parlor doors, asking me to play for Miranda to sing at his next service, and this was the song he asked for.

Well, this was his next service, and it was being sung. But not by Miranda, and another man stood in the pulpit. And Tom was—no, he was *not.*

If there'd been a way to get out, I'd have bolted. But we were across the church from that small, convenient door, and Jane and I were tucked in between Andrew and Ian. I saw Ian's hand lying on his leg, gradually tightening over his knee until the knuckles showed white, and I wished that he would take my hand or that I could take his. Jane's hand had moved into Andrew's.

The windows were open and in a little silence we heard gulls crying. I wondered nonsensically if the eagles knew what was going on. I hoped they were making their great, slow arcs above us in the brilliant September sky. I would look for them when we went out.

Mr. Clement's words were short, but I gave him no credit for that. We know all those things, I felt like shouting at him. Saying them won't bring anybody back. They shouldn't have died. Why can't you say that? Why can't you say, "God, why did this have to be your will?" You can't, because God had nothing to do with it. Admit that, for once. Maybe even Tom would admit it now. We used to argue about it. . . . Admit that God, if He's all lovingkindness, wouldn't have taken Tom away from Meg and Dougal, and all the people he was going to help in his life. No, God wouldn't do that; but Patrick would. It was Patrick who slung the hatchet at Miranda's head and dyed the bright hair red, and stopped the voice forever. Not God directing Patrick's hand. God doesn't want them now any more than He wanted my mother then.

My silent ferocity got me through it, and at the graves I was thinking more of Ian and Andrew than of myself. But I forgot to look for the eagles.

Some of the women had gone to The Eyrie and prepared a meal for the mainland visitors to have before they went back on the *Pearl*. For a little while the house was filled with a subdued air of good fellowship among those who were not intimately concerned, but relieved to have the services behind them. Meg and Dougal were there, silent and dignified, and the seminary students clustered around them. Jane and I acted as hostesses, pouring tea and coffee, urging food on people as if our lives depended on it.

It was nearly sunset when the party went back to the harbor. Ian and Andrew walked with them. Meg offered to help with the dishes, but we wouldn't allow it, knowing she wanted to be with Dougal in their own home.

I went to my room before the brothers came back. Jane and Andrew wouldn't need my company, and Ian certainly wouldn't want it. But Charlie went up with me, and I was touched by his fidelity; I sat by my windows holding him in my lap, and watched the light of fire opals fade in the west and the shapes of the spruces turn into flat black ink designs against it. I had come to know those trees as individuals during the summer.

Between the spruces and myself everything sank into obscurity, until the farm was only to be guessed at. Meg and Dougal would be sitting silent in the dusk, and my throat ached.

The crickets went on and on, and in Weir Cove the gulls were excited about herring. After a time I heard the brothers' low voices as they rounded the garden wall. I went to bed then, and sank into sleep as the farm had sunk into the dark, pastures and barn and all.

I awoke when the windows were gray with the first light, to the full awareness of an extremely personal problem. If I could have turned over in bed at that moment and composed myself to die, like the figure in *Thanatopsis,* I would have done so. I lay there with my hands on my belly and tried to think if I felt any different there. When I'd been surrounded by death I'd fought like an animal to live, and now, with a possible new life within me, I could see death as the only escape.

But what else *was* there, if I was pregnant by Patrick?

Then I rejected the theory; it seemed that I was still fighting. I got up and dressed. With a little time to myself, I might be able to think. But when I opened the door at the head of the back stairs I smelled coffee. Wearily I hoped it would be Andrew down there, if it had to be anyone. He almost always managed that smile, no matter how bad things were.

It was Ian. We nodded silently, and I let Charlie out, and when I came back my coffee was ready. "I forgot to start the oatmeal," I said in dismay.

"Never mind. What will you have with your coffee?"

"Nothing," I said. "Thank you."

"I wanted to talk to you last night, but I was afraid of disturbing you." He sat down opposite me. "You have a right to know what to expect. First, there'll be no trial. Patrick's in the state hospital at Augusta for observation, but he's obviously—" He stopped, and I was both embarrassed and hurt for him. "Well, he was quiet when I last saw him." He rubbed his forehead and went on. "But living in a world of his own. None of us on the outside exist for him." He pushed away from the table and went to the eastward windows and stood there with folded arms. Sunrise was edging the morning clouds. "So life will go on for all of us, after a fashion," he said. "All of us that are left, that is. When does your school open?"

"In about two weeks," I said.

"Will your position be compromised because you've been involved in this business?"

"I doubt it. They'll be sick at losing Miranda, though. Everybody loved her, and her voice. It won't be the same place. I dread going back."

"Your work will occupy your mind," Ian said. "Your music." He came back to the table. "One thing I thought about last night was music."

"I *am* sorry!" I said. "I expected you'd want some privacy. I wish you had come and got me."

"Never mind," he said. "Maybe tonight... Are you planning to leave tomorrow?"

I said with brittle honesty, "I've planned to leave more than once. I suppose this will be the actual time. But there's one thing I have to talk to you about first, simply because there's no one else I can talk to about it. I don't want to burden you, but I have to mention it."

"We owe you something, Seafair. My brother tried to murder you, remember?"

"*Someone* did. Not Patrick. Anyway, I had only myself to blame. Just as in this other case, except that the results may be much more long-lasting... I have to get this said, so I might as well plunge. I slept with Patrick. We made love."

His thoughtful, listening expression didn't change. "For the same reason you stayed. Because he asked you to."

"Because I *wanted* to," I said. "I was in love with him. I didn't know I was a substitute for . . . somebody else." The blood came up my body in a rush and flooded my face. "I want you to know it wasn't an act of—of cheap opportunism."

"I don't believe you'd be capable of any such act, Seafair," he said. "Considering what's been done around here in the name of love, I can't condemn you for taking the most natural step. Are you carrying?" He was so low-keyed he made it easier for me.

"It's too soon to tell. It never occurred to me until this morning. I know that it doesn't always happen the first time, but it could."

"How soon will you know?"

"In a week or so."

"What will you do if it's so?" He began filling his pipe.

"Resign my job. Ask you for a loan—a loan *only*—and go away somewhere to have it." At the moment *it* was an abstract concept to me.

"And then give it up for adoption?" He was just as impersonal. But it was a slap that rocked me to my senses.

"*Patrick's* child? And *mine*?" At that moment *it* ceased to be an abstraction. "Give it up? I couldn't!"

He said, "Have you considered what your life will be, unless your parents are extraordinary? Even then you would still have to cope with the community, society, and so forth. You'll be barred from teaching in most places, unless you can be a convincing young widow, and there'll always be somebody to turn up the truth and use it to damage you, all in the name of morality."

"I haven't thought about any of that." It was my turn to get up and prowl. "I just know that if it's so there was nothing sordid about it, and it was my free choice, so I have to do the paying."

"The child pays also." He sat back from the table and watched me pace. "Stay here until you know, Seafair. Then if it's so, we'll be married." He cut off my exclamation. "It'll be a legality for the child's sake only. He'll have a name and legitimate support. You can do what you like after that, but wherever you go you'll both be looked after."

I was still arguing incoherently. He got up and led me back to the table, turned out my untouched coffee and brought me some fresh and hot. "Drink that, and drop any Puritan ideas you have of needing to be punished and of getting yourself out of this. Because you can't do it alone. You can tramp off with your chin in the air, but the time will come when you'll damn yourself as several kinds of a fool for not accepting my offer."

I couldn't tell him that alone I would still have some wisp of pride. His way I would be the victim of his already overburdened sense of responsibility. Like Adrienne. —But he was right. Alone with a baby, I would be as far out of the world as Patrick was, and worse off because I would know it. All the cheap paper novels read secretly in my girlhood surrounded me in a fluttering packlike birds of prey attacking.

Charlie barked outside the shed, and when I went to let him in I kept on going, and didn't come back until there was nothing else I could do.

he brothers began to go through Patrick's things, as Jane and I did Miranda's. The clothes were to be given away where they'd be the most useful. The personal things would go to the attic. I could choose what I liked, and I chose nothing. I had the bracelet she had given me, and she had been wearing the pin I had given her.

Patrick's journals were to go into the Museum. The tragic irony was that, in uncovering the bodies where he had buried them in the pit, Andrew and Mr. Gillis had turned up a soapstone spindle-whorl and a bronze pin for a cloak, which matched indisputably those found at a Viking site in Norway. Patrick's proof had been only about one day's digging away from him.

Ian was now faced with having to decide whether the dig should be filled in forever and grown over, or if Patrick's work should be carried on by someone else. At dinner that night he called for a vote on it. "You're in on this too, Seafair," he said when I was silent.

"For God's sake, let it be *yes*," Andrew said. "Let the archeologists take it over. Otherwise the grove will really be haunted and the island will never be free of it."

"Tom and Miranda deserve better than that," Ian agreed.

It was the last part of the journals that gave the story of the murders. This is what Patrick had been writing so busily in the days when we were alone. It began as a confused record of dreams and nightmares, the means of death varied between imagination and reality. He had the *Lorna Doone* sinking without a trace in the moonlit bay; he saw a train disaster with bodies strewn around in bloody fragments. The ramming of the *Marjorie Osborne* provided him with a new series of dreams as his brain fought to keep the truth from him. Well, it had masked the truth efficiently enough in his waking hours, but enough had broken through his defenses when he was asleep so that he'd had to write it down to get rid of it, and this was how we found out what had really happened. . . . Remembering the morning on the Bowsprit when he'd pretended to walk overboard, I wondered now how much had been pretense; if unbearable reality had been close to breaking through.

He had met Tom and Miranda in the kitchen, as he told us. They were writing their notes. They told him simply that they were in love, and what they intended to do. From then on Patrick wrote as a bystander, a helpless witness. The murderer became *he*. When *he* realized what was going on, there was something like an earthquake in *his* brain, a dreadful rending and shaking that nearly knocked *him* flat. Tom's face became monstrous to *him*. Miranda was as horrible as a walking corpse.

"It was as if I were experiencing it myself," Patrick wrote. "I knew *he* was going to murder. *He* couldn't help himself. I watched Patrick watching *him*. Why didn't Patrick stop *him*? I couldn't do anything. *He* attacked Tom, who flung *him* off so hard *he* bruised *his* face against the sink. But *he* bounded up again. Nothing could subdue this madman. *He* sprang on Tom like a leopard. Tom was borne down under *his* weight and struck his head on a corner of the laundry stove, and while he was half-stunned *he* knelt on his chest and strangled him.

I felt bound hand and foot. This was the most ghastly dream so far. "It took so long to kill Tom. He fought so hard, and he had a strong throat."

Miranda jumped on *his* back, grabbing *him* by the hair, all in a silent frenzy. *He* had flung her off and stood up to face her. "*Murderer!*" she spat at *him*, and turned to run. *He* seized that hatchet and threw it. It struck the back of her head and split it open. "I can never forget the sound of that," he wrote. "I cried to Patrick, but he had disappeared."

As the powerless observer he watched the murderer wrap Miranda's head in her old plaid coat to soak up the blood, and carry her across the moonlit field, accompanied by *his* misshapen shadow like a tame monster, and down into the grove. Then Tom went, slung over *his* shoulder. Last, *he* took their luggage to the grove, and tore up the notes, and scattered them over the bodies like flower petals. Then *he* began to shovel dirt.

It was almost daylight when *he'd* finished the burial. *He* had then meticulously split some kindling, laid *his* hand on the chopping block, cut off *his* left forefinger, and swung *his* hand around to spatter blood through shed and kitchen.

"The madman was both tough and brilliant," Patrick wrote. "He left nothing undone. He would take any step to achieve his purpose. The result was a masterpiece of credibility."

The Patrick who roused me that morning had almost succeeded in wiping out the conscious memory of his own actions, and he could account for the blank spot by believing he was the one who had been knocked down and stunned, and that they had fled and left him there. Otherwise the account was true. Tom had been strangled, and Miranda's skull shattered. The luggage was there with them, and the old plaid coat, and the officers found most of the fragments of the notes. The journal thus closed the case for good, as far as the law was concerned.

But I was never to forget that the whole bloody debacle had taken place while I slept to the scent of stocks and the sound of crickets. The granite walls had shut out any noise from the ell, even for Charlie's sensitive ears. . . . And I would remember, too, my fantasy of boatmen with bare skulls for heads, raising black sails.

Ian and Andrew went back to business. Meg began coming at her usual time. She had lost much weight, but she had a rugged obstinacy, and she had Dougal to worry about.

By now the newspapers had the story, and parties of reporters hired boats in Rockland to bring them out to the islands. They weren't allowed to land on Drummond's, or on Bannock either, but one group succeeded in sneaking into Steeple Cove, and made sketches of the church and the new stones in the cemetery before Dill Kalloch drove them off with his scythe. He'd been mowing along the wall.

Fortuitously my father was laid low with one of his late summer colds when the story first appeared in the headlines, so he had to settle for sending me imperious letters. Phoebe wrote one herself, hinting that my father's demise would be on my head if I didn't come home. Used to his colds, I wrote assuring them that I was not going to appear in the papers giving my own exclusive story of what happened, or go into vaudeville on the strength of it.

In a week I knew I wasn't pregnant, but blessedly on time as always, regardless of everything. I went to the harbor in the late afternoon to walk home with Ian, so I could tell him.

We had reached the pasture when I told him, and he stepped off the road among the goldenrod and asters, and sat down on the wall. "I'm sorry," he said. "This may sound selfish or inhuman, but I was beginning to count on it."

"Why?" I asked, taken by surprise.

"Because I'm going to miss you. Jane will be going home after a while, and when she comes back it will be to her own home here. In the meantime Andrew and I will be—" he waved his hand toward The Eyrie. "Rattling around, you could call it. . . . Neither of us can play the piano," he said with the first spark of humor I'd seen for weeks. "And then I'd begun to look forward to the child. I was even thinking that you might stay on, and take the school here next year. You want to work somewhere. Why not here?"

"Do you like me that well?" I asked in honest curiosity. "I'm not just a nuisance or a liability? Or is it the child you're thinking of? A little Drummond who should be raised at The Eyrie?"

"There's that," he said slowly. "Another Drummond. But yes, I do like you that well, Seafair. . . . I'd make no demands on you, of course."

"That's no marriage for a healthy man," I objected. "You're too young to throw your life away like that. You need to move around a bit and give yourself a chance to fall in love. I know you can't think of it now, and I don't believe I ever will again, for myself, but the time will come for you. It *has* to."

He actually laughed aloud. "Thank you for the advice. It has the proper big-sisterly tone. It's nice to be treated as a mere lad instead of an old duffer."

"I thought I sounded like a maiden aunt, myself. The advanced kind who prides herself on plain speaking."

He got up and we walked along. We both glanced instinctively toward the farm, and then away again. "Meg grieves for Patrick," he said. "She can't hate him. She says she's lost three children in all."

I looked steadily at the sea. He said, "Can your family spare you at Christmas?"

"The sky will probably fall in Fern Grove," I said, "but yes, they can spare me."

He said nothing more until we reached the corner of the garden wall, when he said mildly, "Since you advise me to get out around more, I may come up to see you at the college this fall."

"I would like that," I said.

"In October," he said. "We'll hire a rig and explore the countryside."

"Yes." I was blinking and my nose wanted to run.

"Look at that," he said, pointing at the empty flagpole. "It's time we started remembering the flag in the morning."

"The Old Colonel must be very displeased," I said, wiping my nose.

One night when Andrew returned from Bannock he came into the dining room where Jane and I were setting the table, and said mysteriously, "I have something to show you." He beckoned us out to the kitchen, and there stood two barefoot black-haired young boys who had been crying, but who now stood staring at us with the defiance of young captive princes. Charlie sniffed excitedly at their toes.

"Hello, Dennis and Michael Dolan," Jane said. They didn't answer, but they didn't lower their heads in shyness, either.

"We're going over to the farm to Meg," Andrew said. "I think perhaps the horses might be a help, not to mention Hero." He went with them at once, leaving Jane and me making the most of our astonishment; as a matter of salvation these days, one made the most of everything that came along, and this was more deserving than the usual run of daily events.

When he came back, alone, he told us what had happened. "They showed up at the store and said Rosaleen had gone. They didn't know what it was all about, and neither did I. I went to the house, and the bird had flown. Nell Duffy, next door, told me a couple of reporters had sneaked ashore on Eider Point to see what they could find out from some women picking blackberries. Nobody else would tell them anything, but Rosaleen must have made some sort of deal, because when the women all came back to the village she packed up her belongings, put a note under the sugar bowl saying, 'Squireen, take them,' and left while everybody else was getting supper. So nobody actually saw her go except the boys, and she'd threatened to slice their ears off if they followed her. Poor little devils came to me."

"Do you think she'll be back?" Jane asked. He shook his head. "Not by what she's taken. She's struck out to make her fortune. And somehow I can't worry about it any more."

In October when Ian came to the college he told me the boys had settled in well at the farm after a little trouble at the first, which was only natural. They were wretched with loss, and so were the Finlays, each pair resenting the other pair. But in time the children's helplessness gradually penetrated the Finlays' sorrow, and roused their parental instincts.

"We could never get them away from Meg and Dougal now if we wanted to," he said.

"What if Rosaleen shows up?"

"She can whistle, for all the good it will do her. Andrew's had the Finlays made their legal guardians."

I had to ask a bad question, one that asked itself often in my waking hours, and always in my bad dreams, which were many. We stopped to rest the horse by a little blue lake, and when we were walking around it under the pines I said, "How is Patrick?"

"Not rational, but calm, because he is completely withdrawn. I see him every two weeks, and Andrew goes on the alternate weeks. Each time Pat's farther away from us, both physically and mentally. But sometimes I think that deep inside him there is a core of perfect sanity, in which he is in hell."

I put my arm through Ian's as we walked; it was the only gesture I could make, I certainly couldn't speak.

"I saw him yesterday," he went on, "and when I left I thought of that thing from *Lear* ... remember? 'O! Let him pass; he hates him/That would upon the rack of this tough world/Stretch him out longer.' "

I nodded, my mouth tight. Otherwise it would have been shaking.

"I wish he could die," he said quietly. "I'm sure Andrew feels the same way, but we can't say aloud to each other that we wish our brother would die. . . . I can't say it to anyone else but you, Seafair."

The news came while I was at The Eyrie for Christmas. Ian had seen Patrick only a few days before, when he had gone to the mainland to make the trip back out with me on the *Ocean Pearl*. But the end had come suddenly, as if all at once the brain and body had refused to go on any longer. By New Year's he was with the other two in the churchyard, lying beside Miranda, where he wanted to be.

For me as well as for Patrick it was a release. I think I had felt married to him, and I couldn't forget that his last lucid words were said in tenderness to me; mine was the last name he ever spoke.

epilogue

The other day I saw a long-legged black-haired young man running across a pasture with a new calf in his arms and the distraught cow chasing him. My stomach seemed to roll itself over with the impact of *déjà vu*. But the dog with them was a collie, not old Hero, and the Skye terrier cheering them on was Calum, not Charlie. When the man had almost reached us I saw the bright blue eyes, freckles, and grin of Michael Dolan. My eleven-year-old Miranda hopped down off the top bar of the gate to open it for him. She wears overalls and goes barefoot all summer, and has a dutch cut, because otherwise I'm forever cutting pitchy snarls out of long silver-blond tresses. But she's not all tomboy. For years she intended to marry Michael if he'd wait for her, but since he's become engaged to Elmer's Ginnie she wants to be either a nurse, a concert pianist, or the first woman to cross the Atlantic in a Swampscott sailing dory.

We have a Patrick too. He's fourteen and goes lobstering summers in his Uncle Pat's peapod. He wants to be a doctor. He's dark, and likes to think that's his Indian blood; he also wants bagpipes for his birthday. The younger three, Henry, David, and Sara, are content for now to be explorers, with Andrew's children, of every tide pool, cave, and glen. Their universe right now is the island, as much as it is the eagles' domain. And they will no doubt attempt to climb to the eagles' nest on schedule. I think Pat has already tried it.

They are all stable, I think, because Ian and I are stable. That's not to say *staid*. We have our moments, even if our marriage started off sedately enough. You could call us late bloomers. Anyway, there's much love floating around The Eyrie, as well as music, and the noise of overflowing streams of young Drummonds, Swensons, Ansons, Peases, Joys, Schofields, and Kallochs. Though all these island children prefer the shores for play, they sometimes run freely through the part of the oak grove that is separate from the fenced-off Norse settlement, where at this moment a runologist is deciphering a newly discovered stone. The familiar ghosts of the grove disappeared almost overnight long ago, as if everyone were anxious to let them go.

To paraphrase Emerson on gods: If we meet no ghosts, it is because we harbor none. So there are none here, even when at night I light my candle by the hall mirror where once I saw, or thought I saw, the image of a lover.

about the author

Brought up in the suburbs of Boston, Elisabeth Ogilvie was exposed to Maine at an early age and caught a bad case of it. She seldom strays far from her habitat, and for good reason: it's as close to heaven as you can get. There's beachcombing; collecting Indian artifacts on her home island, which was an Indian campground for hundreds of years; unusual birds to keep an eye on; the neighboring woodchuck and the cock pheasant who crows under her windows in the morning like a rooster. Sometimes a moose takes a short-cut through her backyard, and there's mackerel fishing when the spirit moves.

Miss Ogilvie says she wants to spend a year in Scotland when she no longer has two Australian terriers to worry about. In the meantime, what with reading and writing and the whole outdoors, she doesn't have much time to think about travel.